IVOR

Cicely Gill

Mallard Publishing

First published in Scotland by Mallard Publishing 2014

Text copyright © 2013 Cicely Gill

ISBN 978-0-9531014-5-0

Printed by Clydeside Press, Glasgow

To Nicky, with love

Acknowledgements

Many thanks to: my husband, Nicky Gill for use of his painting as the cover, to Stuart Gough for painstaking reading of the MS, to Phyllis McGowan and Sue Goldsack for their constructive criticism in the early stages, to John Weir for being a helpful and supportive computer wizard par excellence, to Andrew Binnie for help with the e-publishing process, to Claire Wingfield, literary consultant, Edinburgh for sound help and advice with my first draft and to all my friends and acquaintances who showed enthusiasm when I said I was going to publish a novel.

Contents

Chapter I Discovery   1

Chapter II Different perspectives   7

Chapter III Digging deeper   11

Chapter IV Don't tell Zara   21

Chapter V Deep water   31

Chapter VI Drawing blanks   41

Chapter VII Smoke and fire   49

Chapter VIII A smokescreen of water   59

Chapter IX If you are lost, use a map   69

Chapter X Matching odd socks   77

Chapter XI Zara won't take a telling   89

Chapter XII Brothers in arms?   99

Chapter XIII Two jigsaw pieces   110

Chapter XIV Who's in debt to whom?   121

Chapter XV Party time   131

Chapter XVI A bit of this and a bit of that   142

Chapter XVII More information but what to do with it   153

Chapter XVIII Pass the word along the line   163

Chapter XIX Biting off more than you can chew   176

Chapter XX It's hard to find things out   192

Chapter XXI More than one game of chess   207

Chapter XXII Action follows decision   219

Chapter XXIII What's locked can be unlocked   230

Chapter XXIV Darkness gives way to light   246

Chapter XXV Checkmate for some   266

Chapter XXVI The importance of children   278

Chapter XXVII Endgame   282

Chapter I Discovery

Zara stared at the muddy object being held out to her and tried to breathe but it was as if she'd forgotten how to.

'Is it a dinosaur bone?' she heard her godson say.

'No, no Ben, not a dinosaur.'

'Ness and I found it in the river bank.'

'You'll need to show me where.'

Zara stood up and carefully placed the bone in the carrier bag that had contained their picnic and then put the bag in her rucksack making sure she zipped it up. She was fighting a growing conviction that the bone was human. She hoped and didn't hope that there would be more.

'Ness found it,' Ben was saying. Zara walked in a kind of dream, saw herself moving over the grass in step with her own shadow.

'It was here,' Ben said. 'Ness had to wrench it out of the mud. It's big isn't it?'

Zara swallowed hard and turned her attention to the hole and the paw marks around it, deeply etching the mud. She felt unbalanced. She was seeing chopped up corpses but trying to focus on preserving a crime scene. In five years as a free-lance investigative journalist, she chided herself, I should have learned how to do "detached".

'Get me some big stones, Ben. We need to make sure this spot can be found later.' She looked hard at the surrounding ground but there were no other signs of skeletal parts.

'There you are, Aunty Zara. Can I make a circle round the hole? Will there be a dig here? Ness would...' He stopped and following his gaze Zara noticed a man standing facing in their direction. Was he watching them or did she just imagine that? Had he seen the bone? He was heavily built with flying grey hair and a sunken jaw that hinted at lots of missing teeth. He wore an old gaberdine raincoat with a leather belt. Zara moved away from the spot like a mother bird deflecting an intruder and began digging at the edge of the river with Ben's stick. Ben came and stood beside her looking very serious.

1

'See in Miss Potter's class,' he said, 'we made pictures and maps of the river around here'. Zara held his eyes. 'The river's changed. It must have been that storm. I think,' he began to whisper, 'that the bone has washed down the river and we might find the rest of whatever it is higher up'. Zara smiled. 'Can I take the bone and show it to Miss Potter?' Zara made an apologetic face:

'I'm afraid not. It will need to... I'm going to take it to my friend Professor Katerina Pond. It's her job to identify bones.' Ben looked put out:

'If you can take it to your friend, why can't I take it to my teacher?'

'No, Ben.'

'But she might know what it is. She's very good at knowing things.'

'Sorry. It's important. I'm going to have to give it to the police. Her stomach lurched as if it wanted her to give up her half of the tuna baguette she'd recently shared with Ben.

Zara told herself she was over-reacting: she'd seen some gruesome specimens in her time. She remembered the rats that had fled away from a body she'd discovered in an empty shop. She'd been hoping to speak to the owner but the rats had been his last companions as he had bled to death after a burglary gone wrong. The incident had given her a horror of rats, the suddenness of their movements, their amazing speed. She remembered then, a detached arm she'd found in a rubbish tip. She'd been looking for a number plate but instead found this limb still dressed in its shirtsleeve lying by itself on a pile of car seats. She'd been shocked but also excited at the idea of a story. She had not found anything else on that occasion but the SOCOs had soon discovered a suitcase containing the rest of the body. It had never been explained why the arm had been in a different place. She imagined the scene: "Oops Willie, you forgot the arm! You'll forget your head next," as someone pitched the limb from the boot of a car after the rest had been carefully stowed in the case.

But to Zara, there was something particularly bleak about this bone. *Don't think about the bone* brought the image sharply into focus. She was fairly certain it was a pelvis. Where were the thighs, the ribs and the head? She thought particularly about the head. And was the fact that there was this one dislocated bone an indication that the body had been dismembered? Katerina would tell her. But did she really want to know? A bit of her would have liked to go back to how her life was at the beginning of the afternoon.

She had been half-promised a series in the Herald, in-depth articles looking at the possible patterns of certain crimes in Glasgow. The first article was about the prevalence of knife crime and the effects of some of the counteractive measures. The second was to be about arson and the business community.

However, she could feel a sense of excitement when she thought about the bone. She wondered if it would take her off course. She smiled to herself: if it happened it would not be the first time. What was it she had been about to do when she became involved in MacWilliams and the empty shop? Marrying Ted. An instance where crime had paid her wonderfully well in helping her avoid a doomed partnership. Four years ago and twenty-five, instead she had hunted down an extortion gang with a little help from Des, her friend in the police. She smiled again: he wouldn't like her putting it like that.

'Can I take the photo?' Ben was twisting her arm because she wouldn't let him take the bone to school. She handed him her phone. She checked the result. 'That's brilliant.' They smiled at one another and then suddenly, they both became aware that the staring man was now ten feet away. He was frowning as if he wished they weren't there and he walked a little way towards the water and then back. He moved as though he were hurting inside.

'Found anything, sonny?' he addressed Ben. Zara shook her head faintly and Ben replied,

'No, nothing. Just poking about'.

The man was muttering but it was difficult to catch his words:

'If the tree... fire... perhaps...'

'Have you lost something, mister? I could help you find it if you like,' said Ben. The man rubbed his lips with his index finger and tried a smile but it didn't work on his face.

'It's okay, sonny. Probably didn't lose it here. Just checking. Hole in my pocket.' He shook his coat as if it might not be clear what he meant. Then he turned abruptly and squinted at the grass and then at the birches and thorn bushes round about.

Zara concluded that he was a down-and-out who'd remembered having a fire in the vicinity and had thought there might be some empties around. She went a little way off and took out her notebook to write a description of the disposition of trees and bushes to give reference points for the hole.

When she looked up Ben had disappeared. She threw a stick for Ness and then glanced at her watch. Barney would be back from work. He was a social worker now and she was more flexible time-wise. Which was why she was looking after Ben.

Zara opened her mouth to call and then realized the man was also gone. She told herself it was a coincidence but her imagination began to spiral. She could feel the bone sticking into her back and it was as if it were nudging her saying, you stupid woman, you let the boy out of your sight.

The park was still sunny and dotted with strollers. There were mums with prams on the benches up on the path and a few smart people coming at a pace and gait that said, I don't have time to meander. I need to get to the gym. No Ben. Twelve minutes gone.

Zara walked up and down over the space of ten yards or so. Every time she turned she expected to see him. Ness, oblivious, punished herself with her continuous game of 'fetch'. Fifteen minutes.

She called Ness, relying on the dog to set off in the direction Ben had gone. Ness trotted off towards the bridge at Gibson Street. Zara followed. Ben had a habit of disappearing into the trees and reappearing a moment later. Zara tried to push the idea of kidnapping out of her mind and broke into a run.

The sun still shone; the park was still fresh and green, the usual effect of more rain than sun. She found it hard to believe anything bad could happen in such surroundings. Still no sign of Ben.

As the bridge came into view, she remembered the tunnel. Disused and belonging to the railway, it was not bricked up and Ben had always been warned off entering it. That's where he'll be, she thought. The tunnel was known to be used by criminal gangs. There were said to be hidden rooms within the walls. Zara had never had reason to discover if this were true.

At last she arrived at a point where she could see the tunnel entrance and suddenly Ben shot out, stopping short when he saw her.

'I followed the man,' he said, 'because I thought he was looking for the bone'.

'Not good,' said Zara. 'You got me worried. You…'

'The man disappeared through an iron door but he saw me and shouted, so I ran back.'

'Dangerous,' said Zara, wanting to hug Ben but not wanting to make him too anxious. She looked past him into the tunnel. She could just see the iron door.

'Wait with Ness. Don't follow me. Just stand here where I can see you.'

'But you said it was dangerous.'

'I know. I'll be careful.'

She crept forward, making no noise on the rough ground, stopped a few feet from the door and listened. There were two voices. One belonged she was sure to the man with the flying hair. The other was commanding; she felt his power. She crept closer. She couldn't help looking upwards to see if there were any bats. She had a mortal fear of bats as well as rats.

'Did you find out…?' She missed the end of the sentence.

'Never mind that, boss. I need to tell you…'

'If it's anything to do with…' A loud cough drowned the rest of that sentence and then the same voice went on: 'I've told you, I don't want to ever hear about it. It's your secret'. Zara pressed herself against the door.

'But Joe, this woman. I'm sure…'

'It could be anything.'

'Supposing she … They may …'

'Was I there? Did I bury anyone?'

'I could go to prison.'

'If you're that bothered' –more coughing –'and don't talk to me about it again or…'

At this point Flying Hair started to shout in a hoarse voice. The other man shouted back and there were sounds of objects being thrown.

Zara thought it was a good moment to leave.

She walked slowly till she re-joined Ben and then walked quickly but Ben seemed incapable of hurrying and kept kicking stones and shooting off into the bushes. She noticed that whenever he came out, he looked back.

'What's the matter Ben?' she said at last.

'It's that man.'

'What man?'

'The shuffley man with the funny teeth.' Zara looked back but could see no one.

'Ben it's too late for games. Your dad will have the tea ready and...'

'Did you hear them behind that door?' asked Ben as if she hadn't spoken.

'Sort of,' Zara said. 'It was mixed up. Hard to understand.' She paused:

'The man saw you, Ben, you said?'

'That's why I keep hiding. So he doesn't see me.'

'Why should it matter?'

'Oh it doesn't matter. It doesn't matter,' said Ben turning a cartwheel in the middle of the path.

Zara gave up talking and just forged ahead in spurts, stopping to let Ben catch up with her. They reached the top of the steps at Kelvin Bridge. Home straight, she thought but then Ben ran all the way back down again.

'I thought you believed in keeping fit,' he said when he saw her face on his return.

'Come on,' said Zara. She didn't quite know why she felt so anxious. She looked along the route they had just taken. No one.

Ben was better on the pavement and walked beside her practising his whistling. They reached his home and she groped in her bag for her key.

'That man was following us,' said Ben as they walked up the stairs.

Chapter II Different perspectives

Barney stood by the stove, rangy and un-stooped at six foot three. His hair was mainly dark with flecks of grey. He was stir-frying vegetables because Ben wouldn't eat salad and Barney had a thing about 'raw'. The chopped up sausage in the other pan was a concession so that Ben would eat the veg.

'Oh', said Ben with mock disappointment, 'I thought it was going to be tripe'.

'Not today', said Barney, 'but we do have rice pudding for afters'.

'Lucky Nessie then.'

Ben went straight into the bone story:

'It was really exciting, first we found the bone...' Zara kept interrupting:

'To be fair, Ness found the bone.'

'Okay first Ness found the bone and then we'd just started looking for the rest of the dino...'

'Except that you know it isn't a dinosaur. If it were it would be a fossil and this is a real bone. Anyway it's too small to be anything to do with a dinosaur.'

'It could be a vertebra,' said Ben looking hard at the object under discussion which was now sitting on the kitchen counter. Ben walked up to it, hands behind his back. He'd been given strict orders not to touch it.

Zara shivered although she was perfectly warm. Barney's kitchen was cosy, its surfaces littered with plants and utensils made of hospitable wood. Red curtains hung at the window. A blue and yellow water-colour of a Hebridean beach graced one wall and on another was hung a calendar showing a different prehistoric animal for every month. It was not the kitchen Barney had shared with his late wife who'd died of cancer two years previously. Maureen. He'd moved house in the process of moving on. In the midst of this cosy brightness, Zara felt the bone appeared alien and desolate. She was prompted to leave to take it to Katerina.

'There was a funny man as well,' Ben said suddenly. 'He was looking for something but he wouldn't say what? I'm sure he was looking for the bone?'

'Unlikely', said Zara quickly. 'What makes you think he might have been?'

'Because he was looking for *something*. We were just picnicking and Ness happened to find a bone but he... looked as if he'd lost something important.'

'Is that why you followed him?' Ben nodded.

'You followed him?' As Barney became anxious Ben became less talkative. Zara noticed a quick expression cross his face which she couldn't immediately interpret.

'Just a little way. He didn't see me. I was hiding behind bushes.' Ben's fingers were all crossed behind his back.

***

Katerina was very pleased to see Zara but much less pleased to see the bone. She affirmed at once that it was the pelvic bone of a young female and added that off the record, she thought it had been in the ground for about ten years, that it seemed charred and that it was cracked. Then she folded her arms and looked at Zara.

'Police now, then?' and when Zara hesitated she added, 'Though I suppose for you that means contacting Des Harris?' Zara avoided her eye but in a mock-sheepish way.

'We help each other out. You know that,' she said.

***

Zara had to leave a message for Des as he wasn't in his office. She didn't want to give the bone to anyone else since it was only if Des was in charge of the investigation that she would have any chance of getting to know anything further, so when she returned to update

Barney on the situation she still had the bone. Ben was in bed and Barney greeted her frowning, gestured her to a chair and threw a photo-copy of what was obviously a page from a school exercise book across to her.

'Read that,' he said. 'I'll make some tea, though when you've read it you may feel you need something stronger.' He shook his head at her when he realised she still had the bone.

Ben's writing and today's date. Homework. The title was 'An Exciting Event'. Barney put the kettle on. Zara began to read:

"I followed the man with the missing teeth at a distance. I'm sure he was looking for the bone and I wanted to see what he would do next. My Aunty Zara was still poking about on the river bank and I didn't think she would miss me. The man turned left under the bridge and I ran and hid behind a tree. He did not continue towards Great Western Road but left the path and turned in towards the mouth of the tunnel. I could feel my heart going pom, pom pom as dad and Aunty Zara have always warned me never to go into the tunnel but I couldn't help it, I suddenly found myself crouching down beside a pile of dirt at the entrance and listening to footsteps.

"The tunnel had an echo so the man's boots went bang bang bang as he slowly walked along. I counted twenty paces. Then there was the sound of squeaky hinges and I saw a bar of light. I crept forward. The man had his back to me. I crept nearer. I wanted to see beyond the door before it shut. I could make out the figure of a short man leaning against something. I could see a knuckleduster ring on one of his fingers. It was shining. I heard a voice say, 'Jim? Come in you – something too rude to put in my homework. Jim was about to enter when something made him turn. In a flash he picked up a half brick and threw it at me. 'Get out,' he shouted, 'and don't come back, ever! You wee barstud'. I ran as fast as I could across the uneven stones but all the time I was thinking, when can I go back and find out what's behind that door?'

Zara was defiant:

'He could have made most of it up: he loves writing stories!' Barney's face was set in a way she remembered from back when they had worked together as volunteers in a project for homeless men. Barney never liked the risks Zara took and he became more and more outspoken about it as he gradually fell in love with her. As a way of saying no to Barney, she had gone out with Ted, a PhD student who had been funded to research the project. Then Barney had overstretched himself, contracted pneumonia and ended up in hospital being nursed by Nurse Maureen.

As soon as Barney became involved with Maureen, Zara and Barney had become really good friends again and had been ever since, Zara supporting him during the time Maureen was ill and dying.

Being Ben's godmother, the child had naturally turned to her when his own mother had died. Zara had continued to help while Barney trained as a social worker. She was still helping out.

But recently she sensed Barney was thinking along the old lines again and unfortunately she had encouraged him by occasionally staying over and sleeping with him. She should have known better: there was too much danger in hurting him – and Ben. She would have to make up her mind properly first.

Today, the look she was getting said all of this and more: please don't take risks; please look after yourself for my sake and for Ben's. What he actually said was,

'Tomorrow. Early. Police. I don't ever want to see that bone again.'

Chapter III Digging deeper

Zara sank into a deep exhausted sleep until the early morning when she woke with a start, fumbled for her clock and saw it was only four-thirty. She turned over thankfully.

But now she was held in the grip of a dream which kept her tense and anxious. She was walking through tall grass and could hear a tractor getting nearer. She could see a gate in the distance she had to reach, but her legs would not take her there. Her limbs were paralysed. She looked down at her legs: her bones were exposed. She sat bolt upright in real terror, holding onto her duvet as if onto a ship's rail in a storm.

The bone. Her mind suddenly re-played her initial waking and alerted her that all was not well. She leapt out of bed and ran through to the living room. There was the bag containing the bone on the mantelpiece where she had left it. But where was her carriage clock? Nothing there but the dustless square on which it had stood.

She had woken to the thief leaving. She looked around for other evidence of loss but all the electronics were in place. The little box, also on the mantelpiece which contained an eternity ring inherited from her great grandmother – she sometimes wore it for luck – was still there. She slipped it on feeling she might need it.

Bizarre or what, thought Zara. Although the carriage clock was valuable it seemed an odd thing to take on its own. She sat down and tried to think rationally. She was crippled by fear but she needed to examine the carrier bag. Taking the simple possibilities first, the burglary had to be connected to the bone...

She felt her body rise to an upright position and glide across to the mantelpiece. Gingerly she opened the bag. There was the carriage clock at the bottom. On its own. Simultaneously she heard the sound of a window banging and felt a slight gust of wind through the open door to the back bedroom... and the fire escape. The burglar had had easy access. Liking to air the flat, Zara had stupidly left the window ajar, and had forgotten, as usual, to close it. Will I ever learn, she wondered.

Although it was not yet five, she went to the kitchen and made herself some tea and toast. She knew she would not get back to sleep; she might as well spend the time writing down everything she knew about the bone for Des. If she gave him a clear concise report it might mitigate the fact that she had lost the key evidence.

She began to record what had happened in the park but stopped, thinking of Barney and pondering on whether to leave out the bit about Ben and the tunnel.

When she woke two hours later she found she had only managed to write 'Ness found a bone'. She sat and mused. Frustrating though the break-in was, it did deepen the story. It meant, surely, that the strange man in the park, the 'Jim' of Ben's story, knew she had the bone and must have followed her, not only to Barney's but subsequently to her own flat. It meant that his suspicions were aroused by Ben's following of him, that he was perhaps thinking someone was interested in *his* interest in the bone. Maybe, and this was complete speculation, whoever Jim had spoken to in the tunnel, hearing that Zara had the bone had detailed Jim to follow Zara and Ben. Whatever the case, recovery of the bone had been thought vital.

***

Zara rang Des on his mobile.

'You're in luck' he said. 'I'm just leaving court. There's been a cock-up. Someone forgot to get the chief witness out of the gaol. Case adjourned.' He named a small café they both knew in the Merchant city.

She had arrived before him. 'Mine's a latte with cream and chocolate,' he said by way of greeting.

'So what's new?' said Zara. There was always this spark between them. They had gone out together a few times some years before and loved each other's company but then he had met and married Pam in a matter of weeks. He did not talk about his marriage and Zara wondered if it was a sore point. She felt he was still attracted to her but he was very loyal to his wife.

It was Des she realized that was stopping her make up her mind about Barney, even though it seemed she couldn't have Des. He always adopted a brisk tone with her now as if to emphasize that they were meeting on business terms only. Zara understood but it rankled with her and sometimes made her bloody-minded.

'So where's the bone?' he asked when they had exchanged a minimum of pleasantries.

'It's turned into a carriage clock,' said Zara trying not to look apologetic. Des glanced at his watch.

'Zara, if this isn't serious, I don't have time.' She told him the story backwards starting with the break-in.

'This guy Jim, you'd recognize him by his teeth?'

'Absolutely.'

'There's a lot of people called Jim... You'll need to show us the locus. Ben is probably right about stuff being washed downriver. There'll have to be an extensive search. I'll need to take a proper statement from you. At the station.' He fell silent looking at her. Then he said,

'Why the fuck did you lose the bone, Zara?'

'I'm sorry.'

'But then,' Des went on, 'you never did try to make anything easier'.

'But I can still be useful to you, helping you with your enquiries.'

'Keep out of it,' said Des, recognizing her sardonic tone. 'There's no way this looks like anything but murder. And one dead person can lead to another. I don't want you mixed up in this.' Zara's hackles rose. 'If you want to be a detective, join the police force,' Des continued. 'Don't start dabbling around under the pretence of being a journalist or a criminologist.' He accented this last word as if being the second, was even worse than being the first.

Zara glared at him trying to resist the temptation to drag up instances where something she'd said had given Des a lead or the famous occasion two years previously when she had solved a murder case virtually single-handed. He had called it luck, said she just been in the right place at the right time, had had a head start because the murderer, like her, often travelled on the number nine bus. His defences were endless and silly and boiled down to the fact that he was sore because she had succeeded where he had failed, something she had never failed to ram down his throat.

'I'll do what I have to do,' Zara growled. 'Don't I get any thanks for being a good citizen and reporting a suspicious situation?'

'Zara!' Des was impatient now. 'Don't go in a huff.' He hated it if she hinted at her own value being dismissed. He drained his mug. 'I'll need to get back. Come in and make your statement after ten-thirty. I'll be free then.'

***

Katerina had phoned Zara to tell her she'd been called in as an expert witness and that she was due to go to the locus later that morning. Zara determined to be there too.

'Hi Jamie, this is Zara. Where's Des? I'm meant to be meeting him at the locus. Any idea when he's going to show?'

'The bone in the park you mean? That locus? He's just left. He was waiting to hear from Professor Pond.' Zara rang off relieved. She had given Des such an accurate indication of where the bone had been found she was feeling he might try to cut her out. Des had told Katerina he needed someone who might be able to determine by studying the mud and vegetation washed down, how far the bone was likely to have travelled and therefore where else they might start looking. Zara wondered if her friend was already there surveying the river.

She left Barney's house quickly and made for the park. She'd called in to update Barney but only just caught him leaving.

Zara was dressed in welly boots, water-resistant trousers and a waterproof jacket with a hood and large pockets one of which held her camera. As she swung her leg over the fence separating the path from the river she saw an intent figure down by the water with a magnifying glass in her hand.

'Just here?' The professor indicated Zara's four stones. Zara nodded. The professor flung open a file of poly-pockets each containing a plan of the river section by section. Zara smiled to herself: she knew Katerina had a digital record at home but that she felt more at home with hard copy. Each page was a detailed study of the geological composition of the bank and the flora and fauna living in or on it, plus the currents in the water. 'I haven't touched anything. I was warned not to, but I can see evidence – she pointed to a bedraggled leaf and stem – that would indicate that the bone, and the mud washed down along with it, came from about a hundred yards upstream.'

She flipped to the relevant river section in her file. 'See this plant. It only grows here. It's the only one on this section of the river and there's not another example for the next couple of miles where there's a substantial clump. So a hundred yards up is where I would start looking.'

'Couldn't the bones have come to rest somewhere in between?' asked Zara.

Katerina smiled. 'That's a good question but look at the current, – she pointed at the page with her finger – see how it starts near the bank but then takes a middle passage as the water gets deeper. Anything from the bank would not come to rest till the current either lessened or veered back near the bank again and here'- she indicated where they were standing – is where it does just that.'

'And that storm we had a few weeks ago, that would have been sufficient to dislodge a lump of bank?'

'Oh yes, the greater the volume of water, the harder for the bank to hold. I'm really intrigued by the fact that I've been studying this stretch of river for a year and I've never found one bone.'

'What's the weirdest thing you have found in the river would you say?' Zara could feel an article coming on.

Professor Pond thought for a moment. She was used to giving only considered responses.

'Once, quite far underground,' she said, 'I was looking for evidence of river seepage. I was with this inspector whose job it was to make sure the tunnels were still safe. We were right under the Clyde and suddenly my torch picked up something white.'

'A bone?' asked Zara.

'A skeleton. The scary thing was that the inspector had been along that route three weeks earlier and there had been nothing there.'

'Rats?' asked Zara, her hand going towards her mouth.

'Most likely. They never found out anything more. Dental records didn't show up anything but then he – it was a 'he' – could have been foreign. But for a long time the public kept coming forward with possible explanations.'

'Any effects beside the body? Clothes?'

'Strangely...' but at this point the professor broke off. A car had stopped. The police had arrived.

'You'll need to tell me another time,' said Zara quickly. 'We'll get together soon.'

The professor nodded but was already turning her mind back to the reason she was there.

Zara looked at Des and saw that he was not pleased that she had been talking to Professor Pond but she didn't care. She always took any opportunity she could and to hell with the consequences. She didn't hold people's annoyance or frustration with her against them and she didn't expect them to hold grudges either. She smiled at Des trying not to look like someone who had got in first and said, in as humble a voice as she could summon up,

'I'll leave you with my friend Katerina then?'

'Okay, okay.' Des cut across her.' He took the professor's arm and moved her a little way off. Zara was more amused than irritated but felt her best policy was to keep a low profile.

'If you need me, captain,' she shouted after him. 'I'll be here.' She went and sat on a tree stump and delved into her pocket for her cheese roll. Zara never went anywhere unprepared. She would skulk, she decided, and then follow them, armed anyway with her information from Katerina which she fully expected Des to act on. If bones were found, Zara wanted to be there with her camera.

Des and the professor were 'Pondering' (Zara smiled to herself) the section plans but this delay might be enough to give her the chance of getting ahead, she thought. There was the team as well: it would be difficult to avoid the team if she waited.

She made a snap decision: she would take a chance that they would be going the hundred yards upriver. She uncurled her body and silently glided back over the bank towards the fence. Des she perceived to be in one of his tight moods which meant his focus would be extremely narrow. He would have forgotten her.

Gaining the path she walked casually until she got to the other side of the bridge on Gibson Street. She scanned the banks: she had not recalled quite what a marshy exposed area this was. Down below the wall which bounded the path was not a place people walked.

She climbed the wall and dropped down, refusing to consider how she would get back. She knew she was risking Des's anger: she could be contaminating a crime scene but then up till a few minutes ago, no one had known it was one.

Zara flexed her shoulders and rolled her head trying to let go of the tension she felt. She looked about her, gauging the distance, so many yards to the bridge, so many after. Then she looked for the plants. At first it seemed impossible but then she realized there was one place where the water had scoured round and taken a great bite from the bank and on the edge of this, clinging almost, Zara recognized the plants Katerina had found evidence of lower down the river. She was impressed.

Here then was the obvious place to start digging. She could see also that it would have been relatively easy to dig here whenever the body was buried, heavy, but muddy rather than stony. She thought if she positioned herself back in the undergrowth beside the wall she could watch the progress of the diggers and if and when something was revealed she would leap out and take a photograph.

Zara wondered what was keeping Des and the team, and decided they would want to explore the area surrounding the first bone very thoroughly. But since it was evident that that one had only lodged superficially, it seemed to her it would be a relatively easy matter to determine whether there were others thrown randomly out of the stormy river.

Zara had only just stationed herself behind a stand of giant hemlock when the investigating team rolled up. Professor Pond went straight to the spot where Zara had been standing and pointed at the plants. Des told the team to start digging. Because Des and the professor were both facing the river, it was impossible for Zara to make sense of their conversation.

The men were working in the water at the river's edge under the assumption that they were looking for something buried in a bank which had turned into a channel. Zara could only make out that they were probing rather than digging.

Zara felt excited and was sure they were going to find something. She eased her weight from one leg to the other to avoid cramp. At that moment there was a shout and then a waiting silence while everyone's eyes were on one particular spot while one of the team members lifted mud carefully away. It sucked resistingly, as if unwilling to give up its treasure, having looked after it for so long. Shuttering was put in place and a pump now drained the key area. Zara watched, unexpectedly shocked as one by one each bone was removed and carefully labelled. Professor Pond stood very still.

Zara suddenly stepped out of her hiding place. Holding her camera at the ready she marched towards the site and took three photographs before Des had time to turn around.

'Oh you're back,' said Katerina as if it were normal for Zara to be there. Zara had seen Des open his mouth to expostulate but Katerina's presence prevented him from being as curt as he would have been had he and Zara been alone.

'Looks like we have a crime scene,' he muttered. Zara took it as a warning-off.

The bones had been buried in a bunched manner as if the burier had been in a hurry and had wanted to dig as small a grave as possible. They had the same signs of blackening as the pelvis had had. Zara expressed this last thought out loud and Des retorted,

'We've only got your word for that.' Zara looked straight back at him, opening her mouth to attack but then she caught beneath his tart words the genuine feeling of compassion which she knew fuelled him to do his work well. He was trying to stay with what had to be done and quell the picture in his mind of the young person whose bones were all that remained of them.

Chapter IV Don't tell Zara

When Zara left the crime scene – but not she mused, necessarily the scene of the crime – she went at once to find her friend Spike. She tried four places before she came across someone she vaguely knew as Munchy. He was sitting on a bench looking at a photograph. Zara came up behind him.

As soon as she spoke, he whipped it into his pocket but not before she had taken in the image of three men all staring straight at the camera. They were outside but there was no identifiable background. The men, it seemed to Zara, were obviously mates. She would have thought nothing of it except for the fact that Munchy so obviously did not want her to see it.

'Friends of yours, Munchy?'

'Er… no.' Hesitation, so, although not friends, he knows them.

'Rellys?' Zara made her voice sound casual. Munchy's hand went to his pocket again.

'It's my dad and…' The hand came out of the pocket as his voice trailed off.

'Did you want something?' he asked her.

'Just to know where Spike is, said Zara turning round curious to know what had made Munchy close up. Someone she didn't know was walking towards them. He wore shades and she could make nothing of his face. Munchy told her where Spike was, rising as he did so, to meet the newcomer. Zara felt he wanted her to leave.

***

Munchy had said Spike was living in luxury for a week: a middleclass couple had unofficially allowed him to stay in their garden shed in return for him keeping an eye on the house and working on the garden.

It was quite a way for Zara to cycle but she enjoyed it, privately dubbing such occasions as one of her own personal mystery tours.

Munchy had told her the house was at the top of the hill in the complex residential district north of Dumbarton Road and that the garden had a monkey puzzle tree by the front gate which was wrought iron and had obviously been replaced quite recently. There were bright red rhododendrons on the drive.

Zara jumped off her bike and took it round the side of the house which was on a corner. She lent the bike against the garage and started across the extensive lawn. She could see the hut and here was Spike coming out with a kettle in his hand. He looked up and smiled, no surprise in his face: it took a lot to surprise Spike.

'How's Munchy then?'

'I didn't ask. I just asked for you.' Spike took down another mug from the shelf behind him.

'How's Ben and Barney then?'

'They're fine, Spike. I see you've landed yourself a holiday?' Spike told her the story.

'It was a case of one good turn deserves another,' he began. 'I saw smoke coming from that window there.' He indicated with the mug in his hand. 'I hammered on the back door and the lady opened it saying "No odd jobs…" So I said, "Just to tell you, missis, your house could be on fire and I don't mean the toast." I followed her in and she turned and ran for the stairs. Smoke was pouring through the door of one of the back bedrooms. I shouted to her to stand back and I opened the door wider.

'Do you know what Zara, she'd only left a mattress airing beside a three bar electric fire. The foam had started to melt. Lots of smoke damage; no flames. I looked up to see if there was a smoke alarm; there was but it obviously didn't have a battery in it. I wondered if they were as careless about house insurance. I unplugged the fire, closed the window and the door. The floorboards were smouldering.' Zara shook her head.

'You shouldn't have gone in, Spike,' said Zara. Spike shrugged his shoulders.

21

'I went downstairs and she hadn't phoned the fire brigade yet. She was looking as if she wasn't going to. 'What will my husband say?' she said.

'Thank god the house didn't burn down?' suggested Zara. Spike smiled.

'Then she decided to introduce herself: "Caroline by the way," she says, "Caroline". Then she phones the fire brigade. I said, "What about phoning your husband" and she said, "He'll be in a meeting. He always is" and sure enough he was in a meeting and sounded quite angry at being called out. I could hear him saying, "Caroline! No I can't get away. It's a very important meeting. I'm certain you'll manage".

'So then we waited here in this hut for the firemen. Tea and biscuits, milk and sugar. She got it all from the house before they arrived and I stayed on till Charlie, her husband got back because all the neighbours seemed to be out and she was in a state of shock by this time. It turned out Charlie had sacked their gardener the week before and there was a lot needed doing so I got the job after all in spite of Charlie referring to me as another lame duck.'

'He doesn't sound pleasant,' said Zara.

'To be fair,' said Spike, 'she answered him back'. "We were the lame ducks this time, Charlie," she said. Told him not to be so ungracious. I didn't think they got on that well.'

'Like a house on fire perhaps,' said Zara. Spike laughed.

'You can see I'm living the life o' Riley here. Caroline took me to the cupboard and made me choose stuff to eat. There's a little fridge for drinks so I've got sausage, eggs and bacon and... I could feed the five thousand.'

'She didn't give you a microwave though.'

'She offered but I said I'd stick to me primus and me own pan. She's all right but he's an odd character.'

Zara never found it difficult to talk to Spike but after half an hour he clapped her knee and said,

'You didn't run me to earth to listen to stories. What is it you want? Information or advice?' She grinned at him. He was teasing her. This was the question she had asked the homeless people when they came to the project in the early days and Spike had suggested it might be more fruitful if she allowed people's wants to come out naturally in the course of conversation. He'd done this by just chatting and not answering her direct questions until he felt like it and then in his own way. She'd learnt quickly.

'Do you know someone called Jim with missing teeth? About your height. Wears a belted gaberdine. A little bit of greyish hair flying at the sides. Red cheeks. Brown boots. Saw him by the Kelvin, downriver from the bridge at Gibson Street.'

Spike's face had been open and attentive but as she mentioned the Kelvin something closed. It was so small Zara didn't register especially, as she was busy dodging a honey bee.

'Jim you say,' said Spike carefully. 'I do know a guy who fits that description.' He paused. 'Anything else you want to tell me?'

Zara hesitated and then told him what had happened at the river and about the subsequent finding of the rest of the skeleton. Spike whistled and shook his head. He paused again then:

'You say Jim was looking for the bone. How do you know that and how – I'm just curious – do you know his name is Jim?'

Zara hesitated again and then told Spike about Ben going into the tunnel.

'So Ben heard someone call this guy Jim?

'That's what he said.'

'That's what he said?'

'How do you mean?'

'Well you told me you found out about Ben's adventure from a story he wrote.' Zara nodded. 'It was a *story*. It could be all true, partly true or not true at all. You've got a bone. That's true.' Zara looked at the grass but didn't immediately contradict him. 'But everything else you've told me is speculation. Your Jim could have nothing to do with the case and was probably just irritated at you poking around his patch. Presumably you've given the bone to the polis; if Ben wants to see bones, take him to the museum.'

'But I lost the bone, Spike!' Spike hit his head with his hand.

'More tea, Zara? I'm getting too old for these carry-ons.'

Spike was very interested in the burglar story and laughed at the bit about the carriage clock in the polybag.

'Sense of humour then, this burglar?'

'But I need the bone back. I was wondering if you could ask around and see if anyone you knew could threw any light on it.'

'Were you?' said Spike concentrating on his tea.

'I know it's a long shot,' said Zara but if as you say, you know Jim...'

'I didn't say I knew him, just that I could think of someone who fitted that description.'

'Not one of the old crowd, is he?' Zara had prided herself on knowing everyone within the parameters of her project.

'No he's not.' Spike changed the subject and started talking about previous times and situations, which was what usually happened when they met. Then he told her more about Caroline. 'All my dealings have been with her. Sometimes I feel he disapproves but he doesn't interfere. I'm the "temporary gardener" at the moment and I'm "sorting the shed" in the evenings – that's what the neighbours have been told in case anyone gets worried about my being here.'

Zara knew better than to press Spike: if he could do anything he would do it. She said goodbye. She had to pick up Ben from school.

***

As soon as Zara was safely away, Spike locked up the shed and hurried as fast as he could to see a man about a bone. He had known from the beginning of Zara's story that she was talking about Bill Mason but because of Bill's situation he hadn't wanted Zara to know more than was necessary. He was dying of cancer and hated hospitals. Was meant to be having chemotherapy but he kept arriving for it on the wrong day or, if he got the day right, was not fit enough to take it.

Spike had been made aware recently that Bill had something on his mind. He was an alcoholic trying not to drink because of the treatments. He had started to talk which was unusual for him, not very coherently but sufficiently to give Spike the notion that the man might be in serious trouble if he were to tell the whole story to the wrong people.

Spike had known exactly what Zara was talking about because he had already seen the bone. Bill had come to Spike's special shelter. They had sat by Spike's fire and Bill had held the bone close to his chest saying, 'I didn't kill her'. This didn't bother Spike unduly because he knew the cancer would get Bill before any court did even if he were to confess to a murder. Not that Spike believed Bill had murdered anyone anyway. He could see he wasn't that kind of person. "They had it and I had to get it back," he'd said. That was another sentence that made more sense now.

A gleam had come into Bill's eyes as he remembered the break-in: "Silly bitch. Walk in, walk out. Why do people leave their windows open onto fire escapes? Not that I couldn't have got in the front door if I'd had to." Spike had asked him if he'd left fingerprints on the carriage clock. "So what if I did?" Bill had said. "It wasn't her bone and I didn't take the clock did I?" Spike imagined even so that there would be no fingerprints on the bone or the clock. He tried to rehearse a possible future scenario:

'See if the polis come...'

'Why will the polis come? I've got no form!' This was true. No one had ever caught Bill. He was a specialist in his own field.

'That woman will tell the polis,' Spike had said. Bill had let out a wail.

'I need the bone. I need the rest of her. She's not at peace. I didn't kill her.' Spike realised there was a lot more to the story but he knew he would only learn it gradually. He hoped he had time.

'Bill, me old friend, that woman could see it was a human bone. Why would she not take it to the polis?' He smiled to himself now, knowing it had been Zara.

'Well, she hadn't, had she? Otherwise I wouldn't have got it, would I?'

Spike hadn't been able to argue with that.

***

As always when Zara left Spike she thought of her own father. He had died when she was ten. They had been picking brambles on a railway bank and reaching forward for a particularly large juicy spray he had lost his balance and rolled down onto the track.

The trains ran past the end of the garden day and night and Zara knew the timetable by heart. Her father was over six foot and weighed a good sixteen stone: she hadn't a chance of moving him. Wanting to stay with him but leaving, the climb back up the bank seemed to take for ever. Her mum was out but Zara knew she had to phone the station to see if they could stop the train. Instead of saying, 'There's a man on the line', Zara said, 'Has the 10.42 left yet?'

'You've missed it hen. Just left a minute ago.' Zara's house was only a mile from the station.

Afterwards, she could not remember how she had told the man what had happened. The next thing she knew the train was approaching. She stood halfway down the bank willing it to stop. Was it slowing down? She couldn't tell. Then she could hear the brakes and slowly, slowly the train advanced, coming to a stop just touching her father's body.

She should have been elated but she knew he was already dead. She knew it had been a false hope. She had seen how dead his head had looked. It must have been the first part of him to hit the line.

There were only odd pictures she remembered from the aftermath: Aunt Doris at the funeral saying what a great thing it was that the train hadn't mangled his body. She'd once seen... Zara had had to leave the room, overcome with nausea.

It was true her father had looked very peaceful when they'd brought him home. Asleep, rather than dead. However in retrospect, for Zara the central drama had been watching the train stop and she could not rid herself of the idea that if the train had not reached him he would still be alive. She played the scene in her mind and though she always knew she was not in any way to blame, she would try to recall for instance if she had asked her father to try to reach those particular brambles.

She and her mother had grieved hard and together. The first year had been grim but then they had moved away. Neither of them could bear the sound of the trains any more.

Going to a new school in Glasgow, swapping the country for the city, had all helped Zara to move on. As luck would have it, her mother had been in the middle of teacher training when the accident had happened. She managed to finish and get a job.

Strangely, Zara reflected, it had been Aunt Doris who had been partly responsible for initiating Zara's interest in detection for she had "stolen" a photo of her brother, Zara's dad, from Zara's bedroom on the day of the funeral.

There had been a lot of relatives at the house and it could have been any one of them but Zara kept noticing that Aunt Doris looked uncomfortable in a way that didn't quite sit with grief. Then she clocked that the photo was missing and she became so certain her aunt was the culprit that when the opportunity arose of searching her aunt's bag and coat, she did so and was not at all surprised to find the photo.

But she didn't take it back. She bided her time and when she next saw Doris she asked her casually whether she had seen anyone with it. Her aunt had denied seeing it but did not meet Zara's eyes. Zara realized how much she was excited by her role as an investigator. For the kill however, she turned thief and liberated it from her aunt's dressing table about six months after her father's death. Then she took great pleasure in telling her aunt that the photo had turned up.

Why did Spike make Zara think of her father? He was considerate. Although – or was it because – Spike had lived in the street for more than thirty years, he had an amazing capacity for supporting people. But he was no minister without a collar and would defend a body with his fists if he felt they were in the right.

***

Zara arrived at the school gate just as the children were beginning come out.

'We're going to my house today,' she said. 'Barney's got a meeting.'

'I know,' said Ben.

'You can watch telly while I do some work with a tape.'

'Will you make me a burger?'

'Well…' They were turning into Zara's close. She could see someone ahead of her just reaching the bend in the stair. Tall but slighter built than her father. She realized she did this: compared all men with him. But this man was black. She raced Ben up the stairs. The man had stopped on the landing to find his key. Not a visitor then. Her new upstairs neighbour perhaps? The flat had been empty for months.

Zara was going so fast she almost bumped into him. He turned. She apologized, her eyes travelling up to his face. He was a very good-looking African man, hand already extended towards her.

'I am Doctor Andrew. I live above you I think.'

They were standing at Zara's door. She released her hand to find her own key. 'Zara. Zara McDonald and this is Ben. Would you like to come in for a cup of tea?'

28

'That's very kind but...' She had the impression he was slightly shy of her.

'You'll be busy unpacking,' she improvised for him to cover his possible embarrassment at refusing.

...but I don't drink tea,' he said his face breaking into a slow smile.

'What about coffee then?' He followed her in and she invited him to sit down but he remained standing looking about him and then he moved over to the window to look at the view.

'Same view as yours I should think,' said Zara.

'Mine is better. Higher. I can see the hills.' He was right. The low-rise flats opposite meant she only had a glimpse in one corner of her panorama. 'You know the names of the hills?'

'It's the Campsies.' He repeated the words after her. She asked him if he'd been in Glasgow long and noted a minute hesitation before he answered.

'No. Before, I was in England.'

'You had a practice there?'

'I... I did.' Although the sentence was finished, Zara wondered about the stammer, wondered whether he'd left a sour relationship behind him.

'And you?' he was asking. 'What do you do?'

'Free-lance journalist,' Zara answered automatically.

'I buy the Herald. You have articles in there perhaps sometimes?

'I have had,' said Zara. 'They are mostly about crime. Angles on why people commit them, unsolved cases, trends.

'I see. Very interesting. Please tell me when you are having another piece published. I would like to read it.' What a polite man, thought Zara. Or just behaves like one.

Ben had been about to switch on the television when Doctor Andrew asked him about the drawing on Zara's mantelpiece. It was of a dog in a bowler hat. Ben explained that his teacher had written a list of objects on the board and asked everyone to pick three and draw a picture including them.

'And what is the third object?' asked the doctor after a lengthy perusal of Ben's picture.

'The sun,' said Ben, delighted that Doctor Andrew had not guessed. 'See all the yellow. That's the sun shining.'

'It is very good,' said Doctor Andrew. 'It reminds me of a game I used to play with my brother. We would each draw pictures with lots of objects in and then swap them. After two minutes by the clock, you took your picture back and rubbed one object out, carefully, so it looked as though nothing had ever been there and then swapped again and you had to see if you could see what was missing.'

'Can we play it now?' asked Ben

Zara, seeing no reason to interrupt, gave them both a drink and a biscuit and put on headphones to listen to an interview tape.

Chapter V Deep water

Zara had come away from her visit to Spike with mixed feelings. He'd
more or less admitted he knew Jim but he'd seemed reluctant to ask
him about the bone. Was this to protect Jim or to protect herself, Zara
wondered. She supposed it was not a pleasant subject to question
anyone about and if Spike did not know him well... Maybe the guy,
Jim, *was* the murderer and had realized his burial place had been
discovered. And what sort of murder could it have been that had
resulted in such remains? Where was the head? It troubled Zara that
there was no head. No dental records then.

She wondered too about Ben's story. He'd been asked to write about
an adventure but there had been no ruling regarding truth. Had she and
Barney jumped on the bits of Ben's story that fitted their own
perspective? Unless they asked Ben himself, they had no way of
knowing fact from fiction. Something was worrying Zara already: the
name Jim. Perhaps that was just the name Ben had given him in the
story but maybe it wasn't the guy's real name. 'I know someone who
fits that description,' Spike had said.

Zara decided to take Ben to talk to Des. Then she remembered she
hadn't told Des about the tunnel. She flushed with annoyance at
herself. Her four walls were pressing in on her; she decided to go and
sit in the park for a bit. It was calming to watch people idly and
speculate on their lives, or look out for animals – squirrels, deer –
which she might just be lucky enough to see.

It wasn't till Zara saw the man again that she realised she had been
drawn back to that same spot. He stood at the same slightly bent
angle, very still, but now he was making straight for the place where
Ness had found the bone.

Zara thought quickly: maybe if she managed to get close enough
without being seen, she might hear something useful. If she was seen,
she would brazen it out.

She made a long detour so she could approach the river bank side-on
and then silently crossed the fence and came nearer and nearer to Jim,

hiding behind trees and bushes and feeling foolish although there was no one else there.

She stood motionless, listening. 'Jim' was talking to himself again but she could not hear distinctly enough to catch a whole sentence. She doubted anyway whether Jim's speech was that coherent. She was struck by the fact that he looked ravaged. That was the only word for it. He looked like someone in the grip of a nightmare.

A bird suddenly darted in front of her causing her to lurch backwards nearly losing her balance. The noise made Jim look up.

'You haven't seen a black glove, have you?' Zara said the first thing that came into her head.

'No I haven't.' The voice was gruff. Zara pretended surprise.

'Were you not here the other day, when I was with my godson?' The man's eyes were immediately guarded. She realized he hadn't recognized her which was strange since he had followed her to her flat. Jim's face registered withdrawal, irritation and panic all in quick succession. Zara remained calm.

'Sorry did I make you jump? I know when I'm looking for something I get very pre-occupied. If you see a glove, give us a shout will you? It's one of my cycling gloves and I get sore hands in the...' but the man had turned away as if she were of no more account than a stray dog. Instinctively, Zara felt sympathetic but then reconsidered: he could be remorseful, and still a murderer. But she didn't really think he looked like one.

Perhaps, she thought, he had been close to the victim and that was why he was passionate about finding the bones. Looking at it that way, he must know something. I'll need to tell Des he's still searching she decided, as well as about Ben and the tunnel.

Zara walked away slowly only turning when she was about thirty feet away. The man was standing looking after her scowling. Maybe he's the murderer after all, thought Zara.

**

The next morning Zara lay in bed structuring her day. She would phone Barney before he went to work and arrange to talk to Ben after school and depending on what he said, decide with Barney what they should tell Des. Then possibly – hopefully Zara thought – they would ring Des and arrange an interview. .

She got up. It was pointless lying there putting 'ifs' and 'buts' into a situation when there was so much that was assumption. She was about to ring Barney when she changed her mind: it might be better to write everything down first. Who knows, she might gain some clarity.

Then she realized she had left her special notebook in the glove compartment of her car which she had used late the previous afternoon to get her favourite honey from a shop a mile away called the "Tree Bears".

Zara ran downstairs to the street and headed up to her car which was parked thirty yards away on the opposite side of the road. Parking was not fun in her area and she kept convincing herself that she didn't need a car and then finding herself in situations where a car was vital: like a car chase. She grinned to herself remembering. It could probably be recorded as the slowest car chase in history but in the end she had been instrumental in helping the police box in Jack Deakin, and this had led to his arrest and subsequent committal.

She was surprised to find the car door unlocked. The glove box was wide open and stuffed casually into it, half in, half out, was the bone. She sat in the passenger seat and stared at it, unwilling to believe it was real. She glanced in the rear-view mirror and shivered. Was this Jim's work again or had Spike recovered it and left it for her? But Spike would have come to her door or asked her to fetch it from him. Whoever had done it was also giving a clear message: that she was no match for them when it came to surveillance.

She reached for the bone and then made a snap decision. She would deliver it to Des now. That way it couldn't go astray again. She moved over to the driver seat and started the car. She wondered if she'd turned the cooker off and then remembered she hadn't had it on.

***

Des was in his office, not too busy but his face did not exactly light up when he saw her.

'Congratulations, Zara. Have you taken up wizardry? So where was it this time? Did you find it or was it the dog again?' He looked alarmed when she told him the truth. 'I don't like the way your involvement in this seems to deepen. You can see for yourself how dangerous the people are who did this murder

'Supposing,' said Zara as if he hadn't spoken, 'I had some more facts to add to the case. Information that might help you.'

'Something you omitted to tell me earlier?' Des was quick and knew her too well. 'Okay, sock it to us. It had better be good. I'll leave out the warning about obstructing the course of justice for now.'

He had lots of questions about the tunnel which of course Zara could not answer properly since her story was dependent on Ben's.

'What worries me,' said Des eventually, 'is that that tunnel has been used in the past by major players in the Glasgow crime world. If it's one of them, we are looking at real trouble and let's hope nobody in this story got a proper look at Ben'.

'What would they do to him?'

'If you heard one of these guys had eaten their granny, you wouldn't dismiss it out of hand.'

'People like that must have had terrible childhoods,' said Zara, not wanting to believe she'd let Ben near anyone who might be so monstrous.

'If you're going sociological on me, then I should imagine his mother was a drug addict, his father an alcoholic who used his son as a punch bag when he wasn't verbally abusing him and who might well have taught him to be cruel.'

'You've someone specific in mind then?' asked Zara.

'Might have,' said Des, continuing his list of dark possibilities. Zara put her hands over her ears – to shut him up, not because she was squeamish. When he did not stop, she shouted,

'You're getting too cynical!'

'You're talking out of your arse, Zara. We've got bones, we've got the evidence pointing to the possibility that there was a murder and now you give me something which possibly brings in one of Glasgow's nastiest criminals.

'You're talking about Malloch aren't you? Tell me what you know about him then, if you want me to believe he's that bad.'

Des closed his lips together in a thin line.

'No, Zara, I don't want to whet your appetite. Can you get Ben down here today? He'd probably enjoy coming to the station from what you say about him. And for god's sake don't tell him it's about a murder enquiry.'

'It is then, is it, for definite?' It was quite obvious that forensics had come up with something conclusive or Des wouldn't have spoken like that.

'Yes, forensics confirmed certain things. Remains were placed there about ten years ago. There is no sign of the body having been hit with a blunt instrument. Only charring. The question seems to be, if the person had died in, say, a house fire, why would she – it is a she – have been buried secretly? It points to something untoward but who knows what at this stage.'

'But she could have been knifed and bled to death. Or poisoned.'

'Absolutely,' agreed Des. 'And we may never know but we will need a statement from Ben and then follow up what leads we have.'

'You're not going to pull out all the stops on this one though?'

'Things happen in this city every day. They pile up. Obviously if we know there's a killer out there, we have to act appropriately to keep the streets safe for others.'

Zara held up her hand. Des was beginning to go into police-speak. She was becoming irritated.

'Des I really need to go now. Don't want to keep you back. Shall we bring Ben in after school?'

***

Ben was thrilled to be involved. Zara told him the inspector was interested in his take on the man with the missing teeth. She and Barney had to say they'd read his story but Ben hadn't minded that. They said nothing else so they couldn't be accused of putting words in his mouth. He seemed happy to go with Des and a female officer, DC Worth, for his interview and Zara heard him ask if he could try on some handcuffs afterwards. Des had replied that they were for criminals and that Ben was an important witness.

'Come and see the paddy- wagon,' DC Worth said to Ben. Des spoke to Zara and Barney:

'Ugly. If Ben's right about the guy in the tunnel wearing a ring like that, it points to the person I mentioned earlier.' Barney looked questioning but it was obvious Des was not going to expand. 'Anyway', finished Des, 'it gives us a reason for asking a few people some questions but I don't think we'll need to trouble Ben again'.

***

'Or you?' Zara mused at the unsaid part of Des's speech. She was quiet, leaving Barney and Ben, refusing an invitation to eat with them. She felt tired and unsettled. Fragments of conversations, ideas, suppositions were all jostling for space as in an angry sea: she wanted to get home.

She pictured the last third of the soup she had made two days ago. She would heat that up and follow it with some cheese on toast – if she still had some toast-able bread. Then she would watch a film or a nature programme she had recorded but never watched. She could almost feel herself cosy among the sofa cushions. Maybe later on when she had recovered a bit, she would write up everything about the Bone Case in her notebook.

She loved the way the close was always warmer than the street, as if she were home already. She entered the flat and immediately turned on the radio, filled the kettle and switched it on. Consequently it wasn't till she had sat down with her mug of tea and, having heard the news headlines, turned the volume down so the music became a relaxing background, not until then, did she hear an ominous sound coming from the bathroom.

She could not believe what she saw: the bath was half full of murky water but, she noted, the taps were off. A large object floating agitatedly round and round made her look upwards. A hole had appeared in the ceiling. Plaster, the object was plaster and as if to confirm this, another piece fell with a splash and was followed by a torrent of water it had, up till then held back. Something was preventing the water going down the plughole? She felt around and retrieved her flannel which had a habit of sliding into the bottom of the bath when she wasn't there.

Then she ran out of the flat and up the stairs. She banged on Doctor Andrews' door. There was no response. Out, unconscious or dead – whichever it was Zara had to get into the flat. Banking on it just being the Yale she had to contend with, she took a run at the door and found herself in a heap in the hallway on the other side.

In the bathroom, she found both taps full on, the bath overflowing and the water finding rapid egress through the ill-fitting floorboards. Taps off, plug out, the water mercifully started finding its way down the hole.

Zara gazed at the sodden floorboards. She wondered how long the water had been running and where Doctor Andrew had gone in such a hurry. A medical emergency perhaps? But surely making sure the taps, cooker, fires were off should be part of the professional training of someone whose job it was to be on call? You imagined doctors to be practical people.

As was usual with questions she couldn't immediately answer, Zara put this one on the back-burner and went to look at the front door. She was an old hand at forced entry, so she was not surprised to find that the lock still worked after a fashion. She looked around for a screwdriver but not seeing one she was loth to start going through drawers. What's the point of being able to break into someone's house if you're going to baulk at looking for a screwdriver? she asked herself.

She sat down wondering what to do next, half thinking that Doctor Andrew was almost bound to come back, could only have slipped out for bread or milk. Surely at some point he would remember he had been running a bath. Zara contemplated waiting till he returned for ten whole minutes and then became bored. She looked round for paper and pencil to write a note.

It was then she became aware of the whistling sound the landline makes when you haven't put the receiver back on its rest properly. Zara's curiosity picked its way quickly and delicately over her scruples: she dialled 1471 and wrote the number down on her leg in such a way that it was hidden by her trousers.

She was in the middle of writing the note when she heard feet on the stairs. She had left the door open so that her presence would merit less surprise but Doctor Andrew still looked aghast to find her sitting on his sofa. He quickly composed his face, remembering, Zara guessed, that she was the woman who only yesterday had invited him into her flat for coffee.

'Coffee?' he said smiling. He looked at Zara as if he had discovered another quirk in the Scottish culture regarding the speed with which you had to repay hospitality.

'Please,' she answered smiling back. There was a silence after he had put on the kettle and she took it that he was inviting her to explain. After all there was nothing untoward about entering your own front door but sitting pensively on your new neighbour's sofa having forced entry...

'You left your bath water running,' Zara began. Doctor Andrew dropped the mug he was holding but it merely bounced. 'My ceiling is down. Fortunately most of the water that came through was contained in my bath. How long were you out?' He consulted his watch.

'I'm not sure. At least... I am so sorry. I will of course pay for the damage.'

'Are you insured?'

'Yes, yes. I am insured. Of course.'

Zara didn't think he was. He was being polite, trying to make it less of a big deal.

'So where did you go in such a hurry?' Zara adopted a teasing tone, but she was in journalist mode, her information muscles itching.

'Oh I just had to see... what time, the... bank closed.' Zara's face said, 'That took so long?' 'And then I realized I needed bread and milk and there was a queue.'

Zara sucked in her cheeks to stop herself from laughing. She had found out enough for now: something serious had happened. He wasn't going to tell her what it was but it was so serious he hadn't even realized he wasn't carrying any shopping.

'I'm sorry about your lock but I think a screwdriver...'

'It's fine, it's fine. Don't worry. Thank goodness you were in.'

'I wasn't in,' Zara laughed. 'Nice coffee.'

He was on edge and she assumed he wanted to assess the damage and clear up. 'You'd best come and look at it from below,' she said putting down her mug. I think there's a de-humidifier in the back of my hall cupboard, if you'd like to borrow it.'

Chapter VI Drawing blanks

A night's sleep – or was it the night itself? – had crystallized the fragments in Zara's mind and she woke up with a clear plan in her head. It was backed by the bloody-minded certainty that she was not going to bow out of the Bone Case. Everything Des, Barney and by implication, Spike, had said to her, merely confirmed her determination.

It had been the same in the Jack Deakin affair. People had told her she wasn't a detective and suggested she stick to developing her considerable talents as a journalist but she heard condescension and became mutinous. Underneath that though, there was an instinct which told her to follow her nose and in the Jack Deakin case this had proved very effective.

This morning, something inside her was flashing a blue light over the charred nature of the bones: supposing the girl had died in a fire but she was collateral damage – that dreadful phrase – that needed to be hushed up? Usually in a house fire, it was a case of the chip pan or the smouldering cigarette and everyone was sorry and any victims were duly and ceremoniously buried. Would you want to cremate someone who had died in a fire, wondered Zara. There had to be a reason why this particular woman had come to such terrible grief.

Where did the fire fit in? She thought of her projected article about city fires: she would investigate some of the unsolved cases where arson appeared to be the name of the game. She would be able to tell Des and Barney this was her focus and this might get them off her back.

Added to these thoughts, was the 'Jim' factor. Zara wondered if perhaps Jim had been responsible inadvertently for the girl's death and feared discovery. Or perhaps he had been responsible and it had affected his brain. Whatever the truth, there was *something* significant in the man's behaviour, some clue to the situation.

She decided to start by interviewing someone from the council planning committee, regarding a site over which there was currently some controversy. A large building in Slater Street had burned down ten years previously and it had taken till now for the site to be sold and a new building – the inevitable office space – at last proposed.

'You can try the publicity officer, but something tells me he won't want to talk about it, a new guy called Rawls,' said Mickey McDowell, Zara's city council connection.

'Okay, if not him who?' asked Zara.

'You might try Charlie Steading. He's an ex-councillor but he was on the planning committee for years. He's a miserable bastard though!'

Zara phoned Rawls immediately and was blanked by his secretary. Mr Rawls apparently was not taking any calls concerning that particular planning proposal. Especially, she emphasised, he was not taking calls from the press.

'But I thought he was the publicity officer,' Zara persisted.

'Exactly,' said the tart voice. The connection was severed.

Zara had better luck with Steading. There was the minutest hesitation before he said he would be delighted to give an interview. Would Zara like to come to the house? This afternoon? He had a business, Techprod, and did a lot of work from home. Zara went online and searched for Steading's business but found there were more mission statements than product information. Doesn't use his name, she thought.

The first surprise was where Steading lived. She seemed to be following the road that had led to Spike. Then, she had had no address as such, just directions about hills and trees. She could hardly believe it when it turned out to be the same property. She remembered Spike's comment about the man of the house being an oddball. She wondered if she would meet Caroline. However the door was opened by Mr Steading himself and there was no sign of any other living creature.

'Come in, come in, my wife's at the hairdresser's.' Zara instantly didn't believe him: the way he said the words, he might as well have said that his wife was in the hall cupboard. She smiled politely and put her hand absently to her own hair.

Mr Steading's eye followed her hand. 'You've no need of a hairdresser, Miss – what was your name again?' Zara decided to ignore the hairdresser remark.

'Zara MacDonald. Call me Zara.'

'Charles, Charles Steading. Pleased to meet you.'

He offered her coffee or tea and the speed with which he brought it argued that it had been waiting on a tray just inside the kitchen. She sat down on the enormous sofa and looked up at the cornices which were picked out in green and gold. The sofa was pale grey with green and gold cushions. Zara bit back the temptation to say, 'Nice place you have here, Charlie,' and instead brought out her notebook and dictaphone.

'It's very kind of you to give me your time. Are you happy being recorded?' The man nodded. 'Do you want me to fire questions at you or shall we have an informal chat?' Was it the word "fire" in Zara's sentence that evoked a response in Charles Steading's body or just a reaction to Zara's direct approach? Zara felt excited.

'Whichever you prefer. Milk and sugar?' Why was it she kept hearing subtexts? And why should such a very pleasant man engender such a strange feeling in her? She had not liked the way he said the word "sugar".

Zara opted for direct questions but Steading failed to answer directly and went off into tangents about resources and petty restrictions, how these days you couldn't move without Health and Safety slapping you on the wrists, followed by the "dreaded dragon Litigation".

She listened intently as was her habit – you never knew when a person was going to let drop some important but subtle point that might lead somewhere – but no little gems were forthcoming and she decided it was time to rein him in. So far she had nothing and she was determined to get something. Des had once accused her of being able to get blood from stones and although he had meant she was ruthless, she had felt complimented.

Zara realized too that she was being manipulated. Mild-looking Mr Steading had no intention of giving anything away. However, through his flannelling, his protestations, his head-shaking and tut-tutting, she felt she sensed the shadow of an elephant in the room.

Why had he allowed her to come then? Zara hazarded it could be an attempt to make her think he had nothing to hide. She'd asked what the procedure was with a site where the building had been subject to an arson enquiry and whether there was for instance, a specified time-lag before something new could be built. But words like 'procedure' seemed to send Steading into bureaucratese of the paragraph-four,-subsection-twenty variety. She suppressed a sigh.

'To go back to something you said earlier,' she lied, 'can you elucidate regarding the discoveries made in the various fires we've talked about?'

'What I said was,' Steading suddenly became a little sharp, 'that discoveries in these cases tend to prolong investigations. The discoveries may be of displaced money, weapons...'

'Or perhaps bodies?' asked Zara. 'Was there not some possibility that a woman – someone who'd previously disappeared – had been found at ...' Zara consulted her notebook but watched Steading out of the corner of her eye, '... in the Slater Street ruins? I think I read it in the Evening Times archives'. She added the last bit to give Steading a way out. She'd seen his hands grip his chair when she'd said 'woman' and then relax when she said 'Slater Street'. He shook his head.

'I think you would find that that was merely newspaper hype.' She widened the net.

'It's sad isn't it when a landmark business suddenly disappears – in a puff of smoke as you might say?'

Steading's face brightened.

'This is why the council, then and now, always wants to erase these eyesores as soon as possible and move forward. It's no good regretting the past.'

'Rosemary Street. That was a big jeweller's store wasn't it? Zara went on as if Steading hadn't spoken. 'Burned to a shell in six hours. That must have been a lot of petrol.'

Steading didn't bite.

'My mother and father bought their wedding rings there. Sizes 'L' and 'T'. And their names were Lorna and Terence.' He smiled absently. Was he losing his mind or getting worried? She continued:

'They found evidence that ceilings had been knocked through in the upper floors which allowed the fire to be sucked upwards very fast. Work to install a metal spiral staircase was being done on a weekend so as not to disturb business but although the ceilings were down, the staircase had never arrived. And then the fire. They knew it was that way because the rubble had been left in bags in the old stairwell. If the ceilings had fallen in on their own, there would obviously have been rubble all over the place.'

'Very sad, as you say,' said Steading slowly. 'I remember reading about that. Extraordinarily unlucky but just the sort of thing the papers would make hay with. Was that the Evening Times again?'

'That was the Herald.' Silence. Zara was aware of Steading shifting in his seat and wondered whether he wanted her to leave but didn't want to appear to be hustling her out. She decided to ignore that possibility.

'Charles, I wonder if you'd like to comment on the fact that there have been ten major fires within a mile of the city centre going west in the last ten years, five of them ten years ago. In your day, did the council worry about this? Did they think things could be improved? Was there a message there someone wasn't hearing or am I being too much of a conspiracy theorist?' A tight smile from the ex-councillor.

'Obviously, the council is always looking at ways of improving negative statistics. I don't think our averages were or are much different from those in other major cities.'

'No conspiracy then?' His look was pained.

'Are you suggesting not only that some of these fires which were thoroughly investigated at the time and found to be accidents were not in fact accidents, but also that there might be a *pattern?*'

Zara let the question hang in the air and then she said,

'No connections then. I suppose I'm thinking that when the city centre is all built up, it's hard to find a place to construct a whole new enterprise – unless you create one. Did it never cross the council's mind that this might be happening?' Zara didn't like playing these cards; they were almost throwaways in the hand she held, but she might as well play them as concede.

'Rest assured,' said Charles, 'nothing like that goes on at the council. You've been reading too many crime novels and no one but no one died in any of the fires you mentioned'. He turned as he spoke. Someone had entered the room. A tall woman, well-groomed without being stand-offish, stood staring quizzically at the two of them.

'Are you talking about McKelvie Buildings, dear?' she said.

Charles Steading stood up producing a smile from his taut face. 'Caroline, my dear, meet Zara, Zara MacDonald. She's a free-lance journalist come to convince me that arson is rife in the beautiful city of Glasgow.' Caroline walked forward and shook Zara's hand.

'Pleased to meet you,' she said and then as an aside to her husband, 'Come on Charles surprise me, what's new?' Zara picked up her bag.

'I must go. Nice to meet you, Caroline. Thanks for the interview Charles. You've been most helpful. Here's my card should anything occur to you that might interest me.' Zara realized she'd gone into formal mode but she couldn't help it when she was riled. Charles peered at the card and then looked up at her as if to say, '*Me* get in touch with *you*?'

***

Zara hurried home. She wanted to go through the tape while she could add body language notes, the weight of this statement, the light dismissal of that. After that she wanted to see Spike again. She didn't like coincidences and wanted to find out whether Charles and Caroline

45

Steading popping into Spike's life could in any way be connected to them popping into hers.

Zara was certain Steading had been alarmed by her suggestions about arson and he had visibly tightened when Zara had mentioned the possibility of a woman's body at Slater Street but his reaction may have merely been the irritation of a man who wanted to look back on his working life as a vision of seamless integrity. There was though, she felt, something curious about McKelvie Buildings.

Why had Caroline thought she and Charles were talking about that particular fire out of all the others? There was the odd way she'd looked too, almost as if she would enjoy it if her remark discomforted him. Not a happy relationship, Zara had concluded from the bare exchanges she had seen. Curious, she thought, how pretending to be pleasant ended up sounding so much nastier than plain nasty.

***

Charles Steading woke with a jerk about two in the morning. He felt very hot and he could still see flames though his eyes were open. He turned his face to the pillow to stop himself from screaming. He should never have allowed that MacDonald woman to come. He'd just begun to feel clear of the nightmares which had haunted him on and off for so many years.

The irony was that he had never even seen the fire. Just been told about it. The man who'd told him had been trying to gain his trust: he'd told him an awful secret which he wished he didn't know, but now he was so embroiled... He was sweating. At least Caroline was still asleep. Ever since he had woken with the words "McKelvie Buildings" on his lips he had been afraid of giving something away.

***

Zara found Spike easily this time. He was sitting on his favourite bench in a bit of park near Kelvinbridge.

'Your drawing room is looking particularly nice just now.'

'It's the way the sun comes in the windows.'

46

'You've not had that leak fixed though.' Zara waved her hand at a puddle.

'But what do you think of my new wallpaper?' Spike looked appreciatively at the bed of roses in front of them. 'You can't beat roses,' he said. 'Chocolate?' He pulled a couple of Mars bars from his pocket and offered Zara one. She reflected on the irony of him always giving her something. She hadn't eaten chocolate for weeks but she wasn't going to disappoint Spike.

'Like my new coat?' Spike stood up and did what Zara took to be a twirl. 'Belonged to Charlie Steading but it doesn't stop it being a good un.'

'You look a million dollars in it, Spike. It looks hardly worn.' It was a black leather car coat. On closer inspection, it was worn at the cuffs and seams enough to stop a man like Steading feeling comfortable about wearing it outside his house.

'How did you come to be in that area, you know, the day you saw the mattress fire?' Zara asked, seizing an opportunity but genuinely curious.

'I was looking for Munchy. He was meant to be collecting something from Steading. Then someone gave *me* a fiver to deliver a message to Munchy asap. Fiver's not much to you but it seemed okay to me for a walk in the sunshine.'

Zara wondered why someone like Steading should use someone like Munchy as a delivery man. A parcel or a letter she wondered. Not intended to be trackable anyway. Just a message perhaps? As in, Friday's off – or on? She realized it was easy for her to suspect Steading of wrongdoing because she had not taken to him.

'I suppose it was the man that took the bone that brought it back?'

'Aye,' said Spike.

'You could tell him the police found the rest of the bones – apart from the head.'

'He knows,' said Spike. Zara shrugged. She was used to the underground information service being as efficient as that of the people who were paid to know. Even though Zara could see Spike wasn't being forthcoming, she pressed on: she could learn from what he didn't tell her as well as from what he did.

'Does he need to know who the bones belong to?'

'I didn't ask him.'

'You mean he already knew?'

'He didn't tell me.'

'Have the police spoken to him yet?'

'He's in the hospital.' Zara gave up. She could tell from Spike's gruff tone that he was protecting someone but she didn't know whether it was Jim or herself. She could ask Des if he'd spoken to Jim. There was definitely a connection there. And Munchy, where did he fit into the frame?

Chapter VII   Smoke and fire

Before Zara could phone Des, he phoned her. She thought he would
be merely giving her the details of the forensics but he asked her out
to dinner. She was surprised and suspected an ulterior motive but she
was not in the habit of turning down gift horses concerning good food.
He gave her a time and a place, asking if they suited and when she
agreed, he made to ring off.

'About the forensics,' said Zara quickly.

'DNA shows up girl, North African origin, going by remains of
jewellery still attached to the vetebrae, aged circa twelve, they reckon.
Look, I'll fill you in with the un-gory details later, okay?'

Back at the flat, Zara decided to begin assembling notes for the article
she had in mind about arson and prime sites in the centre of Glasgow.
She had material on ten sites. The one that interested her the most now
was the McKelvie Buildings, because of Caroline's casual remark.

She thought about Steading. His attitude had been arrogant and smug
and there was obviously something not good between him and his
wife but Zara had no more than a feeling that he might be implicated
in any way. The feeling was at its strongest when she recollected his
response to her saying, 'A woman was found at Slater Street'. He
hadn't liked a woman being brought into the frame at all and he had
shown this later by stressing that no one had died in any of the fires.
But he had made it sound like a defence of the city, as in, tut tut,
things like that don't happen here. Zara had felt something was being
withheld.

Then there was the Munchy factor. From her knowledge of Spike and
his compatriots, she knew that a messenger taking something from 'a'
to 'b' didn't necessarily mean the messenger was in any way involved.
Often the point would be that they weren't involved. It could be very
useful for *I know nothing* to be true. Zara wondered if Munchy would
tell her more than Spike had. But on what grounds could she ask him a
question? Maybe she was just tired but suddenly the whole business
seemed intractable. Why was she beating her brains out over a few

bones? Even if she did find out their identity, it wouldn't bring the girl back to life.

Zara was suddenly overwhelmed with sadness. It was too late. A life had been terminated with as little thought as it takes to terminate a phone call. She kicked her chair viciously but merely succeeded in bruising her heel. A girl of twelve for goodness' sake! Only now were Des's words getting through to her and they were making her despair.

Zara blinked sullenly at her notebook. Maybe she should just accept what everyone around her said, that she should stick to journalism and leave policing to the police. There was Ben to think of. The 'Jim' character had seen him twice that afternoon and if he at any point thought that a threat might be needed, he might think of using Ben. Spike could have been warning her off for her own good, knowing things she wouldn't even want to know.

Malloch. For the first time she allowed herself to think about him. She had never crossed his path but she knew one or two anecdotes about him, one from Katerina involving a foot found in the sewers. Katerina had pinpointed a metal deposit on the flesh of the ankle which she surmised correctly could have been made by the grip of someone wearing a ring made of a particular silver alloy.

At the time Malloch was known for wearing a lot of silver jewellery. Also it was at a time when he still did a lot of his own dirty work. It was allegedly the only crime he had gone down for and though he was successfully implicated, he was not actually charged with the murder. Apparently Malloch was so disgusted he threw all his jewellery in the Clyde and only wore gold thereafter. He was known for brutality and keeping his word and at least three Glasgow murders were commonly attributed to him.

Zara went cold again thinking of Ben and the tunnel. She felt confused and unable to concentrate. She went to the kitchen to make coffee. She paused, her hand on the kettle. From above she could hear the unmistakable sound of water boiling. A metal pipe in the wall meant that sound travelled down very distinctly. Suddenly she felt a cup of coffee with her new neighbour would improve her mood. And she did need to ask for an update on the bathroom ceiling situation.

Zara tapped unceremoniously on Doctor Andrew's door. He looked surprised but pleased to see her.

'Please come in,' he waved her past him. 'I am just making coffee. You would like... oh I know you prefer tea. I am afraid...'

'Coffee is absolutely fine,' said Zara. He indicated she should go into the living room.

'You are wanting to know about our ceiling?' said Doctor Andrew placing a mug of coffee in front of her. His interrogative statement was casual and it was difficult to tell whether his sentence construction was a result of English not being his first language or an attempt at post-modernism.

'Yes,' Zara replied, not wanting to sully the relationship with polite-isms, 'that is if you've got anywhere. It's early days'. When he didn't speak, she shifted her ground. 'To tell you the truth, I heard your kettle and I didn't like to think of you drinking alone.' He laughed.

'You are quite right in fact. I drink far too much coffee. Fortunately not alcohol or I would be pulled over every night.' Moslem, thought Zara, or just not Glaswegian.

'A guy who can plumb and plaster is coming to give me an estimate tomorrow about ten a.m. I was going to come and ask you about access to your flat.' Zara thought about sharing with him just how easy it was to access her flat but decided the story had too many nasty edges. She didn't want to end up telling Doctor Andrew she had discovered a bone belonging to a North African twelve-year-old especially when she didn't know what Doctor Andrew's country of origin was.

'I can be in whenever,' Zara told him, 'but what about you? Hasn't your job started yet?'

She could see him hesitate. 'Actually it would help a lot if...'

'If you want me to show him the damage, that's fine.'

'I would be very grateful. Very, but it seems the wrong way round. I should be doing you favours.' Zara raised her mug.

'It's just being neighbourly. I'll let you know when I need you to help me shift a piano.' He nodded smiling. She wasn't sure this time if he knew she was joking.

'So how did you come by this plumber/plasterer?' asked Zara, wondering how someone new to the city had managed to find a reliable artisan.

'I phoned my landlord. He is very helpful. I phoned him and he gave me a number.'

'Who is your landlord?' asked Zara.

'He says to call him 'Joe'. His business is property. He has owned this flat for about fifteen years. He said a previous tenant had complained about the taps and he had meant to get them fixed but somehow it had slipped his mind. He will pay though. He says not a problem for him. And definitely not a problem for you,' Doctor Andrew added smiling. It was a beautiful smile and Zara had a feeling that the doctor was not truly aware of its power. She found herself looking at his hands – long fingers, elegant but capable. Gentle, she thought.

'Can I ask you a boring question, Doctor Andrew?'

'Andrew.'

'Oh sorry, I thought...'

'No, no. I was called Doctor Andrew in my previous practice because I shared it with my brother James but no please call me Andrew. So what was the question? Ah, you want to know where I am from? Of course you do. We have to be able to place people to feel safe with them. Even with the mobile phone, it's where are you? First question. I am from Egypt.'

He stood up and went over to his desk. And this is my wife and daughter at her parents' house. Zara took the photograph. She had missed it on her reconnoitre of the room as it had been lying down partly obscured by papers. The face that met hers was beaming and confident and belonged to a tall graceful body. The child was a girl about five years old.

'So your wife is not with you just now?'

'Her parents are not well. I had some difficulties in getting a job there. I thought I could get one easily at home but – the smile again – here I am getting a job more easily in the UK.'

Zara handed him the photo feeling a pang of disappointment. The best ones were always taken.

***

Des was already in the restaurant at a table at the back where he and Zara would be relatively private. It was an Italian restaurant where the waiters knew them both well.

Was it her imagination or was Des looking at her as if she were a woman rather than a professional? She found she didn't mind and decided she would relax and enjoy herself. There was too much seriousness in her life at the moment. Because of this, as soon as they had ordered the food – however long Zara looked at the menu, she always ended up having cannelloni – she asked him for the details of the forensic report to get it over with.

Although the bones were charred, the forensic team had concluded that the victim had not died in a fire. The condition of the neck vertebra had suggested a blow to the head of some force – but of course the head was missing.

The strange thing was, there was still evidence that burning had taken place in two separate loci, one inside a building. A glue such as might easily have been found in an office had melted onto the tarsals of one foot and some plastic had stuck to the ribcage. Small pieces of evidence which might or might not lead to a "where" or a "who". Also the DNA testing had narrowed down the geographical origin of the bones to North Africa, possibly Egypt.'

Zara sat up. 'You're sure?'

'Absolutely. Why shouldn't I be?' Zara shrugged. If she told Des the strange coincidence that the guy in the flat above her came from Egypt too, he would just mock her.

'We have quite a lot to go on,' Des continued, 'especially considering the amount of time it's been since the murder happened. I've worked on far colder cases than this.' The food came and she told Des about her interview with Charles Steading:

'I went to see an ex-councillor today about suspected arson at prime city centre sites. I'm doing an article on it'.

'And?' Des was focusing on his sticky chicken wings. Zara had settled for soup as her starter.

'He said that "no one but no one" died at any of the sites I ran past him – he really stressed that – but he looked quite tense when I queried the fact re Slater Street on the basis of an archived newspaper article. I was lying: it was McKelvie Buildings the article had been about but I wanted to see if he was rattled by the idea of a body.'

'So you have some notion that the victim died in one of these fires, possibly McKelvie Buildings?'

'Actually, what the article said was, "No one who had the misfortune to be in that building would have had any chance of survival. It was such a great conflagration". Zara smiled at him. 'When there's not much truth about, you have to use what you can get.' Des laughed. He appreciated her tactics when they didn't interfere with his operations. 'I suppose I was thinking of bodies because of finding the bone. It would be an amazing coincidence if there was a connection between the victim and one of those city fires. I suppose I was just trying to shake Steading's confidence and the easiest way to do it was to imply people had died there.' Zara sat for a moment enjoying her first mouthful of cannelloni.

'I know it's a long shot but it seems to me that in a normal house fire, there are both survivors and victims and usually the victims are mourned and buried by survivors officially, not carted off to some hole by the river. Of course it's possible that this just happens to be one of these cases where someone started a fire and then felt sufficiently guilty about the result to try to destroy the evidence but to me...'

'Okay, so give me a possible scenario with your limited jigsaw pieces. I can't tell the sky from the sea from where I'm sitting.' Des was humouring her, she knew. He wanted the evening to remain pleasant.

'In my scenario,' said Zara, 'someone would need to get rid of a person, hands off. The crime would not fit. There would be nothing to link the person with it. One of the city fires would have left a body the way you get it from the crem. But supposing something went wrong?'

'What makes you think that? Just because you are interested in two different stories, it doesn't automatically make them linked.'

'I know that,' said Zara. It's just a handy way of thinking about it. There's Jim. He haunts the bone site. He wanted the bone as you might want to reclaim a person. He's obsessive. Spike knows him but he won't tell me anything. I think he's protecting me but he may well be protecting both of us. There's some information there we haven't got.'

Des regretfully ate the last of his carbonara. 'We spoke to "Jim", of course, but there was nothing he said that sounded suspicious.'

'What about breaking in and stealing the bone?'

'There were no prints and he denied seeing the bone. And by the way, his name's not Jim, it's Bill. We interviewed him in hospital. We went by the missing teeth. He did admit to seeing you and a small boy by the river bank but interestingly, he denied anyone had followed him to the tunnel. All we have from the two interviews, Bill's and Ben's are the bare facts that Bill was in the tunnel and that Ben followed him and saw the man with the knuckle-duster.'

'Malloch' said Zara. Des ignored her.

'We have no evidence that ties the bone to him. Nobody saw him with it.'

'You go your way, I'll go mine,' Zara said. 'Do you want coffee?' He nodded and she signalled the waiter.

There was a silence and Zara realized that Des had no more to say on that subject of bones but she had the feeling he was holding something back.

'What is it you want to say?' she asked puzzled. Des blew out his breath looking serious and then grinned.

'If we could get onto a lighter note...' Zara inclined her head, curious. 'Pam and I, as people say these days, are pregnant.'

***

In a different part of town, the following conversation was taking place: 'I need to kill two birds with one stone. There's a budgerigar out there whose tweeting is getting on my nerves. Check.' The speaker moved his queen.

His opponent sighed inwardly. 'Why are you telling me this?'

'Like to keep you in the loop. Just being friendly.' The other man knew that both these statements were patently untrue. He hated when his self-styled friend talked in riddles but he didn't like 'direct' any better. He moved his king out of check.

'I want DI Des off that case. I'll need to give him another. What I want is something that looks like the beginning of a series. Something to get him rattled. Something to focus all his attention on.'

For several years now, the chess games had been a way of ruminating for Malloch. He claimed chess helped his thoughts towards clarity.

'Checkmate,' he said suddenly, moving his bishop and clapping the other man on the shoulder with a hand that felt like a sledge-hammer. 'Thank you, Boris. Once again your help has been invaluable. I'll send you down another case of the whisky. Really helps the game along, does it not?' Then he picked his mobile up off the table and made some quick calls.

Boris, whose name was not Boris, felt fear rise in his gut. He should just turn this guy over to the police. It would be worth it to get a decent night's sleep without pills but he was too afraid of the consequences. He didn't want to be dead yet. It wasn't a case of either his body or his reputation, it would probably be both.

Chapter VIII   A smokescreen of water

Zara ended up inviting Des back to her flat. It hadn't been part of her plan but the evening had gone so well and she wanted it to continue. What had made it especially good, was the fact that they'd disagreed but it hadn't altered the basic tenor of the occasion. She thought fleetingly of Barney but then put him out of her mind. This is professional, she told herself.

She'd opened another bottle of wine and they'd sat on the sofa, both of them, unbelievably relaxed, so much so that Zara didn't want to spoil it by saying something like, 'How long are you staying?' But Zara was doing all the drinking – Des had muttered something about having to use his car later on.

Their eyes locked as they laughed at an anecdote from months ago and she realized with a jolt that she never really even thought of Des as married and here he was going to be a father. She had a tremor of guilt. She realized that up till tonight she hadn't totally ruled him out of her list of possibles.

Zara liked things to be clear once she thought she understood a situation: 'Does your wife know you're here?'

'She's in Venice on a hen night. Back tomorrow. I'm meeting her at the airport at 5a.m.'

'That's a "no" then.' Zara raised her eyebrows suddenly seeing the whole evening in a different light. 'So you're just filling in time here because it's hardly worth going to bed if...'

Des looked at her squarely.

'Did I not seem as though I were enjoying myself? Were you looking for something more?' He put his arms round her shoulders, pulling her body towards him. She would never know whether he had been joking at that point because that was the moment his phone rang. He glanced at his watch: it was 3a.m. He listened and then said, 'I'm on my way.' Turning back to Zara he said, 'They got an earlier flight. If I go now I'll just beat them'. He kissed Zara on the neck and then summarily on the mouth. 'And you'll get some kip after all. Sorry to have to leave so suddenly.'

***

A knock at the door. Zara thought Des must have forgotten something but it was Spike:

'Sorry Zara, I know it's late but I can't find Bill. I know he's been haunting you. I just wondered...' Zara reached for her coat.

'He'll be at the river Spike, won't he?' They fell into step together, Spike not speaking. Zara thought him particularly agitated. It wasn't like him. He wouldn't answer any of her questions as they made their way to the park and walked along the Kelvin scanning the banks. It was a restless shadowy night, a small breeze ruffling the river. There was no one around as if there were some reason for the place to be unfrequented on this night.

Zara pulled a roll from her pocket and tore it in half:

'A bit old but...' Spike muttered thanks but still didn't speak. They went through the tunnel under Kelvin Bridge on Great Western Road. Zara was getting cold and tired but at every corner she was relieved at not coming upon a lifeless floating log or a silent lump on the bank. Until they found the latter.

They both stopped dead and then went forward quietly as if unwilling to disturb someone in sleep.

'He came here to die,' said Zara but Spike was staring hard at Bill's stiff body, anger growing in his face.

'He may have come here to sit but I'm not convinced someone didn't help him die.'

'What makes you say that?'

'The way he's sitting and the fact that he's soaked to the skin. I reckon he was dunked under and then left to catch pneumonia or more likely die of hypothermia, having been given a large dose of – Spike lifted an empty bottle of whisky which was lying conveniently near.

Zara was beginning to agree:

'If he'd fallen in himself and tried to scramble out, he'd never have ended up in this position – as if he's just missing a fishing rod.'

They had not touched him. Zara took out her mobile and dialled 999, handing the instrument to Spike.

***

It was very late by the time Zara got to bed, after the police had taken statements and Bill had gone off in an ambulance but she was totally unprepared when she received a phone call from Barney the next morning. He'd met Spike by Kelvin Bridge underground.

'Go and see him, Zara: he's in a terrible state.'

Zara was all set to rush out when she remembered she'd promised Dr Andrew she'd wait in for the plasterer. She was worried but she did not see what she could do about it. She tidied up and put on a wash and was contemplating cleaning the windows – a sure sign of severe stress – when the buzzer went.

Although there is no 'plasterer design' as such, Zara felt all the world knows what a plasterer looks like and this guy did not fit the bill. He looked as though *he* had fallen off the back of a lorry. He peered at the ceiling or where the ceiling had been and asked if she had a stepladder so he could test the strength of what remained.

'Quite straightforward,' he said to her. 'Can I look upstairs now? You've got a key, ye'?'

Zara accompanied him to Doctor Andrew's flat and stood while he took stock of the bath. 'Looks like the guy just went out in a hurry. Okay for the likes of me. Not so good for you. Landlord asked me to check if the overflow was working and if the washers needed renewing.'

'When you live in a flat like this you never know what's going to hit you from above or below,' said Zara, one ear to the guy's laconic talk but her mind on Spike. She couldn't remember exactly what Barney had said.

'...in two or three weeks, to make sure it's dried out,' she heard the plasterer say.

'I'll give you my phone number so you can contact me directly.' Zara was standing by the window looking onto the street and heard someone sound a horn.

'That's my mate. He's parked on a yellow line. Usually gets away with it at this time of day but...' His hand was on the door handle, waiting for the number but impatient.

For some reason, after seeing him out, Zara went back to the window. There was something familiar about the driver but she couldn't think what.

***

It wasn't until about one in the afternoon that Zara left the flat to search for Spike. First her mother had phoned regarding an aunt visiting from New Zealand and then Zara remembered it was the last day for paying her electricity bill. When she found Spike, he was drunk. She knew him to be a recovering alcoholic but she had never known him to succumb. He wasn't apologetic: he was still angry.

'It's that fucking bastard that's behind it.'

'What bastard, Spike?'

'The one that made Bill get rid of the body. Bill had nothing to do with it. He was just a look-out – you know, whistle if the coast's unclear – but he saw...'

'What did he see, Spike?'

'I don't know. That's what he said. They'd have some plan and he probably had to signal if... I don't know, Zara. I wasn't there. I only know what he told me.'

'Spike, why didn't you tell me this earlier? Or tell the police?'

'He only told me yesterday. He was in hospital but he wanted out. I couldn't persuade him to stay and neither could the doctors. He said he had to get back to the river. It was them that killed him. Made it look as if he fell asleep and died of hypothermia but it was them. You'll see when the mortuary men have done their job. You'll see. It was someone who knew he was too frail to survive a night soaking wet, outside. And I reckon they also frightened him to death. He had the look of someone who'd died in terror.'

'But why would anyone want to kill him?' asked Zara.

'Because the burden had become too much for him. The burden of being in hock to Malloch.

'And why was he in hock to Malloch?'

'Things going way back. I'm not even sure...' Spike's eyes looked past her for a moment. 'He didn't know who that body was but he knew it was not an accidental death. He saw the body in McKelvie Buildings.'

'McKelvie Buildings?'

'It was moving he said.' Spike continued unaware of the effect the words had had on Zara. 'He couldn't believe it. Lit up by the flames it was. Its arms went up as if asking for help. Must have been the effect of the heat. Bill didn't think. He dashed out of his hiding place across the street and found an open door. It was like a janny's office and the body looked as if it had been left with a broom in its hand.'

'A twelve-year-old cleaner?' Spike nodded, not really taking in the implications, and took another swig out of the half empty bottle of whisky. Zara cursed herself for not having got to him sooner. She had never seen him so upset.

'He rushes in thinking, this person should be dead but she's moving. The fire hasn't completely taken hold here, though there are cracks in the walls from heat from the rest of the building. At first he can't see why the person is alight and then he spots a can of something inflammable and realises the body has been doused with it and the rest will create an inferno when it explodes, not leaving much evidence behind.'

'Bill takes his coat off and throws it over the girl – she's not very big – and runs out. By now the fire brigade has arrived but they are on the other side of the building. He runs back to his hiding place and puts the girl down. Only then does he realize just how dead she is. She didn't die in the fire, he can see that but what can he do now?'

'How did he keep the secret all this time?' asked Zara. 'It's incredible.'

'Drink. He swallowed it down every day of his life for nine years.'

'And then?'

'His liver. Cancer. They told him to stop, the doctors, and he tried but then he got the nightmares. That's when I began to notice something was wrong but even then he never said anything that I could make sense of – till yesterday. He knew that bastard would take him out if he told anyone the secret. No one knew where she was buried, no one and I don't know how that bastard got to know about Bill's illness but someone told him and it was too risky, someone in a weak state like that might talk. He couldn't even wait for Bill to die naturally.' Spike wiped his eye.

'So what made Bill dispose of the body? Why didn't he just abandon it? He hadn't killed the person after all. He could have gone far away and then phoned the police.'

'He panicked. He has a daughter. Never sees her but that's by the by. He knows what it means to have children. He couldn't leave her but he was afraid, because he suspected that the bastard who'd caused the fire had something to do with the body. He phoned him.'

'Phoned who?'

'Malloch, Zara, but you don't want to know. Don't get involved with him. I am not telling you anymore.' Zara looked at him in the ensuing silence.

'And you're not telling the police either?'

'The police know about Malloch. More than I do. I don't expect I could tell them anything they didn't know.' Zara could see Spike might close down in spite of the drink.

'Okay, Spike, I'm sorry. So what did Bill do, poor sod?'

'He phoned him, like I said and he said, "Just *disappear* the body. A car will come for you. I don't want to know where you bury her. Think of a place. The driver will have a spade but don't let him know which direction you are going in after he's dropped you."' Zara was angry and shivering at the same time.

'And Bill did this?'

'He couldn't see what else to do. The guy made him feel it was his fault, spoiling a good plan, not sticking to his brief.' Zara put her arm round Spike.

'Will the police be releasing Bill's body?'

'Later today. His daughter's been let know but she's in England.'

'You want me to help?' Spike nodded and took another swig from the bottle.

***

It wasn't till much later in the day that Zara was able to contact Des. He was either out or otherwise occupied. She left messages for him to call her back but he didn't. Maybe he was embarrassed about the way the evening might have ended. There was no point in thinking about it: she didn't know.

She spent the day helping Spike with the funeral arrangements. The daughter, Brenda, was on her way up and had said she was paying for everything. Spike had given Zara's mobile number to the police – not that he'd ever used it himself but he had it among the important pieces of paper he always carried with him.

The funeral was scheduled for Wednesday. It turned out Bill was Roman Catholic, 'though how he can be a Roman with a name like Mason I don't know,' Spike had said when he told Zara about the priest wanting to do the last rites one time when Bill was caught in the hospital. Bill had succumbed it seemed.

Eventually Zara managed to speak to Des who said he could give her half an hour. When she asked if that was him finishing his shift, he snorted:

'With what's going on in the city just now, it's unlikely I'll ever leave the station again.' They met in a little café across from the building where Des worked. He eyed her with a look that held curiosity and exhaustion. 'Shoot,' he said.

'You've seen Spike?' Des nodded. 'You agree with him it's murder?'

'If you're talking about Bill Mason, yes, no, I don't bloody know, probably, is the answer.'

'Did Spike tell you it was Bill who...'

'I know what you think about Bill and the bone, but this has fuck all to do with that.'

'How can you be so sure?' Des looked at her for a moment and Zara could see he had bitten back whatever sarcastic remark he was about to make:

'Supposing I told you there had been three attempts to drown people in the Kelvin last night? Zara looked suitably shocked. She could see Des was not joking. 'The first was our man Bill and we got the call, as you know, from Spike. We were treating it as an accident in spite of what Spike said until we had another call.

'A woman had gone to Partick police station, soaked to the skin. She claimed she'd been dragged into the river on her way home through the park and held under the water for some time. No, her clothes weren't taken off,' added Des anticipating Zara's question. 'The woman lay there trying to get her breath, expecting each one to be her last but then suddenly the man wasn't there.

'And as if that wasn't enough, a gay guy was found, again soaked to the skin with a knife mark against his jugular. He's asthmatic and he'd lost his inhaler in the confusion. If it hadn't been for another gay guy coming past, he would have been a goner too.'

'Attempted robbery?' suggested Zara. Des thrust his bottom lip out.

'Nothing fits all three but they are too similar to rule out the possibility that one person or one group is behind them. If it's some mad man on the loose we should be expecting more. We're lucky we didn't end up with three bodies. One's bad enough.'

'Won't there be fingerprints to tie the three assaults together or not as the case may be?'

'There are none. The woman said her man was wearing a mask and gloves. And his voice was obscured by the mask. Not that he said much apparently.'

Zara thought, obstinately she knew, that the whole business could still have something to do with Bill's interest in the bone about which he seemed to know more than most but she could see Des was on a roll. Plus there was what Ben had reported the voice had said in the tunnel: 'I'll kill you if…'

'So what about the bones in the river, are you still…?'

'That will have to go on the back-burner for now. Not forgotten but we have to concentrate on catching whoever was responsible for last night. He may do more. Whoever was responsible for killing the girl in the river isn't likely to be striking today.'

Zara compressed her lips. She hated when Des was so sure of himself but she thought, if I'm right we are still looking for the same killer. I'm just going from a different angle. She was acutely aware that she had decided absolutely to continue her pursuit, whatever Des did.

She was quite glad on reflection, that he had not stayed the night as she really didn't like him today. *Now* would have been much more difficult if *then* had been different. She looked at him, a quick flick of her eyes, to see where his mind was: hundred per cent focus on the job. That was Des. She knew it was just his way of working and, without getting into a gender argument, the way most of his male colleagues worked.

Zara felt she had a logical mind but she also used hunches far more. She had evidence of them working so why wouldn't she? It was no different if you ended up in a blind alley, from getting there on a logical basis.

Zara didn't know what her next move was going to be but it would be secret. She would use the material she had. She didn't think Des knew the story of the fire yet. She had been going to tell him because she didn't think Spike would have, but she'd keep it a little longer now. She knew there was a big piece of the jigsaw missing. And perhaps they were looking at more than one jigsaw.

Chapter IX If you are lost, use a map

Spike had told Zara that Bill's friends would feel happier getting together after the funeral in the park rather than in the lounge of a pub where they were not usually welcome. And the daughter Brenda had agreed. She was very "agreeable". The park was Bill's garden – Spike had put it to her like that.

The turnout was big and Zara felt at once she was there with two hats – the mourner's and the investigative journalist's. As she handed round sandwiches to the folk hunkered on the grass, she wondered if Des would put in an appearance. People who were part of the jigsaw often turned up at funerals.

The crowd was sad and amiable with it. No visible alcohol due to the law but there was the inevitable half bottle in the inside pocket. The food made up for it. It was being supplied on a continuous basis from a nearby restaurant. Zara wondered about a daughter who never came to see her father but who could spend a hundred or two on a funeral tea. Spike smiled at her elbow, following her eye and discerning her train of thought.

'The son, guilt money. Couldn't make the event. Important business meeting in Geneva.'

'Poor Bill,' said Zara.

'What's more,' Spike added, 'neither Brenda nor James knew their dad had cancer'.

Zara sighed. It was easy to picture, less easy to judge. Bill hadn't either a mobile or a fixed address. A man in a suit with commitments in Geneva would find it hard to contact such a father. Brenda had three children and a husband who worked on the rigs. Bill's elder brother had gone to Canada as a young man. His younger sister had died of a heart attack in her early sixties.

There were one or two surprises. Zara spoke to a man who said he'd taught Bill to play the fiddle many years ago. They had busked in Buchanan Street.

'He could sing too.' Munchy had joined the conversation. Zara was taken aback. She had thought the fiddler was talking about a time before Munchy was born but Munchy was a man of undefinable age and Zara didn't know him at all well. He had been absent from Glasgow when she had been working on the Project.

She suddenly became aware of eyes in her back and she turned to see a tall thin man with pale eyes looking intently at her. She recognized him as the person who had approached Munchy and made him uneasy when she had been asking where Spike was. As soon as he realized she was looking, he withdrew his gaze but in an odd way, as if the light in his eyes was being depleted gradually from the back of the sockets. Zara also noticed how nobody except Munchy stood close to him and when he wove through the crowd to the food table, he cut an invisible swathe on either side of him.

'Who's your friend?' Zara asked Munchy.

'That's Screw,' said Munchy cheerfully. 'Stephen Crewe,' he added, just so she didn't think the name had any negative implications. 'Mate o' mine. Been away.'

'Chicken wing?' the voice, which belonged to Screw, made Zara jump.

'You're all right,' she said. Something about Screw's hand proffering the plate made her feel distinctly vegetarian.

'So sorry to hear about Bill,' Screw was saying. His voice was pleasant in tone and timbre but Zara didn't like it.

'Did you know him well?' Zara was trying hard to stay polite.

'Very well. Over the years. Lost touch recently...'

Zara's attention was suddenly distracted by Spike who was about fifteen feet away. He had his thumb nail between his bottom front teeth and was drawing it upward the way people do when they have food stuck. Zara watched mesmerized. Her memory wasn't working properly. Then she recollected how she felt. The proximity of Screw made her feel afraid. Spike was warning her.

69

She remembered now, it was a code they had shared on the Project for when she was about to get into deep water and he knew something she didn't. She detached herself as casually as she could and walked away, purposely not towards Spike. She busied herself passing a plate of food around, chatting briefly with people till she accidentally on purpose, came round to him.

'Keep out of that guy's way,' he said between gritted teeth, head down as if inspecting the pizza slice he was about to take. Zara slid away quickly, grateful that Spike had eyes in the back of his head where her safety was concerned.

She was torn. She felt certain that Screw was a jigsaw piece but she recognized that Spike's warning was real and that not to heed it would be foolish. She wondered if Munchy were safe. He was doing his best to be cheerful, that was his personality but she felt he had been hard hit by Bill's death. She was aware Munchy and Bill had spent a lot of time together lately. Spike had told her that Munchy had visited Bill every day when he'd been too ill for even him to stay out of hospital.

Zara looked round at the people present who obviously felt Bill had contributed something to their lives, enough to make them want to pay their respects, tell his daughter what a good man he was. Zara stood feeling the warmth generated by all these friends and acquaintances of Bill's. She felt she knew him a little now. He was no longer a stranger hunting for something but a human being with a heart.

Then she turned round and went cold. Screw was gazing at her again as if he could see right through to her bones.

***

Back home, Zara pondered on what she had so far. She took a large piece of paper and plotted everything diagrammatically. Bill's story went into a central box and from it there were lines linking boxes called 'Fire' and 'Body'. From 'Fire' she drew a line to a box marked Steading and from that to a smaller box called Munchy. Reluctantly she made a box for Screw.

Zara hesitated but realized she needed a box from Steading to Spike but here hesitance told her there was a different relationship between them than between Steading and Munchy.

She was uncertain as to what value to give the tunnel story. She wondered here about taking Ben to see Katerina: maybe he would say something more about his experience if he were excited by Katerina's fossil collection.

She made a box for Malloch. She made it big and placed it at the top, dominating everything.

Next to the word 'Body' in Bill's box, Zara drew a line to a box named 'Forensic report'. Then she allowed her mind to play over the diagram. She noticed she had placed Munchy between Steading and Screw. This could indicate Munchy as go-between. Was Screw important or was there another line to another, at present missing, box? Would Screw lead directly to Malloch? She didn't know. Then she felt she needed another box for Bill's own death or murder. It felt much more macabre drawing Bill's box and she didn't like the way the box marked Malloch hung over it in a menacing way.

She looked hard at the 'Forensic' box. She had written 'Charring times two'. She shut her eyes and tried to visualize scenarios that made sense: Bill reaches the spot by the Kelvin. Although the body is small it still represents a lot of digging. Bill imagines Brenda as a child. There is no way he can break the body so it fits into a smaller hole but he thinks if he lit a fire...

Perhaps he hopes the girl comes from a culture where riverside burning is part of the death ritual. He lights a fire. It's easy, he's used to it, can do it in all weathers, even knows where there is some old dry timber. He digs while the body burns.

His heart is heavy, the smell is wrongdoing personified but he keeps digging. He is driven by the spectre of Malloch which prevents him considering going to the police. He can see a murder being pinned on him and he can't see further; his mind is too panicked. What, Zara wondered, did Malloch have over Bill that made him so frightened.

'Plastic on the ribcage,' Des had said. Had Bill wrapped the body in a mac – he'd carried a rucksack in the park – in the mac and then into the bin bag. Zara couldn't see Bill putting the body straight in with no intermediate covering. She smiled to herself. It was as if there were a code of behaviour all right-minded people knew for dealing with such a situation: 'How to disappear a body with due respect'. Ethics were funny things: even when people were doing wrong they could be trying to do it right.

Zara gazed at the diagram feeling pleased with her work. It gave her a sense of where she was. It was strange how a diagram could do this. It was a map in progress. She had reached a river certainly. One of the crocodiles was called Malloch. She did not yet know where it was lurking.

***

Zara had decided to go and feed the ducks. She had half a stale loaf and she had been sitting still too long. Later she would get back to organizing herself vis à vis articles she wanted to write. At the moment, she didn't know where to begin.

She found the ducks very therapeutic and loved the quiet quacking that accompanied their so silent swimming. The sun made patterns on the water, the trees reflected themselves and the whole scene was a constantly shifting colour-and-light show.

Nobody disturbed her thoughts and soon she had recovered her equilibrium and turned for home. She could not help remembering Bill as she passed the place on the river where Ness had found the bone. She hoped the man was at peace now in spite of the troubled waters he'd left behind him.

Turning her face away from the river she came face to face with a man, an African with a familiar face. 'Doctor Andrew,' she greeted him, 'Have you...?' but the man had walked straight past her, if anything quickening his step.

She stopped and thought: the only difference between him and the man who had brought down her bathroom ceiling was that this man had a strange injury to his cheek. A new injury, the blood not quite congealed. But why would Doctor Andrew not speak to her? Was he embarrassed because of the ceiling? He hadn't seemed embarrassed yesterday. Had he been deep in thought and not immediately recognized her? But she had said his name. However, Doctor Andrew, she reminded herself, had left both bath taps running and gone out. Maybe not recognizing her was part of the same amnesiac behaviour. She smiled. It was amusing to have such an odd neighbour.

***

Zara remembered she was looking after Ben that afternoon. She decided she would take him to visit Katerina as Barney was not due home till seven-thirty. She decided not to tell Barney where she was going as he might say no to Ben having anything more to do with the Bone affair. She justified herself by using the argument that she would say nothing to lead Ben to talk about the bone: she would just hope he talked about it with no prompting.

Ben was delighted to be going to Katerina's. He was fascinated by the fossils in the museum and Katerina had a whole room full of them which spilled out into the hall and onto her patio.

After being given a conducted tour, Ben sat between the two women sublimely happy with his takeaway hamburger and chips, the meal he wasn't usually allowed. Ness was poking around in the long thin sliver of garden that Katerina was lucky enough to possess as part of her basement flat.

'She's found a fossil,' Ben shouted as Ness appeared from the middle of a hydrangea bush bearing a piece of rock in his mouth.

To Ben it was a magical repeat of the bone incident. Katerina tried to explain that Ness hadn't *found* the fossil in so much as it had already been found once and had somehow got into the garden from the house.

'You have so many, you can't keep track of them.' Ben nodded as he spoke in an adult way. 'Well done Ness,' he said, patting her head as she paused momentarily in her investigations. 'I think you should definitely take Ness next time you go on an exploration. She's so good at finding things.' Zara opened her mouth to head him off. She wanted to be squeaky clean if she had to answer to Barney later but Ben came in at an odd angle: 'If she'd been with me in the tunnel, she might have found something really exciting. She might have gone into that place where the man with the missing teeth disappeared'. Ben was looking at Katerina, telling Katerina because, Zara supposed, he thought she was less conversant with the story. 'I only got a glimpse in the door before Jim – that's what I called him in my story I wrote for school but he was actually called Bill - I heard this voice shout, 'Bill' – before 'Jim' disappeared. If Ness had been there, she might have dived in and brought out a really useful piece of evidence.'

'Maybe,' said Katerina.

'I just saw this man, well his nose mostly and his hand was moving like when you're excited' – 'Barney is always telling Ben not to wave his hands about at the table, it's too expensive,' Zara put in – 'and I saw this ring on his' – he indicated his index - 'this finger. There was some sort of light and I could see this ring with lots of angles, glinting like gold treasure and then the voice shouted 'I'll kill you if...' and I ran away as fast as I could.'

'Good thinking,' said Katerina. There was a silence.

'You know' said Ben, 'I think we should call her 'Ivory'.

Who?' asked Zara though she thought she knew the answer.

'The owner of the bone. You can't go on calling her "the bone girl". It isn't very...'

'You're right Ben. It's a good name. We'll do that if and when we need to.' Ben was away down the garden again. Zara turned to Katerina:

'My god. How beautiful he should come out with that.'

'And there's no way he made up that story,' added Katerina.

'It underwrites Spike's conclusion about Bill's death not being an accident,' said Zara. There was a silence and then she shrugged her shoulders.

'Have to wait and see what the pathologist says,' said Katerina. Then, 'You were going to tell me about the forensic report on the bones. Did it mention the pubic bone being cracked?' Katerina asked.

'Why would that be significant? Wouldn't there just be cracking with the heat?'

'What I'm thinking,' said Katerina looking grim, 'is that that sometimes happens in female genital mutilation, FGM for short, and you say the girl could have been from North Africa'.

'Yes, there were wee bits of beads found from there,' said Zara. A dreadful chill went through her body, starting in her sexual organs and rising to her throat. Her hand found her mouth.

'I'm just saying it's a possibility,' Katerina added trying to soften the shock. Zara's eyes were looking into the far distance. FGM. Now she realized she might have touched the bone of a girl for whom this horrific ordeal had been a reality. She felt sick and powerless. Katerina handed her a glass of water. 'Ben's coming back,' she said. Zara managed a smile.

Katerina was so practical but sensitive with it. Zara rose to her feet.

'Come on Ben, we need to get you home. You can come and see the fossils another day.'

'And me,' said Katerina.

***

Coincidentally, Zara bumped into Doctor Andrew on the stairs and she was initially wrong-footed by his cheery greeting. She recovered by the next turn of the stair and said,

'You were deep in thought when we passed each other in the park today.' Even in the dim light of the stairwell, she could see his surprise was genuine.

'I was not in the park,' he said. She looked at his face: there was no sign of injury. What she had seen was far too deep to have been magicked away in a few hours even if he were a doctor. He felt her scrutiny.

'What is it?' he asked. 'You must have mistaken me for someone else'.

'Yes,' said Zara, her words coming slowly, 'this man looked like you but he had a strange injury to his face. And I can see you haven't'. She added this last to try to lighten the tone but she saw that Doctor Andrew now looked very agitated as if a whole jumble of anxious thoughts were colliding in his mind. Then he obviously made a decision. His face cleared.

'That could have been my brother,' he said. 'He is also a doctor. His name is Doctor James. I told you of him.'

Zara nodded. 'I remember now. 'Have you seen him today?' The doctor jumped, then re-composed himself so quickly that Zara wasn't even sure she'd seen it happen.

'Yes. In fact, I have just seen him.'

'And did he have an injury to his face?'

'Yes, yes, he did.'

'It must have been your brother then?' Zara was half-teasing.

'He had an argument with a door.'

'I see,' said Zara. 'I'm sorry about that'. The doctor continued up the stair.

'Neighbours,' she thought. 'Why are they always such peculiar people?'

Chapter X Matching odd socks

Spike picked each object up in turn for the fourth time in a row. The entirety of Bill's possessions lay before him on the ground. Brenda had wanted nothing. She had mentioned a ring of his mother's she'd thought he'd had but when Spike knew nothing about it, she left the matter.

The grey rucksack was grimy and battered but Spike thought he could use it, at least till it fell to pieces. The contents were forlorn. A toothbrush – hardly used. Spike smiled and shook his head. Bill's mac, a tent of an affair, his "home in wet weather" he'd called it. Sundry socks, odd ones. Bill had a thing about socks: 'You never find a pair', he'd say but as long as the sizes matched it didn't matter to him. There were eleven socks and one pair of underpants.

Apart from these things there was a mug and a tin plate, a knife and a spoon. Bill, unlike Spike, didn't stretch to the sophistication of a frying pan and primus. There was one photo of his children, heads together looking happy; when they'd been about seven and nine.

Spike rested, the photo still in his hand, and for a moment re-lived the funeral tea. He'd felt on edge ever since yesterday afternoon, from the point when Screw turned up. The only time he'd ever seen Screw before, was in the company of Malloch. It worried Spike that Malloch was sufficiently interested in Bill's funeral to send a representative for he was certain that's what Screw had been. He was especially alarmed at Screw's interest in Zara. He knew that not telling her about Malloch was risky because she was always fired up by secrets but he felt the longer he could stall her attempts to investigate Malloch, the better. He'd meant to have a word with Barney about it all but Barney hadn't been at the funeral as he'd expected. He'd had to go to court with a client.

'Hullo Spike.' Zara's voice coming so close on his thoughts made him jump. 'Bill's things?' She squatted down beside him and picked up the photo that had fallen from Spike's hand.

'Nothing here worth keeping,' Spike said suddenly and began cramming everything into an old bin bag. Zara watched him in silence. The socks disappeared and then he began stuffing the mac in.

'Wait,' said Zara. She had noticed a piece was missing from the bottom corner at the front of the garment. Two things came together in her mind: plastic fused to one of the bones mentioned in the forensic report and her own image of the body being wrapped in something...'Supposing Bill had wrapped it in this mac to bring it from the fire in McKelvie Buildings but then discarded it when he placed it in the fire by the river – if indeed that had happened – but perhaps a piece had caught, torn and melted. She wondered if the mac could be tested against the plastic found fused to the bone. Spike seemed indifferent to whether she took it or not.

'Giving it to Des, are you? That's all right then.'

Zara wanted to ask more questions about Bill and the girl's body but she didn't want to be insensitive. Spike would know immediately if she circled the subject and he might withdraw if she asked too bluntly. No alcohol today to take away his inhibitions. What she really wanted to know of course was more about Malloch. Des had warned her off too. She guessed they both seriously wanted to protect her but she didn't want to be protected.

'Munchy might like the socks,' Spike said suddenly, 'but he's not very good at hanging onto things. I'll keep him a couple for old times' sake though. He picked out two of the thickest ones with no holes. Given an in, Zara capitalized:

'Munchy wasn't looking too hot yesterday.'

'Took it hard, did Munchy. They were good pals.'

'I know,' said Zara. 'I felt that.' Pause. Then, 'Who was the guy you warned me off? Is he a friend of Munchy's?

'Some friend!' said Spike. 'Munchy told me he took his photo of his father. The only one he had. He was that upset on top of the death and everything.'

'Why would Screw want the photo?' Zara tried to keep her voice even.

'Don't suppose it was the photo so much as the fact it meant a lot to Munchy. Blackmail value.' Spike paused. 'I don't know why the guy was at the funeral.'

'You mean Screw didn't have a motive for being there?'

'Who knows?' said Spike looking away. Not a good liar, thought Zara. It didn't matter: she knew now that Screw was important just because Spike was refusing to talk about him.

'He's part of Malloch's team then?'

Spike looked really upset. 'You'll take the mac then, Zara? I couldn't wear it. I'd feel I was disguised as Bill!'

***

Zara made straight for the river bank. She was wondering if she could prove there had really been a fire near the burial place. Her memory was that the police had not combed the ground around but had stopped when they had found what constituted a skeleton. Except for the head. From what Des had said, the head was presumed to have drifted down river like the pelvis.

She was hoping to find charred earth. She stood on the little stony beach and thought about where she would put a fire if she had Bill's task to do: not near the river, near the wall. Dryer and more sheltered. She looked around for a digging implement and found a rusty metal stake. She decided to dig in ten sample spots and if she found nothing, she would go home.

The ground was hard to dig. She removed surface stones and then used the stake as a drill. She didn't think she would need to go far down for ten years. After four attempts she stood up feeling defeated. She hated to draw blanks. She took a step back and surveyed the ground pretending to be Katerina. If there had been a fire, might there not be evidence in the way the vegetation grew? Maybe there was a plant just waiting for a charcoal feed. Or one that hated charcoal.

She chose a place where the prevalent plants seemed to end abruptly and scrabbled out the stones. There was a darker colour showing. She took out more stones and widened the area. It was becoming sticky and black and instead of more stones, there was a layer just over an area about three feet by two, of black dirt.

She lifted a sample between her finger and thumb. Charcoal. She lifted a larger sample and took out her magnifying glass. There were tiny broken bits of something different. Bits of bone, thought Zara collecting some and stowing them in a plastic bag in her pocket. Only they've been trodden on and sunk down through the years. She took a copy of the Metro from another pocket and spread it carefully over the exposed area. Here we go again, she said to herself, covering the newspaper with random stones.

***

'I've got evidence that connects Bill Mason to the Bone Case.' Zara in her excitement had forgotten that Des had marginalized her take on the situation in the face of the strange business of the three drowning attempts which put Bill Mason in a different context. Or so Des liked to think.

She had wavered as to whether she should go straight to the station or ring first but since her evidence was hard, she felt she might as well present it physically: she couldn't put the bits of bone down the phone and she knew Des would have to give them a cursory glance at least.

He looked grey with big bags under his eyes and as if the coffee he'd drunk to wake himself up had sent him into a manic overdrive. He didn't speak, merely held out his hand and Zara gave him a small clear plastic bag through which you could see the crushed pieces.

'So you've been back to the site and found more bits? Is that it? Or is this another body?' He passed his hand over his head as if to make room for more information.

'Same bit of the river that was excavated but about twenty feet away, near the wall. In black mud. Looks like a fire was lit. As far as I could see,' Zara added, playing humble.

Des nodded.

'Okay. This is "the bones were burnt twice" theory?' Zara nodded back.

'And I've got Bill's mac. There's a bit missing. I thought it might match the plastic that was found fused to a bone that was mentioned in the forensic report.' Des's eyes actually shut: he didn't want to divide his energies, he didn't have enough of them but he answered,

'I'll see to it. Get it checked'. He held up his hand as Zara tried to interrupt, 'and I'll let you know but meanwhile will you promise to do *nothing?*'

'Thanks for your time, Des.' Zara wore her I'm-not-answering-you-if-you-don't-treat-me-like-an-adult look.

***

Zara came away feeling hostile. She felt everyone was trying to block her – Des, Barney, Spike – and consequently she wanted to do the opposite of what they suggested. She decided to walk back home and was deep in thought in the middle of Great Western Road when a voice called her name. She didn't immediately recognize it and turned round to find Munchy grinning at her. The photo she thought. I must ask him about the photo.

'Nice funeral, wasn't it?' There was a one-legged pigeon hopping behind him.

'Is that yours?' asked Zara. She recalled seeing a one-legged pigeon near the food tables, along with a lot of two-legged ones of course.

'Fond of me but I wouldn't go so far as to say it's mine,' said Munchy.

Zara wanted to tread carefully. Spike had ended up refusing to talk but maybe if she went about it the right way she could get some information from Munchy.

'A terrible shame, what happened,' said Munchy. 'I've rarely seen a man go down so fast. He ought never to have got the cancer. Too much on his mind, that's what finished him, if you ask me, not that anyone ever does.'

'He talked to you, didn't he, when he was in the hospital?'

'A lot of it didn't make sense of course but he was very troubled about that night, that particular night.'

'What particular night?' Zara had not really thought that Munchy would know as much as Spike.

'I was there at the McKelvie Buildings. I saw Bill dive into the building and come out again. I couldn't believe my eyes. He should have got a medal. There was flames and smoke and I don't know how he could have seen anything.' Zara pretended to look mystified.

'You think he was looking for something?'

'I'm not suggesting nothing. I only know what I saw.' Munchy sounded injured.

'Go on then, Munchy, what else?' He looked thoughtful:

'If you want, I could take you to the spot where I stood. Zara had looked at it before but...

'What were you doing there?'

'Likely as not I'd been on a message for someone. I can't remember that far back.'

'You'd been a message at the Steading's when Spike came looking for you.' Munchy took the change of tack in his stride.

'That's right. I'm cheaper than the post office. Same day delivery. Confidential. Nothing written down. Mrs Steading says to me, "Have you got a degree in message delivery, Munchy?" and I says to her, "I teach it, lady, I teach it." Zara smiled. Her face was calm but her mind was racing. It seemed too good to be true being taken to the site of the crime or rather part of the endgame. Zara felt it was an opportunity she could not turn down.

'When?' she said, 'When can we go to McKelvie Buildings?'

Munchy looked up at the sky as if to an invisible clock:

'How about six-ish, tonight? I'll be outside the Mitchell library. Inside if it's raining and we'll walk round from there.' Zara thanked him.

'I'll be there,' she said. Afterwards she realized she had not asked him about the photo.

***

If Zara considered Des's caveat at all, she dismissed it as irrelevant to what she was about to do. How could there be any danger in going to look at a site where something happened ten years ago? She told herself it would probably be a waste of time but she felt she could not turn down the chance of learning something new, some little piece of information to help sort the jigsaw.

Munchy was waiting. He had a way of blending with his surroundings, never looking out of place, not invisible but "eminently overlook-able", Zara described him to herself.

'Let's go', he said, as if they were at the start of a great expedition. It was spitting with rain. 'Don't worry. I have an umbrella big enough for both of us. He flourished a large golfing umbrella. 'You'd be surprised how people abandon perfectly good articles. I can't just leave them to rot, can I?' He unfurled the article with a flourish: it was so big she didn't even have to walk close to him.

They walked down towards Anderston station and then veered across the confluence of roads. Then they were in hotel land, multi-storey buildings in concrete, ugly and impersonal on the outside. One large area remained unoccupied. It was even more of an eyesore than the buildings except for the buddleia growing from cracks in the old foundations. Inadequate wire fencing surrounded the site. You could still make out where the walls had been, though every loose piece of rubble had been cleared away. Munchy kept walking and they turned a corner.

'This,' Munchy indicated with a wave of his hand, 'was the front of McKelvie Buildings and this close is where Bill was standing when he saw the body, the girl's body, the girl. This here was a line of little shops at the bottom of the tenements. All closed now. Bill came out of the entrance and dived across the road.'

'Was the fire well caught by then? Weren't the fire engines here yet?'

'They'd arrived but not at the front. The seat of the fire appeared to be more at the back. Not so noticeable, I suppose, for if you were starting a fire. Not that I've ever started one myself,' said Munchy. 'Five floors of flame and Bill goes in there. He should have had a medal.' Zara began to wonder if Bill had passed the baton on to Munchy. Was he too becoming obsessed with what had happened that night?'

'So then what, Munchy?

'I couldn't believe what I was seeing. The flames, the heat. It was like Clydebank in the blitz. By now there were other folk watching but I just saw Bill. He didn't seem to see anyone. Just dived back out with something wrapped in his coat. Smoking it was. And then it was raining. You know how people don't see nothing in the rain and it was getting dark. It was all shadows and flames. I just watched Bill.'

'Why didn't you go and help him?' Zara asked. Munchy paused looking straight back at her.

'That I don't know. It's a fair question. Why didn't I? I don't know. It was a strange night. Such a strange night.' Another pause. 'I saw Bill get a phone out of his pocket. Wasn't his phone.'

'Didn't have one?'

'Didn't have no money to fund one, did he? Anyway he phones and after a little while a car comes round the corner and he and the thing he's carrying disappear inside.'

'I see,' said Zara. 'And do you know anything about how the fire started?'

'Petrol,' said Munchy. 'Lots of it.'

'How do you know that?'

'Just that way it went up. Poum poum! Poum poum!'

'But you don't know who did it?'

'If I'd known that I'd have been phoning the papers and getting some dosh for my story.'

'But you're saying it had to be arson?'

'Is the Pope a Catholic?' said Munchy. 'Well, is he?' Zara nodded. 'Look,' he said, 'I need to go round the corner for a slash. Take the umbrella and hang on, I won't be more than a minute and then I'll walk you back to...' He was already disappearing into a lane.

Zara stood surveying the ruins lost in thought. She could see the building in her mind's eye, having found photos in newspaper archives. She saw flames and the figure of Bill and...

Because of the umbrella, she was totally unaware of two guys approaching from behind. One knocked the umbrella forward so it covered her face and the other hit her on the head with a blunt instrument. As their footsteps receded, Zara lost consciousness.

***

The first person she saw when she opened her eyes was Barney. It was at times like these when she realized that Barney was 'family' to her. She could think of no one she would have rather seen. He smiled with relief to see she recognized him.

'Who told you?' Zara heard her own voice as if from a distance.

'Munchy phoned me on your phone, in a terrible state. He said he came round the corner of the lane and saw these two guys mugging you and he ran and shouted and they took off. Then he phoned for an ambulance.'

'Am I in the Western?' Barney nodded. 'Where's Ben?'

'Fortunately he was at a friend's when I got the call so I just phoned to say I'd pick him up whenever I was through.'

Zara tried to think back but the effort was too great. 'Thank god Munchy came back,' she said at last.

'Came back?'

'He'd been showing me the ruins of the McKelvie Buildings and explaining what... he saw Bill...' Zara faded into silence when she saw Barney's expression.

'You're saying you arranged to meet him?' Her face said 'Yes'. Barney shook his head. 'I'll need to talk to you later.' A nurse came in and asked if Zara felt up to making a statement to the police.

Zara could say nothing. She had not seen her assailants because of the umbrella. She had not heard them come up. As far as she knew, the street had been empty. Her purse had not been taken but she thought that was because Munchy had re-appeared just at the right time.

'It would have been more useful if he had appeared a minute or two sooner, wouldn't it?' one of the police officers said. Zara felt confused, then irritated.

'You're not implying Munchy *waited,* that it was a *plan*? Why on earth would he do that? And if it had been planned why didn't they take my purse? Not that there was anything in it?'

'No credit cards?'

'I don't walk around the city with credit cards except when I'm going shopping.'

'And on this occasion, where were you going?' Zara suddenly felt very tired.

'I don't think I can answer any more questions just now.' The officers exchanged glances and got up.

'We'll be back,' said the one who'd suggested Munchy might have waited.

Because it had been a blow to the head, Zara was kept in overnight. Xrays showed no internal damage. She was told she was very lucky – an inch or two nearer this or that...

I expect, thought Zara, they always say that, just to make sure you are more careful the next time you have occasion to get in the way of a blunt instrument coming at you from behind.

But she did wonder about the officer's query. And if he were right, thinking back, someone must have actually told Munchy to look for an opportunity: that's why he'd said six instead of going straight away – he'd had to consult and get given a plan. Zara's head told her to stop thinking but another part of her said, 'A warning from Malloch'.

Chapter XI Zara won't take a telling

The following morning, Zara had just finished persuading her mother, who had been informed as next of kin, that she didn't need to rush over to Glasgow to see her daughter who was very well now and leaving the hospital asap when Des blew in, even before the doctor came on his rounds.

'How did you know I was here?' asked Zara frowning.

'How do you think?'

'Barney?' Des nodded. 'Are you here as a friend or a police officer?'

'We're here together. The friend asked the police officer if he could accompany him.'

'The friend was worried but the officer wants information?'

'You've hit it on the head.'

'Wrong story, Des. They hit me on the head. Apparently.'

'What's particularly worrying is that there were no fingerprints or footprints at the crime scene. Nothing to tie two guys to that location.'

'Particularly worrying because...?'

'Because what looks like a random mugging interrupted, turns into a planned operation. Random muggers don't wear plastic gloves and neither do they haunt such relatively unfrequented places. People leave those hotels by car and taxi. Never many pedestrians around there.' Zara's mind went back to her misgivings of the night before but she said,

'You're going to say 'I told you so.'

'I'm not,' said Des sighing instead 'but mainly because I want you to remain sweet and answer my questions'. Zara nodded and then shook her head.

'I can't remember anything.'

Des put on his patient face:

'I spoke to the two officers who interviewed you last night and they say you said you met Munchy and went with him to the site of the McKelvie Buildings. Why did you do that?'

'I wanted to get a better picture of what happened that night.'

'What night?'

'The night the McKelvie Buildings burned down.'

'What's that got to do with anything?'

'The bones taken from the Kelvin were from a body taken from the McKelvie Buildings by Bill Mason. Munchy saw him go into the building and come out. But the body was already dead.'

'How do you know that?'

'Spike told me. Bill confessed to him before he died.'

'Can I ask why you didn't tell me?'

'I haven't had time,' Zara lied. 'Anyway, you said you were putting Ivory's case on the back burner –that's Ben's name for her, by the way –I thought I'd give you a break.'

'Neat name,' Des acknowledged.

'I thought you were hunting down serial drowners.'

'I am,' said Des. 'The woman who managed to drag herself to Anderston police station turns out to be a drug addict and...'

'So she must be telling lies?'

'Zara, desperate people will say anything to get money and anyway my job is to consider all options. Nothing and nobody are sacrosanct. She tells the officer at the bar she was having a quiet fag near the duck pond, when she was pushed from behind.'

'No umbrellas or blunt instruments, I hope?' Des looked sulky. 'Oh go on then, tell us the full story.'

'She fell into the water and as she struggled to get out, she was held under for a count of about twenty and then heaved up for air and then held under again. After that she was thrown onto the bank and then she saw flash after flash and realized someone was taking photos of her. At that point some guys came past and the photographer ran off. She was so short of air she lay there for about half an hour she said. Then she found her handbag, had a fag to steady herself and then came to the station.' Des looked at Zara.

'Well,' she said, 'and?'

'I don't believe a word of it.'

'What do you mean?'

'I think it's meant to make us think there's a psychopath out there who likes to drown people but isn't very good at it though they may improve with practice. Someone wants the police to concentrate on this...'

'...and not on the questions relating to Bill Mason? You believe now it wasn't an accident?'

'It wasn't an accident and neither perhaps, was you getting hit over the head.'

'You're implicating Munchy?'

'Possibly, but not inevitably. The two guys following you might have been unconnected to Munchy but even if that were the case, it's still worrying. Why, Zara, do you think, anyone would want to hit you over the head?' Zara's face was expressionless:

'Malloch wants me to stop poking my nose in?'

'Yes, Zara, exactly,' said Des in a tired voice, 'but there's a certain group of people whose profession is to protect the rest of the population from such people. They may not always do it very well but at least they go in equipped to deal with violence'.

'Your bullet proof vest wouldn't have stopped you getting bashed on the head.'

'There would have been two of us so that situation would have been unlikely to arise.'

Zara didn't know whether it was because of the blow to the head but Des's words, meant to be protective, made her feel stubborn and bloody-minded.

'Did you find out about the mac and the bone splinters?' Des glared at her from under his eyebrows.

'Yes, you were right. Bone was part of the fingers. Plastic matches what was found on one of the bones. Good work for an amateur.'

'You're just jealous. Aren't you going to thank me?'

'Thank you,' said Des in a neutral tone. 'Police are following a relevant line of enquiry. Your information has been most useful.'

'So you know who had Bill Mason in his pocket and you suspect Munchy of being part of the same set up?'

'These people are pawns, Zara. They are neither here nor there. Look at what happened to Bill.'

There was after that a long silence.

'The SOCOS went and looked at your new site where the splinters were found and the forensic team concur with your conclusion that a separate fire took place there. I mean, it looks as if the body was burned twice.' A shudder went through Zara. 'Look, this is why you shouldn't be involved. You don't have to take it on.'

'Were you going to say any more?'

'Just that the connection to the fire in McKelvie Buildings will be investigated. We're keeping our ears close to the ground. If possible, we want them to think we've swallowed their bait but we have people we can ask.' Des stopped and stared at Zara.

'What?' she asked.

'If I promise to keep you in the loop will you back off? You're in no fit state to risk your life out there.' Zara looked back at him and then lowered her eyelids. He took it as acquiescence.

'How's Pam keeping?' trying to make her voice sound pleasant and lull Des into thinking Ivory's case was not the only thing on her mind. Des launched into a long saga about hospital appointments, high blood pressure, tests, babies' names, buggys, cots and feeding options till Zara felt quite drowsy. At last he went away. She hoped he hadn't thought she was bored.

***

Zara was back home, lying on the sofa thinking about everything. She could not understand why she continued to feel so drained and edgy. She was loth to believe Munchy was on the wrong side. He seemed so cheerful and helpful and had seemed so upset about Bill and then about her own assault. Also she didn't like to feel she could be so wrong in reading a character.

The doorbell went and she jumped and started shaking but from the intercom came Spike's voice. She felt a rush of pleasure. She stood at the open door to greet him. His face was grey and when she took his hand it shook.

'Spike, whatever's the matter?'

'I met Barney.' Spike held her arms and appraised her. 'Zara, I'm sorry. How are you? I'd never forgive myself if... it's my fault...'

'How could it be your fault, Spike?'

'I've been too busy drowning my sorrows. You're playing with fire, Zara.'

'I know *that,* Spike.'

'Tell me from the beginning. Barney just told me bits and he was upset, he wasn't making sense. Said some guys hit you over the head and then ran off and you were opposite the McKelvie Buildings?'

'I don't know why everyone is making such a fuss. I had just asked Munchy to show me exactly what Bill did on the night of the fire. Munchy was there, he said. He saw it all.'

'Spike's face had gone even greyer. 'You asked *Munchy* to show you? What did you ask that little rat for? *Munchy?*'

'I thought you liked Munchy. He seems so harmless and...'

'He's weak, Munchy is. Does things for the wrong reasons. Doesn't think ahead. Lands in shit but somehow wriggles out.'

'Was he a friend of Bill's?'

'He was. I don't know how much Bill told him, mind, but I think he really was upset when... we all were... are...'

Zara heard the kettle click off and got up again to make tea. 'I asked Munchy because he was obliging. No one else would talk to me. You and Des kept treating me as if I were six but Munchy was quite happy to meet me and take me there.'

'You met him by chance?

'I met him by chance the day after Bill's funeral.'

'Yesterday,' said Spike.

'Yesterday and we arranged to go six o'clock that evening.' Spike looked thoughtful. 'Munchy talked me through the whole incident,' Zara went on, 'to where Bill gets in the car. Then he – Munchy that is – said he wanted a slash and disappeared decorously round the corner and that's when it happened. I didn't see them coming because of the umbrella Munchy had lent me. And then I woke up in the Western.'

'Does it hurt still?'

'Just a dull headache or more like the memory of a headache.'

'And what did your pal Des say?'

'He thought Munchy was at it.' Spike was silent. He agreed with Des but he knew Zara too well to imagine he would gain anything by voicing this opinion. He would just need to keep a better eye on her.

'If you need help, Zara, you can always come to me. You know that.'

'But you wouldn't talk to me, Spike, and you weren't at the McKelvie Buildings fire.'

'Nor I was.' Spike bit his lip with his bottom teeth. Neither was Munchy, he thought, but he didn't say that to Zara. He decided to give Munchy a bollocking and see what his reaction was. He felt he might be able to ascertain whether Munchy was a thinking cog in Malloch's machine or whether he was an underling who was only good for fetching and carrying.

It crossed his mind that Munchy had taken a message to the Steadings: Mr or Mrs, he wondered. Munchy had better look out too. Malloch was only okay when he was on your side. In the following silence, Zara suddenly remembered a question:

'Maybe you could tell me, Spike, why Bill Mason had to jump when Malloch asked him?'

'That's an old story, Zara and it has nothing to do with the price of fish.'

'Tell me though, Spike.' Spike sighed.

'It's just one of those things from the past. Malloch lied in Court and Bill's father got off a murder. He hadn't done it mind but he would have gone down but for Malloch.'

'So why did Malloch do a good turn?'

'He didn't. He just saw a good blackmail opportunity in prospect, so to speak. Had Bill's father on a string for the rest of his life. And now Bill.' Zara looked sad. 'I keep telling you, Zara, you don't want to know about Malloch: there's no happy endings anywhere.'

***

Later on that day, Zara opened her door to Ben and Barney who was carrying a large rucksack. Ness stood between them looking eager. Zara watched Barney head for the kitchen and start taking food from his bag and putting it on the counter. He'd wanted to get Zara from the hospital but she'd said she would take a taxi. In the event, she'd walked feeling the sort of freedom you only feel when you escape from an institution.

'You didn't tell Ben?' Zara hissed at him while Ben was through in the bathroom but Barney had been economical with the truth. He'd told the boy that someone had tried to take Zara's purse and in the struggle she had fallen and that a passer-by had seen she was unconscious and phoned for an ambulance.

'Have you got an egg on your head, Aunty Zara?'

'Feel,' said Zara

'It's nearly as big as the one I had when I fell down the stairs when I was three.' Zara watched as Barney took a sleeping bag out of his rucksack.

'This is for Ben. He's going to sleep in your spare room.' Ben picked it up and went off. Barney lowered his voice. 'We got it today for going camping and he wanted to try it out. I said it wouldn't be a proper trial in his own bed. There's space enough for him in your spare room to go the whole hog if he likes and sleep on the carpet whereas in his room at home...' Zara raised her eyebrows.

'And you?'

'I'm sleeping on your sofa.'

'I don't get a say in all this?'

'That's right. One, I promised Spike and two, I can't trust you to lock your windows.'

'I'm quite all right,' protested Zara leaning back in her chair.

Suddenly there was a small crashing noise and Zara leapt to her feet and stood shaking. Barney had his arms around her in an instant.

'Sorry,' shouted Ben from the bedroom. 'That funny metal pot fell off your shelf, Aunty Zara. It sort of jumped as I went past it. It nearly fell on my sleeping bag but not quite. It's not broken though.'

***

'Ben has opted for the bed,' said Barney coming through from saying goodnight to his son and carefully shutting the living room door behind him. 'He says he thinks the earth will be softer than your floor so it's a fairer experiment if he sleeps on the bed and pretends he's in a meadow of soft grass. He says is it all right if Ness sleeps on the floor.' Zara smiled a 'yes'.

'You don't feel nervous leaving him in the room the robber entered?'

'The windows are locked and alarmed. I don't believe you've ever used your alarm system but it does work.'

'If you're just going to lecture me, I'll read my book.'

'Zara, I just want to understand what you're about.'

'I've been trying to understand that for years!'

'Zara, Spike says these people are dangerous. Of course I have no right to control what you do, though, as you know, I wouldn't turn down the opportunity to be more permanently on hand when you make decisions.'

'Is that like some backhanded proposal?'

'It's partly about Ben's safety too. I'm not talking about whether there's an "us" or whether there ever will be but I do want to be assured that you are not going to do anything that will put Ben at risk.'

'You have my assurance.'

'But how do I know that for certain? You can't even look after yourself. I have to think of Ben.'

Zara's head began to hurt, not exactly physically, more a sense of everything in it moving chaotically in too small a space. She put her hands over her ears.

'We were only in the fucking park, Barney. Same as always. You can't put reins on a ten-year-old. You've no idea how quickly he disappears. If you don't think I'm...' Zara stopped, appalled at the way the conversation was heading.

'Let me put another point to you,' said Barney, in a softer voice. 'Ben has not forgotten the bone. I keep thinking he has or at least that it's gone into his ordinary memory store of things that happened in the past but then he comes up with a question or a statement. Like last night he said, "The girl, Ivory. Was she older than me?" and it always seems to be when he's in bed. I don't like to think of him having macabre images – like about his mother's death, thought Zara – before he goes to sleep.

'Last week he said, "I know what happened now. She was an African and she died of starvation but she belonged to a tribe that burn dead bodies by the river so that's what her family did. It's very sad." And when I looked at him as if to say, What was sad? he said, "I thought people just starved in *Africa*. She could have had my dinner if I'd known she was in Glasgow."'

'I'll be careful.' Zara sounded subdued.

'It's not just that,' went on Barney. 'He's interested. He wants to know who the girl was and why the police are still involved, why they were interested in the tunnel. He likes his explanation of the girl's burial but he can also see it doesn't entirely add up with what's happening and of course now he tends to think anything that happens relates to the bone so your getting injured – even though I described it as an accident – sets his imagination going. He thinks the muggers thought you had important information about the bone in your bag.'

'Well there's an idea,' said Zara. 'DC Ben got any more of them?'

'There you go again,' said Barney, 'treating it all like a game. Sometimes I wish you'd take life a bit more seriously.'

'Barney, if I took life seriously,' Zara answered, 'I wouldn't get out of bed.'

***

Somehow they managed to turn the evening into a pleasant and relaxed one, more because they wanted to, not because anything had been resolved. Then Barney made himself comfortable on the sofa and Zara went off to bed. But not to sleep. She found herself going over and over the facts as she knew them, looking for bits she'd missed: the dead girl, the burial, a connection –there had to be one –between the death of the girl and the McKelvie Buildings fire. Or at least a connection between the people involved.

Going back to the fire itself, the body complicated things but possibly confirmed arson, since people aren't usually so lucky as to have to hand an appropriately hot fire just when they have a body to dispose of. Further, you wouldn't fire a five storey building to burn one small body. This meant the two incidents were linked in one way but not in another: the idea of arson to release a vacant prime site was still a runner, with Malloch and Steading in the frame for that. But it also meant Zara had to look further, one, for a reason for Ivory's body being disposed of in *this* fire and two, a reason for her death in the first place.

Zara held it all in her mind and then she let go and all the pieces swirled into disorder as she drifted off to sleep.

Chapter XII Brothers in arms?

Spike could see Munchy did not like the sight of his clenched fists, reddened with tension. Munchy liked to please everyone.

'I'm sorry about your pal,' he said before Spike could get a word in. 'I was only helping her out. She was desperate to see where Bill had been that night and I thought, Spike's upset...'

'I'm not fucking interested,' said Spike, his face remaining impassive. 'I just want to tell you that if anything else happens to her and you're anywhere near, I'll hold you responsible and – he held up his fists – here's two blunt instruments I might use if I think it's necessary. Who put you up to it?' Munchy looked – or pretended to look, Spike couldn't tell – hurt.

'It was nothing to do with me. I was just helping the lady out. I came back round the corner and there was these two muggers. I don't know what would have happened if I hadn't come back.' Spike looked hard at Munchy, loth to believe him.

'Did you mention your little arrangement to anyone?'

'I might have.' Munchy's eyes flickered right and left. Sometimes he chose honesty because he thought it might just get him into a better place with his adversary. 'If I'd mentioned it in company, anyone might have used the information.'

Spike leaned up to him: 'So, just supposing that's what happened, who just might have got to hear, entirely without your help of course?'

'Well I wouldn't know that, would I? I didn't recognize them, the two guys that run off. They don't work for...' He stopped. Spike smiled.

'They don't work for Malloch? Is that what you were going to say? Munchy if you're ever interrogated by MI5, remember to get your jaws wired first. You are too easy to read.' Munchy looked startled then shifty.

'I never seen him, not since my daddy's funeral. I mean never. He doesn't deal with the likes of me. I only ever seen him once. And that was from a bus.' Spike smiled again: Munchy never travelled by bus.

'So it was Screw then? Your friend Screw. He set you up. You gave him the info, he knew just where you and she would be and then he had a couple of heavies waiting to do the business. Perhaps he told you might get your photo back.'

'I wouldn't ever hurt a lady,' said Munchy. 'Never in my born days.'

'What's Screw doing out anyway. I thought they'd thrown away the key.'

'He got out on good behaviour.'

'That'll be right,' Spike shook his head. On balance he was inclined to believe some of what Munchy said. It was quite possible that he had offered to help Zara from a wish to be part of the drama and also possible that he had relayed the information to whomever he was next talking to, Screw a strong possibility. Screw might have used the information, quite without Munchy knowing. Anything to do with Malloch was difficult to work out: he always played a game of bluff and double bluff. Spike had seen Munchy's eyes change at the mention of the name Screw: he felt he had his answer.

***

Two hundred yards down from the Rum and Rocket, a pub frequented on occasion by Charles Steading, stands a strange church with a corrugated iron roof. It was built in the thirties on a gifted piece of land and the roof material was a result of the church members running out of funds.

Sometime in the fifties, the members dropped out or died and nettles took over but in the early 2000s the Church of the Rainmakers bought the building for a song and renovated it keeping the roof because it fitted their ethos: their raison d'être was to pray for rain anywhere in the world where the rains and therefore the crops had failed. When it rained on the roof of the church it was seen – or rather heard – as a blessing and celebrated in a ritual of listening, praying and rain-singing.

If it wasn't raining, every so often someone would get to their feet and start a clapping pattern which was meant to induce the rain but it was generally felt that the best way of bringing it on in the dry places was by waiting till it poured in Glasgow and then saying, 'Lord, lord, can we have some more of that and over in Africa please?' One of the regular members of this church was Doctor James.

The most unaccountable presence in the congregation was the occasional appearance of Charles Steading who was overtly welcomed by Doctor James though secretly his heart fell. Steading always had a message for him delivered in a jolly voice – Steading's version of being holy – which the doctor received with a radiant smile reminiscent of his brother's but with a shadow in it.

The Sunday following Zara's assault saw one such meeting between Steading and the doctor at the Rainmakers' church. Before attending, Steading had met Screw in the Rum and Rocket and Screw had given Steading a message for Doctor James. Screw was still in the pub when everyone came out of the service. Steading went straight home but Doctor James had to pass the pub and he met Screw coming out. Screw sized him up at once for a worried man and said to him,

'You look as if you could use a drink, my friend'. Doctor James had only met Screw once before and had found him genial. He accepted the invitation.

'I need a …,' said Doctor James straightening his first two fingers and pointing, thumb held back.

'That is easily found, my friend but can you pay for it?' Doctor James took off his platinum Rolex.

'Would that be enough?'

'That would do.' Screw was imperturbable. 'I take it you want it soon.'

'Tomorrow at the latest.'

'This evening then. Meet me here again at seven.'

'You have saved my life,' said Doctor James. Screw doubted this but didn't say so.

Doctor James did not know, because of Malloch's way of keeping people apart, that Screw and Steading knew each other but Screw knew that Doctor James knew Steading and that he had just been given a message at the Rainmakers' church. He put through a call to the Boss.

'This one I think we will allow to play out, although I am grateful for the tip off,' said the voice at the end of the line. 'A score here might be a good diversion at this present point in time. Don't shiver, Screw, the weather's not chilly.' Screw shivered again. He was tough but Malloch's voice always struck through him like ice.

***

Zara woke on Sunday morning with a delicious feeling of languor. She always felt the slight change like a larger outbreath: you might end up being busy, but that was your choice. She stretched her toes into a cool part of the bed and wondered if it were eight o'clock or nine. Should she have another snooze or wake up a bit more and read her book or – even more active – get out of bed and make herself a cup of tea? Then she heard a voice and remembered that her home was extra-inhabited. She shrank back under the bedclothes.

For Zara the idea of living with other people always seemed more attractive when they weren't there. Sharing space, even thinking about it sometimes, brought on claustrophobia. Why was that? She did love Barney, she was sure of that and she had a real bond with Ben. She was already his godmother.

Was it picturing their ménage in Barney's flat that was the problem? There would be no room for a room to be hers and hers alone and she needed that. But supposing she up-ended Barney and Ben from their established home into somewhere new and bigger and then it didn't work out? Zara's skin went gooseflesh-y at the thought. Ben had already lost one mother.

She heard their voices more distinctly now:

'I like staying here with Aunty Zara but I like our house better.'

'Why is that?' Silence, then:

'I think it's because all my stuff's there.'

'I see,' Zara heard Barney murmur.

'Couldn't Aunty Zara come and stay with us?'

'She could if she wanted to.'

'Doesn't she want to then?' Silence.

'It's a bit more complicated than that.'

'Ah, something I'll understand when I'm older?' Zara detected a hint of sarcasm.

'She likes space,' said Barney. 'She wouldn't have enough space.'

'It's not because she doesn't love us then?'

'No, no. It's not that. She does love us.'

'Definitely?'

'Absolutely definitely.'

Zara had to turn her face to the pillow to soak up her tears. She lay perfectly still for another fifteen minutes and then made waking up noises – drawing the curtains back, switching her radio on then off. She heard Barney move towards the kitchen. Suddenly she caught a waft of bacon smell. Barney had been waiting for her to surface so he could cook a Sunday breakfast. It would be worth moving in permanently with Barney and Ben to have those Sunday breakfasts every week, said Zara's stomach firmly.

She took a shower and then back in her bedroom selected a red tee-shirt with puff sleeves and a pair of black jeans. She wrenched a brush through her hair, looked in the mirror and decided to leave her long locks loose. She liked the look of them hitting the neckline of the tee-shirt.

Barney's timing was as excellent as his cooking. They all sat down to fried egg – yolk just on the verge of runny for Zara, set for Ben – mushrooms, slightly brown but not burnt, halved cherry tomatoes, hot and peppered, and lean bacon with crispy edges. Also black pudding, flat sausage and chipolatas. Also potato scones. They ate in a state of dreamy concentration, Duke Ellington in the background – chef's choice. To Zara it felt very traditional and made her mind turn to picnics.

They decided on Mugdock Park and Barney went out for rolls. When Zara heard the door she thought it was him returning but it was Doctor Andrew whose face she saw first. She stood back to let him in. Barney followed: they had met on the stair.

'About the plasterer,' he said. 'I forgot to ask you when we last met. Very remiss of me. I am sorry.' Zara put her hand to her head thinking 'What plasterer? And then she remembered but of course it had happened before Bill's funeral and before her assault. She wondered if Doctor Andrew's life had been equally full.

When Zara had ascertained that everyone knew everybody else, she related to Andrew what the plasterer had said.

Barney was looking puzzled, then suddenly he slapped his knee: 'I've seen you somewhere before. Was it at a seminar or a meeting of some kind?'

'Your face looks familiar too.' Zara wondered whether the doctor was just being polite.

'I wonder,' said Barney. 'It's going to annoy me now if I can't...'
Zara thought the doctor was beginning to look uncomfortable.

'I know, it was that conference last month! Wasn't it?'

'What's a conference?' asked Ben.

'Just to do with my work,' Barney answered. 'A bit boring for a picnic Sunday.' Ben looked huffy.

'It's to do with Ivory then,' he said daring the grown-ups to lie to him.

'Would you like to come with us to Mugdock Park?' asked Zara turning to the doctor in a desperate attempt to switch the conversation.

'That's very kind of you but...'

'No buts,' said Barney. 'Just say "Yes". He was answered with a beautiful smile.

The day remained bright. On the way to the park, Doctor Andrew answered Ben's questions about Egypt. Barney was quiet. Although Zara knew he had been genuine in encouraging Doctor Andrew to come on the picnic she wanted him to know the doctor was married. She felt this question had lodged itself in Barney's mind.

'You'll be able to phone your wife and say you've been on a real Scottish picnic,' she said, suddenly realizing as she said it how irrelevant the statement sounded.

'This is different from an English picnic?' asked Doctor Andrew.

'No cucumber sandwiches,' said Barney.

'No hamper with caviar and champagne,' said Zara.

'No dog called Spot,' added Ben, patting Ness.

'What is there then especial about a Scottish picnic?' The doctor was perplexed.

'There's a tea-room in case you run out of food,' said Ben filling the gap when the grown-ups seemed unable to. Everyone laughed. Elaborate, thought Zara but he knows now. She realized how much she did not want to hurt Barney.

Although they all set off together, on the route they took through the woods, Barney was some way ahead with Ben who kept rushing off and back, Ness following him, barking excitedly.

Zara wanted to keep things light so she questioned the doctor about his new practice. She had told him already she was a free-lance journalist and when he politely asked what she was currently engaged on she did not for some reason mention her current obsession with prime site arson attacks. She wasn't sure why.

They came together by the water and ate their rolls and drank tea from a thermos. Ben and Doctor Andrew had juice. There was fruitcake and Doctor Andrew asked Zara for the recipe.

'It's very easy', said Zara. 'One step only – to the shop round the corner.'

On the way back, they all played frisbee. Doctor Andrew was very good because he was tall and Ness was always willing to retrieve when the frisbee flew off into the distance. Then, because they had made themselves thirsty, they decided to do the only Scottish thing and visit the tea-room.

It was on the way to the tea-room that Zara fell into step with Doctor Andrew and asked him what the conference had been about where he had met Barney. She heard his voice falter as he struggled to sound normal and calm. She looked up to see his face had changed colour completely.

'Well,' he began, 'it was about...' The doctor opened his mouth wide and then sneezed into a large handkerchief five or six times. 'Hay fever,' he apologized. 'Never had it before I came to the UK.'

'You were saying?' persisted Zara, when he'd recovered sufficiently and put his handkerchief back in his pocket.

'Was I... what was I...?

'...about the conference.' Doctor Andrew sneezed again and had to lean against a tree. Fortunately for him the tea-room was now in view and Barney and Ben were waiting for them a few yards ahead.

Doctor Andrew was silent during the tea and soon excused himself to the Gents.

'Hay fever,' said Zara when Barney asked her.

'Really?' said Barney, interpreting a subtle twist in her lip.

'Yes,' said Zara. 'Amazing what brings it on.' After a time, Barney went to look for him but he had gone. They returned home without him.

***

Nine-thirty Monday. A drizzly night. A man with a revolver waits behind the trees. His desperation gives him clarity of mind. He stands rock still and wills himself to invisibility. His eyes are on the road before him. His target will walk towards him and he will fire at his head. Two shots: kill and confirm. He hears his own breathing and he has to force it not to quicken. He waits for his quarry to appear in the empty space. Sweat trickles down his back.

Then there he is, He recognizes the coat. But the man is coming from the wrong direction. The shooter can only see his back. He cannot shoot a man in the back. He shouts, 'Oy!' The man turns but as the two shots ring out he ducks instinctively. The first bullet grazes his shoulder, the second whistles over his fallen body, the face turning towards the shooter.

It's the wrong face. He has shot the wrong man. His brain guides his feet. He plunges through the trees to the river. The revolver flies into the water. The now gun-less man finds the road, forces himself to walk, to take a circuitous route home. Nobody has seen him he is sure.

He had thought his plan was watertight. He'd phoned Steading saying he had the money and to meet him at nine-thirty at the Rum and Rocket. Knowing from previous assignations where Steading was likely to park, he had positioned himself in the shadows between the parking and the pub. What had happened? Had he merely lost his nerve? He had really thought the man was Steading.

He was comforted by the belief that there had been no witnesses but unfortunately for him, in this he was wrong. He had been seen by Screw who had had the opportunity to put two and two together, having sold the revolver to Doctor James and then fortuitously hearing from Steading that he was to meet the doctor on the Monday night. Steading was late. Too late to get killed and not in time to see the victim.

Someone in the pub had dialled 999 as soon as the shots were heard. Police and ambulance were on the scene very quickly. The injured man was taken to hospital.

Screw affected surprise to Steading at the non-appearance of Doctor James, and Steading, not knowing about the revolver transaction did not connect the shooting with the doctor. He had a drink with Screw and then went home.

***

Ben was in bed. Zara and Barney were discussing Doctor Andrew's strange behaviour at Mugdock Park.

'He seems so polite, I think the fact that he disappeared without saying anything is very significant.'

'Any ideas?' said Barney, knowing Zara would be bound to have some.

'It was after I had asked him what the conference was about. He sneezed and after that he seemed uneasy.'

'I talked about the conference too,' said Barney. Perhaps he thought he was getting the third degree. I only had a short conversation with him on the walk, about the prevalence around Glasgow.'

'Prevalence of what?'

'FGM.' said Barney. That's what the conference was about.'

'That is a coincidence,' said Zara. 'Katerina was saying that the pubic bone being broken could mean FGM'.

'How do you mean. What pubic bone?'

'*The* bone. The charred one belonging to the North African girl, to Ivory. What an opportunity. We can ask Doctor Andrew all about the process.'

At that moment there was a knock on the door.

'Andrew! We were just talking about you. How's your hay fever? You weren't carried off by a big sneeze after all then?'

'I am very sorry. Always I seem to be apologizing to you. You must think me very rude. I was called away...'

'Of course,' said Zara. 'Your work. Were you on call? A doctor's life...' Doctor Andrew looked very relieved as Zara took the burden of having to explain away from him. He accepted a cup of coffee, refusing the beer Barney offered him.

'I need a clear head,' he said. Zara did her best to reclaim the relaxed feelings they'd all had the previous day and felt she was doing well when the doctor's phone rang.

'Andrew, Andrew, you must come now!' The voice was loud and upset, the whole room could hear it.

'Hang on for a minute. I'm with someone,' the doctor said with a trace of tension and turning to Zara he added, 'It seems I am destined to be called away from your delightful company. I hope we will...' He was at the door.

But Zara's landline was ringing. As she listened to the voice her face became pale.

'I'll be right over,' she said and crashed the receiver down. 'Someone has shot Spike,' she said, 'outside the Rum and Rocket.' Barney hugged Zara to him. 'He's okay,' said Zara, 'that was him on the phone but I must go and see him.' The doctor backed out of the door and disappeared.

'Don't take the car,' said Barney, 'you're too upset to drive'.

'What?' said Zara putting on her jacket. She was not understanding Barney's puzzled expression.

'You should have seen Andrew's face when you said about Spike, Barney said. 'He looked as if he'd seen a ghost.'

Chapter XIII   Two jigsaw pieces

The nurse who had triaged Zara the week before had also triaged Spike. She looked bemused to see Zara again. Spike was in a state of shock and was being kept in overnight but his wound had been a lucky one, not touching an artery.

'You spoke to the police I take it?' Zara asked after she had made sure of Spike's relative comfort and wellbeing.

'I couldn't tell them nothing, could I? It came out of the night – a shout and a shot. Why the guy shouted I can't imagine but if he hadn't I think I'd have been a gonner. I had a sort of sense where the shout came from and I ducked. Good job I ducked, eh Zara?'

'I'm very glad you ducked, Spike.'

'Why would anyone want to shoot me, Zara? I've not led a perfect life, god knows, but I've never done nothing to warrant a shooting.'

'Nothing to do with Malloch then?'

'He's capable but what's the motive? Even he has to have *some* motive.'

Zara racked her brain. It felt to her like when you lose something and precisely because it seems to have vanished out of the universe, you know there is a simple explanation.

'Okay, Spike, tell me the story from the beginning.'

'Well, it was drizzling a bit, so I put on that coat of Steading's that Mrs Caroline gave me...'

'Spike we've got it! Whoever shot you, thought you were Steading. Done and dusted. God wasn't out to get you today. Bet the police haven't got there yet.'

'They don't know where the coat came from, Zara.'

'This gets interesting. I wish you'd got a better look at the guy. You didn't see him *at all?*'

Spike closed his eyes recalling the moment: 'Not really. All I can say is, where the shout came from, I sensed a figure just for a split second, you understand. There was something... It was tall this figure... I can't see a head... could have been a balaclava job but I don't think so. Dark it was quite dark. It was just a split second...'

'Maybe you'll remember better tomorrow, Spike.' Zara could see he was tiring. 'If you get out tomorrow, do you want to come and stay at my house for a few days?' Zara knew he would say 'No' but she had to ask.

'They are arranging for me to go to a hostel. Don't worry, Zara. This is nothing.'

***

'Do you want a lead on the attempted murder of John McLure, aka Spike?' Zara's voice. Des was on night shift and his division had actually been at the scene because there had been a call for back-up.

'Our officers have already got a statement.' Des sounded stiff. Maybe tired, thought Zara, I know I am. She continued as if she had not been snubbed.

'I was just in seeing Spike myself and I wanted to make sure you knew he was wearing Charles Steading's jacket at the time.'

'*Steading's* jacket?'

'Yep. A gift. Spike did a bit of gardening and Mrs Caroline, as he calls her, gave it to him. I know because I saw him the day after he got it. He was quite chuffed then but maybe we should make a habit of looking gift horses in the mouth.'

'So your take on it is that someone was out to get Steading?'

'That would seem possible,' said Zara. 'You know Steading then?'

'He's an ex-city councillor,' said Des, a bit too quickly Zara thought.

'There must be more than one Steading in Glasgow. Why do you assume it's him?' she asked. Des's voice changed.

'Look Zara, thanks but I'd better go and get on with catching the crims. And Zara, leave it to us, please!'

Zara hung up. She felt pleased: she'd done her duty and now she was free to follow her own track. She turned to Barney who was still dressed and awake even though it was late now: 'Let's discuss the doctor connection,' she said. 'I need to go over what I know already because something's nagging me, a missed link somewhere...'

Because Barney had been on the picnic with Doctor Andrew, he had become intrigued, though usually he would have lectured Zara for getting involved in dodgy things.

'I'm all ears,' he said.

'I first became aware,' Zara began, 'of Doctor James's existence when I mistook him for Doctor Andrew. I met Doctor James as I was crossing the park and I spoke to him thinking he was Doctor Andrew. Not surprisingly he passed me by. Later that day I saw Doctor Andrew and asked him why he had blanked me and he hesitated a bit and then said it must have been his brother. Then I said that the only difference between them seemed to be a nasty facial injury on Doctor James's cheek. Doctor Andrew said he'd walked into a door.'

Barney smiled. 'Well it's women that fall over hoovers isn't it?'

'Then,' said Zara, smiling back, 'there's Doctor Andrew's behaviour at Mugdock Park and also tonight with the phone call. I wouldn't mind betting it was his brother calling him tonight and maybe he got a call at Mugdock too'.

'Brothers are allowed to phone each other.'

'Yes, but on both occasions the results were dramatic.'

'Doctor Andrew did not phone his brother or anyone else for that matter in our hearing.'

'No, but he left us and maybe coincidentally his brother phoned him and he had to leave in a hurry.' Zara paused. 'He didn't like us talking about the FGM conference. I wonder why that was. I'm beginning to think,' said Zara, 'that there is a connection between the doctors and Ivory but that means there's a connection between them and Malloch'.

'Malloch? *The* Malloch?'

'The very one. The one that neither Spike nor Des will tell me anything about.'

'It seems a long shot,' said Barney. 'It's an extraordinary coincidence if in the whole of Glasgow, of the people that are involved with Ivory, one of them should be living above you, when you were the person to find the bone.'

'Absolutely,' said Zara. 'Who says there isn't a god?'

'Or you could just be plain wrong.'

They both became silent and thoughtful. Zara was still trying to hunt down the missing link:

'I have two pictures in my mind: One, Doctor James walking through the park and two, another picture which I can't grasp.'

'Which bit of the park are we talking about, Zara?'

'The bit where... I see him coming down the path from... well he could have come from Gibson Street or from the path that goes under the bridge. Who else have I seen...?'

'Ben,' said Barney.

'Ben coming back from the tunnel? I didn't see him come. He suddenly appeared but interestingly, when I think about his homework story, I *do* see him. I wonder if that's why it didn't click properly, because I didn't really see him.'

'So,' said Barney patiently, 'are you any nearer making a link?' Zara pushed out her bottom lip in a cartoon 'glum' position:

'Let's go back to Ben's story. What did he see in the tunnel? There was Bill, a very grumpy Bill; there was a door, and all Ben saw through the door was a dim figure with a raised hand and - Ben particularly remembered this – the gold knuckle-duster ring on it. He told Katerina about it, how sparkly it was. Don't worry, I didn't prompt him. So, what if Doctor James had come from the tunnel too?'

'Zara, you do sometimes grasp at straws. You'll be saying next that the injury to the Doctor's face was caused by the knuckle-duster.'

Zara was jubilant. 'Barney, you star! It adds up. It may be ridiculous but it does add up.'

'Speculative addition.'

'You know it makes sense.'

'Whichever way you look at it, it's not pretty,' said Barney. 'I hope to god you're wrong. What worries me is...' But at that point Ben woke up wanting a glass of water, Zara and Barney realized it was now two o'clock in the morning, so they all went to bed.

***

By morning Zara had become preoccupied with the shooting. She wanted very much to know who had thought they were taking a pot-shot at Steading but she didn't think Des would welcome her asking. If he were not too hassled and in a good mood he might just tell her what the SOCOS had picked up.

Or, who knows, there might have been an arrest. Maybe they caught someone fleeing from the scene. The weapon would have been thrown away. The bullet had been retrieved from Spike's shoulder and so the police would know if it was from a sawn-off shot gun or a revolver but even if they dragged the Kelvin – the most likely depository – and found the weapon, it would probably be a model easily obtainable on the black market.

***

Steading had been interviewed to see if he thought anyone was out to get him. In fact he had been able to be quite honest about his movements. Yes, he had been in the Rum and Rocket, having a pint with Stephen Crewe just after nine-thirty p.m., luckily not just before. Then he had gone home. Wife would vouch for that (even though she was visiting her sister at the time).

He did not tell the police he had had a rendezvous with Doctor James not because he wished to protect him but because he was protecting his relationship with Malloch. He had not yet spoken to him about the shooting affair and he hadn't either, spoken to Caroline about the jacket.

He hadn't spoken to Caroline about any of it because she wasn't party to his involvement with Malloch regarding Doctor James. He couldn't explain to her that Spike having the jacket made him a target. She would immediately want to know why he, Steading, was the real target.

How he wished he had never started playing chess with Malloch. He often felt he was being used as a messenger boy but Malloch knew so much that could be used against him. The guy was always so casual: "if you happen to see James, perhaps you could…" But it was the iron fist in the velvet glove. The best policy was to say nothing. Secrecy, he had always found was the best policy. He crossed his fingers and hoped this problem would go away.

***

Des had told Zara that footprints at the tree positioned where the shots had been fired from were from trainers that were new and that could have belonged to half Glasgow: the soles had developed no distinguishing features. Found in anyone's possession they would not have been incriminating in themselves. There were no cloth threads on the tree trunk and the shooter had dropped nothing in his flight. The gun had been found but it was unlicensed and untraceable. Nobody had admitted to seeing the gunman either shooting or running away. It was being assumed that Spike had nothing to do with the incident except to be the unfortunate recipient of a jacket.

Des and his team were treating the case as attempted murder. He seemed stumped and Zara had the impression he was willing to speak to her because he thought she might have something more for him.

She was left with two questions. Who would want to kill Steading and why? And in tandem with this, was the connection between Doctor

James and the tunnel (and therefore Malloch) anything to do with the Steading angle?

She took out her chart and studied it. It looked likely that there was a connection but she had no direct evidence. She drew another box and labelled it "The Gunman" and then put arrows through Spike's box and towards, but stopping short of, Steading's. Try as hard as she could, she could see no connections. She concentrated her thoughts instead on the two doctors. After two cups of coffee and three oatcakes, she decided she needed more material. She even began to sympathize with Des. Needing a complete change, she took the hoover out of the cupboard and applied herself to the lifting of dust.

Hoovering could become like a meditation for Zara: she pushed and pulled and watched as the carpet became evenly devoid of specks, threads and scraps. She even took the machine down the sides of the sofa. There were usually felt pens there (Ben) and sometimes money so she felt with her hands first and pulled out half a dozen drawings.

She couldn't recollect having seen them before but close inspection told her they were by two different hands. The stethoscope was a giveaway: Ben and Doctor Andrew the day they'd first met him. The stethoscope had a funny hat on top of it. Ben's drawings were full of random objects. She tried to remember but she hadn't been listening. Some game or other. She put the paper into a box of things that were Ben's and went on with her hoovering. She was lulled into a world without thought.

Consequently she almost overlooked a folded piece of paper half stuck under her door. At first she wondered why it hadn't been put through the letter-box and then assumed it had been delivered while the storm door was open and she was in the flat. Hand delivered: could just be junk mail. She opened it with trepidation.

KEEP OUT! THIS IS NOT FOR YOU TO HANDLE. YOU ARE NOT SAFE, she read. No signature of course. Her first thought was that it was from the person behind the assault near the McKelvie Buildings. She realized it was the first time she had admitted to herself that the assault had been planned not random. She shivered.

Zara put the hoover away and sat down in the living room. She looked at the note, holding it by a corner, thinking about fingerprints. Don't panic, she said to herself. This could be a useful clue. She thought about other mail she had received in the past week. Something sat on the edge of her consciousness. She went to the mantelpiece. There, a note from Doctor Andrew, the day after the plasterer's visit. 'Called but you were out,' it read. 'How did you get on with the plasterer? A'.

She compared the two notes: different paper, different pen, different writing. Why anyway would Doctor Andrew send her an anonymous note? Her heart thudded uncomfortably in her chest. The bone. That bone! She sensed it invading her space as if challenging her awareness. At least it couldn't be from Bill – it hadn't been spirited from the "Other Side".

She turned the paper over and over and noticed that it had been torn off, the bottom half of a piece of A4, she guessed. There was writing along the tear so only half the letters were visible but she could see that the words read: 'FGM ruins lives: help to stop it now.'

She closed her eyes as if she could make the words go away. Doctor Andrew. The piece of paper was torn from a handout at the conference perhaps. Zara tried to stay calm. Coincidence. It was absolutely reasonable for a doctor, especially one from Egypt to have an interest in FGM and how could Doctor Andrew possibly have anything to do with Ivory? I must stop trying to link things that don't link, she said to herself.

She took a deep breath to calm herself down. She would take the two notes to Des and get them tested for fingerprints, and to see if it was the same writer in both instances. She supposed she must tell Barney. Maybe he wouldn't want to stay if the flat wasn't safe: if it wasn't safe for Zara, it wasn't safe for Ben.

Zara phoned Des who told her to leave the notes at the station as he was too busy to see her. She was happy with that and after she'd delivered them she went to see Spike again. But Spike had left the hospital. Leaving the building she saw a one-legged pigeon and looked round for Munchy. The pigeon appeared to be looking round too but Munchy was nowhere to be seen.

She decided on the spur of the moment to go and call on the Steadings. This time it would be a surprise visit. Steading might feel a little less cocky having been almost killed the night before. She didn't know what she would say to him but that didn't bother her: she would think of something.

When Zara rang the bell at the Steadings', the door opened immediately and Steading himself stood on the threshold. He looked taken aback.

'Just a word,' said Zara smiling.

'I have nothing to say to the press,' said Steading.

'About what?' said Zara.

'I thought...' Steading began, 'I thought, sorry, I thought it was about something else. If you want to talk about fires, I've got five minutes only'.

'Can I come in?' asked Zara. He held the door wide. 'It was something quite small,' said Zara, 'and I was passing so I thought I'd drop by'. She made a play of retrieving her notebook from a deep pocket. 'Now last time I was here, you told me a great deal about...' she stopped and consulted her notes. She could feel Steading getting edgy. 'Yes, here it is. You said that in the time you were a councillor, there were, let's see, ten fires in the centre of Glasgow. That's right isn't it?' She looked up. He was scowling.

'What's your point?'

'I just wanted to clarify exactly the dates at which you became a councillor and when you finished. Just to tie up...'

'Tie up what?'

'Is it a problem?' asked Zara. 'Maybe you can't remember?' A telephone rang in another room and Steading's wife appeared.

'Charles, you're wanted. Not on the phone, you idiot. You should have been there half an hour ago. I can't believe you're still here!' To Zara, Steading's wife sounded irritated beyond the minor issue of being late for something. Steading responded by yanking his briefcase off the floor so violently that the metal zip of a side pocket caught Zara's arm and immediately she had a bright red scratch which started bleeding profusely.

'Go!' shouted Mrs Steading. 'Go on before you faint.' Steading backed towards the door glowering at Zara. 'He can't stand the sight of blood,' his wife said apologetically.

'I'd be glad if you didn't come here again. Invited or not invited. You're nothing but trouble.' Steading did not apologize for Zara's injury.

Zara was surprised at herself but she was feeling nauseous as she stood watching the blood ooze out of the cut. It felt like another assault. Mrs Steading was propelling her towards the bathroom. She allowed herself to be tended, watching deft fingers dab with cotton wool and select a plaster.

'Cup of tea?' said Mrs Steading relinquishing Zara's arm. Zara nodded.

'I'm sorry, Mrs Steading, to have invaded you like this.'

'Caroline.' Zara watched Caroline prepare a tray much in the manner she surmised that she had prepared one for Spike. 'Let's go into the garden,' said her hostess. Zara scented an agenda and felt excited. However she decided she would present her agenda first.

'So what did you reckon on Spike getting shot on account of wearing your ex-husband's, sorry your husband's ex-jacket? That still doesn't sound right,' Zara tried to laugh off her blunder but she could see that what had been not even a wild shot in the dark but a genuine slip, had turned Caroline's face pale.

'Spike? Jacket?' she was confused. Zara realized she had not been told the story and proceeded to fill her in. 'The police didn't speak to you then?' Zara finished.

'I was away till this morning, down at my sister's near Manchester. I expect they'll be in touch.' Zara thought that Caroline's pupils had dilated.

'Poor Spike,' said Caroline. 'Is he all right?' Zara nodded. 'That's a relief. I shall always be grateful to him for saving my house.'

'He told me that story,' said Zara. Then she had to satisfy Caroline's curiosity as to how she knew Spike. After that there was a pregnant pause.

'I'm wondering who wanted to kill my husband,' said Caroline.'

'No ideas come to mind then?' asked Zara. Again a pause.

'The past, if one goes into the past. He was after all a man with position and responsibility. Such people always have enemies...'Are you thinking more specifically, Zara wondered.

'Nothing to do with the questions I was asking last time I was here for instance?'

'What?'.Caroline seemed to have gone into a reverie.

'Last time I was here I mentioned the McKelvie Buildings fire and that was the point you entered the room as I remember it. You seemed interested in the fact that we'd been discussing that.' Caroline looked Zara straight in the eye:

'I know nothing about the McKelvie Buildings fire – except that there is something to be known.' A long silence.

Chapter XIV Who's in debt to whom?

'Are you married or in a partnership, Zara? Do you mind my asking that?'

'Not at the moment.' Zara plumped for the easy answer. The two women had found it easy to talk to each other and Caroline was dropping to a deeper level.

'Do you think Zara, that if you felt a relationship was dead, you should move on or does loyalty come into it?'

'If the relationship was dead for you, why would you stay in it?' Zara answered.

'My sister,' said Caroline, is in a dead relationship. We talked about it a lot when I visited her. If certain things came out, you see, she might lose financially. Would you, Zara, take finance into consideration?'

'I suppose,' said Zara, 'it depends on the individual case. Personally I would get out and be poor but then I have an inbuilt belief in my own capacity to survive. I've always been very independent. Probably makes me unliveable with.'

'I don't know what I'd do if it were me,' said Caroline. Zara's antennae stood up.

'It sounds,' said Zara, 'as if there is a specific obstacle standing in your sister's way. Is it something she has no control over?'

'Yes and No.' Caroline glanced up the lawn as if she expected someone to appear suddenly and catch the two of them. 'She's having an affair with an unsuitable guy.'

'If she's married, there's a case for saying any candidate's unsuitable,' Zara observed, keeping her face blank.

'You're right of course,' said Caroline. 'But even overlooking her marriage, walking off into the sunset with this guy would be out of the question.'

'Because?'

'Because of the wife's father.'

'Your father then as well?'

'Yes, yes.' Caroline looked surprised as if she'd forgotten her own connection. Or was it because she was lying and finding it difficult to stick to her own story, Zara wondered.

'And how would he have reacted to the news? Died of shock or cut her off without a penny?

'Possibly one after the other.'

'So she's too fond of her father to do that?' Caroline hesitated.

'There's something else.' Zara raised her eyebrows. 'Her husband is in debt. The wife bails him out with her father's money.' Zara expelled her breath.

'Families, families. How complicated can you get? I suppose in the end, I would ask myself if I felt changing things would make me happier and whether I would want to look back on the situation and feel I'd dealt with it honestly.' Caroline looked pained.

'My sister is not a bad person.'

'I'm sure she isn't,' said Zara. 'Maybe she needs a little extra courage.'

'Another cup of tea?' asked Caroline, pouring from the china pot when Zara nodded. Caroline's hand was shaking.

'Are you fond of your sister?'

'Of course but it's that she relies on me for support and I don't know what advice to give her.'

'I'm sorry.' said Zara. 'I don't know what else to say. Does your husband have a take on it?'

'Charlie? No, no, he knows nothing. I couldn't possibly tell Charlie. That's why I'm speaking to you. I can't bother him with emotional stuff. He says that's just for women.'

Zara got up. She needed to get out of the Steading's house. She was afraid Caroline might realize she'd given herself away. However, she wanted to leave the door open: she looked round desperately for inspiration.

'Your clematis. Will it bloom soon? I would love to come and see it full out. I imagine it's spectacular.' Caroline looked strangely grateful.

'Come any time. It should flower within a week. Give my good wishes to Spike,' she said at the gate and I'm sorry about the argument with Charlie's briefcase. He has a facility for rubbing people up the wrong way so to speak.' Zara laughed and waved her way down the road.

***

Zara came away from her visit to the Steading's running her conversation with Caroline like a tape through her mind: "My sister is not a bad person"; "I couldn't possibly tell Charlie". She smiled to herself. Simple she thought, but relevant? All she really knew for certain was that it was Caroline that was having the affair. But was that part of the jigsaw or just an extraneous complication?

Was Doctor Andrew involved in any way with any of this? Obviously he was entitled to be concerned about his brother but she didn't want him to be bad. An Egyptian doctor who had a commitment to the FGM issue and no more.

Zara reached home, took down her file with her chart in it and also a clean sheet of paper. Then she put on the kettle. She needed a new updated chart to look at alongside the original. First she drew a rectangle for McKelvie Buildings. Above it she placed a box for Steading and above that, one for Malloch. Below the McKelvie Buildings box was one for Ivory and below that, a box for Bill. On the right of Ivory was a box each for Doctor James and Doctor Andrew.

She had broken her rule of only giving people boxes if she had strong evidence of their involvement but she was frustrated.

Looking at her chart, one thing stood out: how Malloch was distant. Zara had the image of someone who, like the man who could finger a nuclear button (to compare great things with small), was in charge, powerful, but able to do things without being seen. He could be somebody who had many schemes in operation at once and a man like that would be in a position both to help people but always at a price: he would also call in favours.

Tentatively she drew in a dotted line from Doctor James to Malloch, reflecting that the line might not go all the way directly to him but that it probably came all the way from him. Through Steading perhaps.

Zara pondered on the Doctor James connection. Looking at the ninety-nine per cent probability that Malloch had a hold over the doctor, what was the most likely basis for that? Money, Zara's mind answered without hesitation. A young doctor in a foreign country accepting a loan from a dubious source. Or if he were a gambler perhaps, losing money and unable to pay the debt.

Suddenly Zara's mind switched the characters in Caroline's story: if it were Caroline having the affair, was it Steading that owed the money? Why was he in debt? Was he being blackmailed? Did Malloch have a way to drop Steading in it regarding breaches in regulations in the Planning Department? It was all plausible but she had no evidence. And Doctor James and his possible vulnerabilities were still a mystery.

***

'I've got a match for your two notes. Does that make sense to you?' Des on the phone.

'It makes sense,' said Zara, 'but not a sense I'm very happy with'.

'I don't like the way we can't exclude the possibility it's the same people who assaulted you – and that puts Doctor Andrew in the frame with, I'm afraid, Malloch.'

Although Zara could say nothing to counter Des's claims, she did not feel them to be true.

'It may not be as simple as that,' she said.

'I'll need to see this Doctor Andrew of yours, Zara'

'No,' said Zara automatically.

'Did you not think this through? It's the obvious next step.'

'When will you see him?'

'As soon as I can get to him.' Zara could only shrug her shoulders in frustration.

***

Much as Zara enjoyed having Barney and Ben in her home, after a week she began to feel edgy: she wanted her space back. At least, she thought it was that but another voice inside her said she was afraid of liking it too much and then having to re-adjust to her singleness. She tentatively put it to Barney that she was fine now and that maybe Ben would like to be back in his own place. Barney agreed but she could see his reluctance. Still, he knew that just now, accepting Zara's wishes was the best thing to do. They left that day.

***

Zara was intrigued to see what happened after Des had been to see Doctor Andrew.

'I'm having a little bet with myself,' she told Barney. 'I think he might knock on my door after Des has been.'

It was seven-thirty in the morning and after Barney and Ben had left. Zara heard tramping on the stair, feet passing her door and a distant but definite knock on the door above. She resisted the impulse to listen to the rise and fall of their voices and turned on her radio.

Twenty minutes later, she heard Des depart. Ten minutes later, there was a knock at her door and Doctor Andrew almost fell in when she opened it.

'Zara,' he began – he looked distraught – 'I am so sorry about the note. I didn't know what to do and I did the wrong thing I know but I was trying to help you'.

'It's the story of my life,' muttered Zara, pouring him a cup of coffee without asking whether he wanted one. She remembered she had to bear in mind that Doctor Andrew didn't know that she knew anything about anything and furthermore didn't know she knew Des.

'You should have just spoken to me.' Zara decided to be dignified and magnanimous but a bit self-righteous. 'I was frightened,' she said. I was assaulted last week in the street. I'm sure...' - she just recovered herself in time - 'I'm sure you can understand how your note read like part of a campaign. The police will want to speak to you, you know. I had to tell them.'

Doctor Andrew hung his head. 'I am sorry. It was very foolish of me and the police have already been. The inspector was very polite and he said he would speak to you about whether you wanted to press charges.'

'I'm not unapproachable, am I?' said Zara, driving her advantage home. 'I thought we were becoming such good friends, I can't believe...'

'Believe me, I was desperate. I was not thinking straight. I had already given you a sample of my handwriting. What sort of criminal is as stupid as that? I am not a criminal, Zara. I am just the unfortunate recipient of information I would rather not have.'

'If it's criminal, you should inform the police. And if it's criminal and you tell me, I shall have to inform the police otherwise I shall be breaking the law too.'

Doctor Andrew's eyes widened at Zara's stolid declaration of the workings of Scottish justice. She could see he was thinking hard.

'It is my brother,' he said at last. 'He owes money, he is entangled with a woman and he is trying to hold down a job. I feel if he can only hold down his job, it is his great chance to climb out of this situation. I am supporting him to do this.'

'So is it that the creditors won't wait for their money?'

'They have threatened my brother's life.'

'So why doesn't he go to the police?' Zara was enjoying playing dumb.

'These people are worse than loan-sharks, Zara. What they do is ask my brother to do something for them and say they'll forget about the money if... but he is refusing. So far.

'So they wouldn't like it if he went to the police?'

'They would kill him. Shoot him dead.'

'Do you know who these people are?'

'No. I don't want to know because then as you say, I would have to act on the information and my brother would never forgive me and would be in great danger. You see my dilemma.' Zara nodded. 'So I panicked,' he went on. 'I thought perhaps you knew something.'

'When did you think that? Was it on Sunday at Mugdock Park?' The doctor's eyes betrayed him. 'Your brother rang you when we were there, didn't he?' The doctor sighed.

'You and Barney had both been questioning me about FGM and I felt you might just keep questioning me and I would reveal something. I had to leave.'

'Why should that subject bother you? We were just asking you about something we understood you were well-informed on,' said Zara. 'I can tell you, you aroused far more suspicion by leaving than you would have done by staying.'

'I know. I can see that now but can you accept that there is nothing to worry about. I just freaked but I can see now I was imagining that you knew more than you did. People have disappeared – Doctor Andrew made full eye contact –distressing cases but my knowledge of it is under wraps. Data protection and all that. I am so nervous these days, my brother rings me night and day, everything extra is a strain and I am likely to overreact.'

'I am sorry I can't be more help to you,' said Zara genuinely moved by the doctor's distress. 'You are obviously very attached to your brother.'

'We have been like that,' he held up two fingers twisted together, 'since we were born'. 'I am his elder by a year only but I have always felt protective towards him.'

'Can I ask you about the woman?' Zara thought she might be able to get *some* information that wasn't of a criminal nature. 'You said your brother was entangled?'

'Yes, he is entangled but he will not tell me who the lady is and this worries me because I think it means there is something not okay about the whole affair. For all I know, she might be involved with the money business. It is all too much.'

'Has it been going on a long time?'

'It all started nine or ten years ago. That's when they met but although he was attracted to her, nothing happened. Then they met again a few years later and the thing took off. I know in my bones it is unsuitable.'

'You mean perhaps the lady is married?'

'I think so, yes but I know nothing and my brother goes wild if I say anything negative about the liaison. He says if he didn't have it, he would die.'

Zara was inclined to believe the Doctor James story although she was not certain Doctor Andrew was telling the whole truth. The only link to Malloch was the knuckleduster injury. She wanted something stronger, preferably something which would put Doctor Andrew firmly in or out of the frame.

After the doctor had left, Zara turned over the visit in her mind. She remembered Doctor Andrew had not shown any surprise when she had mentioned her assault. Was that because he already knew about it? But of course Des would have used it as a lever. Even so, one might have thought he would have commiserated with her. Perhaps the fact that he didn't just showed how normal that type of activity was in the world he had been dragged into.

She also realized he had not answered her question about FGM, why the subject should bother him. Was that part of his general distractedness or had he been consciously suppressing something?

There was a knock at the door. It was the plasterer.

'Haven't come to do the job,' he said. 'Too soon, but can I leave some plaster here? I had some left over from another job and I thought it would just about do your ceiling. Save me carrying it around in the van.' Zara directed him to put it in the hall cupboard which she had fortunately cleared out in a frustrated mood in March.

When he left she went to the window. The van was parked in the same place: it was the same driver. She watched the plasterer saunter down the street and as he got into the van, the driver's head turned. Zara took down the van's number and let the curtain she had been hiding behind fall. She rang Des. He answered immediately.

'I've had Doctor Andrew at my door protesting innocence but something else... The plasterer came. – You know how the bathroom ceiling fell in? – He was just leaving some plaster but guess who was his mate driving the van? Munchy! I've seen him before in that van.'

'What are you telling me? That Munchy knows a plasterer? As far as I know, plastering isn't a banned occupation in this country.'

'Wait,' said Zara, 'I will make sense, just listen a minute. When my neighbour Doctor Andrew talked to me about the plasterer he said he was someone his landlord knew. I want you to check on who the owner of the flat is'.

'Zara, why shouldn't a landlord know a plasterer? It seems quite reasonable to me.'

'Okay, it's a hunch on my part but it was you who suspected Munchy of being complicit in my assault. If he was and if he is now driving around a plasterer who is going to be working in my bathroom, I think that fact deserves some attention.' Des was quiet for a moment and then he said,

'Did you have someone in mind for the owner of the flat?'

'Malloch comes high on my list,' said Zara.

'Okay, I'll run a check.'

'Thanks, and Des? If I'm right, I want a reward.'

'What's that, another dinner?'

'I want to know at least one salient fact about that man.'

Chapter XV Party time

The phone rang: it was Zara's contact at the Herald wanting to know if she could move her deadline forward for her first article. Zara made a face at the phone but reconciled herself to spending as long as it took to finish the article. She worked well under pressure and anyway she just had to tighten up the opening paragraph and make sure the ending was vibrant, actually drew some conclusions, and made readers want to read her next piece.

Reluctantly she sat down at her desk. She did need money coming in and sooner than she had originally thought. She wondered about asking Noreen at the Rialto Café down the road if she could have some shifts. Her savings were going to run out in a few weeks. Perhaps she should set herself to work at her writing for at least two hours every morning. She used to do this. She shook her head. It was the bone that had wrecked all that but she couldn't help it. Two hours later she had finished a workable draft of the article.

However Zara now felt stuck. Because the article was as good as finished, the case was crowding her again. She had to go out and talk to someone, anyone, who might be able to cast a small light on it. Grabbing a sandwich, she headed for the park and looked for the one-legged pigeon.

After ten minutes she was lucky enough to spy it hopping on the fringes of a flock surrounding the fountain. She followed it. She realized it must have an inbuilt clock timed to monitor Munchy's day: it actually looked as if it knew exactly when and where he was going to appear. Zara was intrigued; the pigeon seemed to be waiting now, so she sat on a bench and waited too.

Sure enough, after about fifteen minutes, Munchy appeared with bread in his pocket. He did not look surprised to see Zara but then he always looked pleased with life, as if it gave him just what he wanted all the time. Zara wondered if it was because he didn't always see round corners.

He hailed her with a smile as if it were the most normal thing in the world for her to be waiting for him. Did he know exactly whose house the plasterer had gone into she wondered.

'Munchy,' she was as direct as usual, 'who were you working for this morning? I saw you driving a van'.

'That was Pete. His mate's off and Pete's lost his licence temporarily so he asked me.'

'He asked you?'

'Well you know, orders come from on high, don't they? I just do what I'm told and take the money.' He grinned.

'Who is your boss, Munchy?'

'He's a big shot, he is. I hardly ever get to meet him but he knew my dad. I take my orders from Charlie Steading.

'Charlie Steading?' Zara kept her voice neutral. She wanted to reassure Munchy that it was okay to talk to her about those people: 'So who's his boss then?'

'You want to see him? I've a job to do tonight. I could take you where you could see him. He wouldn't see you!' Munchy became excited. 'He's having a party. Very posh, so I hear, and he wants me to keep a watch on who's there; for an hour; until the real man comes. It's in a big house with lots of rooms but I'm in a shed outside. You'll need to come between nine-thirty and ten-thirty.'

'So how do you keep watch?' Zara felt the necessity to be patient.

'CCTV. If I see anything suspicious, I phone him. You come to my shed, I'll show you the Boss.' Munchy looked triumphant. Zara wondered, not for the first time, if Munchy was stupid rather than bad. Had he been a pawn in the game of her assault rather than a willing participant? Why would Malloch use someone like him? She didn't ultimately care. It was an opportunity she was not going to miss.

The house was in Bearsden. Once again, Munchy's directions were made up of pictures: hills, corners, trees. The house itself was apparently considerably concealed by a tall hedge but Munchy said it was the only one with lions on the gateposts. Zara wondered if Munchy could read and write. Had he actually passed his driving test, for instance? Very possibly not. She assumed fake driving licences were as easy to forge as fake passports.

She remembered the photo and plunged straight in:

'Munchy, you were going to show me a photo, that day... you know when... I was looking for Spike... we were interrupted.' Munchy looked uncomfortable.

'Oh yes.' Doesn't want to talk about it, thought Zara.

'I think you were going to tell me who was in the photo...'

'Well, it was my dad and the Boss and... I don't know who the other guy was. The guy that took the photo is dead.'

'The Boss? You mean Malloch?' A faint nod. 'So where are they? What are they doing?'

'They're in the army aren't they?' Munchy seemed quite irritated.

'Is there something wrong?' Zara asked. She didn't like Munchy and found it difficult to stay friendly.

'Screw took away my photo didn't he? And now I don't have a picture of my dad.' Bastard, thought Zara.

'Who is Screw?'

'You don't want to know,' replied Munchy, kicking a stone at his feet.

'Was it just malice or does he want something from you?'

'I don't know,' said Munchy.

Zara left, her mind in a ferment: Munchy's dad and Malloch. An old liaison. Malloch's loyalty to his friend's son – if you could call it that. What army though and when and who was the third man? Would finding him...? Zara went over the conversation she had just had: 'The man who took the photo is dead.' Was that significant? How did he die?

It was like something and nothing. Zara felt the way you do when you are trying to grasp a dream: some image she needed to remember, some connection she needed to make. She realized she had been very disappointed not to see the picture again. She took this as a sign. She let her mind play over the evidence she had: there had been something in the photo that she'd seen before quite recently.

***

Zara had been phoning Barney every night since he had stopped sleeping at her flat. It was to keep him happy: she didn't feel the need for it but she felt deceitful saying, 'I'm fine, goodnight' if she was then going to be sneaking off to watch a party in Bearsden. She rang a friend who lived nearby and made a date to go round. A white lie was better than a black one: 'Going to see Corinne, may stay over', sounded okay to Zara. She would leave Corinne's before ten which would be fine as her friend had to get up at six to get to work on time in Edinburgh. Zara had her mobile. What could go wrong?

Des phoned. What he told her made her evening seem much more formidable:

'Zara. The flat does not look as if it belongs to Malloch, although I would be stressing 'look as if', but the white van is traceable to him so there is a connection. Here's your salient fact: he's never been the same since his daughter was killed by a hit-and-run driver. She was ten. The driver got off on insufficient evidence. Malloch was a bad man before that but that death changed him for the worse. Will that do? Fair exchange?'

'Thanks Des,' said Zara overwhelmed by the quick fire volley of information. She had been scribbling as he spoke; he hadn't given her much but at least she'd broken the taboo.

Inside, Zara was nervous. It seemed strange to her that the day she was to almost meet Malloch should be the day when Des gave her information on him. She didn't like 'too good to be true'. Still, she decided, she was going to keep her assignation with Munchy.

She would find Malloch's house before going to Corinne's, then when she went to meet Munchy, she would leave the car in the next street as a precaution.

***

Zara found the house easily and drove cheerfully back to spend time with Corinne. Whilst there she received a text from Barney, 'Thanks for message re where you are tonight. Enjoy. Catch up tomorrow. Love, B & B'. She felt a bit guilty reading it and thinking about what she was really going to be doing. She did not tell Corinne, playing out the whole 'I-won't- keep-you-up, I've-an-early-start-too routine and waving as she left, to the friendly figure on the doorstep.

She parked the car under some trees on a small piece of waste ground. There were houses. The area didn't look unfrequented. She was wearing, as Munchy had suggested, a dark mac and a cap, (Barney's: too big) because Munchy did not want anyone wondering, should anyone care to, why he was entertaining a woman when he was meant to be working. A mate he could explain away to the retinue of wheelers and dealers who clung to the edges of Malloch's life, people who tonight would be dressed up as wine waiters and takers of jackets, bouncers who would only look like bouncers should they have someone to bounce.

Approaching the house, Zara could hear music but it was not at a level at which neighbours would start phoning the police. She wondered whether Malloch presented as an ordinary neighbour from whom you might borrow that cup of sugar Glasgow folk are traditionally reputed to run out of or as someone you could ask to water your tomatoes while you were on holiday in Spain. Perhaps everyone said a polite 'Good morning' but otherwise gave him a wide berth. Who would be at his party? She would soon see.

Munchy had mentioned a side gate where the bins were. If she entered here, there was a line of laurels and rhododendrons all the way along to the shed where Munchy was located. She looked to left and right. No one. She opened the gate and went in.

The door of the shed was not evident and only one small window with a blind betrayed a chink of light. You would hardly have noticed the shed at all if you had not been looking for it. The shrubs were not overgrown but they were doing their screening job very well.

Zara stood in front of the door suddenly scared. Supposing it wasn't Munchy inside? Why would Malloch go to all the trouble of getting his guests on film? So he could blackmail them at a later date? She listened hard. Someone was moving about in the shed and she could hear the low hum of electronic equipment. She turned the handle of the door slowly and silently – a stouter door she noticed than on an ordinary garden shed – and peeped through the crack. Munchy. She opened it further and stepped inside.

There was a bank of screens, one for each room, Zara supposed and Munchy sat idly in front of them.

'You made it then. Come and join the party.' He had a can sat beside him and Zara reckoned it wasn't the first. He wasn't drunk but his voice wasn't as quick as usual. Zara took possession of the only other chair.

'Where's Malloch then?' she said, not wanting to waste any time. She didn't know how long she'd want to stay: she wanted to leave before the real security man came. Munchy surveyed the screens and then pointed at one.

'That's him. Back view. Wait 'n' he'll turn round in a minute.'

'That's Steading he's talking to,' said Zara. Munchy looked sideways at her and she realized she'd just told Munchy she knew Steading when she'd implied she didn't know him earlier. Bad move, she cursed herself, I need to be more careful.

The head that Munchy claimed was owned by Joe Malloch was large. The hair was shaved and the ears protruded giving the impression of an outsize gnome. A bull neck and a broad back. Heavy arms imprisoned in an expanse of kingfisher-blue shirt. Zara's eyes travelled down to the hands: there was the knuckle-duster ring on the right index finger. She held her face expressionless.

Suddenly the head swung round and Zara jumped as she felt as if the eyes bored right into her. She was gazing into the face of a man from whom all good spirit was drained. His eyes had an opalescent quality, neither one colour nor another. Despite, or maybe because of a long scar down the right side of his right cheek, he would have been good-looking if he had been good but Zara felt she was looking at a living embodiment of hatred and distrust. Then he smiled and she felt a chill spread through her body.

She watched him pass from guest to guest playing the beneficent host. Then suddenly he wasn't in the room any more. This made Zara edgy: she wanted him where she could see him. He didn't re-appear in any of the other rooms.

'Where do you think he's gone?' asked Zara.

'Oh I dunno. Perhaps he's looking at the CCTV coming in the gates. That's the only one you can see from the house,' said Munchy.

'The gates! All the gates?' Zara was horrified.

Munchy waved his hand at two screens at the side which Zara had taken no notice of because nothing was happening on them. 'State of the art,' he said. 'You can pick up anything on them even in the dark. You can process the film and work out a good picture. My mate Woody what's usually here, he told me.' Zara got to her feet.

'So he'll have seen me arrive?' Munchy blinked.

'I suppose he will.'

'Definitely stupid rather than bad,' thought Zara realizing as she blamed Munchy, that she had been just as stupid.

At that moment there was a footfall and then the door was flung open. Simultaneously Zara dived, taking advantage of the fact that the incomer would blink at the light and also not know which direction she was coming from.

There was an exclamation and a clutching at her back and Zara was caught by the mac but fortunately it was undone and she managed to twist herself free, sliding out of the sleeves, stumbling on the threshold and out into the dark bushes. She made for the fence, not the gate, vaulting over with an ease she would not have imagined possible. She made herself stand in the shadow for a second to gauge where her pursuer was and then ran across the next door garden, trying to keep her breath soundless. Her heart sounded very loud but she presumed she was the only person who could hear that.

Gaining her car, she started the engine and slid away without putting on the lights till she was well clear of the street. She hoped there was nothing incriminating in the pockets of the mac. She supposed Munchy would either say it was a very nervous friend of his or that he knew nothing about her.

Turning onto the main road back to the centre of town, she noticed a police car travelling in the opposite direction and managed to relax enough to smile at the idea that they might be going to Joe Malloch's.

***

Des showed his ID at the door and he and his colleague, Jamie, strode passed the bouncers and went from room to room looking for Malloch. He was holding court in the main lounge.

'DI Desmond Harris,' said Des flicking his badge towards Malloch. 'Neighbour phoned ten minutes ago, saw a figure jump over your fence into his garden. Wondered if everything was all right. Anything to report?' Des was taking the opportunity to take in as many faces as possible. He saw Steading because, even though he had his back to him he was facing a mirror.

'Gentlemen,' Malloch was smooth and unruffled. 'I was about to call you myself though I wouldn't have expected the honour of a visit from CID. Would have settled for a couple of uniforms. However, since you're here, maybe you'd be interested in helping us identify this person on the CCTV. Could be who jumped over the fence. I'm quite choosy about who comes to my parties. Hence the footage.'

Des was taken into a small back room with two screens showing the gates. Grainy and very dark though the picture was, Des saw immediately that it was Zara. He shook his head.

'No, doesn't ring any bells. 'Nothing missing from the house or garden?' He stood poker-faced.

'Nothing so far as we can see. It's a good job the dogs were caged though. She could have been…' Des waved his hand: he didn't want to hear the Malloch making a black joke about missing limbs.

'We won't spoil your jollifications any longer then.'

'Sorry you've had a wasted journey,' said Malloch, raising his glass to Des.

'Don't mention it. We were in the area as it happened.'

Leaving, Des caught sight of Munchy peering from the gate. His curiosity was obvious from his face. Des kicked the kerb and Jamie looked at him questioningly.

'Two and two make four,' said Des, his hand on Jamie's arm guiding him past Munchy. 'Not always what you want. You don't need to know,' Des added as Jamie opened his mouth. Jamie didn't pursue it: he had recognized Zara too.

***

Zara did not have a good night. On the one hand she felt she was on an adrenalin high because of her narrow escape and the whole adventure of being on Malloch's premises. She kept re-living her dive through the door. Also, the image of Malloch haunted her, together with the information about his daughter's death. She felt she was at last on a track: not at the endgame by any means but as if she'd found an orientation for the route she should take.

It was as if a hole had been identified: there had always been something missing. However much Zara had tried to piece the story or stories together from the information she had, there was still a feeling of absence. Yes, there were the fires, there was a particular fire in the McKelvie Buildings which had yielded Bill's story, and there was Doctor James and the knuckle-duster injury, which linked somehow, as Zara saw it. But she did not yet know how Malloch fitted in and was loth to leave the motivation where it was.

Why was this? Zara thought about it, looking up at her favourite crack in the ceiling which was shaped like a heron in flight. What was interesting, she concluded, was Malloch's apparent wish for things to lie, to stay the same with no one suddenly producing bits of information from the past. There was nothing odd about it, it was a very reasonable wish from where he was sitting but Zara scented something and she wondered whether it had anything to do with his daughter's accident.

***

Eight o'clock. Zara still in her pyjamas. A knock at the door that wasn't the postman. Des looking thunderous. He stood in the middle of her living room:

'Well?'

'Well what? I didn't see you flash your ID but you don't sound very friendly.'

'What were you doing at the Malloch's last night?'

'Munchy tell you?' Zara was surprised at the speed information travelled.

'We were called to the house. A neighbour saw someone climb the fence. Malloch showed us your picture on his CCTV.'

'He didn't know who I was?' Zara's voice was anxious.

'No, but he soon will and it will be a face to a name. Remember he has already had you assaulted without ever having set eyes on you. In some ways he has a better network even than us. Anyway I don't suppose it would be too difficult to break Munchy. A Mars bar would do it I reckon.' Zara couldn't resist smiling. 'The situation is not funny.' Des resumed his angry-parent stance. 'What has to happen to you for you to realize you can't mess with Malloch? I know I have no personal claims on you but I do value your life. I would like you to be around for a little longer. Look, I would say this to anyone, if you want to stay alive, just leave Malloch alone.'

'If he's so dangerous, why don't you arrest him?'

'He's a very clever man. I wish he worked for CID. He always puts lots of layers between himself and any crime he's involved in. He's never there. For instance: McKelvie Buildings. There is no evidence to tie him to the event.'

'What about Bill's phone call?'

'The word of a man who can no longer be questioned? If we asked, Malloch would deny receiving the call, he will likely have made it from someone else's phone or one not in his name and he would probably say he was in Dundee or Dalry quietly playing chess.'

'He plays chess?'

'He's an excellent player we hear. Plays against Steading.'

'What strange pieces of information you collect!'

'Is your kettle broken?' asked Des sitting down at last. He didn't know if he was getting through to Zara but he had realized, as usual, that the angry method only drove her in the other direction: he was going to have to be a little more subtle.

***

It was late the following afternoon and Zara was looking after Ben at her house. He had opened his box, as he usually did and shuffled through everything, as he usually did. Zara was otherwise occupied when she heard him say,

'Will you play that game with me that I played with Doctor Andrew? He was sitting with the drawing in his hand. Zara glanced down and saw a hat that looked like an upside-down flowerpot:

'Got it', she whispered.

'Got what?' asked Ben.

'Just that I've seen a hat like that before recently.'

'It's called a kepi,' said Ben. 'They wear them in the French Foreign Legion,' he added, pleased to know something Zara didn't. 'Why are you so excited? Has it got something to do with Ivory?'

Chapter XVI A bit of this and a bit of that

Charlie Steading came out of the Rainmaker's church and turned dispiritedly towards his car. He had wanted to meet Doctor James but he wasn't there and hadn't been seen since that last time when he had asked him for money. Doctor James had never given him a telephone number – his way of keeping a little bit of control, Charlie supposed. Not seeing Doctor James, who had a habit of complete regularity at the Rainmaker's, gave Charlie a windy feeling. Could Doctor James have anything to do with the attempt on his life? He could not bring himself to believe that the man had stood behind a tree with a gun. He seemed such an amiable person. But his lying low did seem a possible pointer towards guilt.

He felt angry: he'd only asked the guy to pay a debt and not to him, he was just the go-between. He felt injured when he thought of the doctor and venomous when he thought of Joe Malloch. More and more he wanted to drop him in it. He didn't care any longer about consequences.

This change had come about partly as a result of a recent shock. A former colleague of his had been in the Beatson hospital and Charlie had visited him there and hardly recognized him. He couldn't believe how 'a touch of bowel cancer' (his colleague's phrase) could alter a man so much.

After seeing Henry, Charlie's kidney pain seemed to get worse and he'd had more headaches than usual. Or was it that he was now monitoring them? Last week he had felt so scared he had actually gone to his GP who had put him in for the usual blood tests and scans. It was not a world he wanted to become familiar with. And what would Caroline say if he had cancer? Would she care? He didn't think so.

His relationship with his wife had always been complicated by the fact that it had been her money that bought their original house. Would he love her if she were suddenly poor? The question made him sweat but he reminded himself he hadn't any idea how rich she was until they came to plan the wedding.

He'd met the parents before that and had been impressed by how well-turned out they were but every man's allowed one good suit and Charlie had never been a good judge of what was 'class' in regard to clothing.

Then after he and Caroline were married he had been asked to meet Archie, Caroline's father. He was taken into his father-in-law's study and shown the extent of the estate. Archie said he was doing it because his wife was not in the best of health so he wanted Charlie to know how the land would lie in the event of her death.

It was then he learnt the true sum of what Caroline would inherit and the message that came over loud and clear was that he needed to be a good husband and not give her any reason to stray. Charlie thought this was just an old man's way of saying, 'Have enough sex to produce some heirs' and he felt only too competent to fulfil that, but time had gone by and no children had appeared. Caroline would not talk about it and he didn't want to force her to talk.

He had though, gone secretly to see if *he* was infertile but he was not. Then he tried in a roundabout way to try and reassure Caroline that he didn't mind (though he did) whether they had children or not.

'They might have your nose!' she'd said. He knew it had been a joke but it remained a niggling memory. And it was about this time that he became irritated by Caroline's money. He had a decent salary at his job as a public servant but he wanted something more adventurous, wanted to start something of his own. Caroline would have expedited that side of things for him but he wanted to be independent for once.

This was how, after he had been working only two years at the council, a man he'd met through playing chess had intimated to him that there were other ways of acquiring capital. Somehow it had been put to him in a way that seemed acceptable: if you could put in a word here or find out a bit of information there. But first there had been the matter of the car.

'I've a friend who needs a garage for his brand new motor he's inherited from his father who died of a heart attack about a week after buying it. Friend's going abroad and doesn't want to waste money on garaging. He's willing to let me use it in return for a home for it till he comes back,' his chess opponent had said. 'He owes me but I don't need a car.'

Eventually, when Charlie was thoroughly used to the BMW, the chess-player, aka Joe Malloch, had told him that his friend had found a new love in the Bahamas. He didn't want the car but it would be useful to hang on to it so that if he were to come back to Glasgow...

Looking back, he could hardly believe he'd bought such stories. That had been the softening up: then had come the big favour. By this time he was involved with the planning committee and had access to all sorts of confidential information. Even then it was as if he were being brain-washed. Joe always made everything seem okay.

For instance, it wasn't until after McKelvie Buildings had burned down – the fifth in a series of city centre fires – and a business associate of Malloch's had procured the ground to rebuild, the previous owners having gone bankrupt because they had been inadequately insured, that a chance remark of Malloch's had made Charlie suddenly see connections and worse, see how he had become a part of the whole evil structure.

He went over the dates of meetings and favours and presents and began to understand that another chess game was being played, a game which went on and on, one where he thought he was winning but where he was a mere pawn.

He had tried to extricate himself, spoken to Joe man to man, told him he could no longer be a party to what was happening. Joe Malloch had looked at him very seriously, clapped him on the shoulder and said he understood. Charlie's relief was huge but a month later, just when he had started to feel he could rely on a full night's sleep, Malloch got in touch to ask if Charlie would do him the honour of coming to a small select party, just a few friends. Implication: for old times' sake.

Charlie went. Took Caroline with him. She'd been included in the invitation. Charlie assumed the inclusion of Caroline made it a kosher do but afterwards he realized it had been a hook. Caroline had thought Joe was charming and had been intrigued by the odd assortment of people – An African doctor, a Welsh accountant who'd just returned from China, an ex-ballet dancer who ran a nightclub in Paris.

Only afterwards Charlie saw how the trap had been laid. Invitations flowed and Caroline always wanted to accept them. Charlie could not think of ways of refusing without telling her the whole sordid story. Things reverted to the old pattern.

There it was, the pain. It was always worse when he was thinking about Malloch. Could one have cancer of the conscience, Charlie wondered.

He thought sadly about his business, the one he'd set up using Malloch's money and support. The man had been most helpful in finding him outlets, smoothing the way past obstacles. The business had been a success and he had enjoyed and still did enjoy his involvement in it but at this stage, Malloch's help seemed as irritating to him as the idea of Caroline's had been in the past. I still haven't done anything on my own, he thought to himself.

***

When Zara arrived at the Steading's house, Caroline did not appear surprised to see her. She had rung and asked for Charlie and been told he was out but on arrival she found she did not even need the excuse of wanting to see the clematis in bloom.

This time she was given a cup of coffee in a room on the east side of the house where the morning sun poured through a French window which was open.

'You get a very good view of the clematis from here', Caroline said smiling.

Zara smiled back appreciatively and then went for the jugular.

'How's your sister? Have you heard from her since I was last here?' Caroline's eyes flickered.

'She's in a really bad state. The guy she's having an affair with is in the most terrible trouble.'

Zara kept her voice level: 'How terrible?'

146

'He tried to solve a problem but it didn't work out and now he thinks all he can do is leave the country.' Her feelings are withdrawing into some sad place inside, Zara thought. 'He wants me to go with him.' She said it softly and Zara didn't know if she'd realized her slip.

'Your sister to leave? Where for?'

'Somewhere… somewhere in Africa.'

'Somewhere in Africa?' Zara repeated the words, not because of what she felt they must mean to Caroline but because of what had come together in her mind, suddenly like two boats crashing in a dark harbour: Caroline was having an affair with one of the doctors?' Zara kept her head.

'Do you know what the guy did? Was it a crime?'

'Yes, yes. I couldn't bear it if he went to prison!'

This time she did realize and she put her hands over her face and wept, her body shaking as what had been hidden came to light. After a while she came to and dried her eyes childishly with the back of her hand.

'He didn't tell me but I overheard… he was talking in his sleep. He said, "They know about the gun," 'but Caroline added, 'I don't know who *they* are. It could be the police or… someone else.'

'Someone else being?' asked Zara.

'I don't know,' said Caroline, tears forming again in her eyes. Stay with her now, analyse later, Zara told herself.

'Do you want to tell me how you met him?'

It had been at a party of Charlie's business associates, a very strange crowd, Caroline had thought but she had found it exciting because she didn't go out much. She had felt a sympathy for him. His English was not perfect but the slips he made, made her laugh and they laughed together as she gently corrected him. 'I need to keep you by me as my support and guide, he had said.

Meant just as a compliment, the words had shot through Caroline as deeply as if he'd said, 'Marry me'. She brushed off the remark with a riposte and the conversation turned to, she remembered, Africa. He told her about his country, Egypt, the beauty of it, the high hopes he had for it, how much he missed it.

Then it seemed he was gone. She had expected Charlie to have his number or that he would be at the next party but she did not see him again for a year. When she'd asked Charlie about him he'd been offhand and she'd felt he would be suspicious if she pressed him since he obviously could not begin to imagine why Caroline should be interested in contacting him. A little place in her heart was from thenceforth reserved for him and she fabricated a lush garden in Africa through which they forever strolled.

But she had met him again and looking back, she thought, it seemed a weird coincidence. She had been going down to the Lake District to meet a friend and spend a couple of days at a guesthouse while Charlie was at some business conference in Manchester. He was to drop her off, drive on and pick her up on the way back.

However on the second evening he phoned and said there was a change of plan. He found he needed to stay on a day but she was to get her friend to drive her to Stockport and then drive the BMW back to Glasgow, only she would be giving a lift to someone she'd met before. Did she remember him, the African doctor she'd met ages ago at a party of Malloch's? Would she mind very much?

'I wondered why,' said Caroline to Zara, 'the doctor couldn't take a train or a plane but I was so excited I just said 'Yes of course'.

'We arrived in Stockport and found the address where the doctor lived I suppose and there was my car and Charlie and the doctor having a beer. He looked older than I remembered but that was not surprising given the time lapse since I'd seen him. I thought he looked anxious but there was genuine pleasure in his eyes when he greeted me and I felt time just fall away as they say in the movies.' Caroline laughed self-consciously. 'My friend had left, it was about four o'clock so I suggested we got going. Charlie was Mr Affability, he said, "Buy her a nice dinner when you get to Glasgow. I don't want you taking my wife for granted."'

Caroline glanced at the clock. 'You wouldn't like a sherry would you? I know it's early to be drinking but it's this story, I'm not sure I can tell you without a bit of liquid support.' Pause. 'I've never told anyone before.'

'Go ahead,' said Zara but I'll just have an orange juice if you don't mind. I need to stay sober.'

'Oh why?'

'I may have to look after my godson later,' Zara replied off the top of her head.

Caroline came back with a large sherry for herself and a glass of orange for Zara.

'This is special but not alcoholic,' she said. Zara thanked her: she was beginning to like Caroline. The storyteller resumed:

'Everything we said to each other made us laugh. He had this enormous suitcase and he was wearing a dreadful red and yellow tie. I remember saying it's a good job he wasn't hitch-hiking. And he said, "I'm really a travelling salesman. My suitcase is full of..." not silk ties?' I asked. And he said, "No. Two hundred and fifty thousand condoms!" I felt as though we were setting off into the future together instead of just going on a car ride to Glasgow. Underneath the conversation there was this huge wave of sexual feeling. At that moment I did not care about anything else in the world except being with him.' Zara could see from Caroline's eyes that she was reliving that scene in the car.

'All the way up he told me funny stories from medical school. I remember one.' Zara nodded encouragingly thinking it was best to let Caroline chat away. She would be more likely to say something useful.

'Just before his graduation,' said Caroline, 'one of his fellow students, Keith, had told him the department was getting a new skeleton and that if he liked he could take the old one – Keith knew he had a particular interest in bones. He didn't think twice. It didn't occur to him it wasn't a serious proposition. He took the skeleton and left. This is what he *said*,' said Caroline, noticing the scepticism in Zara's face.

'Sorry, go on,' said Zara frightened of a sudden withdrawal.

'Well, the following term,' said Caroline, 'of course nobody was back and no one ever found out what had happened until a long time after. ' Zara nodded. 'Apparently Keith met another old student, Spicer, at a conference and Spicer asked him in the most benign and casual way if he knew anything about the disappearance and Keith told him thinking it would be history but Spicer said, "Can you get it back for me?"' Zara laughed. 'Keith tracked down James who had a very small flat and was using the skeleton as a hat and coat stand. Keith had a drunk friend with him who talked to the skeleton throughout the visit and was quite distressed at the idea of leaving it until he knew *he* was coming with them. "It's just that he's so like my brother," he kept saying. "It could be my brother. He's got his hangy way of standing." Zara laughed again and Caroline resumed:

'We reached the outskirts of Glasgow in time for dinner and he asked if I knew a good restaurant he could take me to and I said, "How about I knock you up something at my house?" And he replied, "Knock you up? Curious expression. Yes, please knock you up," and I said, "James, your English has not improved!"' Zara was so relieved it was not Andrew who was the lover:

'So did you make him an omelette?'

'No,' said Caroline, blushing into her sherry glass, 'we went straight to bed'.

***

Zara had to talk to someone. Obviously it would not be Des and it couldn't be Barney either because there were now bits of the story he didn't know. It would have to be Katerina. Zara felt she had too much information swirling about in her head: she needed someone detached and level-headed to be a sounding board.

She phoned and offered to bring round a take-away but Katerina said she had exotic left-overs from a friend's party and that there was far too much for one. She'd be grateful if Zara could help her out. When Zara arrived, Katerina had a variety of food set out on the patio.

'This is for starters,' she said. 'There's more in the oven.' Zara was glad she had had a small lunch. 'This is what you get when an Italian marries a Moroccan – and they are both chefs!' Katerina added.

After a third time Zara had asked Katerina what a particular dish was and Katerina had said she didn't know, they both just enjoyed the tastes and smells and Zara began to lay out the story, some of which, of course, Katerina knew.

'What I'm looking for,' said Zara, 'is connections. Somehow the doctors – or at least Doctor James, are linked into this story which I have reason to believe involves Malloch and a man called Steading.' Zara explained to her friend a bit of what she knew about Malloch's reputation and how Steading was mixed up with him.

'Also, I've now discovered one, that Malloch, Munchy's father and someone as yet unidentified were all in the French Foreign Legion together and two, that the doctors have a connection to the French Foreign Legion as well. Zara told Katerina about the drawings.

'Could you not ask Doctor Andrew if his father was in the Legion?' asked Katerina.

'You mean Malloch might have been in with him?' Zara digested this. 'It's possible. So, okay we have a line-up, apart from one missing identity but no story. Maybe something happened back then that makes sense of what's happening now. Who knows?' said Zara. The two friends sat silent, thinking.

'Bill is an incidental,' said Zara at last, 'though he is important because he saves a crucial piece of evidence. I feel sure the doctors know about Ivory, but I don't know how or why she is in the McKelvie Buildings fire.'

'Have you thought any more about the possibility that Ivory was a victim of FGM – remember the cracked pubic bone?' Zara hit her head with her hand.

'For some reason I remember and then I forget. I think it's because I don't want Doctor Andrew to be implicated in any of that. He was certainly upset when I tried to ask him about a conference he'd been at.' Zara thought for a minute. 'Doctor Andrew said he didn't want to talk about FGM because he was afraid it would lead him to mention his brother.' She laughed. 'How to give yourself away without really trying.'

'But why would Malloch be involved?' said Katerina.

'Doctor Andrew did tell me his brother was in a lot of debt. Maybe Malloch is owed money and now is calling in a favour. That time I met Doctor James in the park he looked like someone with a millstone round his neck.'

'I'll get the rest of the food,' said Katerina. 'It might help us think better.'

Zara began again, having chosen a little bit of this and that. She didn't want to feel stuffed.

'Caroline was – is – so smitten by Doctor James. She was just longing to tell someone about it all, like a fourteen year old. She was so excited when she found she was to drive him to Glasgow. I think now she's getting high on the secrecy. They've been having a clandestine relationship for all these years, on and off. Her relationship with her husband has gone cold and she resents him being in her life. Also she resents his relationship with Malloch although if it hadn't been for him, she wouldn't have met Doctor James.'

'All of which is interesting but perhaps not material to solving the case,' said Katerina chewing thoughtfully on a spicy bean dish.

'Hm,' said Zara, 'you're probably right but Caroline could be useful as a giver-away of information. Does she know though what Doctor James has done?'

'You think you've connected Doctor James to Malloch but you've said yourself, he's a man with many pots on the boil and his involvement with Doctor James may be nothing to do with Ivory at all.

'Um' said Zara. You are probably right.' She helped herself to a ladle or two of aromatic lamb and another piece of unleavened bread. They both ate in silence.

'Stuck,' I think, is the word I'm looking for,' said Zara.

'Well at least you know that, that you're stuck. You could be walking down a blind alley,' said Katerina.

'I'll have to talk to everyone again – Steading, Caroline, Munchy, Spike, Doctor Andrew. I wonder if I could get to talk to Doctor James.'

'However,' said Katerina, 'one thing you do know is that Doctor James believes himself to have committed a crime. Are you going to tell Des?'

'I suppose,' said Zara.

'Otherwise aren't you withholding information?'

'I suppose,' Zara nodded.

Chapter XVII More information but what to do with it?

When Des took Zara's call he was holed up at the station feeling totally frustrated. He had interviewed for a second time, the woman who had been held under water, and had found contradictions in her story. When he pressed on a point or two, she had admitted to inventing the whole assault. She was angry. She hadn't liked the guy who'd come to ask her to do it. He'd promised to pay her money before and after. She'd not received the "after".

'A bit of politeness never hurt no one,' she kept saying. 'I've got my self-respect the same as everyone else. Dipping yourself in the Kelvin and walking through the streets soaking wet isn't funny. I can't think why I done it.' Des couldn't think either. He was too tired. He gave her two biscuits and another cup of tea, making sure it was hot and had the required amount of milk and sugar.

He'd realized he would have to interview the other two victims again. Was everyone in the city in the pay of Joe Malloch? He gave an audible groan but there was no one in the office to hear him. Knowing the truth about the prostitute meant it had been easy to demolish the story of the gay man. That left Bill Mason in an entirely different light: it made his death seem intentional and if it were intentional, it might have to do with the bone and therefore with the McKelvie Buildings fire.

Des remembered what Zara had said about Steading and he decided he would talk to him again using the attempted shooting as a pretext. If the hoax drowning attempts were connected to Bill Mason, this could put Malloch in the frame. It meant they had most probably been a ruse to take the police's mind off something else. The fire in McKelvie Buildings? The ruse had certainly worked, gained Malloch a bit of time. But for what? Des asked himself.

Then there was the assault on Zara. If Malloch knew she was interested in the fire, he would have no compunction about warning her off. Des squeezed the thumb of his left hand with its four fingers. The gesture felt to him as if it could stop something nasty happening.

Perhaps things with Malloch were going to be resolved. Perhaps soon, but Des knew he had to tread carefully.

He didn't want any more dead bodies. Zara's face inevitably came to his mind but Barney was in the picture too, looking distraught. Des did not want Barney to be wearing that face. It came as a minor shock to him, seeing clearly that there was no way he had a claim on Zara. He felt he knew with certainty how Barney felt about Zara but how Zara felt about Barney was still a mystery to him. He berated himself for getting side-tracked by sentiment: it was at that moment that Zara rang:

'Des, I need to speak to you. It's very important.'

Des asked Zara to come to the station. He felt even tireder now. He hadn't questioned Zara on the phone and hadn't snapped at her but he hoped very much she had not been visiting Malloch again.

Zara told the story plainly and clearly, as near to Caroline's own words as she could remember, interspersed with Zara's own questions at the time.

Des listened, alternately drumming his fingers on the table in front of him and balling his fists tightly. Zara wondered if he did that when he was interviewing suspects.

As she finished, he jumped in.

'So this connects Doctor James with Joe Malloch. It sounds as if he's called in a favour. Unless the doctor is a bad character in his own right.'

'She'd told me previously, when she was pretending it was her sister who was having the affair, that he was in terrible trouble but I had the impression it was about money. He's in debt but that sounds ongoing. Caroline said he gambled.'

'That's one of Malloch's specialities. He's behind several gambling dens and as usual he's not in evidence but knows what's going on and if a likely person gets into financial difficulties…'

'Loses, you mean?'

'Yes, loses, he'll accommodate them and then, down the line, that's when he calls in the favour. Lots of men who were not bad people have been caught this way and ended up pressured into taking part in a crime. Not necessarily a big part but an essential part, something where it's useful if the actor appears to have no connection to Malloch.'

Des's brain was sharply focused; he could sense his mind working, dragging bits of information into a more coherent picture.

'Thanks for the jigsaw piece, Zara. 'Every little helps.' She looked grateful, he thought, but then she said,

'I'll leave you to get on with it then,' in that ironic tone she used when she was pissed off. Des sighed again as she closed the door behind her.

***

Zara was actually feeling a bit guilty about having dropped Caroline in it. She realized that if Des went to question her, Caroline would know it was Zara that had put the police onto her and she would be appalled at what would appear to her a broken confidence. Zara mentally shrugged her shoulders. Caroline may not have known she was literally playing with fire but she was surely old enough to be able to suspect that a relationship with an associate of Malloch's was not likely to turn out positively. But perhaps she really knew nothing about Malloch's dark side. She would be worried too about Charlie discovering the affair.

Zara rang Barney and invited him and Ben round for their tea. She wanted to do something normal, to hear about what Ben's teacher had said that day and what Ben had found. Ben had always found something. And it was always good to see Barney. Zara tended to forget this till it happened and she felt herself relaxing in his presence.

'We're doing a project about underground railways in Glasgow,' said Ben when Zara asked him how school had been. Zara was momentarily taken aback. Her eyebrows went up and she met Barney's gaze. 'More tunnels,' they said silently to each other.

'We're going to see one next week,' said Ben.

'Not one with trains in I hope?' said Zara.

'No, it's really safe. We're just going to look at where the station used to be. The platform's still there but there's railings all round. We've seen a photo. There used to be more stations than now and there's lots of tunnels that aren't used. Some of them you can store trains in but it's too expensive to maintain them all so they just get blocked up so people can't go into them.'

Zara didn't say, 'Like the one in the park' because she didn't want to open up that conversation. Barney looked at her gratefully.

'So where is it you are going exactly?' he asked.

'Hamburgers! Aunty Zara, you've made me hamburgers!' Ben wasn't evading the question: he hadn't heard it being overcome by the arrival of his very favourite dinner. Zara's hamburgers were even better than MacDonald's according to Ben.

***

Des thought about sending two detective constables to track down Doctor James but the wish to see Doctor Andrew's face once again outweighed the feeling of torpor in his body. He decided to take DC Karen Worth, the newest person on the team. He found himself once again knocking at the doctor's door at eight in the morning.

The way the colour completely left Doctor Andrew's face was very promising: Des hadn't as yet uttered a word. He flashed his card. There was a fleeting look of panic and then the expression went blank. Des couldn't tell whether the doctor was concealing a secret of his own or someone else's.

'You have a brother known as Doctor James?'

'Yes.' Doctor Andrew's voice sounded as if he needed to clear his throat.

'I need to talk to him. Can you give me his address?'

'He's in the process of moving at the moment. I can give you his old address but he hasn't given me his new one yet as he couldn't remember it himself and he didn't want to confuse me by giving it wrong.' Des nodded pretending to buy the story.

'Please phone then and ask him.'

'He's changed his number and he hasn't given me…'

'Doesn't want to confuse you. I understand.' Des's mind was working fast. He wished he had a search warrant but he didn't even have a pretext for one and he wasn't going to start blurring the rules when he had someone new to the job with him. Instead he scanned the room for evidence of another person. There was nothing. No extra coffee cup on the table. No different smell.'

Then the doctor's mobile rang.

'Answer it,' said Des. There was an agitated voice at the other end. It was difficult to tell if it were male or female and Des could not make out the words.

'Can I call you back? I have someone with me.' There was a torrent from the other end. 'I know I said I would call but please I will phone you back in five minutes, I promise.'

'Is that your brother?' asked Des. Doctor Andrew was so agitated he waved Des away angrily.

'Your husband will be fine. Just loosen his clothing and try to find his inhaler. I was coming to see you later anyway. Yes, yes, I will phone back.' The doctor's hand was shaking. Des held out his hand for the phone, punched the last caller's number and when the voice answered, Des asked,

'Is that Doctor James?' There followed a long tirade of abuse and Des decided that the caller had indeed been a genuine patient. Des apologized and said he had made a mistake. The torrent went on: he disconnected the call.

'I'm sorry,' said Des handing the phone back.

'That was very unprofessional, Inspector. I am surprised that an officer of your standing would do such a thing.'

'I'm sorry,' Des said again,' but can I ask why you are so agitated when you've done nothing wrong?' Doctor Andrew remained silent. 'Okay,' said Des, 'what's his work number?'

'I don't know.'

'Does he work in a hospital or as a GP?'

'GP', the doctor muttered.

'Name and address of the practice?' Doctor Andrew shrugged.

'Dal-something Road?' Des sighed, thanked him and rose to his feet.

'If your brother should call or visit you, tell him to come down to the station immediately. I have some information for him I think he would be interested to hear. But don't worry, I'll find him without your help.' The two officers left.

'That was a 'how not to' example, Karen, in case you were wondering', said Des as his phone rang. It was Pam, not feeling well again. Karen looked hard at him: she had never seen him so overwhelmed.

***

She couldn't see any reason why but Zara had begun to have nightmares about the assault. She would wake up having thought she'd heard a 'clunk' noise and she would be rigid in the bed, unable to move. When she had endured it nightly for a week she mentioned it to Barney who had remonstrated with her for being snappy. She'd only had about four hours sleep per night for the last seven days, she told him. She was getting to be afraid of sleep it had become so unpleasant.

'What you need is some NLP,' said Barney. Zara looked sceptical: she always did when Barney started using abbreviations. Nevertheless she listened to what he had to say and agreed to ring the number he gave her and, as luck would have it, the lady therapist could see her the following day.

Everything the lady, Alison, said about PTSD – one of the abbreviations Zara was familiar with – and the brain and how she had stayed in 'fight or flight' mode but needed to get the material processed so she could move on, made sense. She came back from the session ecstatic:

'I'll never ridicule your abbreviations again,' she said giving Barney a long version of her usual hug. 'She had me pretend to watch a film of the incident with my eyes shut. I was feeling really relaxed. I had to start the film before the incident when I was feeling okay and then watch the incident and then go to "afterwards". But guess what? I heard his voice.'

'Whose voice?'

'Someone who was there. Not Munchy. One of the assailants.'

'How do you know there was more than one?'

'There must have been more than one, even if only one hit me. The voice I heard wasn't addressing me. It said, 'There – and not too hard'. The person with the voice pushed the umbrella forward so I couldn't see and pinioned my arm against the handle so I couldn't escape.'

'I can see you're pleased you've recovered some of the memory but why are you so excited?'

'It was Screw. I'd recognize that voice anywhere. And it accounts for why he stared at me at Bill's funeral. It was a well-honed plot. I was not mugged, I was set up.'

'It looks as though we have to accept Munchy played a part in this.' Zara nodded her head reluctantly.

***

When Zara phoned Des with the news that she had recovered a memory from the assault he was both glad and sorry. Glad to have some new information to work on but sorry that, inevitably, he felt, it should involve Screw and therefore Malloch. He updated her:

'I didn't find Doctor James yet – not so much as a phone number.'

'I've got his landline number, if it's any use.'

'Thanks for telling me!'

'I have to admit it had momentarily slipped my mind.'

There was a pause while Des wondered and then asked, 'How did you come by that? Not above board I hope?' Zara related how she had listened to the message on Doctor Andrew's phone when she was waiting for him after the bathroom leak.

She gave him the number. 'Never know what might come in handy, do you?'

'Have a nice day,' said Des, an exhortation which Zara rightly took to mean, 'Thank you very much'.

Des now had two lines of enquiry. First he asked DC Karen to find the address attached to the landline. He surmised that Doctor Andrew had been lying when he had said Doctor James was moving. He might well be in hiding but at least there were now premises he could search. And he could also look forward to an interview with Screw. Screw would deny being there of course but Des would be looking to catch the guy in a contradiction.

***

Zara was going out for a meal with Barney. Ben was staying over at his Gran's. It was unusual. Ben had realized that sometimes you could persuade people to do what you wanted if you played the right cards. Ben's friend Milly had suggested it would be good if Barney and Zara had some time to themselves. She said she'd read in one of her mum's magazines that often the man just hadn't thought to ask the woman out and it wasn't every woman who would ask the man. They might be afraid of being turned down. Ben privately didn't put Zara into this category but he could see there might be something in what Milly said so he'd gone so far as to suggest to Barney:

'See dad, when it's your birthday next week, why don't you go out for a meal with Aunty Zara and I'll go to Gran's'. Barney had smiled, quite a complicated smile meaning good idea, nice of you to think of it, mixed with a rueful why didn't I think of it myself?

Barney was attending a seminar at the Marriott hotel and Zara was meeting him when it ended at five. Depending on how hungry they were, they might go and eat and then go to the pictures or, if they were not so hungry, a drink, pictures and then a meal.

Zara arrived early quite unintentionally. She automatically started walking round the block and when that didn't use up the time, she turned in a different direction. Suddenly she found herself opposite the site of McKelvie Buildings. Without a second thought, she walked to the spot where she had been standing when she had been assaulted. She felt if she stood there long enough a message would appear. She didn't believe in coincidences but she did believe sometimes you could benefit from being in a certain place at a certain time.

She looked around. The only person in sight was a man clawing up litter, a black bin bag in his other hand. She waited till he approached then pulled a Glasgow street map out of her bag and appeared to be studying it. She waited again.

'Can I help you?' The standard Glasgow response to anyone with a map.

'This area's changed,' said Zara. 'There used to be...'

'McKelvie Buildings,' the man interrupted. 'I used to work in that wee caff right there.' He pointed to a row of shops opposite where they were standing: all except one was boarded up. 'All the employees from McKelvie Buildings would come across for a bite. It just died. Just died in that one night.'

'Did you see the fire?'

'Naw. My night off.' Zara thought he sounded quite disappointed. They were there though.' He nodded in the direction of the caff. 'Why do you want to know anyway if you don't mind me asking?'

'Journalist,' said Zara. 'Thanks for your help.' She was already across the road.

She walked past the caff but the windows were too steamed up to see what was going on inside. She looked at her watch. She'd need to come back another day.

Then Zara's mobile rang and of course it was Barney wondering where she was. Zara ran. She hoped he hadn't been waiting. She didn't want to have to explain she'd been back to the site and have Barney huffy all evening.

Unfortunately, Barney had been early coming out so he had had time to wonder about what might have held her up and when he saw her approach he put two and two together.

'I thought you'd stopped playing with fire,' he said gruffly. 'The thought of you going back to that place puts me off my dinner.'

'We can't just go home!'

'Home? Whose home?' Zara ignored the remark.

'Ben would be so disappointed.'

'We needn't tell him. How would he know?'

'You can't lie to your own son.'

'How much you consider Ben,' said Barney. 'How much you love him,' is what Zara heard and she replied,

'Well you'll have to be content with a little less than that.' It was no good hiding her face in her bag. She had said what she'd said. Barney knew better than to comment. He just said,

'Italian or Indian? I think my appetite's suddenly come back'.

Chapter XVIII Pass the word along the line

'I've got some information you might want,' said Munchy to Spike. Spike pretended to be uninterested:

'More gossip is it, Munchy? Will your friends thank you for talking about them?'

'What friends? I have no friends now Bill's gone.' Munchy went silent for a bit and Spike could see he was resentful about something. Hasn't been paid what he thought he was due, thought Spike.

Spike was furious with Munchy because of the assault on Zara but he knew he had to go carefully to get the most out of the guy. He knew also that Munchy was most likely dreaming of a nice fish supper which would have been one of the things he would have treated himself to if Joe Malloch had not been such a mean bastard.

Munchy was resentful. Malloch, on the rare occasions they met always said, 'Never forget what I did for your father'. However this fact had not resulted in help and support for Munchy. Munchy didn't understand why and knew he would not get an answer if he asked. It was a love-hate relationship based on a mystery and it was the reason he passed information against Malloch's best interests.

'It's something I overheard,' said Munchy. 'It was the Boss talking to Charlie Steading.' He waited for Spike to bite.

'A fish supper?'

'One tonight and one tomorrow?'

'You're on,' said Spike nodding for Munchy to continue.

'They didn't know I was there,' said Munchy. 'They were in a booth in that pub they go to, to play chess sometimes and I'd been talking to a mate I know at the kitchen door. I was just moving away but then I caught that voice which of course I'd recognize anywhere.

'I put out me cigarette quick as I realized the smoke might drift up and give me away. You go up steps to that pub so I was standing right below them. They couldn't see me even if they was looking out.'

Spike nodded: he knew Munchy was best left to tell what he had to tell at his own pace.

'It was one of them conversations what's coded like only the people what are having it understand. "I've done what you've asked till now," says Steading and the Boss says, "You've been amazingly helpful. I don't know what I'd have done without you."' Munchy added, 'You haven't got to see his face to know he doesn't believe a word he's saying'. He went on: 'Then Steading says as he wants to terminate the arrangement and the Boss says, "Feel free. Never let it be said that I looked for more than was freely given. I'll be sorry of course but we can't have everything we want in life."

'Then there was this long silence,' said Munchy, 'and I began to wonder if they'd gone but then the Boss opens his mean little mouth again. He says "How's Caroline? Lovely woman, Caroline. A real gem. Always looks a million dollars". And Steading's voice goes all stiff and he says, "Caroline is fine, thank you". And the Boss says, "I've not seen much of her lately. She wasn't at my last party". He didn't say it like it was a question but that was how Steading took it. "She had to go and see her sister," he says and the Boss replies, "If she were mine, I'd keep her on a short leash". And he laughed. I didn't hear Steading join in. It sounded like a threat and Steading, he mumbled something I couldn't hear and then he said, "I don't think I feel like chess tonight," like he knew that would hurt the Boss cos he added, "Or any other night for that matter". Then the Boss says, "Charlie, Charlie, sit down. There's no need for all that drama. Don't let's say things we're going to regret". And Steading must've sat down cos then the Boss says as he actually wanted a piece of advice. His voice dropped and I didn't hear the next bit at all but then I heard Steading say, "That's outrageous. No. No. No. Get someone else to do your dirty work". Then the Boss starts, "And if I..." but Steading interrupts, he says, "I don't care anymore. Do what you like to me. I'm not your tool any longer". Munchy sat back. 'That was it.'

'Fish supper now?' Spike wanted to get Munchy's mind off the conversation between Steading and Malloch because he had no intention of discussing it with him. He thought for once that Munchy was reporting honestly what he'd heard. Rancour had brought out the best in him.

They went together to a joint where if Spike used his charm he could get a free supper at the end of the night, food that would otherwise be thrown away.

'I don't know how you do that,' said Munchy savouring each sauce-covered chip and keeping the battered fish till last. 'If I ask, I just get shown the door.' Spike knew it was because Munchy, however hard he tried, managed to sound self-pitying but he said nothing: he was thinking about the quickest way to get hold of Zara.

***

Zara lay in Barney's bed, letting various thoughts trickle through her mind. The dominant one was how pleasant it was to be there. 'I could get used to this' was one and 'I feel safe' was another. 'Is it love?' brought up images of yesterday where she'd given herself away by implying she loved Barney only a little less than Ben. He knew how much she loved Ben.

But then, as always, her mind swung round to thoughts of independence, how much importance she attached to being a free spirit. If Ben were officially her responsibility, would she have to think of him before she plunged herself into dangerous predicaments? On the other hand, did she want to go on for ever having that freedom but no deep lasting relationship? Could it be that she was not cut out for that sort of commitment but more for commitment to tasks with targets and solutions? How would she know unless she tried it? But she couldn't do an experiment on Ben.

Barney stirred and an arm came over her and held her close.

***

The next day Zara went back to investigate the wee caff which was called La Bella Cippa and was run by Giovanni and Maria Mazzoni or so it said above the door. Zara bought a coffee and sat at the counter. There were only two other customers, obviously regulars. They all talked to each other in Italian but when Maria took her order Zara heard a perfect west of Scotland accent. The woman had very large dark eyes which she rolled about to punctuate what she was saying.

Zara looked around for some way to start a conversation and was suddenly aware that the whole of the wall behind her was covered with photographs. Of Italians but in Glasgow.

'My husband, Gio.' The woman's voice. 'So many photos. He clicks all day when he has the chance.' She sounded deprecatory but her eyes rolled happily. 'Many of these were in the big exhibition at McLellan Galleries showing the history of Italian Scots.' Zara nodded and pointed to a portrait which had to be a younger version of Maria:

'That's a very handsome lady.'

'Then, perhaps.' She rolled her eyes again. 'I have too many worries now to look beautiful.'

'Business not so good?' said Zara nodding.

'Since the fire we might as well have shut up shop. We kept going because my daughter has a hairdressing salon in the back and we pick up some trade with that. Added to which,' Maria said, 'the site across the road was leased to a builder and he had mobile huts on it and used it as a yard, sold materials and all, so we had his employees coming in but it wasn't like the old days and then he moved. The yard wasn't secure. He lost a lot of stuff. So, here we are at the end of the world…'

She stopped seeming to register she did not have Zara's full attention and before Zara could ask the question in her mind, Maria answered: 'We don't have pictures of the fire on the wall: too morbid but Gio took a lot. He saw it from the beginning. He has a collection –'

'Maria!' A man, Gio, Zara presumed, appeared at the kitchen doorway and jerked his head. Maria followed him into the back.

Zara turned her attention back to the photos. She was lost for a moment and then aware of raised voices but the language was *italiano furioso* and when Maria returned looking sullen, her eyes had ceased to roll.

'We are closing soon and going to the west coast. Gio's brother has an ice cream business and we are going to help him.' She spoke as if the fire had never been mentioned. Zara didn't know whether this was coincidental or not but she didn't think Maria would be proffering any more information.

She paid and left wishing them luck. She didn't know if she'd learned anything useful or not but on reflection thought she might as well see if she could track down the collection of photos wherever they might be. There might be other photos of the fire besides Gio's. They might yield some clue. It was worth a try.

She was back in her flat now, the night with Barney already receding and she was about to commit some of her thoughts to paper when her mobile beeped. It was a text from Barney. At first she thought he was getting sentimental but then she saw the message: 'Meet Spike. He needs to see you urgently'.

***

Spike was in his usual place by Kelvin Bridge and he wasted no time putting Zara in the picture regarding the overheard conversation between Steading and Malloch.

'So,' said Zara, 'it looks as though Steading has been giving Malloch information over some considerable time but he doesn't want to any more. However getting shut of someone like that isn't like closing a bank account and it looks like Malloch had another job for him but he won't play ball'.

'Chess, said Spike.

'Absolutely,' said Zara and added that the way he had mentioned Caroline sounded like some sort of veiled threat. 'Caroline is having an affair with Doctor James,'

'That is not good news,' said Spike. 'And Steading doesn't know,' he mused, 'but it looks as if Malloch does'.

'The only significance of the affair might be that it shows a link between Malloch and Doctor James,' Zara went on. It doesn't help us with the body in the fire.

'There are too many jigsaw pieces and I wonder if they all belong to the same jigsaw,' said Zara. Spike nodded contemplatively. They sat in silence for a bit and then Zara said,

'So why was the body disposed of in Glasgow? Maybe Malloch was involved and had to help out. He seems to be one of those 'no job too small' type of businesses'.

'Malloch,' said Spike, 'really enjoys mixing things. He would love the idea of setting up an arson attack and then throwing the body in for good measure'.

'The body is found by Bill and buried elsewhere but no leads as to why,' added Zara.

Another silence.

'And then someone tries to shoot Steading but shoots me and someone, the same person perhaps, assaults you,' added Spike.

'I still feel stuck, said Zara. I'll have to find something soon…What connects the doctor to Malloch?'

'Gambling I'd guess. That's mostly how he gets people under his thumb. Big fish, small fish all get swallowed up,' said Spike echoing what Des had said.

'What worries me,' said Zara, 'is the talk of some new ploy, the thing Steading baulked at. Is it relevant? Would it help us to understand the whole picture or does it relate to some other devious tangent Malloch's involved in?' Spike could offer no answers but he laid his hand on Zara's arm:

'Zara, I was giving you that information to warn you. You've been assaulted. Don't you think you should back off. That it would be better –

'Safer Spike, not better.' Zara squeezed his hand and marched off.

***

Half an hour after Des had left Doctor Andrew's flat, Doctor James arrived at the door.

'Did anyone see you come? The police have just left. They are looking for you. They want your address and phone number.' Andrew scanned his brother's face and gripped his arm. James looked equally agitated:

'They've found out about...?'

'No, I don't think so. I think they've found out...'

'About the girl? Please not about the girl.'

'No', said Andrew. 'That is just my fear I realize. I don't know what they want but it sounded serious. You will have to hide or leave the country.'

'I can't leave her!' James went off in a torrent of his first language which indicated to Andrew what a state he was in. They rarely spoke in their mother tongue, even when alone together. It was a convention they had started when they had first come to the UK and needed to practise English as much as possible. James was looking around the room as if he expected a secret passage to open up and contain him.

'You can't stay here. That Inspector Harris was already wishing he had a warrant. He will be back, I know.'

'Where can I go, Andrew?' His brother looked at him with his beseeching eyes which up till now had always resulted in some positive response but now Andrew was shaking his head.

'I cannot work miracles. You will have to look to God.'

'God or Joe Malloch,' said James.

'You would be better giving yourself up,' said Andrew. He looked at his watch. Work called.

'If I leave here now,' James pleaded, 'you may never see me again'. His voice rose and he held on to Andrew's jacket sleeves. His brother lifted them off.

'I'm sorry. I've done the best I can do.'

James stood straight for a moment and then made for the door. Then he ran back and flung his arms around Andrew.

'Thank you. Thank you. You are the best of brothers and the best of men. Do not forget that.' Andrew listened to James's footsteps all the way down the stairs and then heard the close door slam.

***

Zara felt she could do worse than follow up on the Italian photos. She rang Raffaello, an old school mate. When she mentioned Giovanni's photos he said he'd seen them at the Italian Club. He sounded pleased to hear her voice and, since it happened to be his day off, he suggested they should meet there for a drink.

'Leave your bicycle at home, Zara and walk,' he said, giving her directions. They reached the steps of the building at the same time. He kissed her on both cheeks, held both her hands and told her she was just as beautiful as ever. Although he was only half Italian, he always behaved as if he were two-and-a-half-Italian – Zara was remembering an old joke.

Inside he bought drinks and introduced Zara to Roberto the barman as a free-lance journalist interested in the archive material. Even in the bar there was much to look at:

'Maria,' said Zara, nodding at a portrait of a young woman in evening dress whose half-smile seemed like an encouragement to life. Roberto nodded:

'Gio's wife.' He smiled. 'Everyone wanted to marry her. One man made do with her sister. Not that she was in any way inferior! Billy Gardner that was, his mum was a Calvino. It's him that's the winner if Gio isn't, in any competition we have. Not that they're not friendly.' Zara could see that the portrait next to Maria's was of her sister.

Roberto led her into the adjoining room which also had photo-covered walls and lots of filing cabinets. He looked proud:

'Everything is categorized by chronology, exhibition or competition. So you might have a competition on the subject of 'hats' and all those entries will be in one file. You might wonder at it all being hard copy but this photographers' lark has been going go for a hundred years or more and some folk want the archive to be continuous, not suddenly turning into something you can only see on a computer screen. Not that we don't have a digital archive as well. This is the index,' Roberto went on, his hand resting on a huge filing cabinet. 'You can cross-reference if you want. You can start with a person or a subject or...'

A bell rang and Roberto excused himself to serve a customer. Zara turned to the vast index and looked up Giovanni but the references were so numerous she looked up McKelvie Buildings instead. There were several entries referring to photographs by several photographers, including Giovanni Mazzoni and Billy Gardner. Giovanni's were dramatic –silhouettes of the building in various stages of ruin, one where you could see some roof members had just fallen in and sparks had ignited dust, casting a strange pattern over the doomed building. But no people to speak of, thought Zara.

She turned her attention to Billy Gardner's pictures. At once she felt a difference. Was this a journalistic eye? All the pictures appeared to be clearly motivated. Billy Gardner must have been there from near the start. He had captured flames taking hold and then how the inferno developed, showing the firemen at their work and how they gradually got it under control. It had obviously taken several hours: the last pictures were of a shell.

However, apart from that, there were many shots containing people and they looked as if the photographer had wanted to catch whoever was in a particular picture. Zara didn't recognize anyone but it was mostly backs she was seeing. She selected six and photographed them on her mobile.

'You didn't see me do that, Raffa.' Zara realized that they'd not actually mentioned the fire to Roberto so there was no need to tell him. The fewer people who knew what she was investigating, the better. As far as Roberto was concerned she was a friend of Raffa's having a social drink and looking at the photos because they were there.

'Look at this, Zara,' Raffa was gazing at pictures of an Extraordinary Hat competition. Every kind of Easter bonnet, every kind of workman's cap, hats representing the army and the navy but in each case the wearer of the hat was inappropriate. Zara looked closer, her arm through Raffa's. She pointed and laughed. She was glad to be able to sound casual and normal to disguise any serious vibes that might have been coming off her.

Raffa pointed at a witchy hat made of flowers supported by a none too happy rabbit. Here was a horse in a fire-man's helmet and here a little girl in what looked like an upside-down flowerpot. She was standing to attention. 'That's Billy Gardner's daughter,' said Raffa pointing to this last one. 'Ain't she a looker?'

'Wait till she's a teenager at least, Raffa,'said Zara, closing the file with a snap. She glanced at her watch. She had shopping to do and then she had to meet Ben from school.

'I'll need to go but lovely to see you again. Got a girlfriend yet?' This was an old joke as Raffa had used to pretend he had girlfriends, when all he had done was pass the time of day with them.

'Any time, Zara,' he said kissing her again.

'Raffa, Zara said as an afterthought, 'What does Billy Gardner do?'

'He's a builder.' Her friend looked curious but didn't ask her why she wanted to know. She thanked Roberto and left Raffa ordering an early lunch. She squinted at his body profile. He must be eating the wrong sort of lunch, she thought. The place was beginning to fill up: she made for the door.

***

'Mr Gardner?'

He held out his hand. 'Call me Billy. Zara, isn't it? Come away into my hidey-hole where we can get a bit of quiet. I can only talk to you till the rain goes off. Right lads, keep up the conversation – I don't want you listening to my trade secrets.' Billy led the way to a partitioned cubby hole which contained a chair and a stool. He waved at the chair: 'Be my guest.'

Zara sat down. She felt quite relaxed and hoped this initial feeling meant that Billy Gardner had nothing to do with Malloch and that the photo he had taken at the fire had been coincidental – he happened to have been at the scene; he was a photographer: why wouldn't he take pictures of something so dramatic?

Billy asked Zara questions about who she was and what she was doing and seemed quite happy with the idea of the dictaphone.

His answers to her general questions of a fires-he-had-known' nature, were fairly standard at first though he told one story about a house he had reconstructed where he was told by the owner that a fire had been the only way they could build a conservatory extension, because the house was listed and the windows couldn't be changed.

'I didn't know till after we'd done most of the work. Don't get me wrong, they'd got all the permissions, it's just that I wouldn't have involved myself in something dodgy if I'd known beforehand.' But when it came to the question of what might be the most likely reason for arson he became quite enthusiastic.

'I remember Slater Street,' he said. 'I live nearby and I used to drink with some of the guys that worked there. You'll know it was a whisky bond? There were always lots of jokes about how if you set the place alight, how could you be sure of escaping with enough whisky to make it worthwhile. The guys were always trying to think up the perfect plot. But of course when it did burn down it was no laughing matter. There were a few deaths – you couldn't get out of the windows of course. I don't know if anyone ever found out what really happened.'

'Did you actually see Slater Street burn?' asked Zara.

'No I did not.' Zara felt he had had seemed to stop very suddenly as if perhaps he was going to say, 'but I saw…' She was wondering whether to prompt him when he began again.

'McKelvie Buildings. That was the big one of course. Thank god I had my camera. Always do.' A dismissive gesture. 'Not, that I was expecting it! It was entirely coincidence that I was there at all. We'd been working late and I'd given a lift home to one of the lads. We sat talking for ten minutes and then he got out and I sat and re-read this paragraph in the evening paper. We'd been discussing whatever it was, can't remember now and I re-read it to get a figure into my head. Then I remember – it was dark – the colour of the paper changed, went yellow and I looked up expecting to see a torch flickering but it was the building, the McKelvie Buildings and then there was a series of explosions.'

'It sounds as if you were a good eye-witness,' said Zara. Billy batted an eyelid but Zara had to be quick to catch it.

'A good crowd gathered almost at once. Strange how that happens. No Facebook then. Did people phone each other or what? Anyway lots of people saw what I saw.'

'Did the police ask for people to come forward?' Again there was a minute hesitation.

'Yes, well, I suppose. I didn't make a statement. Didn't feel I'd anything to add.' He was looking out of the window. 'It's almost stopped, the rain... Have you about finished? I need to get back to work.'

'Just one thing,' said Zara 'and thank you, you've been very helpful. As I said, I'm hoping to do a series of articles about city crime. I'll send you a copy when it's all done. But in connection with that, would you be willing for some of your photos to be used?'

Zara waited. She hardly dared hope he would say yes. She crossed her fingers mentally.

'I was in the Italian Club today with a friend and we saw some of your pictures but I didn't get time to look at them properly.' A covering lie to avert suspicion.

Billy drummed his fingers on the leg of his stool. Zara added a bit:

'It seemed from the little I saw that between the pictures of Giovanni Mazzoni and your own, he was more interested in the building and you more interested in the people.'

For a moment she thought he was looking at her questioningly, as if he sensed a subtext but then thought the better of it.

'I don't know, Zara,' he answered. 'I've been taking pictures since I was ten. I suppose I'm bound to have developed a way of looking at people.'

'You weren't recognizing anyone at the fire?'

'Like who?' Billy sounded curious rather than suspicious. Zara shook her head.

'No one in mind,' she answered. He still looked unsure.

'Tell you what,' he said, 'You go back and pick the photos you want from the archive and then come back and ask me. Okay?'

Billy's mobile rang and he answered it with an apologetic gesture. Zara knew the interview was finished. She turned her attention to a photo of a little girl pinned up behind Billy's makeshift desk.

'Yes, I got the card. And the present. How would I forget?' Zara heard him say as he closed the call.

'Is this one of yours?' Billy misunderstood:

'She's my only one,' he replied proudly.

'I meant did you take the photo,' said Zara laughing. Billy nodded. 'It's good,' said Zara. 'Really good. When you get tired of building…'

'It's her birthday tomorrow,' said Billy. 'I video them all.'

The sun was out now, so Zara left thanking Billy again as she mounted her bicycle, dictaphone safely strapped into her bike basket.

Chapter XIX   Biting off more than you can chew

Doctor Andrew was at the door. He looked humble and on edge. Zara invited him in.

'I have a favour to ask you, he began without preamble. Zara nodded for him to go on. I have been asked out to dinner and I am expected to bring a guest. I do not know who to ask and I was wondering if you would be so kind as to accompany me. No strings attached,' he added.

'Of course not. You are a married man, I know. May I ask who the host is?' Doctor Andrew looked uncomfortable.

'It is a Mr Joe Malloch, I think. James knows him.' Zara held onto the door for support and tried to keep her face blank. 'I don't know him,' Doctor Andrew was saying. 'but he is very important to my brother. He wants to stay on the right side of him.' The doctor looked at the floor: 'I quarrelled with my brother and my saying 'yes' is a peace-offering.'

'Is it a formal dinner?' asked Zara wondering about her wardrobe.

'No, no more a buffet and people from different walks of life. Musical people and sports people. This man entertains a lot I hear and likes to meet new people. I thought you might like to come as you are an interesting person and I think for your journalism you like to meet...'

'Okay, yes I'll come,' said Zara, taking a leap she felt, into the dark. 'When is it?'

'It's tomorrow I'm afraid,' said Doctor Andrew.

'You don't give me much time. I'll have to take my best dress to the dry cleaners. – Joke,' she added as she saw the doctor begin to look distressed.

'I will book us a taxi. About eight if that is all right with you. I will call for you if you will be ready.' Zara agreed and he went off. She shook her head. Should she disguise herself, she wondered. But Malloch had seen her image on his CCTV. She was being foolhardy, she knew, but she could not resist the opportunity.

She tried to convince herself that she would be safe as the guest of Doctor Andrew and when she failed she put the matter out of her mind: sometimes you had to take a leap into the dark.

**

Later that day, Zara went back to the Italian Club. Roberto looked a little doubtful at first and muttered something about being signed in by a member. Zara feigned surprise that Raffaello hadn't arrived and asked if she could wait in the archive room. A reluctant yes from Roberto.

Zara quickly found the file and skimmed through the McKelvie Buildings pictures again. She snapped everything she found interesting with her mobile and then went to Roberto and apologized.

'I just looked in my diary again: I got the wrong day, didn't I. Sorry Roberto and thanks for putting up with me.'

'You want a drink, ma'am?'

'No, no thanks. I don't want to get you into trouble. I'll be back another day with Raffaello.'

Zara went straight back home and transferred all the pictures onto her computer. Then she scrutinized each image for the sight of Malloch. If he were there, it was not only evidence that he was involved in the fire but also proved there was a possible link between Gardner and Malloch. Zara had not been entirely convinced by Billy's denial that he recognized anyone.

Even so, she was captivated by all the photos and went through them slowly, enjoying the compositions. This for instance: Billy had caught a solitary figure in silhouette, flames from one window behind him. A hunched but solid man with something distinctive about the set of his shoulders and the loping stride.

Suddenly she realized it was familiarity she was experiencing: it was the man on Munchy's monitor: she had found Malloch. She closed her eyes and opened them again but he was still there. She was ninety-nine percent sure. Des would know. She felt excited. Des could look up Billy Gardner. A connection between Gardner and Malloch might be revealed. Perhaps at last they had a decent lead. She picked up her phone and stabbed in Des's number.

However, although Des's response was exactly what Zara had expected and he straight away detailed D.C. Karen Worth to look up Billy Gardner, and though diligent constable as she was, she subsequently placed on Des's desk all details she thought relevant, at the point where Des put out his hand to pull the sheets across to read, the phone rang: Pam's mum.

'Now don't worry but Pam's been taken into hospital. They may want to keep her even though there's still a month to go.' Des's arm slid across his desk as he slumped momentarily over it. He did not notice the papers fall to the floor. Later, D.C.Karen, trying to be helpful, as well as tidy, filed them so they would not get lost. When Des returned from the hospital, he had completely forgotten about them.

***

Joe Malloch was beginning to feel he had to move to a conclusion. If he did not act quickly, his ground plan would be scuppered. He knew Steading was not as wholehearted as he had been formerly. Something had changed there but Malloch had one more card to play to keep him in line.

He thought about having another talk with the man but was afraid it might make him suspicious. At the moment Steading thought he was in a superior position but that could easily be altered. He had to keep him sweet. If Steading decided to tell all, he could drag the whole edifice down with him. All the years of work, and the contacts, the people who at the moment would come running if Malloch flicked a finger. If only it were possible to do everything myself, he thought. But the truth was he had always enjoyed having lots of pieces on the board. He saw life as a game of chess. If my next move does not work he thought, I will have to come to a serious decision about Steading. A shame though. Who will I play chess with if not him?

***

Zara was coming back from the post office when she met Spike. It was surprising how often he happened to appear, as if he were psychic.

'I wanted to see you,' he said. It's about that shooting. You know you said if I thought of anything else I should tell you? Well, it's been going round and round in my head and I think at last I've made sense of it. Not that it gets me anywhere but it might get you somewhere.' Zara waited. 'It's just that business of what I saw when I looked up in the direction of the shot. You know how I didn't see the face? It was dark I know but even so, well, what I thought was, suppose the man was black?' Zara let out a deep breath.

'Spike, you wonderful man. That makes so much sense. Doctor James! Doctor Andrew said he was in deep trouble. And Caroline mentioned he talked about a gun in his sleep. That's what he could have meant. And that leads us to the question, 'Why would Doctor James want to get rid of Steading?' and the answer could be, 'Because he's in love with Steading's wife'.

'Don't be so hasty Zara. I could be wrong. It was just a thought. It could have been a white man with a balaclava over his face.'

'No,' said Zara. 'You saw what you saw and it was a face but you probably just picked out the eyes gleaming in what light there was. A balaclava would give a different effect entirely.'

'Will you be passing it on to Des?'

'Of course. They could do with a lead or two...'

'If you don't, I will, said Spike looking serious.

'I'll behave,' said Zara. I've been behaving really well lately. You'd be surprised.'

'You take care,' said Spike patting her arm and walking off. He looked as though he would like to believe her but couldn't.

***

After some debate with herself, Zara texted Barney to say she was going to a party in Bearsden and not to worry. His reply was, 'Bring me a doggy bag if the food's good.' She felt he probably thought Bearsden was shorthand for Corinne's. If something happened she thought, this would be her backup. The taxi arrived and Zara and Doctor Andrew – Andrew, he kept insisting – sat back, both of them less than relaxed. He kept looking at her as if he couldn't believe it really *was* her. He was too polite to remark on her get-up.

'I imagine you are good on these occasions,' Andrew said, indicating he was not.

'It depends,' said Zara. 'If I'm unhappy, I might be rude. But I'll try to stay happy,' she reassured him. Zara was running on adrenalin. One moment she wondered why she was there, the next she felt excited about what she might find out.

They arrived. A very spruce Malloch was welcoming in the couple ahead of them. Zara had thought of asking Doctor Andrew to introduce her as 'Maureen' she didn't want to be connected with her journalistic self, wanted to be incognito but then she had changed her mind and decided she stay as Zara. She recognized Doctor James at once because he was almost identical to his brother and then Caroline, standing a little apart with Charlie Steading. James came towards his brother with a big smile.

'Thank you for coming,' he said. 'Let me introduce you to Joe.'

'This is Zara,' said Andrew, 'my very kind neighbour. Zara shook hands.

Then Malloch stood before her and she almost took a step back. The man was overpowering. That and the fact that he had suddenly become 'Joe' took her by surprise. His handshake was firm and measured as if he might be gleaning information but it was not lingering. He looked her in the eye and if he recognized her he made no show of it.

'Welcome to my house,' he said.

'Thank you for the invitation,' said Zara matching his formality.

'Are you a doctor as well?' he asked.

'No,' said Zara 'but I'm fond of diagnosis: I'm in the communications business.'

'Ah, you work for one of the Glasgow papers?' Not just a pretty face, thought Zara.

'Freelance', said Zara. Evening Times. Herald.

'Maybe we'll have the chance of a conversation later. Discovering the truth, an interesting line of country. Do you play chess?'

'I'm afraid not.'

'I'm always on the lookout for intelligent players. It's a passion of mine. Almost, you might say, a vice.'

'Is your wife a chess widow then?' asked Zara without reflection.

'I do not have the comfort of a wife,' he said and making a polite gesture Malloch withdrew to spread his bonhomie elsewhere.

Zara looked around for the doctors and came upon them in an alcove. They had their backs to her and they were arguing.

'You lied to me. What will Zara think? That I brought her here under false pretences. We would never have come if I'd thought...'

'Joe wanted to meet you.' There was a palpably angry silence.

Andrew was obviously thinking things through: 'It was you suggested Zara, that I might bring her. What's that about? I will never forgive you, if you are dragging her into something evil. You are not a good person any more, James. I am ashamed of you. I never thought the police would ever be looking for my brother.'

Zara turned away and sought neutral territory but the two brothers were so deep in their argument that they had not noticed her. Her heart was beating very fast: she had been imagining this was a coincidence and at best might be an opportunity to learn something new from the lion's den, but now she realized it was she who was being observed, and what more? She did not like to imagine. She wondered if she could trust Andrew: even if he were on her side, he might not be much help in a dangerous situation. Perhaps she should leave now before anything happened?

She saw Caroline coming towards her. Did Andrew know who Caroline was, she wondered. Did Steading know about James and Caroline? Zara wished she didn't. She hated dissimulating. But Caroline was looking at her like a long lost friend. Zara pulled herself together. She had better make the best of it. Perhaps Caroline could help her leave.

'I'm so pleased you came! It was Charlie's idea believe it or not.' Charlie's idea? Given him by Malloch? Zara felt she'd just missed her footing.

They stood in a circle, James, Andrew, Caroline and Zara and Zara noted that Caroline directed her attention towards Andrew. She wondered if it were to allay possible suspicion regarding herself and James.

Charlie Steading was standing alone with a plate of food. The buffet had just started. It was a sumptuous spread with courses being brought in in turn. Zara recognized the uniforms of the waiting staff as belonging to one of the most reputable outside caterers in town.

There were not more than twenty people in the room. She saw an up-and-coming stand-up comedian and hoped he wasn't going to perform and a couple of well-known footballers and their wives. Had these people committed crimes, like fraud or were they in debt to Malloch? Did he want something from them or did they need something from him?

Zara helped herself to the salmon pâté which lay on a bed of something she couldn't quite name and someone refilled her glass with white wine. She talked to a woman who said she was an accountant with a firm in partnership with her husband but Zara didn't believe her.

'How do you know Joe?' asked Zara.

'It's my husband knows him, not me.' She laughed. 'I hope he's not expecting an invite back. Our house isn't posh like this one.'

'Nor mine,' said Zara.

'He won't tell me how he met him either,' said the woman whose name was Jessamine, 'except it wasn't on the golf course and it has nothing to do with football or I wouldn't have come'.

'Chess?' said Zara. 'I believe Joe is very keen on chess.'

'Even I can beat my husband at chess and I'm no chess-player. My father was, so I do know what I'm talking about.'

Jessamine went to the bathroom and Zara sidled over to one of the two footballers' wives and plunged in: 'Pleased to meet you. I'm Zara'.

'Kelly,' said the blonde with over-made-up eyes and very high heels.

'It's lovely to meet so many of Joe's friends,' said Zara.

'I don't know him from Adam,' said Kelly. 'It's my hubby knows him. Suppose he's a fan or something. Most people Jimmy knows are football. I'm so glad I've got two girls. Don't get me wrong, if Jimmy didn't eat, breathe and sleep it, I'd have probably encouraged my two to kick a ball about but it's a hundred per cent dancing and swimming till they are old enough not to choose football.'

Kelly's companion, Fiona, didn't know Joe either.

'Who is Joe?' she asked.

'The one that's giving the party,' said Kelly. 'Joe Malloch.'

'Oh the one they call the Boss,' said Fiona. 'I've heard Tommy talk about him but I've never met him. Nice place he's got though.'

Zara helped herself to some spiced chicken which had just arrived. It was surrounded with a garnish of thickly sliced lettuce and avocado. She began to wish Malloch was a good person so she could visit him more often.

She took herself into a corner and acted the part of someone focused on food but her mind was busy. Three women, four if she counted herself, who had never met Malloch before. That figured: it was the men who were involved with him. This was not a meeting of friends but a collection of associates, claimants and debtors. An elaborate stage in a game of stick and carrot. Zara remembered that more than one person had mentioned Malloch's liking for complication, for entwining and binding.

She felt more than ever that she had been invited there for a reason and she wished suddenly she had been more explicit about where she had been going. But Barney would have tried to persuade her not to go. If she texted someone now, Malloch might find it suspicious. Would he have CCTV in the bathroom? Zara put down her fork and secreted her plate on a side table. What would happen she wondered, if she just left. People would think her odd. That wouldn't matter but Malloch, what would he do? Had he got her here to find out about her or…?

Caroline was in front of her again:

'Joe wants you to come and talk to him in the library. He's got something to show you. He was showing it to one of the other guests and he thought you might be interested.' Caroline was smiling. There was no tension or anxiety coming from her. Zara allowed herself to be guided from the room, down the spacious hall to a door that stood open. Inside she could hear the murmur of voices; the lights were soft.

She stepped into a room lined with shelves. It was not large but it was a book-lover's dream and Zara paused and gave a little cry of pleasure. She saw Malloch turn and smile.

'You like my library, Zara? It is a facsimile of a room my grandfather had, and I have his collections, mostly maps and books about exploration.' He was standing beside a table. He beckoned her over. 'I thought you might be interested in this.' Zara looked down on an unusual map. 'It's underground,' said Malloch. 'It's a map of all the tunnels under Glasgow.'

'How very…' Zara started to say but at that moment her phone rang. She was prepared: if it were Barney or Des, she would answer in code. What had started as a game when she and Barney had worked together, and sometimes wanted to communicate when there were sensitive persons in the vicinity, had been passed on to Des but lightheartedly and only once. If it was Barney there would be a better chance of his understanding. If it was Des and he didn't understand he would ring Barney.

It was her mother. Zara nearly threw the phone across the room but collected herself and held the phone out as if resigned to being interrupted.

'Mum,' she said. She saw Malloch read the word 'Mum' across the display and breathed out in relief. Now she had to act, and depend on her mum's bewilderment and curiosity to propel her into phoning Barney. 'Mum, hi. What? Oh, number thirteen. Yes I know it's unlucky but that's the number. She's not at the old place any more. She moved. Yes, I'm sure she'd love to hear from you. Look, I'm with friends. I'll phone you tomorrow. Okay? Take care. Bye.' She replaced her mobile in her bag without looking at Malloch and then turned back to give him her undivided attention. 'Sorry about that. Mums always ring at the wrong time, don't they?'

Malloch looked back at her calmly. His eyes said that that may or may not have been a genuine call but don't try any funny business while you're in my house. It was now nine-thirty-five. The earliest she could expect a response was in twenty minutes. The code was simple but it depended on her mum relaying what Zara had said accurately. There were only two important words and they were 'thirteen' and 'place'. 'Thirteen' referred to the thirteenth letter of the alphabet, 'm', and 'place' was to indicate Zara was at the place of someone whose name began with 'm'. She was relying on the hope that her mother would be so baffled by the apparent nonsense Zara had spoken that she would phone Barney up at once.

'Recognize anything?' asked Malloch pleasantly. 'Obviously there are all the subway train tunnels, the ones in use but also many disused ones. For instance,' he stabbed his finger in the one Ben had approached, 'most people know this one but some of the others are more obscure. And then there are the mines. They are all on here too. Disused, all of them now, of course.' He smiled again and looked at Zara who tried to smile back. Misused more like, she thought.

'A honeycomb,' he was saying. 'I've often thought how exciting it would be to join them all up. An underworld. You'd have an underworld. Of course every so often, there's subsidence and a disused tunnel becomes a blocked tunnel. I find that sad.'

Zara couldn't help hearing Malloch's words as threatening. She had images of him throwing people down mineshafts and forgetting about them.

'Fascinating,' she said. 'I suppose you've explored them all, all these tunnels. Bit like collecting Munros is it? And what about the sewers? Are the sewers here too? How are they all safe when they must be at different levels?' She was beginning to talk too fast and make her fear obvious. In twenty minutes she wanted to be outside in case Des managed to come. Barney would phone Des. Des knew where Malloch lived. Or Barney might come in a taxi perhaps. She forced herself to listen to Malloch. The other man who'd been in the room when she had entered it had gone now. She made herself focus. Then Malloch completely changed tack:

'I didn't ask you in here just to talk about tunnels,' he was saying. 'You seem a very intelligent young lady and I was wondering if you would be interested in an offer I could make you.' Zara was wondering if she had been translated onto another planet. 'A permanent but very part-time job at a full-time wage. You'd be able to do most of it on computer but it would entail being based in Spain.'

'And what would that job be?' Zara heard her own voice as if from a great distance.

'Finding suitable accommodation for business associates of mine. Short term, long term, sometimes in a city, sometimes in the country. It wouldn't be onerous and you would have plenty of time to devote to your journalistic endeavours.'

'I don't speak Spanish,' said Zara.

'That's no problem. You could learn all you needed in a month. And these days where business is international, languages count less, don't you think?'

'Will you be advertising this job in the Herald? With the salary and everything?'

'No, no. I like to do things my own way. How would twenty K grab you with a flat thrown in?

He means it, thought Zara wildly. I'm being commercially propositioned by a gangster.

'I like living in Scotland,' she said lamely. 'All my friends are here.'

'They would love to come and visit you in Spain, I'm sure.'

'But what do you want from me?' said Zara suddenly. 'I may be cynical but I was brought up to believe there's no such thing as a free lunch.'

Someone was filling Zara's glass. Malloch continued to smile.

'Obviously a person cannot be in two places at once, although I can be pretty near to it at times.' Zara suppressed a smile. 'If you were in Spain your interests and commitments would inevitably change but ambitious people learn to let things go and move into the new.'

He's telling me to lay off, thought Zara and he's bribing me. Whatever he's up to now, it's so important I can't be left to mess it up. She couldn't even bring herself to say she'd consider it. All she could think about was getting out. She put her hand to her head. 'I think I need some air,' she said.

'I'll get Doctor James to take you a turn round the garden,' said Malloch evenly. 'But think about my offer, won't you?' He hadn't once shown his claws, she reflected.

Zara did not demur. She did not think she would have that much trouble getting away from Doctor James but she did hope desperately that Barney would have received the message and then act upon it. If no help was there she would just have to run. She had had a rehearsal, she thought grimly. And it was dark. No problem, she told herself.

Doctor James was doing his best to be charming. He said how lucky his brother was to have Zara as a neighbour. He asked her if she belonged to Glasgow and told her what a delightful city it was.

'Always so much going on,' he said, giving a big smile like his brother's. She glanced at the injury on his cheek, now healing nicely and nodded. She didn't want to alert him to her distress by saying anything in the slightest bit negative.

They were walking round and round a gravel path which encircled a lawn with roses on its perimeter and a magnificent central bed of perennials just coming into bloom. Zara saw them but did not register them: she was listening hard for the sound of a car or a taxi. She wondered what Doctor James had been told and what he would do if she attempted to leave. She remembered that he was in the frame for shooting Steading and wounding Spike. Would he be armed tonight? The person who had shot Spike was no novice. She would have to be very quick if she were to come off best.

No car yet. Maybe it was unreasonable to hope and yet she knew exactly how her mum, Barney and Des would respond, if they understood the message. One more circuit and then she would make a move. She noticed the curtains flick in the room overlooking the garden. Someone was watching, not just on CCTV.

Nearing the gate, Zara gathered all her strength. She had just teased Doctor James gently and he was laughing. She did not like it but half measures would not do here. Turning she leapt towards him, kneeing him in the crotch – she had to leap because of their difference in height. Zara recovered her balance instantly and hit the gate as Doctor James howled and lunged at her and in missing, lost his balance. She did not waste time opening the gate but vaulted clean over it. A shot rang out. Doctor James fails again, she thought from twenty yards down the road.

Zara looked right and left. No one was out there. She ran towards the main road. Last time she had dodged into gardens but this time she was banking on Barney. At the first corner she glanced behind her and simultaneously heard a car start up. On impulse she darted into a stand of trees. She stood still hoping the vehicle would go past: they were after her.

She realized her mobile was telling her there was a text. Barney: just the words 'Bearsden but where?' She texted back: 'Tulip Avenue'.

189

She had to keep where she could see Barney arrive but how could she do that with someone from the house tailing her? The car she'd heard had passed her but having reached the corner, it had not moved on. Whoever it was had deduced she must be hiding. What would they do if a taxi turned in? Could she make a run for it?

Now the car was reversing and she could see it had two occupants but she could not see who they were. Were they going to hunt the copse she was in? She had to act. There was no other cover. She threw her shoes into a bush and shinned up the nearest tree. At about twelve feet she was surrounded by dense foliage. She could not see down but she could hear. A car door opened.

'She could be in those trees,' said a voice. Did these men have guns too?

'Better go and see,' said the other. Feet on pavement, feet on grass coming nearer. Zara stopped breathing. The footsteps hesitated below her. Were her shoes visible? She prayed not.

'She's not here,' called the first voice.

'Better look in the gardens then.'

'She could be anywhere by now.'

'She came in a taxi and she didn't leave by car and she didn't go down or up the road.' The second voice sounded very bored. 'She's hiding. We'll just wait her out.'

'Some fucking party,' said the other voice. 'What's his game anyway?' The voice at her feet went on mumbling, half to the man in the car and half to himself.

Zara wanted to mobile Barney again but it was so quiet in the trees that she was afraid the man below would hear her if she moved at all. She was amazed he could not hear her heart knocking on her ribs. The noise of the gun had gone right through her and she was shivering uncontrollably but adrenalin kept her alert, waiting for an opportunity. She heard the flick of a cigarette lighter and made out, as she took courage to part the leaves a red glow beside the car and now the man under the tree was going over, attracted by the idea of having a fag.

She waited till they were in conversation and then she texted Barney: 'Up tree at road end. Watch for car with two men.'

The two men were enjoying their smoke but Zara thought they were still watching. She held on, every minute expecting reinforcements to emerge from Malloch's house. She had an image of herself being gunned down by Doctor James. She would fall out of the tree in a heap. Where was Doctor James? Why hadn't he chased after her? Maybe there were other people out there in the night creeping up on her. She knew how frightened she was when she suddenly found herself imagining her dad. It was as if she could hear his voice saying, 'Zara?'

After what seemed an age, a taxi turned into the road and pulled up at the first house. There was a pause and then the horn sounded softly. No one got out. Was this her taxi? She twisted her neck to get a better view. Now someone had got out of the taxi which was parked under a street light with the engine running; he was walking towards the first house. The guy – it was definitely a guy – was Barney's height. Why was he approaching a house? Was it a ruse to deflect attention?

The men in the car were looking at the taxi, but was it idly, or were they suspicious? Zara strained her eyes towards the figure at the door. It was Barney. It was just her fear that had made her doubt it. He was expecting her to see him from where ever she was and make a dive for the taxi.

Coming down from the tree was much worse than going up, like dropping into a den of wild animals. Zara made the ground with one scraped shin and a banged elbow and crouched where she landed listening for signs of detection. She did not dare to look for her shoes.

There was a clear path between Zara and the taxi and the two guys in the car were facing the house Barney had gone to. Seventy-five yards, Zara estimated. One short spurt. She would have to negotiate the door of the taxi but that was all. She moved silently, running, sharp stones punishing her bare feet. Thirty to go, twenty, ten. She was almost there. She was on the driver side, whereas Barney had got out on the other side, leaving his door open.

Zara dived towards the taxi. Now her hand was on the door-handle clicking it open. The noise disturbed the quiet. She knew without looking that Malloch's men had turned.

Now she was in the taxi – but so were they, having entered on Barney's side. One lurched towards her, making a grab at her body. Zara fought back, hitting whatever limbs she could see with her bag. Then suddenly her aggressor fell forward, his feet taken from under him and before her eyes he shot backwards. Zara heard his skull hit the road. The other man, having taken his place, was pulling Zara towards the door not fully aware of the raging Barney behind him.

Now Barney was kicking at the backs of his knees and then trying to pull him backwards with an arm round his neck. Zara dug her nails into the man's arm with her free hand. She realized with a shock she was scoring into a tattoo of a snake which now had blood coming from its twisting body. She gave a shriek. The man let go of Zara and staggered back. With one huge twist of his body Barney threw him out of the door and fell into the taxi himself, slamming the door behind him.

'Back to the West End please,' he said to the taxi driver. Then he texted Des to say, 'All well, no backup needed.'

'If that had gone to another round, I would have had to blow the whistle,' said the driver, carefully manoeuvring round the man on the ground. 'I take it you're not calling an ambulance.' Barney was still getting his breath. 'You two all right back there. I hope there's no blood. It's a bastard getting it out of the seats.'

Barney hugged Zara to him but neither of them spoke. At Barney's door the taxi-meter registered sixteen pounds. Barney gave the driver twenty.

'Thank you. That was beyond the call of duty.'

'I won't say, "Any time,"' said the driver, nodding his thanks as he drove off into the night.

Chapter XX It's hard to find things out

Steading had been engaged in a drawn-out conversation with the accountant and wanted to sit down but had some discomfort in his stomach. Shellfish, he thought, or was he dying? Whichever it was made bending his body painful. Tomorrow he would get the results of his tests. The thought made him feel sicker. He could hardly keep his attention on the accountant's words and he wondered what time it was and whether he and Caroline could decently leave soon.

He looked round. Where was Caroline? In the bathroom he supposed or maybe Malloch's library. The party had spilled out a bit into other rooms. He had vaguely registered some dancing going on in the glasshouse at the back. There had been an influx of guests who seemed to have been invited for later. A sort of gaiety top-up, Steading thought, except that they were making him feel moody and disquieted. He no longer knew who everyone was. Usually good at names, he had had all the first guests under his belt but he had not kept the name of one person in the second batch.

Zara's disappearance, scuffle and the shot had sent a peculiar ripple through the gathering. No neighbours appeared, perhaps because they were used to ignoring strange goings on at Joe Malloch's. Some of the guests had gone out thinking Doctor James needed help and indeed he had fallen and banged his knee. One of Malloch's minions had taken him off for some first aid. Doctor Andrew was now bereft of both Zara and his brother and found himself being chatted up by the two footballers' wives who were delighted to find he had no interest in the game.

Steading suddenly put down his glass and walked away from the chess bore he had been pretending to listen to. He had to find Caroline and go home. But Caroline was not in the library or in any of the bathrooms. In desperation he cornered Malloch.

'Where's Caroline?' he asked abruptly.

'Your lovely wife? I don't know. She's not run off like the other guest has she?'

At that moment Doctor Andrew extricated himself from the conversation he was having with the footballers' wives and came to join Steading. He addressed Malloch:

'Where is my brother?' Malloch answered him affably:

'He was in the garden and then he was getting a plaster on his knee. Accident prone. Has he always been like that, Doctor Andrew?'

Steading, knowing Malloch, felt his stomach turn. Whenever the man spoke, Steading could always hear a very nasty subtext.

Before all concerned could form speculations about whether James and Caroline were absent together, Doctor James appeared, limping slightly. When he saw Steading he changed direction and then thinking the better of it, swerved back towards the group.

'Last time I ask you to look after a lady,' said Malloch. Steading looked for steel in Malloch's eyes but there was none. He has a bigger plot on hand, he thought. Zara's going is not important to him. If he wants to deal with her, he knows where to look for her.

Steading's stomach lurched uncomfortably.

'I think I might leave soon,' he said trying to sound apologetic, 'but I would like to find Caroline'.

'Obviously a man can't leave without his wife,' said Malloch smiling. 'Now where can she be? We won't send Doctor James. He might find her but he would probably lose her again or perhaps shoot her. Steading, you'd better look for her yourself. All the rooms are open in my stately home. Feel free.' He clapped Charlie Steading on the shoulder. Steading had to resist a strong desire to shake Malloch off: there was something especially creepy about him tonight.

**

'Ben?' Zara exclaimed as she and Barney entered Barney's flat. 'How…?'

'Luckily for you, my friend Matt was round and he gamely stepped into the breach.' Zara was more upset about the fact that she had not thought of Barney not necessarily being free to help her than she was by the incident itself. Matt left saying everything had been fine; Ben hadn't stirred.

'Cocoa, shower, bed,' said Barney looking at Zara's exhausted face. He made cocoa. Zara refused toast but Barney ate four rounds, two with bacon. He said that rescuing people was strenuous when you weren't used to it. Zara said she was too tired to shower but... She yawned twice in succession. They sat in that silence that follows commotion, enjoying the safety of Barney's familiar room.

'Zara, I have to say this. Never again please. Much as I love you, I can't live a life that stressful, that dangerous, for god's sake. I have to think of Ben.'

I'm sorry,' said Zara, 'but I couldn't think what else to do'.

'Well,' said Barney, 'you didn't need to go to Malloch's party in the first place but let's have the whole story leaving nothing out'. Zara gave him a blow by blow account and Barney listened, interjecting an occasional question.

'Malloch wanted you to go? He asked Charlie Steading to arrange it? A likely story.'

'It looks like it,' said Zara. 'I think Andrew was alarmed by the whole affair. I think all he is guilty of, is wanting to protect his brother.'

'And what do you think Malloch was aiming at? Was it just making you that extraordinary offer or was the intention to hold you?' Zara shuddered.

'I don't know. I hope not, the holding I mean. He's such a strange person. He doesn't look evil though his eyes have no warmth in them and he's perfectly pleasant when he talks to you but there's a peculiar energy that comes off him which makes me feel uncomfortable all the time.'

'Nothing to do with the fact that you know that he kills people I suppose? Others would call that feeling 'fear'.' Zara wrinkled her nose:

'Yes, I see what you mean.' She thought for a moment. 'Let's put it this way. I felt an evil intent but I felt it had not yet reached an operational level. If it were 'Hansel and Gretel', it would be where the witch feels the children to see if they are fat enough to eat... but it's not time yet.'

'So when will it be time?' asked Barney looking anxious.

'I don't know,' said Zara. 'I don't know what he wants regarding me. I didn't realize till tonight that I was important in any way. He must think I can upset his plan somehow but since I don't know what the plan is...'

'He won't know you know he's implicated in the McKelvie Buildings fire?'

'Probably not. It's all been intelligent speculation on my part.' Zara drained the last of her cocoa. 'There is a tie-up between the bone and the fire but my hunch is that it's tangential. Doctor James knows the police are after him but he doesn't know why. Remember I told you Spike thought the guy who shot at him might have been black and that was why he couldn't make out his face? Well if that person was Doctor James... But then he will also be worried as to whether the police connect him with Ivory.'

'And you think he is definitely connected?'

'Yes but I don't know how.'

'It seems you've uncovered one plot only to find another, said Barney'.

'But there's a 'something else' that's pressing now. The best I can come up with is that what I know can spoil Malloch's plan whatever that plan is. He may think I've got evidence that would link him to the fire but why is that so important just now? There's something he wants to do now and he's having a job finding pawns to do his dirty work. Remember what Spike told me, what Munchy overheard: Steading wouldn't do it whatever it was. But think what Steading must owe Malloch if he can even ask?' Is it money? Or is it that he could drop Steading in it? But then Steading could drop Malloch in it too.'

'Either way, neither of them would have a chess partner,' said Barney.

***

The following morning Zara left Barney's early so she was home when Des arrived at her door at nine, apologetic. He had received Barney's text when he was in the middle of an attempt murder call out. Then he had had Barney's all clear but was still too busy to reply. Zara had not showered yet. Des was frustrated that she had not let him know where Doctor James was the previous night so he could have nabbed him at Malloch's.

'Okay, I knew he was going to be there but… Sorry. You're right. Too right.'

'If you had been thinking properly, you wouldn't have gone. Someone who has recently been assaulted doesn't go off to a party where the host is probably the man that ordered that assault especially in the company of someone whose brother, on pretty good evidence, we know to be a criminal.'

'I just didn't think!'

'You could have rung me when you got there.'

'Malloch would have known I'd made the call. I might not have got out alive.'

'You would have left with me,' said Des. Zara nodded. Des had a point but it was easier to see it with hindsight. Looking back at the previous evening she could see that she had embroiled herself in a situation which had been dangerous from the start.

Des made her tell the whole story in detail pricking up his ears when she came to anything about Doctor James but he managed not to criticize Zara further. She could see he was genuinely worried that she had been inveigled into Malloch's den. He wanted descriptions of all the people there but although he thought he recognized some of them, he could see nothing there that helped the case except he thought it might be worth trying to find the bullet or the bullet casing, he thought it might tie up with someone or something previous.

But when she recounted the struggle in the taxi and spoke about scratching the guy with the tattoo, he brightened up.

'We'll need to test what's under your fingernails for DNA,' he said. 'That tattoo, could you draw it? I think I know it.'

Des agreed that there was something else afoot. He had been convinced when he'd magnified the picture Zara had sent him: the figure departing from the fire was definitely Malloch.

'This brings another player into the game,' said Des: 'a guy who takes a photo of Malloch at a fire. What's that all about? Have you found out anything about him?'

'I thought you would have. After I sent you the photo.' Des hit his head with his hand:

'Oh my god. I'm going senile. I asked Karen to do a check and... I remember now it was the day Pam was taken into the hospital. It completely slipped my mind. I suppose Karen must have filed the info.' He was so genuinely distressed that Zara didn't even tease him, just asked after Pam. When she felt they could get back to the subject in hand she said,

'I liked Billy Gardner when I met him. He seemed straight forward but he could have been pretending to be completely open.'

'You think he has something to do with the fire?' asked Des.

'No I don't but I think he has some connection to Malloch.'

The phone rang and Zara answered. It was Billy Gardner. Zara wrote the name on the pad at her elbow and passed it to Des. He sat nearer to hear the man's voice. There was no preamble.

'Zara, I've decided I don't want you to use my photographs. Is that clear? Just don't bother going back to the Italian Club, right?'

'Of course. I'm sorry. Whatever you want. May I ask why you changed your mind?' There was silence at the other end of the phone and then Billy Gardner hung up.

Des rose.

'So what do you make of that?' he said. Zara hesitated. She was intrigued by this new move of Gardner's but there was something else on her mind she wanted cleared first:

'You never told me about Screw. Did you manage to question him yet?' Des was at the door.

'Not very successful, I'm afraid. Denied everything. Said that lots of people have a voice like his.'

'But not so disgustingly whiney,' said Zara.

'His alibi may trip him up,' said Des. 'I'll phone you when I get back to the station. See what I can make of the Billy Gardner file. And we'll arrange for you to do the forensics. Don't clean your fingernails and bring in the clothing you were wearing.' He stopped at the door. 'I'll really need to think about the Billy Gardner connection.'

***

Steading stumbled out of the hospital, so agitated he tried to unlock a car of the same make and colour as his own. The nurse, whom he had seen after the consultant had made her pronouncement on the tests, wondered why there was no one with him, though she reflected that people were generally happier at being given an all clear.

'I thought your wife…' That made things worse: he could hardly say to the nurse, who was male, 'My wife didn't come home last night. I don't know where she is'.

He felt dizzy. An all clear but his wife had gone, and on top of that there were the secrets which were held between him and Malloch which he felt he could no longer hold. He could not believe what the man had asked him to do. To him it was a sign that Malloch was facing a dilemma too; it felt as if the odds had changed. There had always been a balance between what each of them knew about the other but now Malloch was trying to involve him in something new, something dear to his heart, Steading thought, which was odd because he'd never thought of him having a heart.

***

Zara sat and looked at her nails. It was amazing that she had not showered. She'd stayed the night at Barney's in his bed but she had hardly been aware of being in it. She'd meant to have a shower, just to rid herself of the feeling of strange hands marking her body but she had fallen asleep mid-sentence on Barney's sofa and he had carried her through to his bed.

'You could have just left me on the sofa,' she had said to him in the morning.

'I was afraid you'd wake up and wonder where you were… and feel alone.' She turned and kissed him on the back of the neck. Suddenly though, she wanted to be in her own flat. She'd had coffee and toast and gone home.

Sitting thinking, she was curious about one thing: when she had dug her nails into the guy and seen the snake, why had she shrieked? The situation had been frightening but her reaction didn't quite add up. It had been the sort of knee-jerk response you have when you are suddenly presented with something fearful; but her situation had been on-going. She sat and thought but she could not get anywhere.

Her mobile rang and, expecting Des she just said hallo.

'Is that Zara MacDonald?' said the voice at the other end.

'Who wants to know?' If her life were going to behave like a B-film she might as well act the part.

'It's Charles Steading.' Pause. 'I don't suppose you would know where my wife is?'

'Charlie, I'm sorry, I've no idea,' Zara picked up at once on the man's genuine distress. 'Would Mall… I mean Joe, not know? She must have gone somewhere after the party.'

'I don't know if he knows but I think if he did he wouldn't tell me.' Zara breathed in and out trying to stay calm.

'Can you think of anyone she'd be with, anyone she might have gone to? She wouldn't be at her sister's?' Zara tried every avenue she could think of but Steading had phoned round all likely contacts. A suitcase had gone. He didn't know what clothes she'd taken. He thought she must have gone home after the party before taking off. But then again he wondered, had she packed beforehand. Her car was still on the drive. Had she gone in someone else's car?

'But', he said, 'she took her favourite toothbrush'.

'I'm sorry,' said Zara wondering why she was. Previously she had felt Steading to be an unsavoury character. Now he just seemed sad.

'Do you know anything about that Doctor James?'

'Not really,' said Zara cautiously.

'I think my wife's run off with him.' Zara stayed silent. James had tried to shoot Steading, she was thinking. James, she thought, had tried to shoot her.

'Did you know Doctor James?' she asked innocently. There was a pause and then he said,

'In a manner of speaking. We sometimes went to the same church.' Zara almost gasped in surprise: there was no way she would have guessed that.

'Really?' she managed, hoping he would go on; he was in such a nervous frame of mind, not his usual self at all.

'It all started,' Steading resumed, 'with charitable giving – to the African community, after one of those natural disasters, famine, war, one or the other or both. They wanted to thank me and after that... I just go occasionally,' he finished lamely. Zara felt Steading was having difficulty concentrating. He's probably wondering why on earth he's telling me this, she thought.

A sudden memory of an African choir came into Zara's mind. Where had she been? It was near the river. She stabbed in the dark.

'Would that be the church down by the Kelvin?'

'That's right.' He was beginning to sound distracted.

'Have you thought of going and seeing if they've seen him?'

Steading hadn't and sounded reluctant. It's probably because that route implies Caroline is with Doctor James and he won't want to accept that, thought Zara.

'Have you spoken to Doctor Andrew?' asked Zara. A mumble. 'I'll tell you what, I'll go and ask him. He lives in the flat above me.' It was Steading's turn to be surprised.

***

As soon as Steading hung up, Zara ran upstairs to the Doctor's flat. She had no idea if he would be there. It was already eleven, but she had not heard him go out.

The door opened savagely at her ring as if the man had been standing behind it.

'James!' he cried and then his face fell as his eyes came down to Zara's level.

'You don't know where he is then?' Zara asked stepping inside without waiting to be asked.

'He won't answer his mobile. He's not at his flat. His car is not parked in his street. He has not turned up for work. I had the practice on the phone. He was due in at eight-thirty this morning. He will lose his job!' All this poured from Doctor Andrew as he sank down on the nearest chair, his head finally meeting his hands, the fingers clutching the skull as if he were holding onto his sanity.

Zara let him be for a minute or so and he gradually relaxed his grip and lifted his eyes to her.

'What shall I do Zara? I am ashamed for my family.'

'Ashamed?' Doctor Andrew did not appear to hear her. 'You must help the police. You cannot afford to protect your brother any longer. He is running away and that won't help him in the long run. He would be better facing up to his mistakes whatever they are.' Zara was probing at random, hoping to get Doctor Andrew to talk.

'But what can I do?'

'Keep phoning him and if you get any leads, phone the police.'

'That man from CID, I should phone him?

'Yes him. You have his number?' Doctor Andrew nodded.

'You knew he was having an affair with Caroline Steading?'

'Yes, yes. He's been talking of nothing else. It's put more important matters to the back of his mind. Like the girl. The body.' Zara held her breath.

'I know about the body, Andrew,' she said in a low voice. Doctor Andrew sat rigid.

Zara's words had alerted him to the fact that he had betrayed his brother's confidence. He looked a long time at his hands. Then he raised his head.

'When I was at home in Egypt, as a boy, I used to sit and gaze at my hands and imagine them sensitive, on a patient's body, listening, as it were, for changes in the breath, in temperature, tensions in the muscle. Above all I saw my hands as a force for good. So much has happened… I do not want to let them down, my hands.' Zara waited. Another silence. What a lot of it in one morning, she thought. First Steading and now the good doctor. Did I miss my vocation, she wondered, wanting to smile but retaining a calm serious face. The doctor began again:

'I will tell you the story. It is painful so please if you know bits already please tell me, and I can leave them out.' Zara nodded.

'My brother had a job in London in a hospital. This is ten years ago. A junior position, he was newly qualified. He was doing well at work and enjoying his social life but a little too well and he spent his money unwisely, gambling.'

'Which is how he met Malloch?'

'Yes but he didn't know at first what was happening. When he couldn't pay his debts, the apparent owner of the joint, which was known officially as 'The Golden Eye', was most accommodating. We know you have a good job et cetera. Before he knew it, he owed not just hundreds but thousands of pounds. The further you fall, the further you fall. He foolishly imagined that he would start winning more than he had lost... Eventually, when he was becoming desperate, he received a message via a third party at 'The Golden Eye', that if he were willing to do a job for Malloch, all his debts would be wiped.'

'I don't understand,' said Zara.

'It is a long story, but all you need to know is that our father knew Malloch a long time back and James had contacted him when he arrived in Britain. I didn't. He was giving James rope, letting him run up debts and then he asked a favour and in return...'

'I see,' said Zara, hoping the doctor would resume.

Andrew had fallen silent and Zara guessed he was suddenly aware he had plunged into a confession which would incriminate his brother still further. He began again:

'The first job he was asked to do, it seemed simple. He just had to drive a car. Pick someone up. It was made to sound like a chauffeuring job. Nothing dodgy at all. He was told to park outside a certain club on the opposite side of the road at a certain time and wait. With the back doors open. He thought that a bit strange. He saw a man standing, looking at his watch at intervals as if waiting for someone.

'Suddenly two men appeared, one either side of the man and hustled him over to the waiting car. One of them said to James, "Drive". He drove. No one said anything else except to give directions. Eventually he was told to stop. The man was bundled out. He had tape wound round his mouth and one of the kidnappers had a knife. He was hustled along to the beat- up door of a house with dim lights. The two kidnappers returned alone. "Drive back," they said to James.'

In the pause which Zara was beginning to recognize as a hallmark of the doctor's style, she rose and boiled the kettle. Her mouth felt very dry and she thought the doctor was in need of a bit of comfort. He managed a small smile when she proffered the mug of coffee.

'The first time I saw James after this incident,' he resumed, 'he was over the moon. "I just had to do a small driving job and now all my debts will be clear", he said. Of course it wasn't like that. And, Zara, the dreadful thing was that it wasn't until James saw he was only going to get a tiny portion of the debt paid off that he seemed to realize he had done wrong, taken part in a kidnap which for all he knew, led to someone's death. My brother did not used to be like this.

'I was living in a different town. I tried to make him promise that he wouldn't do anything like that again but he was too caught up, in gambling mode you could say, and he really believed this was the only way out. I was fed up with the late-night phone calls where he talked without listening, so when he mentioned, almost casually, that he had been asked to supervise a medical procedure, I didn't entirely take in what it was about.

'I had begun to wonder if he were taking drugs, he sounded so spaced out but he assured me he was not. Anyway, I suppose I sort of assumed he was speaking about something at the hospital. With hindsight, it didn't add up because he was also saying that doing this would clear his debt but as I say, I was tired, and tired of listening, tired of his problems.

'I regret now I did not question him more. For my own conscience' sake. I would like to be able to say I advised him against it. But then I didn't know what "it" was.' A horrible stillness had invaded Zara's body. She felt numb, did not want the story to continue – although she already knew the outcome. Doctor Andrew now looked into the past; she could see his eyes were oblivious of her. He was re-living a horror that still haunted him daily.

'I heard nothing for a week,' he continued, 'then I received one of his midnight calls. He was almost inarticulate with fear. It took me several minutes to grasp that he was talking about FGM. He had not, as I told you, been called upon to perform the operation but the family who wanted it done were not satisfied that the procedure would be carried out safely and the father, knowing Malloch – a man with an infinite reach it appeared – had asked if he knew a doctor who could assist if things looked like going wrong.' Zara's mouth was dry. She'd finished her tea but her legs were locked in a sitting position.

'So many things went wrong,' she said softly.

'Wrong, wrong, wrong. There was too much blood. The person doing the procedure was a woman who had done such things back home. My brother saw immediately what was happening but even though he tried, he said he tried for as long… till she… till there was no life left in her. She would have needed a transfusion. He had not thought this through, how he would have needed equipment to be able to help.' Doctor Andrew looked up. Zara shook her head at his expression:

'It was him, not you. You have nothing to reproach yourself with.' He shut his eyes tightly as if to erase an image from his mind and then opened them and looked at her again.

'My brother thinks now that the cause of death could have been a heart attack due to the shock and the pain.'

Zara could think of nothing to say for several moments. At last she said: 'And then?'

'James suddenly found himself on his own. The woman who had carried out the procedure disappeared. James was meant to ring and say something on the lines of "mission accomplished" but when he told what had happened, the voice at the other end said, "You'll have to deal with it. Wait an hour and then phone back for instructions".

'This for me is almost the most gruesome part of the story,' said Doctor Andrew. 'James folded the body up before rigor mortis set in. He folded her up, in order to transport her more easily! He was already in survival mode. He never thought of confessing his part to the police. He thought about his job and his future and how he would be dishonoured if our family knew – not what he had done but that he would lose his profession.'

Zara realized that Doctor Andrew didn't know about the findings at the river or the fire. She was not going to tell him, not now at any rate.

'I pleaded with him to confess, that not to do so would mean his future life would be hell, but he still thought, then at least, he would be cleared of debt and if he could keep the death secret, he could start again with a clean slate. Of course he has been looking over his shoulder ever since. And so have I! And then Caroline saved him, unwittingly of course.'

James and Caroline! The car journey! 'Ah yes,' said Zara slowly, 'I suppose he hasn't told her that story.'

'No, she has no idea. He sees her as a knight-ess in shining armour. And can't see that he can't make a relationship with someone based on such a false premise. What am I to do, Zara? I can't go on with this in my heart. I feel I am going to break.' Zara was saved from having to answer such an impossible question by the ringing of the phone.

Chapter XXI More than one game of chess

After she had left Doctor Andrew's flat, Zara phoned Des and put to him that a visit to the Rainmaker's church – he'd heard of it vaguely but she explained in more detail how it was relevant – might be useful.

'I'm going anyway,' said Zara, 'but I thought you might be interested…' After a brief hesitation, Des said,

'We'll go after you've been to the station. Forensics won't take long.'

***

On the way to the Rainmaker's church, Zara filled Des in regarding Doctor James and the FGM operation. Finding the Doctor was even more imperative now.

The church had regular service times but apart from those, there were always people around as it served as a social centre as well. Zara rather hoped there would not be a service in progress since it would make asking questions more difficult.

Singing greeted them. They stood at the back and smiled at anyone who looked their way. No one seemed at all fazed by their presence. Zara was beginning to enjoy the rhythmic sounds and drift into a mesmerized state when suddenly the singing broke off and a mellifluous voice announced that there would be a break.

Zara and Des were looking at a wall of photographs of a very dry and seemingly vast tract of land, when someone approached them with cups of tea. The woman introduced herself as Martha and did not ask them why they were there. Instead she pointed at one of the pictures.

'There has been no rain here for six years. It used to be a fertile plain. A dam was built…'

Zara left Des to do the listening and she herself sat down a little way away. She started discreetly observing the people present, wondering who would be the most likely person to approach regarding Doctor James. But no psychic powers seemed to be needed: almost immediately a man about Doctor James's age came and sat beside her.

'Excuse me. I haven't seen you here before I think?' Zara gave him her hand and her name. 'I am Paul,' he said gravely.

Zara decided there was nothing to be gained by dissembling. 'Paul, we're here today because we're trying to contact someone. His brother is very worried because he has not heard from him and...'

'Is this brother in UK or Africa? Where please?'

'Oh in Glasgow but... I don't know if you would know him... a Doctor James?'

Paul's face cleared. 'Ah, he is my friend. I see him here often and sometimes his friend Charlie.' Charlie? Zara swallowed and tried to keep her face neutral.

'And have you seen him this week?'

'He was here with Charlie,' he drummed his fingers against his cheek, 'Sunday, last Sunday. And then no. Neither of them'.

'And is that unusual?'

'He is usually here, yes two or three times a week.'

'I see,' said Zara.

'You think there is something wrong?' Paul's face became anxious.

'Perhaps,' said Zara. '*Do you* think there might be something wrong? Would he have told anyone here? Did he seem worried?' Paul nodded his head but now he was smiling.

'He used to come with a heavy face but always leave with a light one. It comes from making the rain.'

Zara listened to Paul telling her how they went about getting God to open the precious celestial sluices for what she thought was long enough: she had her answer. She looked across at Des who was dropping a fiver into a donation box.

'It was for the Red Cross, don't worry,' he said when they got outside.

'I've no idea how to make rain,' said Zara. 'They may be on to something for all we know.'

'He's not been there,' she added as they walked away from the church and down the road that passed the Rum and Rocket. 'Where's your car parked?' Des pointed down the road. As they passed the pub they saw a familiar figure come out of the entrance. He looked left and right but didn't seem to recognize them. It was Screw. 'I can feel a hunch coming on,' said Zara and when Des made a face she said, 'Humour me.'

'Imagine you are Doctor James,' she began. 'You go to the church. Charlie arrives. Stuff the rain, it's their under-cover meeting place. Charlie gives James some sort of ultimatum. He leaves desperate. Walks down the road and who does he meet?'

'Screw,' said Des.

'You're getting the idea,' said Zara. 'And if you wanted to buy a gun quickly who might you go to, for one point only? The answer being, Screw again.'

'Screw also can put two and two together,' said Des, 'and he knows…'

'How does he know?'

'Okay, I have a hunch he knows that Doctor James wants the gun to shoot Steading. Surprising how often Screw is on the margins in these little incidents.'

'Where does this get us then?'

'Not much nearer Doctor James, but another reason for questioning Screw.'

'You'll trip him up yet, DI Des,' said Zara, giving him a mock salute as he got into his car and drove away.

**

Zara rang Billy Gardner. It was just out of badness she realized as she dialled the number but she wanted to be certain of how the land lay.

'Oh, Mrs Gardner? This is Zara MacDonald again.' The friendly voice replying had become guarded:

'What do you want? Billy already told you –

'That's what I was phoning about. I just wanted to make sure everything was all right, I hadn't offended your husband or anything.' Zara was doing her best to sound innocent.

'No, no he wasn't offended. He… he just decided… well, he didn't want the publicity was how he put it.'

I see,' said Zara. 'That's okay then. I understand.'

'He was quite upset,' Mrs Gardiner was becoming more relaxed, 'but then Rose's birthday took his mind off it. He loves doing a film of her party. Does one every year. That's her ten now.'

'Oh they grow up so quickly, don't they?' Zara put in.

'Have you got any of your own?'

'Not yet.' Zara let the conversation wind down, thanked Mrs Gardner and closed the call.

***

Steading phoned Malloch:

'Where's Caroline? I know you know. If you don't tell me I'll go to the police.'

'I don't think you will.' Malloch's voice sounded reasonableness itself.

'Where is she?' Steading persisted.

'A better question might be, 'Who is she with?'' said Malloch.

'Get to fuck! You helped them to leave. I'll never forgive you for this.'

'Everyone has his price. You wouldn't help me with my little scheme so I had to go elsewhere. He may be enjoying himself right now but you know what they say about free lunches?'

'Where is she?'

'I have a little hideaway. A cottage in Sutherland. Remote. Idyllic. Somewhere where you can feel free.'

'Give me the address,' Steading shouted although he knew shouting was not a good plan when dealing with Malloch. 'Where? Where in Sutherland?'

'My friend, don't get upset. We can resolve this. Friends can always find a way. And remember,' he added as Steading continued to expostulate, 'it wasn't me that fell in love with Doctor James.'

***

'The words that stuck in Steading's throat after this altercation were, *We can resolve this,* except he changed the *We* to *I.* What had been in his mind for some time, crystallized suddenly into a plan. He went to his desk and, selecting a key from a ring taken from his pocket, he opened a drawer. From there he took an envelope which also held a key. With this he opened a chest in the corner of the room. He armed the contents, which were papers, onto the carpet. He glanced up: there was no need even to shut the door because no one was coming.

There were many papers – reports, minutes of meetings, letters – but the one thing they had in common was that they incriminated both him and Malloch. Even though the letters were all print-outs of e-mails and sent to his personal address, not his office, by careful chronology, he could show with sufficient clarity which reports or minutes they referred to.

Mostly the information was of the type which would enable Malloch or more likely, one of Malloch's protégés, to get in first on a contract or put in a bid which was going to win out. But apart from this, there was the whole McKelvie Buildings affair. At least half the papers related to this matter: e-mails which hinted, later e-mails which demanded and later still which threatened.

Steading wondered why Malloch had committed so much to such a traceable source. Because he was so bloody arrogant, thought he was invincible under his various pseudonyms, thought above all, he was so powerful people would always kowtow to him, but he'd left out one possibility – that a man might decide that he wanted to die with a clear conscience, so that money would cease to be a consideration.

Steading was surprised at his own thoughts. It was not even as if he believed in a judgment day. He tried to put his finger on it. Part of it, he had to admit, was a strong desire to see Malloch fall and if he didn't live to see it, at least to have taken part in engineering it.

When he had everything in order, he felt almost happy. On impulse, he decided he would mail the whole correspondence to Zara. That made him feel even happier but he did feel he lacked one thing: a piece of evidence which would tie Malloch indissolubly to the McKelvie Buildings fire.

He pulled the phone towards him and reading off a card he'd taken from his pocket, he dialled Zara's number for the second time that day. That woman had been after something: maybe she knew something he didn't. Maybe they could work together.

'Zara? Can I meet you? No, nothing to do with Caroline. No. I think I need to do this face to face. In fact, could you come to my house? I have something to show you. No, you will be safe. Please believe me, you will be safe.'

She had said she would come but he heard her hesitation and could understand it: she rightly connected him with Malloch. He shuddered, seeing as if for the first time what kind of a man this made him. But perhaps he could do something good, put something right. He would not tell Zara everything but he would tell her enough so she could help him, that is if it were within her capabilities.

While he was waiting for her to arrive, Steading thought about writing a letter to Caroline. He would tell her he loved her and that he knew he had been unfair to her, that he was glad he had not told her his secrets but he wanted her to know how much he wished things could have been otherwise. He realized how all the things he'd done to make himself big, had made him small. So many things went through his mind. He felt that none of it was either interesting nor beautiful but pondering it gave him some relief. He reached for a pen but then Zara arrived.

***

Billy Gardner didn't know why he did it: he sent a copy of the photo of the fire with Malloch in it to the man himself. Like Steading, Billy was getting fed up. He wished to move on. What had seemed unalterable some years ago, now appeared able to be changed. He didn't know what the outcome of his action would be. It felt a bit like goading a bull in a ring but he was getting a grim satisfaction from doing it.

Suddenly he felt he'd been suffering all these years for nothing. Just the act of thinking differently changed things. He realized he had been playing a passive waiting game and had allowed his fear to dominate him: fear of the unknown and the unexpected.

***

James and Caroline had arrived at Malloch's cottage the day after the party. They were euphoric. They picked up a week's groceries on their way and when they eventually arrived, went about the small property expressing astonishment at their good fortune.

Someone had been in and aired the beds; there were logs cut for the fire. As Malloch had said, it was idyllic. They had spent time together alone at Doctor James's flat but had never felt this freedom to be themselves.

That first evening they ate a simple meal, drank wine and fell into bed drugged with happiness. The next day they had a late breakfast, walked beside a river they thought sparkled for them alone, had a picnic lunch which consisted mostly of wine and sat outside the cottage in the sun.

'Good sex and good fortune go together,' James said to Caroline stroking her hair as she sat at his feet. 'I want to spend the rest of my life with you.'

But even on that second day, Caroline felt a twinge of irritation when the statement was repeated. He had called in sick to give them some respite but she had a feeling they would be lucky if their 'honeymoon' lasted the week.

Away from Charlie, she began to miss things about him. Some of them quite negative but still, no one is perfect, she told herself. She also began to think more closely about other aspects of Doctor James. One thing troubled her more than anything and she didn't know why.

On the second night when they lay in each other's arms, after making love, she said to him, 'Jamesie, what was in that suitcase... you remember, when I gave you the lift from Manchester?' Because they were lying entwined, she felt the full force of the sudden jerk his body gave.

'The usual. You know, the kitchen sink et cetera. My hair-dryer, my curling tongs. Didn't I tell you at the time?' He laughed but Caroline turned away from him. 'Why do you bring it up?' She felt him try to keep his voice calm. She lay thinking about the answer to his question: the reason she'd brought it up was that when she had told the story of the trip from Manchester to Zara she had realized she was leaving the very large suitcase out of the narrative.

It had been strange how the staying silent had focused her awareness. Subsequently she had also become convinced that Doctor James's tense excitable mood had been only partly a result of being with her again. But she loved him and whenever she had thought of bringing the question up, she'd shelved it wanting to stay in the moment, the romantic all-absorbing moment.

With hindsight she felt there had always been a mysterious fog around that suitcase. Zara at the party, for instance, had looked at her at one point and instantly she had thought of it. There had to be a reason for that. She remembered another thing: when they had stopped for petrol, James had asked her to open the boot so he could check the suitcase was shut. Even at the time Caroline had thought the request strange.

James was lying rigidly staring at the ceiling when Caroline suddenly replied: 'It was Zara. Zara made me think otherwise.'

James sat bolt upright. 'What have you been telling her?' he gasped, his eyes wide as if he could see Zara in front of him.

'I told her how we met.'

'You told her about our affair?'

'I had to tell someone. You told your brother!' Doctor James groaned.

'That is different. He would never give me away.'

'Give you away? What is there to give away?' Now Doctor James turned away from Caroline and looked out of the skylight at the cold stars. Only five minutes ago they had appeared friendly, given him the same sense of security he had been used to in Egypt where they were so much brighter.

Caroline lay musing over what James had said. Up till now, as far as she had thought about the men Charlie had introduced her to – Joe Malloch and James – she had gathered only that Malloch was a powerful business man with his fingers in lots of pies. She had been so unsuspicious that at the party when she had actually seen James with a gun in his hand, she had believed his story that he had taken it from an over-zealous security man in the interests of safety and that it had gone off by mistake. She thought Charlie's primary involvement with Malloch was as a chess player, though she knew there was something else, and that it concerned the McKelvie Buildings. Charlie had always been reticent when she had mentioned it and on occasion irritable:

'You've told me over and over again that you are not interested in my work, so what's changed? It's too complicated. Yes, it is worrying me at the moment, but that's work for you...'

And what he said was true: she had been wont to say to him, 'Charlie, have you not got another topic of conversation? People at the council are paid to listen to you. I'm not.'

Suddenly lying beside this warm man she had thought she loved, she was struck by a horrible fear: McKelvie Buildings.

'You haven't anything to do with the fire, have you?' she whispered and the words went through him like sharp knives.

***

The first thing Charlie Steading asked of Zara was that he had her word she would not go to the police. He was going to tell her a few facts but not in enough detail to be useful at the moment, although, at a certain point down the line, she would be able to fit the jigsaw together herself.

'What do you want from me?' asked Zara.

'You may not be able to give me what I want but I have to ask.' Zara nodded for him to go on. It was evident to her that he was going to tell her the facts before asking his question.

Steading sat at his desk looking drained. He gave her the bare bones of the story:

'I had been approached by Malloch concerning a building contract that was up for tender. It was to develop a site in Slater Street. Looking back it was easy to see that the guy had done his homework. The week before, I'd been on a discussion panel at an event at the local community centre here and mentioned I had a passion for chess. I was asked a question about the maintenance of physical agility as one grows older and I answered that my only agility was as a knight jumping over bishops and queens. Within six days, Malloch approached me at the chess club that I visited two or three times a week.'

'He mentioned cars, and it happened that I was vaguely thinking of replacing mine. "Don't do that," he said. "If it's an upgrade you're looking for, why not let your wife have the car you have now and I can put you in the way of a brilliant motor at well below the market price. As long as you keep coming to the chess club." I thought him quite charming. He played a good game. I was easily seduced. Naïve.' He looked at Zara and she could see the honesty was giving him pain.

'The next thing was, he rang me and told me to come to a certain garage to look at a car. I thought he owned the garage. The car was a BMW with the previous year's registration number. When I'd fallen in love with it, Malloch told me it belonged to a business associate of his who was going to be out of the country for a year but who wanted to have a car for if he should come back for a visit. He owed Malloch a favour or two so he'd said he would be happy the car was being driven rather than sitting in a garage.

'I said yes, in spite of the fact that the car was much heavier on petrol than mine. I told myself at least I wasn't buying a car. Three months on though, Malloch had told me his friend wasn't coming back to the UK. He'd met a beautiful woman and was staying in Hong Kong. He didn't want the car. He wanted to settle up with Malloch and had offered the car as part of the bargain. Steading was welcome to continue to use it for the time being.'

Zara saw that Steading was waiting for an acknowledgement so she nodded vigorously and said,

'I understand.' He began again:

'I was aware at meetings of words springing to my lips which might influence the way things swung re the Slater Street contract. I found myself repeating at tea-breaks snippets of positive information about the firm Malloch had in mind and the odd negative about some of the others. That wasn't all.' Steading gazed at the floor as if he were looking for a way back to innocence. 'The upshot was Malloch's firm – not his personally but the one he had an interest in – obtained the contract. Malloch congratulated me on my effort and said it had been a pleasure to do business with me. It was only then that I realized I had been bribed.' Zara nodded again.

'However, it took far longer for the whole picture to emerge and by then I had all sorts of self-justifying ideas in my head. Caroline had been very pleased to have the old car as it gave her more independence. And Malloch was making a difference to our lives in other ways.

'He had a pal who had built a new hotel in Majorca who wanted people to try it out incognito and for free of course. Malloch always made it sound as if we were doing him a favour which made it difficult for us to refuse anything he asked. When we moved here, a building firm known to Malloch sorted the dry rot at a very reasonable price.

'I could still sleep, if you can believe that, but there came the day when the horrible realization struck me: there was a link between certain fires in the city centre and the sites Malloch seemed interested in securing contracts for.' Zara leant forward in her seat. 'I developed insomnia. I felt resentful and then I would remember the BMW and the dry rot and conclude that the balance was really the other way. It would go round and round in my mind and I knew I had to find a way to get out of Malloch's clutches without bringing him down because if I did that I would bring my own house down too.' He seemed at last to have finished.

'So where do I come in?' asked Zara gently.

'I have a mountain of evidence,' said Steading. 'I want to post it to you. It's time. It really is time.'

Zara nodded her assent not knowing how to respond, too many ideas going round in her head.

'Why don't you go straight to the police?' There was a short silence then Steading sighed and said,

'What I need is some evidence to link Malloch with the fire at McKelvie Buildings and I wondered, because it seems to me you have some idea of all this which is why you approached me in the first place, I wondered if you had any cards in your hand so to speak.'

'Does the name Billy Gardner mean anything to you? A builder by trade.' Zara looked at Steading's eyes not wanting to miss the smallest indication of yes or no. She made a gesture that indicated the click of a camera.

Chapter XXII Action follows decision

When Zara left the Steading's house she thought she saw a one-legged pigeon but she wasn't sure and her mind was too pre-occupied with everything she'd been told, to take note. When she had turned the corner Munchy came out of the hedge and made a phone call.

'She went to his house, Boss. She's just left.'

At the other end, Malloch was irritated by Munchy's use of the word 'Boss'. He'd tried to get Munchy to call him Uncle Joe but Munchy had not taken to that. Some things in life were not worth pursuing. Malloch settled down to being patient.

'Hear anything useful, Munchy?'

''Aven't got xray ears, Boss. I looked through the window, sideways like and there were lots of papers on the floor and he was talking very serious.'

'What sort of papers?'

'I don't know. I wasn't close enough.'

'Well, good work anyway, Munchy. See Screw and he'll give you something. Meanwhile *I'll* need to see *you*. I've another job for you. It's quite urgent. In fact it's becoming more urgent as we speak.'

Malloch had made two decisions which equalled the removal of two obstacles. For one he would use Munchy. For the other he thought he had better engage himself, much as he disliked hands-on operations. Time was getting short. If he wanted to succeed in his ultimate goal, he needed a clearer field.

One other thing bothered him: the arrival of the fire photograph. No message, just this flimsy reminder of that ten year-old affair at McKelvie Buildings. Was it a threat? He had thought the stand-off was still working and certainly he needed it to be working. Although he prided himself on second guessing, he had to admit grave puzzlement. However it did not suit his purpose to get in touch with the guy who had sent it.

Zara was not sure what she should tell Des. She had meant to ask him if he had been able to use the photo of the fire as a way of nailing Malloch but she supposed he would need the paper trail which she now knew Steading had in his house. She had promised Steading she would not tell but…

In the end she compromised. Des answered his phone on the second ring.

'Hypothesis', Zara began without preamble. 'Were you to have a paper trail relating to certain fires at certain prime sites in a city within your remit, would that put you in a position to make any arrests or at least take certain parties in for questioning?'

'It might,' said Des. 'Obviously if and when that day arrives I would want to be the first to know but at the moment we have another trail to follow. Doctor James, we are reliably informed has been staying in Sutherland. If we can nab him when he comes back – and the same source says it will be soon – we may get the answers to many riddles with a bit of gentle questioning down at the station.' Zara thought for a minute.

'I wonder why he's coming back.'

'Go on,' said Des.

'It's just that business Spike told me about when Malloch was trying to get Steading to do something for him. I wonder if Doctor James is now in line and that's the price of his honeymoon with Caroline.' Des's noisy but inarticulate response told Zara that he was not in the frame of mind to entertain her speculations. She was not deterred. 'What about my forensics?' she asked. 'Who was my assailant after the party, DI Des?'

''Jed McCue. He's got form. He's been known to work with Screw on occasion and the two guys are known to do heavy work for Malloch. It seems probable that McCue was the one that mugged you. Getting him to admit it would be a different story.'

'So what are you going to do?'

'Get the guy in for questioning.' Zara thanked him and rang off. As so often when she had a conversation with Des, she ended up feeling dissatisfied.

***

'At least phone your brother.' This had been the beginning of Caroline's campaign. When she realized her relationship with Doctor James had changed utterly, she wanted him to change course, to do something right. He had said that to know where they were would really upset his brother but he was upset himself by the phone calls which he had not been answering and by the anguished messages left on his voice-mail. He couldn't switch off his mobile because of Malloch who seemed to want to talk to him daily.

He would take these calls outside, walking up and down the little path surrounding the cottage. All this beauty, thought Caroline, and all this ugliness.

Doctor James had eventually broken down and told Caroline the whole story. Not the total detail of it, as much for his own sake as for hers. He could not bear to look at her horror-struck face. He wanted to take her into his arms. But she would not come anywhere near him. At night he was sleeping uncomfortably on a sofa half his length.

When Caroline learnt that James's brother Andrew had counselled confession to the police, she threw her weight behind this solution but James was adamant: he would not admit he was cornered. Unfortunately some desperate part of him still believed Malloch would help him.

'Look at this wonderful week he has given us,' he said in an attempt to win Caroline over. Caroline was almost sick. The FGM element in the story had overwhelmed her and she could not conceive how anyone could bring anything in, in mitigation.

He would not tell her what it was Malloch wanted him to do; he just kept saying it was not a criminal act.

'Does Charlie know about it?' asked Caroline. Zara would have asked whether it was part of a plan which facilitated a criminal act but

Caroline was not a criminologist. Yes, James had responded. He thought Charlie had refused to do this. He did not know why. It was not a criminal act.

Charlie had refused. Caroline was heartened by this but also made more afraid. She did not want to contemplate the degree of her husband's involvement. It made her flesh creep to know she had shared a bed with people who… Now she understood why Charlie had been economic with the truth regarding his relationship with Malloch but she worried over her own part.

Could she have known? Should she have asked more questions? Would she have been able to save him from getting in up to his neck? She still did not understand what Malloch's hold on Charlie had been but she was terrified of the insidious power Malloch seemed to have. She hoped she was not in the net.

They still drank wine at night. He thought it was for togetherness but for Caroline it was to dim her fears. On the third night, perhaps with Dutch courage she took her purse, put on her jacket and walked away. James was in a fitful doze. She thought vaguely of getting to the village and then getting a taxi to somewhere bigger and then…

She stumbled onto the road and set off. It began to rain and she was wet through in minutes. She came to a crossroads and panicked. She did not remember it. Right or left? She took left because she could see lights in the distance. After half a mile the road became a track. She turned round. She was now facing east and it was darker. Although she had just traversed it, the road seemed strange to her, the trees black shapes only, bending towards her as if to stop her path. When she reached the crossroads, there was James in his car. She couldn't help feeling relieved. After this incident, she changed tactics.

What had Charlie refused to do? The question kept coming back to her. She slowly realized that perhaps she could put in her pennyworth to hinder or stop whatever it was that was going to happen. She didn't seem able to stop James going blindly forward but perhaps if she could find out even a little clue she could pass it on to someone. Who? Zara? She didn't have her number. Andrew, he was the obvious one but could he be relied on? Ask Andrew to get Zara's number? On what pretext? Didn't matter. She would just have to do it.

She used the same tactics with James that she had used to use with Charlie in the old days: care and concern, overt support until her quarry relaxed into giving something away. She began in a roundabout fashion. First she made James a cup of coffee and since it was the first thing she had done for him since the dreadful night he'd confessed, it went a long way towards making him think she was relaxing her view of him.

'So we'll be leaving when... Friday...?

'I'm not sure. Need to check with Joe.

'I see. So we'll be back by the end of the week and you'll be able to go back to work. Are you not working this weekend?

'Yes but...'

'You can't go on playing at being sick Jamesie.' She forced herself to use her intimate name for him.

'Yes but...' She looked at him with a questioning but reassuring smile. He remained silent but struggling: he wanted to appear normal, she thought.

'Well,' she said brightly, 'we won't be going to that film we talked about. It's only on on Wednesday afternoon and...'

'No, not Wednesday.'

'No, not Wednesday what?' Got him, she thought, and aloud she said, 'Oh, is that the day you have a date with Malloch?'

'It's not *with* Malloch.'

'Okay, the day you do whatever it is you're going to do.'

'I've only got to stand at a bus-stop and speak to someone.'

'Who?' Caroline's voice was casual.

'I don't *know*. He won't tell me that. He never tells… It's not a criminal offence.'

Caroline nodded. 'I hear you James.' She had something: a day, a bus stop. Was it enough to be helpful? Now she had to find an opportunity to phone Andrew. She sent James upstairs to look for something she knew was downstairs. He would look hard she knew: he wanted to please her. She found Andrew's number and transferred it to her phone. Then she texted Andrew: send me Zara's number.

***

Sunday. Zara was with Barney when she received Caroline's text.

'Mrs Steading has found out which side her bread is buttered.' Barney waited. 'Doesn't say where they are but coming back probably at the end of the week and guess what? Something is going to happen at a bus stop. Doctor James is to talk to someone as yet unknown at an unknown bus stop. Just the sort of information DI Des loves.'

'When?' asked Barney.

'We do know the day. Wednesday next. All the police need to do now is to tour all the bus stops in Glasgow till they find Doctor James. Shouldn't be difficult.'

Zara phoned Des who told her to pump the source for more.

'I'm glad you're not thinking of touring the bus stops yourself,' said Barney.

'Don't be too sure. It might come to that.'

'I'm comforted by the fact that you seem to have almost nothing to go on.'

'But Caroline might uncover the whole plot. She's not just a pretty face.'

'I only want you to be safe.'

'I know that.' Zara gave him a quick hug. 'Things to do, places to go. See you soon. If not, later. I'll meet Ben from school tomorrow as arranged.'

Zara walked home humming tunelessly to herself, a habit she had when something was afoot. She felt excited. Whether or not she was going to be involved, there was going to be some outcome, some clarity.

***

Although Munchy was flattered to be meeting Malloch, he was not comfortable as he picked his way into the tunnel where, in the secret place Ben had caught sight of Bill Mason on an earlier occasion, he was to be given his orders.

'She won't believe anything I say, Boss,' was his first rejoinder.

'She will, if you follow the script, Munchy.'

'What if she has the boy with her?'

'You'll need to be a bit creative. Tell him to look after your pigeon for a minute.' Munchy was silent for a moment:

'I suppose. But the other business, it's all very well for you, Boss, seeing it from the general's point of view. You can afford to make jokes when you're not the poor bloody infantry.' He paused. 'I don't fancy the other thing at all.'

'Munchy, I'm not asking much considering. But yours is a vital part. And it's simple. Remember, I'm promising you a little bit more than that holiday in Spain you always wanted.'

Munchy looked sceptical but he daren't say 'No'. If he did Jed McCue would be round with his mate and Munchy couldn't stand up to them. He didn't want to lose any more teeth at his age.

'So it's Wednesday?' He sounded resigned.

'You lack your father's courage, Munchy. I do miss him.'

'Wednesday, you say?' Munchy was trying for 'implacable'.

'Had you anything else planned? Visiting someone in hospital perhaps or seeing your accountant?'

***

The next day, Zara received the parcel of incriminating evidence from Charlie Steading by special delivery. She held the parcel to her savouring its importance and wondering where on earth to put it. Part of her wanted to go through it immediately page by page but another part knew she would need time so that she could do it properly. Also she was conscious of the fact that Charlie had delivered it into her safe-keeping and that he had a plan of his own. The bundle of paper fitted into it somewhere but he had not told Zara where. She left it on the kitchen table while she decided on a good place to put it. Maybe the bank, she thought. She did not want to have to be anxious about it.

She spent the morning working on an article and answering a back-log of e-mails. It became one of those mornings where you think you have a clear space ahead of you but trivial things keep cropping up that you have to deal with. At eleven she had to go out for bread and milk and something for lunch. She could not remember when she had last stocked up the fridge. Her mother rang. There was even a knock on the door from a couple of Jehovah's Witnesses. Zara was beginning to get exasperated. She kept looking at the parcel on the table, wanting to open it.

After lunch she was carrying a cup of coffee to her desk when she tripped on a corner of the carpet which had previously been stapled to the floor. She took a deep breath and went to get staples and a hammer.

'Okay, I give in,' she said to herself. 'Perhaps I'm not going to be able to get on with anything until I've looked inside the parcel.' She took off the outer wrapping. On top of the rectangular block of papers which were neatly housed in three boxes, lay an envelope; written across it in a sloping hand were the words: What I found out about Billy Gardner. She slit it open at once.

Charlie had been thorough. Sifting through the thick pile of material, Zara realized that he'd taken Billy's photography as his starting point and followed up people, places and events. The result was a detailed portrait of the man. Our Mr Steading missed his vocation, thought Zara. He should have worked in CID or been an investigative journalist. She leafed through the pile hoping something would jump out that would help her make the more recent connections she needed but nothing did. Knowing the past was not enough. There had to be another reason for Malloch's present activity. Then she found it: a newspaper story. 'Hit and Run Driver Walks Free'. Zara's heart flipped over. Where had she heard those words before? She knew they were important but she could not think why. At the same time she looked at the clock and remembered school was out early that Monday, some teachers' meeting.

Zara stuffed everything relating to Billy Gardner back in its envelope, picked up the boxes of evidence and stowed them in the back of the airing cupboard. She made sure she had the keys to Barney's flat as well as her own and left. It was only when she was halfway down the stairs that she realized she still had the envelope in her hand. She had no time to go back; she pushed it into her capacious inside pocket and ran.

Nevertheless she felt quite contented as she walked towards where she would meet Ben who, now he was ten, always started walking along the road from the school, not wanting to look young enough to be met. Not that he wasn't always pleased to see Zara. They greeted each other and by mutual consent they began to walk back through the park. Ben asked why Zara had not brought Ness but Zara said she'd been running late and hadn't had time to go and get her.

'Let's go and get her now then,' said Ben speeding up. Zara agreed but then they met a woman called Frances who had a boy, Dan, in Ben's class – the two women had often met at the school gates – and Ben and Dan started to run about, bored with waiting. Zara was deep in conversation with Frances when Munchy shambled up to her. He sounded out of breath and looked worried.

'You need to come,' he said making as if to pull her arm.

'Why?' asked Zara feeling irritated.

'It's… it's… Spike.' The word was electric.

'What? Where? Take me.' She was already running but stopped suddenly remembering Ben she shouted to Frances, 'Look after him till I come back' and 'Ben, stay with Frances, okay?'

The two boys shook their heads at one another and continued their game with someone's discarded football. Frances sat down on a bench with the book she always carried with her but never got time to read. Twenty minutes later she looked up. The boys were still playing. She'd known they were because she could hear them laughing. But where was Zara? Frances needed to get home. She had to make tea and go out to a class when her partner got in. She could do without complications.

She stood up and took a step in the direction she thought Zara had gone in and then felt confused. She didn't really know which way it had been it had happened so quickly. They were near the bridge which led onto University Avenue. Had Zara gone over the bridge?

Frances made a snap decision: she would walk that way and surely meet Zara and be able to off-load Ben. She called the boys over.

***

Zara had jogged along with Munchy who was too out of breath to speak. He just kept repeating phrases like 'on the bank' and 'a bit further along' and Zara started imagining a re-run of what had happened to Bill Mason. They reached a place where the bank was wide and sloping and trees screened whoever was near the river from view. Zara could see a figure kneeling with his back to her. Thinking it was Spike, she saw Spike.

'Are you all right?' she shouted, scrambling towards him.

The face that turned towards her was Screw's: she could not have been more shocked and in that frozen moment she fell forward, pushed hard from behind. Then Screw had a rope round her tying it so her arms were trapped inside. She felt a blow to the head. She was not unconscious but everything was spinning. She tried to scream but no sound would come.

The men waited. No one seemed to have been there to notice but Munchy climbed back up the bank to make sure. Frances was sitting on the bench reading her book and the boys were playing further off. Zara struggled as if in a dream where you can make no headway. Then a van drew up, the sort of van the park's department might use and Zara was unceremoniously hoisted into the back. The doors slammed.

Chapter XXIII What's locked can be unlocked

Barney arrived home to an empty house. He rang Zara's mobile but there was no reply. Then he rang her landline. He left an inquiring message on both phones. At first he was not unduly worried. He knew that Zara and Ben often forgot the time when they were together, especially if Zara started telling Ben a story and he knew that in Zara's mind Ben was safe because he was with her. He was surprised Ness wasn't with them: Zara usually picked up the dog on her way to collect Ben. He decided to leave preparing the tea and go and look for them in the park, taking an eager Ness with him.

He walked from Kelvin Bridge down to the bridge from where Zara had been abducted but saw no signs of her or Ben. He was becoming anxious. All this river business. All this involvement with Malloch. However he couldn't believe Zara would have wittingly taken Ben into a dangerous situation. He wondered if Spike would have any ideas. Where would Spike be now? He walked along looking at the ground, looking up at intervals as if he might conjure Zara and Ben out of thin air.

'Barney, you okay?' It was Spike. The older man came towards him very fast.

'Zara and Ben?' said Barney trying to read Spike's face.

'I'm worried,' said Spike. 'Munchy's been behaving strangely this past two days. I've been keeping a close eye on him but he managed to give me the slip this afternoon.'

'You think he's done something with them?'

'I've no idea what was in his mind. Are you looking for them?' Barney nodded, unable to speak. 'Ben was meant to meet Zara out of school?' Barney nodded again.

They were walking along slowly beside the river, reaching the further bridge again. Spike took hold of Barney by his jacket:

'Tell me everything you know!'

'Zara's been talking for ages about some plan of that man Malloch, some plan she thinks is going off on Wednesday. Thinks she knows something which could spoil his…'

'What's that in the grass?' interrupted Spike. On the bank they could see something red and half hidden. Spike climbed down and retrieved a hairslide.

'That's Zara's. It was a birthday present from Ben,' said Barney.

'There's a lot of footprints here,' said Spike, 'but there's no knowing what that means'.

'I'll need to go home and ring all the parents I know. I don't want to ring the police if there's a simple explanation,' said Barney. Spike nodded, but he was thinking things did not look good.

***

Two hours later Spike found Munchy in a corner devouring a fish supper as if it were his last meal on earth.

'What have you done with them?'

'What do you mean, them?'

'Zara and Ben. I know you've been up to something'. Spike grabbed the fish supper and hurled it to the ground and pulled Munchy towards him by his collar. 'Where are they?'

'I don't know what you're talking about.' Spike pulled the collar tighter. 'It was just Zara,' said Munchy. 'I didn't hurt her.'

'Where the fuck is she?'

'Don't know pal.'

'Where did you leave her?'

'Screw pushed me out of the van.'

'Where?'

'Not far away. Just on University Avenue.'

'And the van went which way?'

'Towards Dumbarton Road.' Spike flung Munchy backwards so hard that he fell to the ground.

'What about the boy?'

'I didn't see a boy.'

'Barney's boy.'

'Didn't see him. He wasn't there.' Spike looked ready to have another go at him. 'I wouldn't do anything to a child. What do you take me for?'

'If you've harmed Zara in any way, I'll put you through a mincer.'

Spike hated going to people's houses but he had to tell Barney what he knew. He spoke into the intercom and asked Barney to come down to the street door; he didn't want Ben, if he were there, to hear what he had to say.

***

Reaching home, Barney had gone systematically through the list he had of the parents of Ben's school mates but the boy Dan was not a special friend so his number was not there. Barney became more and more angry with Zara and frightened beyond anything for Ben. Then the last parent on the list said she thought she had seen Ben playing in the park with Dan. She couldn't remember seeing Zara. The woman knew Dan's mother's number. It was Dan's father who answered:

'I wanted to ring you but Ben said his Aunty Zara would come for him.' Barney swallowed his anger. The guy probably hadn't taken in the story properly. 'I've given him his tea,' the guy went on, 'and I would have rung if it had got any later.'

'And Zara,' said Barney, 'where did she go?'

'I've no idea. My wife said she was talking to a funny little man who was very out of breath. He said she had to go and see someone. Name could have been 'Mike'. My wife got the impression there had been an accident or something.' Barney was trying to compute the time.

233

'So when would all this have happened?'

The man was silent while he tried to backtrack. 'Frances said she'd been in about ten minutes when I got back home. She was in the park, she said, waiting, about twenty. I suppose it must have happened... she must have gone about four o'clock.'

It was now five-thirty. Barney was in two minds. He decided to fetch Ben first and hear the whole story again before ringing the police. But then he remembered the taxi rescue of a few days before so he did ring.

***

Barney felt increasingly uncomfortable as the evening wore on, partly because it was difficult knowing what to say to Ben. He had phoned Des who had had a reaction similar to his own: fear for Zara. After Spike had delivered his message, Barney phoned Des again. Since no one seemed to have been in the vicinity, there were no leads on the vehicle which had probably been abandoned by now anyway. It seemed a safe assumption that Malloch was behind the kidnap. If Screw could be found, he might be made to give something away but Malloch's strategy of compartmentalizing his plans made them difficult to track. The other way in, was to try to second guess what Malloch might consider to be a good hiding place.

This brought both Barney and Des to a new possibility: suppose Malloch was thinking of getting rid of the Zara problem once and for all.

***

Zara felt like a cartoon character. Poum! She falls in the mud. Poum! She's thrown somewhere dark and damp. Poum! The van doors slam. She had been so shaken by the ride, She had not been able to stop herself from being rolled about. She had no idea of the journey except she reckoned they had been on the road about ten minutes but, she thought, she might have been driven round on purpose and might not be very far from their departure point.

Now she did not know where she was. Her feet were tightly bound with a rope which was attached to both her hands making access to her feet impossible. She was on her own, lying on her side. The light was dim and it was difficult to make out her surroundings.

Moving to gain a slightly more comfortable position, she felt something hard and rectangular beneath her: her mobile; it must have fallen from her pocket when they were tying her feet. She found she could reach it and amazingly she just had enough leverage to get Barney's number. But there was no signal. She must be underground. Mentally she kicked herself. Of course, a tunnel, Malloch's favourite stomping ground.

She strained her eyes to make out what sort of place it was but the light from her mobile was only strong enough to cast strange shadows. She inched forward in one direction and found herself suddenly on an edge. She pulled back in terror and pointed the light downwards. A platform! She had nearly rolled onto the line. Now she knew, she could distinguish the faint line of the platform edge stretching towards what might be the entrance if it were not blocked. Did she recall the sound of padlocks being opened and the drawing of bolts? Possibly.

She strained her ears for noises. She thought she could detect the dull rumble of traffic. She could be under Dumbarton Road or Great Western Road but she could equally well be further afield. How long was she going to be left here? The words 'maybe for ever' came to her and she saw in her mind's eye the picture Katerina had painted of the skeleton picked clean by rats. Also found in a tunnel.

She sat up and forced herself to be practical. She had one sandwich in her pocket. Yesterday's but still eminently edible. She knew in another pocket she had a small torch, fortunately not solar-powered and a box of matches, and a pocket knife. Also half of a half-litre bottle of water. She thanked the universe that it had looked like rain when she'd set out, otherwise she wouldn't have been wearing her jacket. Reaching all these things was a puzzle she had yet to work out.

Her mind turned to Malloch and what might be his game. Did he intend to keep her here till after Wednesday when he had carried out his plan? At best he was trying to frighten her and would let her go perhaps in a few hours. Struggling with the ropes, she tried to extricate her sandwich but it was impossible. She found herself dozing – it was hard to keep her eyes open in the gloom.

When she heard the clang of metal, at first she wondered if she were dreaming and then seeing a moving density in the darkness, she hoped it was a dream but in a second the apparition resolved itself into the figure of Malloch shining a powerful torch straight at her.

'Evening Miss MacDonald, so glad I didn't tread on you.' He set the torch down and tut-tutted at the ropes. 'No real need for these,' and proceeded to untie them. 'Get up.' Zara staggered and he had to catch her, holding her arm tightly. His torch indicated a door set in the back wall. Momentarily Zara thought of Ben's description but this was a different place altogether.

There was a clang and a metal door opened to reveal a thin rectangle with rough, once white-washed walls and a sofa wearing a mock tiger skin throw, which hid a large degree of dilapidation. There were pieces of cheap fitted carpet on the floor and a small table with a Calor gas ring on it and a pan. There was a cupboard on one wall which Zara was sure would contain a plate, a cup, a knife, a spoon and a fork. A place someone on the run could hole up in, she thought, or a place you could hide an unwanted person.

'I think we should have a little talk,' said Malloch pushing Zara towards the sofa. He remained standing, switching on an electric light so suddenly Zara was momentarily blinded. Even so, she could not help but smile inwardly at the sheer style of the man: she supposed it was not difficult for a sparky to tap into someone else's wires to get some juice flowing: you just had to know the right people.

She made herself relax. It looked as though it was going to be verbals: she felt she could handle that. Malloch was taking a bag from his shoulder.

'I nearly forgot your tea,' he said producing a box containing a takeaway curry. Zara's taste buds overwhelmed her pride in one second. She gambled on the food being safe: she didn't think poison was Malloch's style. Condemned woman's last breakfast was more like it.

'Don't worry. I'm not being nice. I just happen to know people concentrate better when they're not hungry.' Raising my hopes, thought Zara, so he can dash them again.

'You'll be wanting to know, one, why you're here and two, what's going to happen to you. I'll talk while you eat.' Zara nodded slightly in acquiescence. She thought she might as well play the part of pretending they were both on a level playing field.

'You're here because I don't want there to be any chance of you messing up my plan for Wednesday.' He watched her closely and so noticed she did not express surprise at the word 'Wednesday'. 'So you know already what day and your source has to be either Munchy or Doctor James or maybe Caroline... Yes, Caroline.' This time Zara managed to keep her face expressionless. She had gone into a cold numb place where only her brain operated, not her feelings. If she were going to die, at least she would do so with a clear mind. She knew her feelings would click in if her senses gave her any new information, the sign of any small crack in Malloch's armour, any piece of information which she might use to effect an escape. Malloch was speaking again:

'Wednesday will be a red-letter day for me. I've waited for it for so long. It's not like other things. I know you see me as a business man, out to make money, using people and discarding them and... I am all that.' Zara looked harder at him. She had been expecting a denial. 'Wednesday's different. It's a private matter and unfortunately I'm not able to carry out the plan myself or I would. I have to rely on others.'

'You're not expecting me to help you?' Zara found herself thinking out loud. Malloch laughed.

'You would have been good but no, I didn't even think of you. You turned down my offer of a nice little job in Spain which was pretty kosher by my standards so...'

'…you wouldn't expect me to do something really criminal,' Zara finished for him. He smiled and Zara saw a face completely devoid of feeling. She tried not to let the contempt she felt show in her face.

'Anyway,' he continued, 'my plan will be executed on Wednesday and you will be here so you won't even be able to learn about it on the news. I believe in people getting their come-uppance and if they've done something to me I want them to know how it felt. He paused. You're curious now, aren't you? Let's put it this way, if someone did the worst thing possible to one of your loved ones – those last words sound peculiar coming from Malloch's mouth, thought Zara – would you not want to get revenge?'

'Someone died?' asked Zara.

'Yes. Not rocket science. Someone died. Every day for ten years I have been thinking of this.'

'And you don't mind going for a long spell in the nick if you're found out?'

'But I won't be doing it, will I?' said Malloch. 'What happens will look unplanned. Any connection with me will be coincidental.'
You're madder than I realized, thought Zara with horror.

She put her hands in her pockets in a characteristic gesture and found her notepad. The situation was bizarre enough: if Malloch could do a performance, so could she.

'Two questions,' said Zara, holding her pen poised. 'One, is it your plan to let me go on Wednesday either way or only if you fail?'

'I'm not going to fail.'

'So, in that case you'll leave me here to rot?'

'You can't say I didn't give you a chance.' Zara digested this.

'You mean because I didn't choose Spain, you're leaving me to die underneath Glasgow?'

'Are you sure you're not a chess player? You have a very good brain.'
Zara didn't answer: she was writing down what he said in her
notebook. Malloch started to do up his bag.

'Look, I'll be fair, though I can't think why. I'll let you stay here
instead of locking you out on the platform.'

'And I can start walking to Motherwell or Milngavie or wherever the
line goes or perhaps find a sewerage pipe to crawl along?'

'If you like rats and bats, good luck to you. I wouldn't bother shouting
though. No one will hear you.'

When Zara hear the word 'bats' she shivered and it felt to her as if her
whole body came to a halt. She did not know why she had a bat
phobia but she did and it had been with her as long as she could
remember. Malloch was going out of the door. She didn't want him to
be the last person she ever saw. She shut her eyes tightly and conjured
up Ben and Barney.

'And by the way,' he called over his shoulder. 'It was a photograph.
That's what clinched it. Why I had to act now. Just one photograph.'
She heard his boots on the platform, steady even steps unfaltering in
their progress towards the light. As they faded, she opened her eyes.
She sat still till she was sure he had gone. There had to be some way
out. She closed her eyes again. Silence. Then, as in a nightmare, she
heard the steps again.

Malloch reappeared.

'On second thoughts,' he said,' I think I will tie you up again. You're
just a bit too clever for my own good. Sorry about this. I don't
suppose I'll ever become a gentleman now.' He had been leaning
against the door, some feet from her, so she was unprepared for his
sudden lunge forward. He seized her wrists, forced her arms behind
her and slipped a loop over her hands, pulling the knot tight with one
deft jerk. He took a roll of tape from his pocket.

'Mm? Necessary? I don't know. Make assurance double sure as my
old man used to say.' He wound what seemed to Zara an inordinate
amount of tape round her mouth. 'And now for the cupboard. It's a

239

nice thin cupboard so you won't fall over' and though she kicked out hard he lifted her easily and pushed her into a cupboard built against the back wall. 'Stop struggling or I'll have to knock you out.' Zara stopped. She knew she must choose her battles. She had no chance against him. He not only looked strong, he was overpowering, and his actions ignited her anger: she could not wait for him to leave. First she heard a key turn on the cupboard door, then one door after another slammed and locked as Malloch made his final exit.

***

When he'd gone, Zara spent for a whole five minutes in a kind of trance. Then wave after wave of fear enveloped her and she began to shake. She saw all the people that mattered to her in her mind's eye and wondered what they would do when they found out she'd died in such a weird way. What would they think? Her mother, Barney, Ben, Des, Katerina. She pictured Ben and Barney: Barney must have raised the alarm by now. Would he have told Ben she was missing? If so, Ben would be saying, Aunty Zara will find a way to escape, won't she? What would Barney say? She sat mesmerized.

Then, suddenly, she saw her father, not lying on the railway track but in a field on the other side of their old house, standing under the trees in the place she always imagined him when she thought about him alive. He was smiling at her and she read his thought:

'We can't have two members of the family dying by the railway. Come on now, Zara. Use your loaf.' She knew he hadn't spoken; it wasn't his ghost she saw but even so the words triggered her into action. She was determined not to die.

But first she had to get out of the cupboard. Thank god he hadn't tied her feet. She had a sneaking feeling that it was because some part of him admired her and wanted to give her an even chance. Or maybe he just knew there was no way of escape and in leaving her feet untied he was taunting her with a false hope?

With her first kick she banged her knee as she brought her foot back. Thin cupboard: that's what the man had said. If she had use of her hands... if she could see... The dark was almost total and there was a musty smell which she found increasingly unpleasant. She was sweating with fear. He *had* left her to die. How much oxygen was there? How long could she last? Panic rose through her body and she tried in vain to open her mouth to scream. But again her father's voice came to her: 'Don't give up yet. How do you know you can't get out of the cupboard?'

Zara made herself still and breathed evenly for a minute or two. When she re-focused, she realized that there was more light than she had thought. She was wearing boots and she began battering as hard as she could at the bottom of the door where there was a crack of grey in all the blackness. She kicked rhythmically and then rested. Don't think: just keep doing it, she said to herself.

However, after what felt like about ten minutes, but which was in fact six, she felt she had made no progress. She stopped and leant against the back of the cupboard. She could feel her fear beginning to overwhelm her again and she started kicking furiously to counteract it. There was a sudden splintering noise and a small piece at the bottom of the door broke off. A bar of light. For a second Zara felt hope but this was still no way out. She kicked at the opening viciously, her foot caught in the gap and she felt the cupboard tip and then topple over onto the floor.

She lay for a long moment wondering if she were alive or dead. She had closed her eyes as she fell but now opened them cautiously. Something was different. She was still in the cupboard but she could see. Where was the light coming from? She looked behind her then and realized the top of the cupboard had fallen off in the crash. She could crawl out.

She sat on the sofa recovering, well aware she had only overcome the first obstacle. She still had tied hands and tape round her mouth and she was still in a tunnel with no known exit. She fell into a silent study, unable to think and momentarily dozed off.

A most extraordinary noise woke her. At first she thought it was rats, then she thought she was dreaming, but listening intently she decided it was a human sound, suppressed possibly, but definitely homo sapiens. There was only one other door. It had a crude bolt which she managed to push back with her fingers. Doctor Andrew fell out of what she saw to be an ancient lavatory. Unfortunately his hands and feet were tied. His eyes smiled thanks. His mouth was taped like hers.

'Try to untie my arms,' Zara said. Doctor Andrew could not have understood her words but knew what had to be done. By feel alone his fingers grappled with the unseen knots. Zara waited patiently. Nothing happened. She indicated that they should swap round. Her fingers were smaller and defter but it still took her a good ten minutes before she could work the rope that bound him loose. He struggled then with the tape round his mouth before getting to work on Zara's rope.

'How good to see you,' Zara cried hugging him before untying his legs. They laughed as if it was some bizarre party game. 'I've never ever been so pleased to see anyone,' said Zara.

'When I heard people come in I tried to make a noise but I couldn't. I listened to the conversation and realized it was you and Malloch. I was really confused when you started the banging because I thought Malloch had left but it was such a racket I thought some dreadful fight was going on. And it was just you kicking your way out of a cupboard. I might have known!' Their stories did not take much telling. They had both been kidnapped by Munchy and Screw.

'We must decide on a plan,' said Zara sobering up.

'You think there is something we can do?'

'Has to be,' Zara replied. 'Don't you think we should try to find a way along the tunnel?' She held up her hand and shook it, partly because now she could. 'I'm going to have to think first. We don't know what Malloch's planning for *us*. All we know about his own plan is that it's on Wednesday and there is a bus-stop involved and your brother of course. I want to go through everything I know and see if I can get any closer to an answer. Why don't you have a think too? Make a list of everything you think is relevant: everything your brother ever said about Malloch and his plan, and then we'll put it all together and see if we can make any better sense of it. We've probably got all night.'

Zara took Charlie Steading's envelope from her pocket and started looking for points of connection. Hit and run, she kept thinking. I know it ties in somehow… She became focused. If it was the last thing she did, she would try to work out how Malloch and Billy Gardner interwove. She began underlining the things in the papers before her that seemed significant. Then she wrote down everything she knew about Malloch which only took up a couple of lines. She sat and stared at it all for a long time.

There was something about the number ten that kept cropping up. The fire in the McKelvie Buildings was ten years ago. Malloch had had his plan in mind for ten years. Malloch's daughter was ten when… Zara's heart stopped as she looked again at the casual words she had written down, the words Des had thrown at her when she'd begged him for information: Malloch was bad before but infinitely worse since his daughter was killed by a hit-and-run driver ten years ago. She drew the newspaper article towards her and read. So it was Billy Gardner who had walked free. That meant whatever Malloch had planned was some sort of revenge for what had happened.

To Zara it was perfectly clear: Malloch was going to exact the price. Billy's Rose was going to die: as Malloch's daughter had done and at exactly the same age. Lots of thoughts crowded in. The bus stop, how did that fit? What was Doctor James's part? Was Rose to be at the bus stop? Which bus stop? If Doctor James was just meant to *talk* to Rose, how was she to get killed? Who else was involved? Screw? Munchy?

And Billy Gardner, he obviously had no idea about this. She wondered if, since he had been charged and gone through due process of law he now considered the matter as part of a regrettable past. Zara thought hard. Billy Gardner had wanted to keep control of the McKelvie fire photos. Why was this? Was he afraid any photo going public might be seen as a message to Malloch. If Billy felt his evidence could be used against Malloch… Maybe it was the only card he had to play. What had Malloch said? – 'It was the photo that did it.' But it seemed that far from stopping the man, Billy Gardner had kick-started his enemy's revenge programme. Zara felt cold inside but she forced herself to think of the details.

Why, thought Zara, had Billy Gardner sent his photo now? Maybe he had become fed up with living under a threat and decided to go for broke. Was it just a coincidence that he'd made his move just after his daughter's tenth birthday? What had stopped him before? Fear. Or perhaps the feeling of guilt – Malloch had lost his daughter after all – and a wish to let things rest.

Whatever was happening, was happening on Wednesday, beginning, she surmised, as Rose waited for her school bus. It was now moving fast towards Tuesday. She didn't have much more than twenty four hours to get out, find out which school Rose went to, which bus stop would be hers, what time she would be there.

Zara and the doctor looked up at the same moment.

'Right,' said Zara, 'I'll give you what I've got' and she laid out the connections between Billy Gardner and Malloch and how the past was now catching up with the present. She finished with the sketchy information concerning the as yet unknown bus-stop.

By the time she had stopped speaking, Doctor Andrew's face had become several shades paler.

'I have one thing to add,' he said in a low voice. Zara felt he was incapable of speaking any louder. 'I think I am here by mistake. I think they meant to get my brother.'

'Ah!' cried Zara. 'Of course.' What is wrong with my brain that I did not realize that, she thought fleetingly. 'If they have you safe, then you cannot renege on the deal. Unfortunately for them, their plan is still unsafe since you are Andrew and not James. Though I don't see James pulling out,' she added. They were both quiet for a moment.

'As I see it,' said Zara eventually,' we have only one option. We need to get out of here to alert people. We have to escape along the tunnel'. Although her voice was steady, she felt fear rise through her as she thought of the darkness, the impossibility of seeing bats, only knowing their presence if they brushed into her.

'Can we?' There was both doubt and hope in Doctor Andrew's face.

'There has to be a way out,' said Zara, forcing her panic down.

'We can try,' said the doctor. 'Better than sitting here anyway.' He smiled but he did not appear reassuring.

'Okay. What have we got? Do you have any food with you, comrade?' Action: she needed to meet her fear head on. She stood up and taking her water bottle from her pocket she filled it from the tap which was miraculously still connected to the water supply. 'Now, all we need is a bit of wire and we're out of here.'

***

Des had not been in the office when Barney phoned but someone said they were expecting him shortly and they would get him to phone back. It was Karen who'd answered. She seemed to recognize Zara's name and understand the situation.

'I would have rung my local station,' Barney had said, but in view of what has already happened...' Karen had agreed with him and said she would put a call out anyway with a description. Thank god she always wears red and black, thought Barney and then remembered seeing her in green only the previous day.

It was impossible not to tell Ben. Barney was so jumpy and Ben was so good at adding two and two together. In the end Barney sat down and told Ben what he feared. Ben listened wide-eyed but outwardly calm.

'Aunty Zara will try to escape,' he said. 'You know her. She won't let a locked door stand in her way.' Barney nodded not wishing to deny the boy hope. Ben went silent for a minute and then he said, 'Do you think it was the people who mugged her?'

Barney sighed. 'I think there's probably a connection between them and the man that's behind all this.'

'You mean Ivory's story?'

'That and a big fire in McKelvie Buildings and now there's a link to a man called Billy Gardner.'

'I see,' said Ben although he couldn't have. 'And Aunty Zara was trying to find out what happened and so they removed her?'

'Something like that.'

'What will they do to her?' his voice faltered as he tried to stay calm. He knew if he didn't Barney wouldn't talk to him about it anymore.

'I don't know, Ben.'

'Then we have to find her. We must think very hard where she might be and go and look for her.'

'I've told the police and left a message for DI Des, the officer you met and he'll be looking for her.'

'Good,' said Ben, 'but I shall still look for her myself.'

Barney hadn't the will or the strength to argue. 'Well how about you go to bed now and sleep on it and in the morning you might have a brilliant idea we could pass on to DI Des?'

Ben slid off the sofa and went towards the bathroom to brush his teeth. 'She'll be in a tunnel,' he said. 'Definitely, because the bad man likes tunnels.'

'Good thinking,' said Barney, but which tunnel or at the bottom of which mine shaft or sewer, he mused to himself, in the whole of Glasgow, how was one to know?

Chapter XXIV Darkness gives way to light

Zara's only problem once she turned her attention to escape was 'rats and bats'. Mostly bats. She had visions of brushing through curtains of fur as the creatures hung on the curving roof of the tunnel or as they flew in their erratic-seeming way, wheeling and diving – and squeaking. I must think about a plan, she thought, and push the bats out. They may all be asleep just now or on their holidays down the line at Loch Lomond.

Doctor Andrew patted his pockets and brought out half a bar of chocolate and some wine gums. Zara had her torch and matches. As an afterthought she took the tiger throw. She realized she was banking on the tunnel not being blocked but perhaps Malloch had known the tunnel *was* blocked and that was why he had no fears about her escaping. She had heard at least three bolts drawn when he left, together with an echo-y sound of turning keys and since all this activity would have to have been on the outside of the door... Still, she decided to check: there was no point feeling their way down tunnels in the dark if they could reach the outside close at hand. However, a quick exploration of the door on the platform through which Malloch had presumably disappeared, showed up neither crack nor handle and Zara's torch revealed that the actual line was completely bricked up.

It was twenty-one hundred hours. They started walking leftwards along the platform, soon coming to the slope which led onto the line. Zara was using the torch part of her mobile intermittently but now she switched on her pocket torch to survey what they were entering into.

The tunnel was dark, with water dripping down one of the side walls, leaving a puddle where the tracks had been. She swung the torch round: the brickwork was unbroken and it stretched away into the blackness. The fact that it stretched away gave Zara hope. She stepped down onto the track and started walking cautiously forward, murmuring to herself, 'Bats on holiday, bats on holiday...' Doctor Andrew fell in behind.

'I should tell you,' she said as conversationally as she could make it, 'that I have a bat phobia'.

'I'm afraid of the dark,' the doctor replied and they both burst out laughing.

'You'd better have the torch then,' said Zara, 'and go ahead'. In the event they soon found themselves stumbling along side by side, holding on to each other as a safety measure against falling.

It was slow going as sometimes water lay in small pools, holes made by erosion, holes in which either of them might turn an ankle. At first Zara was just glad that the tunnel continued and she soon became used to the darkness around her, though she was on edge for rustlings and brushings from small creatures she increasingly preferred not to name. After an hour, which seemed like three, she was exhausted. She felt they had perhaps gone a mile. How long these tunnels are, she thought, but if she flagged she saw her dad in the field and a picture of an unknown bus stop with a ten year old girl standing at it. She and Andrew did not speak much except to caution one another.

Then after a slight bend, Zara was aware of a more open feeling around her. A flick of the torch revealed what seemed to be a junction, two tunnels going off at angles. Although this was something new and different, Zara's heart sank: how were they to choose?

Zara walked a little way along one of the tunnels and found a space let into the wall where men could stand if a train went by. It felt relatively dry. She shouted to the doctor. She folded the tiger throw and they sat down on it. She pulled out her bag of food and offered her companion half a filled chapatti.

'Hey, Andrew, this is our second picnic!'

'I am sad it takes this situation before you can call me Andrew.' She could not see his face but felt his voice was smiling.

Zara realized she had fallen asleep when Andrew's voice suddenly startled her.

'Zara,' Andrew was saying, 'can you talk to me? I am afraid of this dark. I think of my country. I used to have nightmares about chameleons. My father would tell stories about them turning into monsters as if they weren't sufficiently frightening just being chameleons'. Zara felt her eyes begin to close. 'He had a whole lot of stories but when he told them he had to wear his kepi.' Zara was wide awake.

'I know that your father was in the French Foreign Legion and that's how he met Joe Malloch.'

'That's right,' said James. 'My father is dead now so I can't check anything but when we first came to the UK, my mother gave us Malloch's name and address. I mentioned before, I think, that they knew each other but they had actually been friends and when my father died, Malloch went to Egypt and spoke to my mother. I am telling you this with hindsight. In those days he was not called Malloch. The stories we heard as children were about a guy called Robinson. When we came to England, James got in touch with his father's friend, now Malloch. I did not. Not for any special reason. I just didn't see the need. Zara was thinking out loud:

'So it was easy for Malloch to ask favours of James?' The doctor nodded. 'And would there be any other connections with the past? Any more kepi wearers?'

'I do not know, Zara.'

'Munchy's father? But you don't know Munchy. And Bobby Gardner? Ring any bells?'

'No, Zara. I only have my kepi stories. I could tell you one and you could see if there was any relevance.'

Andrew was so quiet Zara began to wonder if he had fallen asleep. She felt for his arm to attract his attention. He jumped.

'Tell me a story then,' said Zara, 'about your dad and Malloch or Robinson as he was then'.

'The most dramatic story is of course the one about the lion.' Zara raised her eyebrows which Andrew couldn't see but he detected a minute hesitation before her,

'Right.'

'Yes, I also used to listen with a pinch of salt.' There was a pause while Andrew seemed to collect his thoughts then,

'They had been sent out to reconnoitre the territory beyond the camp. Don't ask me which country. I think my father used to change the location of the story every time he told it. So, they had achieved their mission in good time and on the way back, my father lingered, inspecting an insect in the sand. He crouched there, intent, as the creature carried a piece of vegetation several times its size to a small hole. Robinson had gone ahead but now he turned, wondering why my father wasn't behind him.

'There was a lion focusing as hard on my father as he was on the insect. Robinson fired his gun. Father always said he felt as if the bullet had gone straight through him but of course it hadn't and, I'm pleased to say it hadn't gone through the lion either. By the time my father recovered sufficiently to look, the lion was nowhere to be seen. At first he laughed thinking the whole thing was a joke on Robinson's part but then he saw the footprints – ten feet from where he'd been crouching. This experience confirmed their friendship and Robinson always saw himself in the role of protector.'

'This puts Malloch in a very positive light,' said Zara. 'I like to hear that people weren't always bad.'

'The other story is similarly positive but has a decidedly negative aspect.'

'Go on,' said Zara.

'This time they are on leave, in the Mediterranean.'

'Who are they?' asked Zara.

'My father...' Zara felt Andrew move his legs as if he were uncomfortable '... Robinson, a man known as Sam and another man called Johnny-B who was always taking photographs, even when forbidden.'

'Ah,' said Zara.

'This story is not told by my father.' He sighed before continuing. So, they were on leave and they set off in a boat, purloined… I think that is a word one might use in that situation.'

'Okay,' said Zara. 'A good word, if appropriate.'

'A storm blew up on the lake. It was night. The boat overturned. They managed to right it but my father and Sam could not get on board again. Johnny B was back in the boat holding onto my father and Robinson was holding onto Sam. They held on for an hour but Robinson could see Johnny B's grip on my father was weakening. His hand had gone numb and in the end he had no control over his muscles. Robinson could do nothing unless he let go of Sam.'

Zara let the ensuing silence last. Although she knew Andrew's father had died many years ago she could still feel the son's sorrow. Eventually Andrew resumed speaking:

'The storm abated almost immediately. The three survivors reached land and returned the boat to its moorings. The story was going to be that my father had gone for a swim and been swept out when the storm came but then his body washed up quite soon and at the post mortem pressure marks were detected on his body were he had been held up.

Johnny B couldn't take any more. He confessed not only his part but that of all the others. They were severely punished and for some reason Robinson never forgave Johnny B. He actually went around saying he'd done it on purpose because he was jealous of the friendship between my father and himself. He came to Egypt to tell my mother the story. Also that subsequently he had taken revenge. He had been witness to an incident between Johnny B and another soldier and he spoke against Johnny B and even produced false evidence.'

'What did your mother make of Robinson?'

'She was in two minds. He quite clearly had been very fond of my father and he had come to Egypt seemingly out of respect for him.'

'And she saw fit to give you his address?' Andrew grunted an affirmative and then said,

'Johnny B was locked up.'

'I begin to see,' said Zara.'

'You do?' Andrew sounded surprised.

'I'll explain to you sometime but just now I have to sleep. It all ties up though; a photograph; the boating incident and the bus-stop. It's all part of the same story. Thank you, Andrew, for finishing the jigsaw for me.'

'Will it make any difference though?' asked Andrew. 'I would be so happy if I could help to make things right.'

'Tomorrow we'll see,' said Zara.

***

Unknown to the two escapees, two people visited the thin rectangular room in the tunnel. They were both annoyed. It was six in the morning and they didn't think work started that early.

'Jesus Christ, they're not here,' said Munchy, who was first in the door.

'Don't be a fucking idiot,' said Screw pushing him out of the way but when he had checked the lavatory he shook his head and had to agree.

Munchy sat down on the sofa and pulled open a bag containing two bacon rolls. He handed one to Screw.

'If they're not here, they won't want their breakfast,' he said in a matter of fact voice.

'I thought she'd been tied up. I tied the doctor to the lavatory myself,' said Screw scowling.

'Well you need to go back to knot school,' said Munchy. 'They're not here or are you blind as well?'

''She may be lying dying on the track. She must have fallen off the platform in the dark.'

'Fat lot you care,' said Munchy. 'Anyway the doctor would be able to mend her.'

'You'll need to put on your x-ray eyes and go and look,' said Screw scrutinizing the sofa to see if it was clean enough for him to sit on.

'Piss off,' said Munchy. 'I'm not risking my neck down there with the rats. I was told to deliver breakfast. That's all. I'm not a bloodhound' Screw could see there was no forcing Munchy and since he was not prepared to go himself, they sat on underground until such time as they could decently leave and report back that the prisoners had very much enjoyed their breakfast.

***

Zara awoke about six-thirty but of course it was just as dark as before. She was beginning to feel blind; with the torch off it was equally black whether her eyes were open or shut. She and the doctor shared what food remained. They still had some chocolate left and half a bottle of water.

They decided to continue down the tunnel they were in as there was no way of judging which would be the better option. The dull noise of traffic seemed more prominent now. Morning time beginning Zara wondered, or was it that they were nearer the surface. She had been aware of sometimes going up and sometimes down and of bends to the left and right but since she had no idea where they had been when they set off, this information was no use to them.

After an hour, Zara began to feel exhausted, physically but also emotionally.

'Let's stop for a bit,' she said, although it was difficult to feel comfortable stopping in the dark. They were trying to conserve the torch battery. Zara was walking beside the tunnel wall, touching it to guide them as they went along. Now she leant against it and took a swig of water. Andrew silently divided the last of the chocolate. Zara sighed.

'My legs will give out soon,' she said, 'and I'd give anything to see daylight. Turn on the torch for a moment will you or I'll go mad'.

Suddenly there was a great whooshing in the blackness as if a wind had arisen. Zara shrank back against the side of the tunnel as things flew past her. She screamed loudly and put her arms over her head and face but she could still hear noises. Something brushed her arm and she froze so rigidly she could not believe she would ever move again. Andrew had his arms around her.

'Please, Zara. You are safe,' he said.

Gradually she came back. Everything was quiet. She dared to open her eyes. Andrew gave her the torch as a comfort. Cautiously she switched it on, curious, shielding the beam with her hands. Did the presence of so many bats mean there was something different up ahead? Nothing. She could see nothing. She shone the torch round: just tunnel. But then she caught sight of one solitary bat. It flew past her in haste. Catching up with its mates she thought. It appeared to be flying off to the side.

They both walked forward. Zara was trying to gauge the distance to where the bat seemed to have turned left and after about ten yards it appeared again and then disappeared into the darkness. Zara flinched as her torchlight picked it up. Then they came to a side tunnel. Four or five yards in she saw it stopped: it was not a tunnel, it was a chimney. There was a small irregular lighter shape on the floor.

Looking up they saw, perhaps fifty feet above, that the source of the light was coming through a cover which had been partly dislodged. It was still so early the sides of the chimney were dark but with the aid of the torch they could make out excrescences of moss covering the stonework. Andrew was looking upwards.

'Rungs Zara. My god there are rungs cemented in to the walls! Zara stood unbelieving: could it be that all they had to do was to climb up and out? They laughed but quite hysterically.

They decided Zara should go first and Andrew should wait in case she fell. They could not know whether the rungs would hold. There was a good eighteen inches between each. Zara pulled on the first one to test it and slowly began her ascent.

**

Ben woke at six and remembered at once that Zara was missing. He jumped out of bed and went to make a cup of tea for Barney who was still asleep.

'You've got to wake up,' he said shaking his father's shoulder. Come on. I think I'm having a bright idea. We've got to go and find Aunty Zara.' Although Barney had only been asleep a couple of hours, he sat up and drank his tea and then hauled himself out of bed. No harm in taking Ness for an early morning walk and letting Ben think he was helping.

But Ben had other ideas.

'Dad,' he said, pushing the plate of toast he'd made towards him, 'I'm sure she'll be in a tunnel and since I only know two tunnels, I think we should start with them.'

They were the only people in the park and quickly reached the point below Gibson Street where Ben had caught his first – and last – glimpse of Malloch. They approached together and with caution. Barney did not really believe that Zara or indeed anyone else would be there and Ben was not daunted when they found no one. He had read too many adventure stories to imagine that you found people in the first place you looked.

They came back to Great Western Road where they met Spike who thought Ben's idea was a good one. He said he would follow them at his own pace. Ben wanted to go to the Botanic Gardens where he had been with his class. They'd only been able to look over the railings but he remembered that, further in than they had been allowed to go there had been a padlocked metal door.

As they were beginning to approach the old station, Ness suddenly shot off and started barking at the only other dog in sight. Barney hurried after her, embarrassed. Ben started to run.

However, just as he came within thirty yards of the railings, he saw two men. He hid quickly in a bush. He was sure one of the men was Munchy. Munchy was the person Aunty Zara had been with when she was mugged. Ben had been with Zara once when they had met Spike and Munchy in the park. He craned his head towards the two men, hoping they would say something useful.

'How are we going to explain it, that they were there but they aren't there now,' Munchy was saying and then the other man said,

'Well, we don't need to tell the Boss that. It will just mean more work. If she could escape, she could have done it after we'd been there and if she hasn't...'

'Ben!' Now Barney was shouting his name. He stood still in the middle of the bush. Then he heard another voice, female this time, saying,

'Don't worry, he can't be far away.' But his father's voice was becoming agitated so Ben stepped out, right into Munchy's path.

'Hello,' said Munchy. 'Up early aren't we?'

'Taking the dog out before school,' said Ben in a neutral voice which didn't sound as if it belonged to him. Munchy looked round for the dog and seeing it, seemed satisfied. Ben didn't know if he knew that Zara was his pretend aunt.

Barney was standing with Ness and the woman who had the dog Ness had run after. Ben walked up to them and interrupted them with a stage whisper.

'Those two men were talking about Aunty Zara. She was in that station but they say she's not there now. One of them said...' Barney moved away. He didn't want the woman to think they were mad. 'She was in that tunnel,' said Ben fiercely. Barney wanted to believe him but it seemed too easy.

'I'll phone Katerina,' he said to placate the boy, 'as soon as we get back. She knows about tunnels under Glasgow. We can ask her if Zara could get out if she started from here'.

'There were two people.'

'I know that,' said Barney. 'You said. They were having a conversation.'

'No, dad, I mean the two men were talking about two people. Only one of them was Aunty Zara.'

'How do you know it was Aunty Zara?'

'I just know,' said Ben. 'Being ten doesn't mean you don't know things when you know them.' Barney could not think of an answer to that one.

'Well, let's go home and phone Katerina. I don't have her number here.'

'I think you should phone DI Des.'

'You're right,' conceded Barney.

'If there was a way out, she would find it,' said Ben.

'I hope there's no bats,' said Barney.

'The bats will have to be hanging up asleep,' said Ben fiercely. 'Aunty Zara will fight her way through them whatever. She will,' he added when Barney did not reply.

***

Zara climbed a couple of steps and rested. She hadn't taken into consideration she would be affected by the height and the twilight atmosphere, damp, dripping, slippery, unholy greens, plants clinging as if in desperation to the vertical sides. It was eerily quiet, like, she imagined, the inside of a grave. She was climbing towards the light but what if, when she reached the top she could not shift the cover? She put the thought out of her mind.

She had been counting the rungs, twenty-one, twenty-two. The ground because it was now just a small circle beneath her, looked minute and far away. Even Andrew looked small. She knew he was shouting encouragement to her but the shape of the chimney distorted his voice. Still it was good not to be alone. She had to haul herself up each step and it was really important to make sure each rung could take her weight. She had to reach up and pull hard on the one above her head to consider its strength.

Twenty-five –

'Look out!' the whole rung came away in her hand and she had to twist her body quickly to avoid the rusty metal as it went clanging down below her. She hardly dare look down. There was no sound, reassuring or otherwise. Andrew could have been hit on the head. She hoped he had not been looking up. Zara swayed on her rung. This moment was worse even than the bats. She looked again and made herself concentrate her focus. She could now make out Andrew's body and see his upturned face but he wasn't moving. He seemed to be slumped against one side of the chimney wall.

'Are you all right down there,' Zara yelled but there was no reply and when she looked up, she saw there were no more rungs at all between her and the top.

***

Joe Malloch knew that Screw and Munchy had the wrong man because he had spoken to Doctor James himself. It had been his way of checking if James was captive, as Munchy and Screw had not been keeping contact properly. And he knew they were habitual liars.

The reason for the kidnap attempt had been because the doctor had not been answering his mobile. Malloch had been afraid, as Zara and Andrew had guessed, that the man was trying to do a disappearing act. However, at last he had made contact but only because someone else – Caroline – had answered James's phone and he had botched not being there. When he realized what had happened, Malloch did not let on that he knew that Doctor Andrew had been kidnapped by mistake.

It took all Malloch's patience not to explode. He talked James through the Wednesday mission yet again and promised him, yet again that all his debts would be written off. It would have to do, he decided, closing the call. He felt reasonably confident that James was still on side.

Next he located Screw and Munchy. They were skulking but he knew where because he made it his business to know everything. He was interested to know whether the two men would admit their mistake. They were under the bridge at Belmont Street. It annoyed Malloch that he had to run round after people. Charlie Steading had taken some of the load off him hitherto but he couldn't, he realized now, have engaged Charlie for this. It was all too big to mess up, he thought as he slipped on one of the steps leading from the road to the river.

'So gentlemen, everything okay?' He registered the speed with which their faces went from worried to blank.

'Anyway you can let the good doctor go,' said Malloch, watching their faces.

'Course Boss,' said Munchy immediately. Screw attempted to look disdainful.

'What about the girl?' said Munchy. Too quickly thought Malloch. He's uneasy.

'You can leave the girl there,' he said. 'Take her another meal but don't tell her it's the last.' He pulled out a tenner. Then he seemed to alter his mind and took out another five. 'Buy yourselves a packet of crisps each and a can of coke.' He made himself appear to soften a bit. 'Doctor all ready for his Wednesday duties then?'

'What duties?' asked Munchy. Screw just looked angry. Malloch chuckled. 'Nothing you need know about yet, Munchy. Don't worry. You're doing good work. Your father would have been proud of you.' Screw looked out over the river and ground his teeth.

***

Zara knew she had to stay calm to keep her balance. Surely she had not come this far to fail. She couldn't just let go: there was Andrew to think of at the bottom of the chimney, dead or alive. She counted to fifty slowly: she didn't think she had time to count further. Then she made herself go over both her resources and the exact nature of her physical environment.

Zara had had the presence of mind to go down a step so that she still had something for her hands to hold and the first thing she noticed was that she had been wrong about the rungs: they did exist but they had been sawn off roughly so there were short bits of metal still sticking out from the wall. Also, for some reason they were nearer fifteen inches apart than eighteen. Even so, she reckoned she needed at least four inches to grasp or put her foot on. And one piece wouldn't do: she had to be able to plot an upward progression before she left the comparative safety of the rung she was on. A wave of dizziness swept over her. Hold on she thought. You haven't explored all the avenues yet.

Zara guessed she was about twenty feet from the top. The lid had been displaced by around four inches. If only she could get a bit closer she felt there might be a point in shouting but there was traffic noise and she thought anyone say, walking their dog, would assume they were imagining things if they heard something that sounded like a voice.

She rested her hand on the side of the chimney and was aware of a slight hollow. She scrabbled at it and loose vegetation and gravel fell out. She continued, not daring to hope but a cavity was appearing and Zara realized it was not there by accident. Gingerly she stretched up another fifteen inches: it was the same pattern: she could see the same-shaped stone had been used. They were steps. Perhaps they had pre-dated the rungs.

She stopped to recover her breath. It was hard work digging out and holding on at the same time. Every so often she shouted down to Andrew. If he were conscious but unable to speak at least it would let him know he was not forgotten. She took a swig from her water-bottle and as she put it back in her pocket she felt the edge of her box of matches. Smoke signal she thought at once. But would it rise in this cold air? Maybe it wouldn't go down but would it go up?

It was still early morning: who would be out there to see it anyway? She could tell she was near a road but what road? What was above her – waste ground, houses, a park? But her spirits lifted a little. She had a sort of plan. She could shout, she could throw gravel at the lid and she could send up smoke. Surely with three different signals, she might get lucky.

***

When Barney and Ben reached the house, Barney immediately phoned Katerina who promised to come straight round. As he replaced the receiver, the phone rang. It was Des returning Barney's call. Barney felt Des's reaction was gloomy. Not much to go on, was his first thought. He reiterated all Barney's doubts. Was it really Zara they were talking about? If so who was the other man? All they knew for certain was that no one was in the Botanic Gardens tunnel now.

'I don't have the resources to search all the tunnels under Glasgow on a whim,' said Des. Barney knew he was serious. 'I want to find Zara as much as you do,' Des went on, 'but I think the best bet is to find Munchy and Screw. Even Malloch, though…' Barney grunted. He knew that finding Malloch was a life mission. 'I'll get on to it. Get back to me if you have anything new.'

Ben looked at his father who was trying his best not to look hopeless. Ben took a deep breath: he was about to lie, something he very rarely did:

'Dad, I think you're right. We don't know where to look for Aunty Zara. I'd better go to school. Just let me know at once though when she's found.' Barney was too distracted to think it through. 'If I go now, I'll meet Damon and Ewan. They pass the door at exactly the same time every morning,' Ben added. There were no big roads to cross and there were lollipop ladies all the way anyway. Barney let him go.

Ben ran down the stairs, out and down the road before Barney could change his mind. The school would ring up but by then Ben would be back in the Botanics looking for Zara.

***

Zara had to use most of her energy to focus. She could not afford even to think about falling. She managed to get her feet into the next cavity. Now she had hold of a metal stump about four inches long and was preparing to go up a step. Then she would have to excavate again. Although she was now only twelve feet from the top, each excavation became harder.

When she was ten feet from the top she felt she could do no more. At the last step she had nearly lost her footing. She tried to shut out the vision of falling on top of the doctor but closing her eyes made her feel even more disoriented.

'Plan X,' she muttered to herself: voice, gravel, matches. At that moment she heard a vehicle detach itself from the general roar. It seemed to come nearer. She could hear wheels turning and brakes being applied. Hastily she gathered some gravel to throw. A stone through the gap would be miraculous but she wasn't hoping for miracles. She was waiting for silence, hoping the men, whoever they were, would have some business in the vicinity which would keep them long enough for her to be able to attract their attention.

A gap, then voices.

'Is it two hundred or three hundred we have to plant?' I'm in a park, thought Zara with a flood of relief. A bang. A tail-gate dropping. Now bags being shifted. They must be working here or they wouldn't be unloading. Maybe, thought Zara, they'll stop for a moment when they've taken everything they need off the truck.

Suddenly there was relative silence and Zara almost fell she was so eager to take advantage of it.

'Help!' she shouted. 'Help!' No response. She threw gravel. Nothing. Possibly the sound wouldn't even register on the other side of the lid. Zara held on to the metal spike above her with her left hand and gathered some dead stems from the crevices in the chimney walls. She hoped they would be dry enough to catch alight but damp enough to smoke. She had unzipped her jacket and was depositing them against her chest. She took a scrumpled piece of paper out of her pocket. She needed to light the paper first to give her time to retrieve the stems. The paper would burn longer than matches.

With one end in her mouth, she twisted the paper into a spill. Then she manoeuvred it between her fourth and fifth fingers and took out the matches. Don't drop the matches. Whatever you do, don't drop the matches, she muttered over and over. Concentrating hard, she opened the matchbox and extracted a match. She placed the box in her mouth and struck. Her left hand was aching. She struck again and managed to light her spill. Holding it in her mouth she replaced the matches in her pocket and dug out the dry stems.

This is ridiculous, she thought. But the stems were catching. Please let them last long enough she whispered to herself. She turned the smoking bundle as best she could and held it up high reaching towards the slim hole: if the smoke could escape, maybe she could.

'Help!' she shouted again.

'Did you hear that?'

'Did I hear what?'

'Someone shouting...'

'Where?' Zara couldn't believe it.

'Move the lid. I'm in the chimney,' she yelled. 'Hurry! I can't hold on much longer.'

'Hey Jimmy, there's smoke coming out of the ground over there and... a stone!'

'Maybe it's an earthquake.' The other voice was sarcastic but it didn't matter because Zara could hear feet running towards her.

'There's a lid. Get the shovel.' There was the sound of metal engaging with metal and all at once there was more light. A head appeared.

'I can't see anything.' Another head appeared.

'You must be blind. There's a woman there. Hang on hen. We've got a rope in the back.'

***

When Ben reached the Botanic Gardens, he decided to walk over them inch by inch. He was quite convinced Zara would be there somewhere. I might be walking on top of her, he thought but I'm sure she'll find her way out. He walked slowly backwards and forwards over the grass being careful not to miss shrubberies and places where it was difficult to maintain a straight line. He saw the two men with the truck and was about to avoid them when he saw them stop and

263

look round. Then one pointed at the ground and they began to run. Ben began to run too.

'Stand back son,' said the man with the rope and Ben watched as the man made a slip knot in the rope and lowered it into the chimney.

'Is it Aunty Zara?' Ben asked but the men were focusing on the task in hand:

'Have you got it?' Jimmy was saying. Can you put it under your armpits? You're not injured?' Ben couldn't hear an answer but surely it had to be Zara.

Then the men heaved. Fortunately they were extremely burly. Ben heard them telling Zara to use her feet against the wall if she could, so she wasn't a dead weight. Then Jimmy grasped an arm. It was Zara's arm. He ran forward. Both men had her now and now she was on the grass.

'Ambulance,' said Jimmy staggering to his feet. The other man sat panting. Ben and Zara looked at each other.

'Ben! Ben!' cried Zara. Oh the sight of you!' Ben hugged her tight but then after a moment, he felt her body begin to go limp.

'Doctor Andrew,' she mumbled in his ear. 'Still at the bottom. Injury…' Then she fainted. Jimmy put her in the recovery position with his jacket over her.

'Do you really know her?' he asked Ben.

'She's called Zara MacDonald and…' Jimmy retrieved Zara's mobile from her pocket.

'Lots of missed calls from Barney.'

'That's my dad. Ring him. Tell him Ben's with her.' Jimmy sighed and shook his head but did what Ben suggested. Ben turned to the other man.

'There's another person down there,' he said. The man looked as if he had had enough surprises for one day.

'Are you sure?'

'Aunty Zara said so before she fainted. He's injured.' The two men looked into the chimney again and then looked at Ben intently.

'If there is someone down there we'll need the fire brigade. You are absolutely sure about this?'

'Of course I'm sure,' said Ben springing to his feet and running to the chimney before they could stop him.

'Doctor Andrew? Are you all right?' There was no answer. 'Doctor Andrew?' Ben's voice became distressed. The two men were shaking their heads when a faint sound reached them. 'Hold on,' shouted Ben. 'We're getting the fire brigade.'

***

Ben, Barney and Katerina came to the hospital. Zara was allowed to leave after she'd been checked over. She said she would go home and sleep. The police could find her at home but two officers arrived as she was signing herself out. Zara lied. She told them she and Doctor Andrew had foolishly decided to explore a railway tunnel. They had got lost. It was as simple as that. Just when she was beginning to doubt she would ever convince them, they received a call to a 'domestic'.

'I think we've got what we need,' they said to Zara as they left.

Doctor Andrew was 'comfortable' although he had a broken collarbone and a suspected green fracture to his right arm. Zara had had to plead to see him, arguing that it would be best for the wellbeing of both of them to know each other were all right.

As soon as Zara had ascertained that Andrew was fine, she asked him if he knew what time his brother was meant to be at the bus-stop. He didn't know. He had been unable to contact him.

'Can't you try again?' Zara failed to control her voice and a passing nursed almost pushed her out of the ward claiming she was distressing a patient.

As soon as she was clear of the hospital, Zara took out her mobile.

'I need to phone Des. I understand the plot now. Being a prisoner concentrates the mind.'

.
:
.

Chapter XXV   Checkmate for some

When Zara got through to the station, Jamie answered. He sounded sleepy. He'd been held on and he was just going off duty. 'So you've turned up,' he said laconically. You won't get Des,' he said. 'He's engaged in something a lot more important than catching crims.'

Zara managed a feeble 'What?'

'He's just become a father. He left here half an hour ago. Got there just as the head was appearing. Mother and baby both well.'

Zara nearly dropped the phone. 'Which hospital?'

'The Southern. Look, I have to go. Shall I put you on to Karen?' Zara thought about trying to explain to Karen but didn't think there was the smallest chance of her understanding and even if she were to grasp Zara's drift, she would be most unlikely to act on what amounted to intelligent guess-work on Zara's part. She would be told that the police could do nothing about events that might happen, they were too busy dealing with the ones that had. Still, she felt she had to try. She put the situation as clearly and briefly as she could.

'I've got all that. I'll see what can be done,' Karen replied.

'Fuck all,' said Zara to herself as she hung up.

'Looks like I'm on my own,' she said to Barney, reaching for her notebook and starting to make a list of things to do. They were all back at Zara's flat. She was only persuaded to stop by the appearance of Ben and Katerina with grilled bacon, sausage and scrambled egg.

'Oh my god,' said Barney suddenly, 'Ben, you didn't go to school.'

'I'm not going,' said Ben. 'Katerina wants me to help her with some research.'

'Don't you think Ben would be better off with me today? I could do with some help in the lab,' said Katerina pointedly. Zara agreed. The next twenty-four hours would be critical and not for ten-year-olds.

'We'll start right after breakfast,' said Katerina.

'You'll be all right, Aunty Zara, won't you?' asked Ben.

Zara nodded. 'Ben, you're the best of the best. Where would I be without you?' Ben smiled.

When the two researchers had gone off to Katerina's, Zara returned to her list. She was worried about the Gardner's and wanted to warn them but on the other hand didn't want to frighten them. But she thought if she spoke to Billy, he might have some ideas about what to do. He could keep his daughter off school for instance. She phoned his office number.

His wife answered. 'You're out of luck,' she said. 'He's in Livingstone on a job. Stayed over at his brother's place. Makes sense doesn't it when you've to get up early?' She sounded so chatty and light-hearted.

'How's Rose?' Zara decided to be equally chatty. 'Did she enjoy her birthday?'

'Oh it was lovely,' said Mrs Gardner. 'Such a picture she was. We took her and her friends to the swimming and then we had a bite in town and went to the cinema. She'll be sixteen before we know it.'

This remark spurred Zara on. 'Same with my niece. She's just eight. I think she might go to Rose's school. They live quite near where you are.'

'Rose is at Flowerhill Primary. I always think that's funny: a Rose going to Flowerhill.'

'My niece has just started going on the bus. With a friend. One of the mums sees them off.'

'Oh Rose goes on the bus. It stops just in the next street, Airdley Drive. So convenient.' A pause. She's wondering why I phoned, thought Zara.

'That's good,' Zara responded. 'Anything to make that morning rush easier. Look… um… I just wanted to ask Billy if I could use some of the information he gave me. I just wanted to check. I know I can't use any photos but… Would I be able to get him on his mobile?' Pause.

'Would I be able to get your husband on his mobile?' asked Zara. Another pause.

'You might but he tends to switch it off in the evening if he's socializing and then he forgets to switch it on again when I'm not around to remind him.' She laughs. 'You know what men are like.' She's suddenly not sure about me, thought Zara but she doesn't like snubbing people.

Zara managed to edge her way off the phone and rang Billy's mobile. He didn't answer. She left a message: Phone me. Your daughter's in danger. Make sure she's not left alone. When Barney who was sitting beside her saw it, he cast his eyes to heaven.

'God, I hope you're right about this.'

'I'd like to be wrong but I can't take any chances. At least now we can recce the bus- stop. If Billy doesn't get back to me, I'll phone Mrs G. again. Flowerhill Primary. I wonder what time school starts. We'll need to get there early.'

'We?' said Barney. 'Don't you think you've done enough gallivanting for a bit?' He stroked her cheek softly. 'Zara, I was so worried. I thought you were dead...'

'I thought I was dead too. I couldn't believe it when I saw Ben. I still can't.'

'It was Ben's idea,' said Barney. 'He heard Munchy say something about you in the park.'

Lunchtime went by and Zara became edgy. She sat looking at her mobile, willing it to ring and give her some good news. At three she fell asleep and Barney likewise but woke to ringing. She snatched at her phone.

'Mr Gardner, I'm so glad you've phoned,' she began.

'Leave me alone and leave my wife alone. Do you hear me? I should have suspected you when you came angling for photographs. You're working for that bastard Malloch, aren't you? I'm not intimidated. I went through due process of law. It was an accident. It's past and

269

gone. And you can tell him I'll pull the rug if I hear anything more.' Silence. Zara re-dialled but her call went unanswered. She phoned Mrs Gardner but she hung up as soon as she heard Zara's voice. Zara bit her fingers and walked up and down. It was getting too near zero hour.

'I don't want to go to this bus-stop event tomorrow but I don't seem to be having any luck calling the show off.' Barney made her a cup of tea and sat beside her, when she would sit.

Then Caroline rang. 'I can't stop him but it's twenty-past eight he's due there. Have to go. He doesn't know I've phoned.'

Zara rang Des's mobile. Barney pulled a face. 'I have to Barney. I know the guy's just become a father but we need Des and I know he'd want to be there. It could be the opportunity to take Malloch down. He's not answering. I can't believe he's not answering. He never switches his mobile off.'

'Maybe it's because he's in a hospital,' said Barney.

'Hallo? Des? Listen. It's Zara. Congratulations. I just heard from Jamie. A girl. That's wonderful. Yes, I would say that. And it all went well? Amazing. Nothing like it. Unbelievable.' Zara stopped interjecting celebratory phrases and let Des dance on his high wire. 'I'm really happy for you,' she said eventually 'but I rang up for another reason as well'. The phone suddenly went quiet. 'Des, I'm sorry. I just had to. Des, Des, listen. Of course I did, Des. I rang the station but –.'Zara looked at the phone angrily as the connection died.

'It's hang-up-on-Zara day,' she muttered.

Barney saw her eyes film over with tears. 'You're overstretched,' he said. 'This is all too much to deal with especially after what you've been through'.

'You'll help me though, won't you, Barney. I can't do it without you.'

He hugged her close and, against his better judgment, said, 'I will'. He felt as serious as if he were agreeing to the marriage contract.

***

James and Caroline were at Andrew's. Caroline kept begging James to give himself up. When the errant lovers had appeared at Andrew's door he had welcomed them in initially because he was so relieved to see James in one piece but after, he was at a loss. James seemed adamant about carrying through Malloch's plan. He seemed truly to believe that if he just fulfilled this one last task, everything would come right. Caroline rose and stood in front of him.

'I'm going James,' she said.

'You can't go back to that man.' James looked as if his whole life was crumbling around him.

'I can go back to the house. It's my house.' James went to embrace her but she put up her hand dismissively, picked up her bag and left. James sank down on a chair and tried to think what to do next.

'If Zara comes here, you will have to go on the fire escape,' Andrew had warned him. 'You know where it is? Go and look. You have to get out through the window. Leave it open.' His brother's words came back to him making him feel as if Zara's approach was imminent.

'Why will she come?' James had asked sulkily.

'I don't know. She's unpredictable. I think her mind will work things out.'

***

Zara sat with Barney on the sofa. Barney would have liked her to relax but he knew it was impossible for her. He could almost see her thoughts circling. He could not imagine what she was going to do next.

She got up to go and get a glass of water. When she returned she had a set look on her face; someone is walking about in Andrew's flat. It must be James. I have to go upstairs.

'What's your plan, Zara. Why must you –?

'If James would just not do his bit, the whole thing might fall through. The trouble is I don't know who else is involved… or what the plan is, apart from the bus-stop conversation at eight-twenty but Malloch seems to be keeping the master plan to himself. That's his strength. Don't worry. He's not going to attack me.' Barney shook his head, thinking of the shooting of Spike. 'Well probably not', said Zara, making a face as she realized what she'd said. She climbed the stairs quietly and then knocked very loud. Then she shouted through the letter-box: 'It's Zara. Open up. I want to talk to you.' She listened intently but could hear nothing. 'Right. I'm phoning the police.'

The door opened suddenly and James appeared grey-faced. 'Andrew's not here, Zara. Truly. He's not here. I don't know where he is. I don't know what to do.'

All Zara's pent up frustration boiled over:

'What do you think you're doing? How can you get involved with another of Malloch's plans!'

'I am only going to a bus-stop. How can that be –

'Are you mad,' shouted Zara. 'Don't you know he set McKelvie Buildings on fire? Don't you know –

But James was out of the room. The sudden breeze told her there was an opened window. She wondered why she was being so slow. By the time she reached it, James had disappeared down the fire escape. Zara followed but reached the bottom to find him scrambling up the wall of the back court opposite. He would then be on a road which had buses and taxis.

She ran towards him arriving as he disappeared over the wall. She scaled it, by this time seriously out of breath but, gaining the top, she saw him running away to her left, his hand up to flag down an approaching taxi. She gave up. Luck was on his side. But not for long, she thought. She regained her flat still inwardly boiling.

***

Charlie Steading had been a little disappointed at not hearing from Zara. He'd hoped his information might help her as he had made no progress in contacting Billy Gardner. Instead he had turned his mind to his other plan. A bigger, once-and-for-all plan which would, he felt, finish things and leave no consequences.

And it hinged on a game of chess. Although he and Malloch had parted on bad terms, Charlie knew he could lure him back with the prospect of a game. He too knew that Wednesday was the day Malloch was intent on carrying out his master strategy. He had procured this information from Munchy but he doubted whether Munchy actually realized this.

He rang Malloch and suggested chess that night. He knew the game calmed the man down but also kept his mind sharp. Malloch did not hesitate.

'My place,' said Charlie. 'I'll have the whisky ready.' He had two hours. He wrote Caroline the letter more or less as he had composed it earlier. His pen sped over the paper soundlessly for fifteen minutes. 'I hope you will be able to forgive me,' he put at the end.

Coming to this point in the letter he began to see it had implications he had not foreseen: it implied premeditation. He signed the letter off, put it in an envelope in the bottom drawer of his desk. Then he checked the drawer above where his revolver lay. Ironically, he thought, he would never have had a gun in his house if he hadn't taken up with Malloch.

Malloch came prompt at nine. Charlie poured him a measure of his favourite malt.

Malloch took off his jacket and sat in his favourite chair. 'Ah, Charlie, the best sight in the world, a chess set, the pieces all ready to go. My old friend, to you,' he raised his glass. Couldn't have been more timely.'

'Timely?' Charlie answered innocently.

'Can't tell you much but tomorrow's the big day. Got it together at last. Managed without you. Would have cleared your debts though.'

'Ah well,' said Charlie, 'Money's not everything.'

'Chess is though,' said Malloch, draining his glass. Charlie poured him another.

They began their game and Charlie was careful to play without mistakes: he didn't want Malloch to become suspicious. Jazz played quietly in the background.

'A beautiful night,' said Malloch. 'You certainly make a man feel at home. Tonight's a night to remember, eh?'

'You can say that again,' said Charlie, wishing Malloch would drink up.

The game continued, neither side gaining any particular advantage. There was a point when Charlie thought he might lose his queen but it was a false alarm. His heartbeat returned to normal. It was hard: he wanted to lose but not obviously. He wanted Malloch euphoric, less guarded, because then he might talk.

He found himself wishing Malloch would cheat but he never did – except once, Charlie remembered, and Charlie had noticed and called him on it and he'd said he was just joking, just testing to see if Charlie was on his toes.

Charlie was suddenly overwhelmed by the situation and he stood up and said he had to go to the bathroom. Once there he decided he was only suffering from the three whiskies he'd had without food. He brought back some nuts in a bowl and a couple of packets of crisps.

As he sat down he saw at once that Malloch had moved a pawn. It had not been his turn. It put Charlie a move away from being in check and he could not see a way of counteracting his opponent. He looked surprised – that was genuine – and rubbed his forehead.

'Have I had too much to drink? How could I have…?' Malloch laughed. Charlie didn't like the laugh. It wasn't in the spirit of their usual game but he decided to play along and see if Malloch went into his customary elation on winning.

They played out the last moves slowly and Malloch laughed again and beat the legs of the table with his hands. 'Another game Charlie. You can do better than that. And how about some coffee?' This was usual, Malloch calling for coffee.

Charlie rose slowly and went to the kitchen. He poured the boiling water onto the coffee grounds and waited, humming under his breath. Then he poured coffee into the mug Malloch always used and then into his own. Then he reached for a bottle he had placed on a high shelf. In it were two measures of Malloch's most favourite malt – the one he said he dreamt about. From an inside pocket he took some foil-wrapped pills. One would be sufficient. He did not hesitate: he'd done a dry run and knew the pill would dissolve. He also knew that at this stage in the evening, Malloch would down the glass in one. It was a quirk of his that even if it was something he really loved, he would not linger over it.

Charlie put his own mug and glass on the right, Malloch's on the left side of the tray and carefully carried it through. Malloch was sitting where he had been when Charlie left.

Charlie set the glasses down and the coffee mugs and sat down opposite Malloch again.

'Surprise!' he said. I found the end of a bottle of your most favourite. Here's to us.' He raised his glass. But Malloch just looked at the chess board. Sweat broke out on Charlie's forehead.

'I think I'll just hold off till we've had this game. I like to have something to look forward to,' said Malloch cheerfully. Charlie lowered his glass and grunted. Malloch played his opening move and it was as much as Charlie could do to stop his fingers shaking as he picked up his chosen piece.

Charlie felt as if he were playing in a dream. He watched Malloch and blanked his mind to the whisky in Malloch's glass. He thought if he let the thought in, Malloch would read it. Minutes passed. Malloch was concentrating hard. He whistled under his breath occasionally. He was neither slower nor faster than usual but each second was like an hour for Charlie. He doesn't know, he kept telling himself. He really doesn't know.

Then thinking too much, acting too hard, Charlie inevitably did exactly what he had been trying to avoid: he knocked his queen flying as he moved his rook and had to bend down to pick it up off the floor.

275

His eyes were off the table for maybe two seconds. Returning he thought the liquid motionless. It was impossible the glasses had been swapped. Two moves later he said,

'Check.' He had surprised himself, as he had been playing on automatic. Malloch took his subsequent loss with a good grace and at last lifted his glass.

'Here's to the decider,' he said smiling. They both drank. Charlie smiled back. His hands moved to the chess pieces, placing them back on their starting positions. He suddenly felt very tired. Too much whisky, he thought. His queen rolled from under his fingers and his head slumped onto the table.

Malloch pursed his lips and crossed the room to the desk, pulling on a pair of tight rubber gloves he had discovered along with other useful things like the revolver in the second drawer while Charlie was out making the coffee. For Malloch, the giveaway had been when Charlie didn't call him on the errant pawn. Then he noticed all the little signs of stress. He shook his head as he closed Charlie's left hand – he knew he was left-handed – over the trigger.

There was a movement outside the front window but any noise was covered by the report. There was no question of whether Charlie was dead. Malloch picked up his jacket and left the room. He made his way out through the back door. Reaching the gate he looked either way but there was no one in view. He walked quickly till he came to a busier street then stopped and sent a text. He was smiling. Then he made a phone call.

'Where are you? Well stay there till I arrive. I've been with you since eleven by the way. You got those Rolexes on you? We may have to humour the barman. Then we're going to your house for a night-cap. All right?'

The figure from the window moved into the softly lit house. It was Caroline, her face rigid. She was staring at the image on her mobile phone of Malloch shooting Charlie. It was less unpleasant than looking at the real thing.

***

Malloch answered his mobile on the first ring. He recognized the voice immediately:

'Okay, Malloch. We need to have this out. Where do you want to meet?' Malloch thought quickly.

'Drum and Rocket,' he said. 'I'll be there in twenty.' He smiled and shook his head as he closed the call. 'I didn't even have to do anything,' he mused.

He made another phone call, to the barman at the pub. He was terse:

'For fifty quid. All I want you to do... The man agreed.

When Billy Gardner arrived at the Drum and Rocket, he was greeted by the barman with a smile.

'Long time no see, Billy. What y' for?' Billy was looking round for Malloch. 'Meeting someone?'

'I might be,' said Billy.

'You won't believe this,' went on the barman but just last night we had a man in the dining room who swore that photo we've got on the wall, you know the one of –

'I know the one,' said Billy. 'What about it?'

'This guy said it was one of Gio's. I know you're sure but would you mind coming through and settling it for me. It's worth a fiver to me. Just so I can say to the guy you saw it and –

'Do I get a free drink?' asked Billy following the barman through the door at the side of the bar.

The barman let the door swing to behind them and switched on the dining room light.

'We're closed in here tonight.' The two of them walked over to the opposite side of the room where the photo was. Billy had just raised his hand to point to something when the light went out and in the complete darkness Billy felt a blow to the back of his head before he lost consciousness.

Malloch started dragging Billy across the floor.

'Everything ready?' The barman grunted. 'You know nothing,' Malloch went on 'but in the morning, if you find someone, just help them leave. Not before nine o-clock though.'

Malloch pulled Billy through the far door of the dining room into a back passage with an exit at one end. He took some tape from his pocket and tied Billy up. The trapdoor to the cellar lay open. The chute was in place. Malloch pushed Billy down it.

Chapter XXVI   The importance of children

Barney watched Zara's face. He recognized only too well the point when she had made up her mind.

'There's nothing for it, I'll have to go and speak to Des, baby or no baby.' By the time Barney had opened his mouth to speak, Zara was out of the door.

She had no plan but she didn't want to anticipate that it would be difficult accessing the ward. There were always throngs of people with flowers and fluffy bags, ready to greet the new-born into the tatty consumerist world. Zara thought back to when Ben was born and how much excitement she had felt, an excitement born of seeing a fragile creature just having emerged into the light and witnessing the parents' joy. She did not want to spoil this for Des and Pam but she was thinking of Billy and his wife and… She couldn't bear to think of anything happening to Rose. She bought a card, some flowers and some chocolates. She didn't want to look completely boorish.

She arrived about halfway through visiting time. Both Des's and Pam's parents were there. She felt awkward. She laid her gifts on the already vast pile and joined in the congratulations conversation. Although Des had welcomed her on arrival – he was holding the baby as proudly as a new father can – very soon she could feel his police officer antennae sensing something: her agenda.

She had taken the precaution of writing him a note in case things went wrong. She'd put it inside the Congratulations card. Bad taste, but that way she knew he would definitely get it. She edged over to him under the pretext of getting a close look at the baby who immediately burst out crying.

'Oh dear,' said Des, 'you mustn't be afraid of Aunty Zara. She's not as fierce as she looks'. Zara was only half successful in managing not to scowl.

'Des, I have to speak to you.'

'Not now, Zara. Nothing, I mean nothing, is going to stop me enjoying this time. If you can't behave like a friend, you'll need to leave.'

'Can I have a wee shot of the baby?' said Zara in a bid to get back to calm waters.

'When are you going to have children, Zara?' Pam was asking, too chirpily for her own good, thought Zara.

'Have to find a fella first,' said Zara.

'I thought you had one. Is Barney not...?' Zara dealt with this unwanted question by smiling at the baby and asking if they thought her eyes would stay blue.

Zara handed the living bundle back to Des's mum instead of Des. Then she stood up and said loudly,

'Well, I'm a bit tired. I was kidnapped yesterday and only managed to escape today'. The grandparents smiled absently as if they thought Zara's remark might have been a slightly embarrassing joke but Zara could see that Des though irritated, was also curious. 'See me out, Des, please. I'm afraid of getting lost and finding myself in surgery. I've only got two legs and I don't want to lose either of them.'

The ruse worked in that Des immediately got to his feet but once out of the ward he turned on Zara in a fury.

'Zara, you just can't do this barging in on people, making dramas...' He looked at her face more intently. 'You weren't?' Zara gave him a brief resumé of the previous day. 'Did Barney call the station?'

'Of course he did,' said Zara. 'Even I would have called the station in those circumstances.'

'You're all right, are you? I'm sorry. God, I'm sorry.' Zara took advantage of his sympathy:

'So what about tomorrow? Something is definitely happening at that bus-stop. I can't get Doctor James to back off. I'll need your help. You know what's going to happen?' Des held up his hand and Zara could see he hadn't really softened, he was still shutting the need for action out: his focus was all on the baby.

'Sorry Zara. You're on your own here. I'm off duty and will be for the next two weeks. There are other officers at the station who will be delighted to help you if you have something concrete to give them.'

'Something concrete?' Zara imagined a large paving stone coming down on Des's head.

'Just keep your nose out of it. *He* will get his come-uppance sooner or later without your help.' Zara took a step towards him. A nurse was approaching them. Des stopped her:

'Excuse me. I'm having difficulty getting this young woman to leave. She was distressing my wife who's just had a little girl.'

The nurse's face changed abruptly from friendly to brusque.

'Leave now or I'll call security,' she said. Zara left.

***

Zara walked slowly back to her car. She knew she had to calm down and move on. The most important thing now was to get some sleep and be up early, ready to go to where Malloch's plan was to be executed. She checked her mobile. There was a voice message: Zara, it's Caroline. I thought you might like to know but Malloch shot Charlie dead in our lounge tonight. They had been playing chess and drinking whisky. Phone me if you can. Caroline.

'Caroline? How are you? I'm so sorry this happened. Have you phoned the police?'

'I'm just about to.'

'Don't touch anything. How do you know it was Malloch?'

'I have it on my camera.' The voice was barely a whisper.

'Oh my god! You were there? Shall I come round?'

'My sister's coming over. Fortunately she was up seeing dad so she's very near.'

'Phone the police now. I take it Malloch's gone?'

'Yes. I saw him leave. He didn't see me.'

Zara's mind was in turmoil. She flew home and ran up the stairs to her flat. She was so out of breath it took a long time for Barney to understand, both about what had happened to Charlie and what had happened at the hospital.

'If the police find him now, that will be the end of operation bus-stop,' said Barney hopefully.

'But we still have to be ready,' said Zara. 'If we don't hear anything…'

'Who will tell us?'

'Caroline. Caroline knows about tomorrow remember?'

Before it got too late, Zara had one last stab at phoning Mrs Gardner. She spoke as soon as she heard someone pick up:

'Don't let Rose go to the bus-stop tomorrow morning. Please don't let her go.'

'If that's Zara McDonald, I have nothing to say to you. Please get off the phone now.' The voice was less determined than the words. Zara had the impression Mrs Gardner was reading from a script.

Caroline did not phone and when Zara texted her: Any news? about eleven o'clock, she texted back: Nothing. Sister here. We're going to try and get some sleep. Police guarding locus.

Chapter XXVII Endgame

Next morning, Barney and Zara set off about seven-thirty. Barney had taken the day off and borrowed a van as they didn't want anyone recognizing Zara's car. They were both disguised as workmen with dungarees and jackets with luminous strips. Zara had found them in a skip months ago and thought they might come in useful. They both wore black woolly hats, no hair showing.

They had looked at a map of the street online. Their plan was to halt at the opposite side of the road from the bus stop a little further up. From there, depending on what happened at the bus stop, they hoped they would be able to anticipate quickly enough to intervene – or phone the police.

Seven-forty-five. They had established themselves in a space and bought tea and bacon rolls at a sandwich bar and were now leaning against the van as if they were waiting for the gaffer or just being lazy about starting work. They surveyed the street, looking for anything that could indicate that something was going to happen. Nothing was happening but Zara was certain that something would. Eventually they sat in the van for a bit, Zara looking down and Barney up, the road. Barney went for more tea.

At ten past eight. Rose appeared accompanied by her mother who looked anxious. She too looked up and down the street. Zara recognized Rose from the photo in her father's office. Zara and Barney left the van and stood with their paper cups, now empty. Barney had a tin of paint balanced on the bonnet for extra effect. Why her and not her father wondered Zara. And why did they not wait in a car? It would have been safer. Nevertheless, Zara was slightly relieved: at least someone was taking a bit of responsibility.

A big white van came into sight over the brow of the hill to their right and stopped. There had been other vans, it could be just another delivery van but no one got out. The driver looked down the street. Was it her imagination, Zara thought, or was he looking at the bus-stop?

Zara looked harder at the driver of the white van. Even though he was disguised, she could tell him by his build: 'It's Munchy,' she muttered under her breath. 'Is this going to be another abduction, or worse?' Zara got in their van and moved it down opposite the bus-stop. Then she got out and dialled 999.

'Get down here, she said. There's been an accident.' She gave a street reference and closed the call.

Then out of nowhere Doctor James appears and things happen very fast. Doctor James stands for a moment and then starts swaying. He does not seem fazed by Mrs Gardner's presence. Zara wonders if he has realized the woman is Rose's mother. Then he is speaking to Rose who is looking perplexed. Zara instinctively starts to move across the road. James walks towards her holding his head and then falls sprawling on the tarmac.

There is no one else at the bus-stop. He shouts something and Rose and her mother start moving towards him, off the pavement and into the road till they are standing bending over him. Zara has to wait for a lorry to pass. When she can see again, it appears they are wondering if they can move him onto the pavement out of the traffic but he is a big man. Rose is nearer the centre of the road.

Suddenly Zara shouts and dives across the road. She has seen Munchy's van move off out of the corner of her eye. She throws herself at Rose with both her arms out and they both fall heavily on the ground in the gutter but safe as Munchy's van careers wildly down the hill and over Doctor James. Munchy does not stop. Barney jumps in the van and starts the engine. Zara waves him to go on.

Rose is crying, shaken but only bruised. Zara does not explain: it seems too complicated. She gets up and hands the child over to her mother who is too shocked to say anything but 'Are you all right Rose? Are you all right?' A little crowd gathers. Someone is giving Doctor James the kiss of life but Zara can see that he's dead.

***

Des woke early and remembered he was a father. He lay there in a euphoric daze for a few moments but then he had a nagging feeling there was something he should check. He wasn't due at the hospital till the afternoon as Pam had told him to catch up on some sleep. He got up and went downstairs. Where was Zara's card? He'd thrust it into his jacket pocket. There had been something written on the envelope. He glanced at the clock. It was seven-forty-five.

On the envelope, below 'To Des and Pam', Zara had scrawled, 'One day your baby will be ten.' He snatched the note from inside the card. It contained a street name a date and a time and the words, 'Rose Gardner was ten last week.' Hit-and-run, thought Des, Malloch's daughter. He was already halfway out of the door.

***

As Barney disappeared down the road after Munchy, Zara realized with some force that she had not thought of a plan for this bit. Munchy would go to Malloch. It was their one lead to him. Then she heard the police sirens and saw the ambulance. She didn't need to be here. There was someone shouting.

'Zara what's happening. It was Des coming down the street yelling at her out of his car.' Zara shot towards him and leapt through the opening door.

'Keep going. We need to catch up with Barney. He's in a van following Munchy. It happened. I managed to push Rose out of the way but I think Doctor James is dead. I don't suppose, thinking about it, that Malloch will be too fussy about a bit of collateral. I'll phone Barney. See where he is.'

Fortunately, as a car chase, it was not dramatically fast as the rush-hour traffic was well under way. Barney answered immediately telling Zara he was at traffic lights and he thought probably – yes, Munchy had turned right – he was heading for the expressway. Des kept driving but called in to colleagues to fill them in. Someone obviously asked him how he happened to be there. 'Tell you later,' he answered. Zara suppressed a smile.

'Coming off at Hayburn Street.' Barney again.

'I think I know where we're going,' said Des.

There was a tension in the car. It was partly the immediate situation but partly the old rivalry between Zara and Des. Surely, thought Zara, he has to acknowledge what I've done this time. She looked sideways at him and could see he was struggling.

'Thank god you came,' she said, meaning it.

'Zara, I'm sorry. I should have listened to you,' he paused. 'I was thick too. The pieces were all there. You kept feeding them to me.'

'I only saw it when I had time to think in the tunnel. Malloch gave me an opportunity, if only he knew...'

'Byres Road,' said Barney, and a bit later, 'Crossing Great Western Road... Queen Margaret Drive... heading north.'

'Heading towards Maryhill,' said Des. 'I know the very place. Abandoned garage. The one time we actually managed to bust Malloch, found him with stolen goods. He got off on a technicality.'

'Barney's gone quiet,' said Zara. 'I hope he's okay. This isn't his operational style.'

'We'll have to use our heads,' said Des. 'My guess is that Barney will stop the van just off the Maryhill Road, if Munchy is heading where I think he's heading. Look out for it. I'll drive slowly.'

Zara's mind went blank: she saw her knuckles had gone white from gripping the open window; she couldn't imagine what their next move could be.

'There,' she said suddenly. 'There's the van and Barney.'

Des parked and they both walked over.

'Up there,' said Barney. 'I'll just stay here, if you don't mind. Zara?'

'I'm not missing this, Barney. I want to see the guy nailed.' Des was phoning for backup.

'We can't make an arrest, even if he's here,' said Des. I phoned Armed Response but we'll approach and see what we can see.'

They entered what at first glance seemed to be a junk yard. Drawn up at defunct petrol pumps was Munchy's van. There had obviously been a delay as the post mortem had not begun to happen yet. Malloch was nowhere in sight.

From their post behind a pile of rusting vehicles, Zara and Des saw Malloch suddenly emerge from behind the van. He pulled Munchy from the driving seat.

'Let's have it then. Let's have it.' He looked possessed. Zara shivered.

'I done it Boss. I done it. I ran clean over her and got away. I want my money now and then I'm off.' While Munchy was speaking Malloch was busy changing the registration plates of the van. He inspected the bumper and the front wheels and then backed the vehicle into the lockup behind him and pulled down the door. No blood, skin or hair then, thought Zara. She saw Malloch's face relax a little. He gave Munchy a friendly slap on the back.

'Bravo. I was getting worried. All went to plan then? What about the Doctor?'

'Couldn't see very well out of me side mirrors but I reckon he just got up and scarpered. I heard the sirens but I was well down the road by then.'

'Any witnesses?'

'Naw Boss. Hardly anyone about. The girl and Doctor James was the only folk at the bus-stop. So can I have my money now, 'cause I want to get going.'

'Of course Munchy.' Malloch drew a sheaf of notes from an inside pocket and placed them on an old metal bench that was conveniently nearby. Munchy went to take it but Malloch stayed his hand.

'Hang on. How about a little celebration first.' He walked over to his own car and withdrew from its interior a couple of shot glasses and a half bottle. Zara noticed Munchy's hand kept straying towards the pile of notes but the power of Malloch restrained him: he could not just snatch the money and make a run for it.

Des had his ears tuned to what was going on but he was also waiting for the backup to arrive. Zara could hear nothing different in the traffic sounds but Des suddenly nodded. At that point Zara heard Malloch's voice again: 'Bottoms up, Munchy. She's dead. That's all that matters.'

'She's not dead.' Zara found herself facing Malloch from about fifteen feet. He jumped momentarily then took a step towards her. He had his back to the yard entrance.

'As you can see, I'm not in the tunnel which may surprise you but then if you believe people like Munchy, you're going to get a lot of false information. Rose Gardner is not dead. Munchy killed Doctor James.' Zara was hardly aware of her own words till they came out of her mouth. She had been impelled by Malloch's gloating. She kept her eyes on Malloch. A voice inside her shouted, Fool, fool. She waited.

She saw it all in slow motion – Malloch reaching inside his jacket, the revolver glinting in the light. Before she had time to move, he was beside her, her arm encased in his grip of steel. Then she heard a voice say,

'Armed Response. Put down your weapon.' Malloch did nothing of the sort but instead propelled Zara in front of him towards his car.

Now Zara could see that there were officers all around with guns but it was difficult to see what they could do. They can't shoot Malloch's gun from his hand without the bullet going through me, Zara thought. Suddenly shots went off in all directions and Malloch's car was no longer functional. There was a yowl of frustration from Malloch as he leapt towards Munchy and locked his arm around his head. Zara sank to her knees and found herself supported by Des.

Round two of the human shield strategy but once again Malloch had mistaken the odds. Munchy had managed to lift his money and was set on slipping out unnoticed in the general fracas. He was incensed when Malloch got hold of him and in spite of the gun in his face he summoned all his strength and, pretending to be unable to breathe let his head slump slowly forward then quickly back and forward again in a Glasgow kiss following this with his left fist in Malloch's balls and his right boot in a searing crunch down Malloch's leg. The gun fell to the ground, the police moved in and handcuffed both men.

Barney appeared haggard at the entrance having heard shots.

'Zara,' he said, 'Zara'. He was unable to say anything but her name.

***

When they had made their statements to the police, Zara said to Barney, 'Let's go to Katerina's. That way we only need to tell the story once more.'

Barney was despairing when he heard about Zara leaping out of her hiding place but she had just grinned and said, 'I'm afraid that's who I am.'

That evening while Zara was relaxing at Barney's, the doorbell rang. It was Spike.

'I knew you were okay but I just wanted to see for myself,' he said, looking uncomfortable in indoor surroundings. 'You believe me now then? Malloch isn't someone to mess with?' Zara made a face but didn't argue.

Mrs Gardner invited Zara to tea, to meet Rose 'properly' and to thank her for all she'd done. Billy was there too, affable as when Zara had first met him.

Much later, going through Doctor James' effects, there was information that enabled the police to get in contact with members of Ivory's family who were still in the UK. The father, who had set up the operation was dead but the mother and two sisters were overwhelmed: they had almost given up hope of any resolution.

***

Five months later Zara received a phone call from Katerina.

'Come to the river,' she said, giving directions. 'I found something,' she said when Zara arrived. Zara took the heavy object from Katerina's hands. She knew instantly it was the missing skull. She thought of Ben and she thought of Rose and she wished for live warm flesh instead of a cold bone.

A note to the reader.

For more information about Female Genital Mutilation please visit www.equalitynow.org

For more information about the author please visit www.cicely.co.uk